The
SCANDALOUS
MRS. BLACKFORD

The
Scandalous
Mrs. Blackford

HARNETT T. KANE

with Victor Leclerc

Julian Messner, Inc.   New York

TO THE READER

THIS NOVEL, DEALING WITH THE LIFE OF HARRIET ELY BLACKFORD, IS based on many sources, hitherto unpublished or little known; in some cases suppressed.

Among them is her own account, published—and suppressed—in 1875 in Paris and Brussels, under the title *Le Roman d'une Américaine en Russie* and signed "Fanny Lear." A number of the copies in existence today lack the twenty pages torn out by the Belgian police under the pressure of the Russian Government. Her book includes letters which her lover, the Tsar's nephew, wrote to her.

Other facts were found in research in Russian sources, such as *Krasny Arkhiv* of Moscow, a Soviet historical journal largely devoted to revelation of secret Tsarist documents. Of much help also were various memoirs scattered throughout the press of the USSR and that of Russian emigrés abroad, in the post-Tsarist period.

While the Russian press of the Tsarist days was restrained in writing about the affairs of Grand Duke Nicholas and Mrs. Blackford, American and West European newspapers of the time were free to devote columns to it. Philadelphia and New York dailies of the 1870s and 1880s provided especially full material.

The National Archives in Washington yielded a rich store of information in the General Records of the Department of State, containing diplomatic dispatches to and from Russia for 1874. Later chapters are based on confidential correspondence exchanged between the American Legation in St. Petersburg and

Secretary of State Hamilton Fish on the case of Mrs. Blackford. Finally, a number of Russian contemporaries of Mrs. Blackford and the Grand Duke assisted in the gathering of written and oral reminiscences of the two principals, their friends and associates, and of the general period.

Perhaps no American woman of her day or ours had a career such as Mrs. Blackford's; yet few people have heard of her. She is a remarkable, almost forgotten figure in the untold history of the last century.

ONE

As it bumped through the dusty Philadelphia streets between drays and high-piled military carts, the dingy carriage proclaimed with every creak that it was a hired hack. Framed in one narrow window was a woman in deep mourning, and in the other, a young girl whose blond hair shone out startlingly under the brim of her little black-bowed bonnet.

Against their shabby draperies, with their vague smell of mold and antiseptic, Mrs. Caroline Ely bowed her head to cry in high gasping breaths. She had lost the bright looks that made people turn in her native Virginia, yet even now she made a fine-featured, if faded, medallion. Next to her mother, Harriet Elizabeth Ely sat forward, her dark eyes intent on the busy street. In years to follow, one man would speak for many others when he said of Hattie Ely, "She was the most beautiful woman I ever saw." But on this hot, overcast summer day of 1861, she was a slim girl of fourteen with an engaging awkwardness that came from lack of understanding of her own loveliness. The arresting effect of her braided yellow hair in contrast with her extraordinarily dark eyes was intensified by a skin almost luminously white. The lift of the eyes at the corners, and the curve of her wide, high cheekbones, gave her a look of additional piquancy, which, as a critic later declared, was clearly "out of place in Philadelphia"!

As the carriage moved slowly along the narrow, crowded streets, it passed an irregular file of freshly recruited soldiers in dark-blue uniforms, halted for a moment under an American flag. Fort Sumter was only a few months behind; the war of North and South had barely started. Philadelphia itself was uncertain, divided in allegiance. Southern families had long dominated there,

1

but now the Unionists were shouting fiercely against advocates of Jefferson Davis, calling them traitors.

Leaning back in her seat, Harriet Ely sighed, the black taffeta bow under her chin stirring with her breath. Then, as the carriage went on, she leaned forward again in response to a sudden excitement from the corner. An officer ran past them, waving a dispatch.

"McClellan!" he shouted. "Little Mac's done it—made the rebels give up in western Virginia!"

Philadelphia's bold young General had scored the first Union victory by taking a wide area out of Southern hands. Mrs. Ely raised her head, and her gray-blue eyes met Hattie's. For today, of all days, the street cries carried a personal barb for Hattie and her mother, and the name "McClellan" struck with special sharpness.

"'General George' a hero!" Hattie's voice was low. "There'll be no bearing those McClellans now."

Just then their vehicle swerved to make way for a wide, well-appointed carriage. For a few moments the two conveyances were parallel, and Hattie saw an imposing matron at the silk-draped window of the other carriage. She was startled at the sight of the remote profile beneath the feathers of a close hat. She hoped that her mother would not look up, but now Caroline Ely glanced over. There was a stir of plumes as the elegant one shifted her head, and Hattie's fingers tightened on the handle of the palm-leaf fan she was carrying. *She* must be as aware of them as they were of her! Surely, on this day at least, the older Mrs. McClellan would speak to them. Even though Isabel McClellan was one of the "other Elys," from the father's first marriage, she wouldn't . . .

Hattie's gaze fixed imploringly on the face of General George McClellan's aunt, Hattie's half-sister.

It turned out that she would. There was no sign of recognition as the shining carriage passed quickly ahead. Caroline Ely's hands went to her face and her tears began again, but Hattie's white skin flushed in anger. All her life she had been divided between sorrow and rage when she thought of those other Elys, who would not even admit that she existed. As the only child of an unusual marriage (for the Reverend Ezra Styles Ely's second wife had been twenty-five years younger than her husband) she heard

2

and saw a great deal, and what she observed, Hattie Ely seldom forgot.

Ezra Styles Ely, originally of Connecticut, had come to Philadelphia from New York in 1814, and soon met the daughter of Philadelphia's great merchant, Samuel Carswell. The wedding had been an important social event, and the couple had taken an imposing ivy-covered Georgian house between Fourth and Walnut. One of their daughters married a Patterson of Baltimore; and Isabel had married Dr. James McClellan, uncle of General George. The well-to-do Dr. Ely rose rapidly in the organization of the Presbyterian Church, and was famous for his charities. He worked tirelessly to put up the first building of Jefferson Medical College, and then gave tens of thousands of dollars to support it.

But then came mistakes in judgment, bad times, an ill-fated expedition to the West, and the death of his wife. When he came back to a smaller church, he was a sick and defeated man. He had been accepted in the social circles of Philadelphia not so much for his achievements, but as the husband of a Carswell, and with this link gone and in his drab days, he was no less dignified, yet not the worldly figure of earlier years. Then, in the eyes of his children, he had done the unforgivable thing: he had married again.

Hattie glanced over at her mother, remembering suddenly a remark she had heard about "Dr. Ely's second wind." The more respectable people were, the more they said such things behind their hands. Still worse was the attitude of her father's first family. As if she understood her daughter's thoughts, Caroline murmured:

"You'd have imagined they'd really be glad to have him taken care of. And it isn't as if the Holmeses of Virginia weren't as good as anybody in Philadelphia."

"Mother, you know what Philadelphia thinks of anybody who isn't from Philadelphia. They wouldn't receive an archangel if he hadn't been born here." Her quick mind asserted itself, and she smiled impishly. "Or *are* archangels born?"

Caroline frowned. "Please, Harriet Elizabeth." Her daughter was sometimes so . . . well, frank—almost like a Northerner. As usual, she ignored the rather frightening precocity of Hattie's mind. She cleared her throat. "We're coming to the cemetery. Remember if any of them speak, you are to curtsy like a lady; if they don't, you are not to show by one muscle of your face, miss, that you realize they haven't recognized us."

Hattie's bright head went up, but she checked her impulse to retort and waved her palm-leaf fan resignedly. "Yes, Mother."

Against the sky, the dark clouds hovered about a half-lost sun. The still trees and bushes shone with a metallic brightness in air that had more than a hint of coming rain. Beside the open grave, the mourners stood awkwardly in two separate groups. Not less awkward was the perspiring young minister, Dr. Black, unhappily aware that the two families facing one another across the piled-up earth could not be mentioned in the same sentence. He coughed nervously.

"We are gathered to pray for one of our city's greatest souls." What a time he had had in preparing his remarks! Dr. Ely had been a celebrated figure, certainly, yet celebrated for things so bitterly charged, so much disputed. Gingerly Dr. Ely's young successor in the pulpit in Buttonwood Street told of the Elys who had come to America from Plymouth in 1660, to settle in Connecticut, as Puritan as "the rock-bordered soil of New England." One early Ely had gone west to found the Ohio town of Elyria. Ezra's maternal grandfather was a minister, chaplain of Congress; his other grandfather was of the cloth, and his father as well.

"Ezra Ely was a forceful, distinguished writer. I need only mention his treatise *A Contrast between Calvinism and Hopkinism*, his *Conversation on the Science of the Human Mind*."

Hattie's dark lashes lifted momentarily, and her eyes searched those around her. She could not help thinking that her father could have preached a far more eloquent sermon at his own funeral. Wasn't Dr. Black going to mention the other book, the really famous one that had sold in the tens of thousands here and in England and Ireland—*Visits of Mercy?*

But of course not. Long ago Hattie had begun to sense how he had shocked people with that account of his missionary work in New York among beggars, thieves, and street women. Until Caroline intervened, Hattie had read several times through the well-filled pages. Her father had approved that reading. . . . She recalled his words about temptation, his stern language in the book—"Flee Youthful Lusts"—and his advice to parents. He had

4

written as he had so that they might beware: "For many never caution their children, from fastidious delicacy, until it is too late—too late forever."

No one could say that *she* hadn't been cautioned. Half frightened, half intrigued, Hattie wondered often about such matters. She knew no young man at all, though now and then she was aware of those who looked at her from a distance. In books, she came upon pictures of soulful gentlemen, long-haired, in tights and with swords. Sometimes in daydreams she would stand with an elegant young personage at a pillared entranceway like the one the McClellans had. She pictured him as a Southerner, a young plantation heir from Louisiana, or even an adventurer from the Texas plains.

Guiltily, she returned to the present, the smell of moist earth and flowers and death. It was dark and clayey in the wide hole; what would it be like down there, locked away from the world? With an effort she made herself listen to the minister. He was talking now of Dr. Ely's eloquence in the splendid pulpit of the Third Presbyterian Church on Pine Street; but he said nothing of the furious fight in the congregation over Dr. Ely's coming, when half the members protested against a minister who wrote too vividly about scandalous subjects. Some had claimed that the young Dr. Ely actually seemed to enjoy his adventures among these fallen women, and there had been a split, with repercussions still to be heard in Philadelphia.

Dr. Black mentioned Dr. Ely's "courageous experiment in the West." That had been the bad turn, Hattie reflected; that changed everything. Ezra Ely had put all his money into a grand project for a "Mother University" for Presbyterians, far out on the banks of the Mississippi. Proudly, he had seen a town go up with the name of Ely, Missouri. Then, soon after, the Mississippi flooded; a dozen other troubles broke upon him, and everything collapsed. (It was said that the ghost town left from the pious project had given Mr. Dickens subject matter for *Martin Chuzzlewit*.) After that, a minor pulpit on Buttonwood Street, and a bare living; in time, serious illness, a scant pension, supplemented by Caroline's small funds. The pension would be gone now.

The girl's thoughts came in a rush. She'd been cheated; for her there'd been nothing like the life that Ezra Ely provided for those first children. And her father himself . . . He had said very little as he sat huddled forward in his chair, living in his earlier memories. Why couldn't he have shown more feeling for her? He hadn't cared that she was there; he had hardly known it. But sometimes those eyes would go directly to her, and in a way that she could not explain, Hattie had been sure he was passing judgment on her, finding her wanting. Once she had hinted her fears to her mother, and the blurred lines had intensified in Caroline's face. "Don't say such a thing, child. That's not true." She should not have hinted how she felt. It wasn't nice, or genteel, and Caroline judged most things by those standards.

The minister went on: "Dr. Ely was never anything but generous, almost overgenerous." At those words Hattie looked directly across the open grave at her tall half-sister, and read the look of satisfaction on the placid face. She recalled one of Caroline's friends murmuring, "Ezra must have given away some fifty thousand dollars." Fifty thousand! . . . How she and Caroline could use that, or only part of it! Then with a rush of emotion she remembered the gold pencil. . . . Years earlier, during one of the worst periods in their fortunes, she had gone with her father and mother to a meeting at which another churchman appealed for badly needed funds. While the plate was being passed, Hattie watched nervously; she knew they had nothing to give. But when it came to them, Ezra Ely reached into his pocket to bring out a shining object—his gold pencil, a present from his old congregation, engraved in commemoration of a happier day—and placed it in the plate.

"And so he is in that home of blessed relief, in that life after death." The mourners glanced anxiously at the scudding clouds, and as a huddle of workmen lowered the casket, the rain struck, a windless leaden fall on the heads and shoulders of the crowd. Partly in sorrow, partly in protection, Hattie's arms went around her weeping mother. In the group across the grave, several of the Elys opened umbrellas against the rain; Caroline and her daughter stood there more miserably alone than ever.

After a pause, it was Isabel McClellan who came forward to extend her gloved hand to the minister.

"Let me thank you for the family," she said, without looking in Caroline's direction.

The minister's assistant approached with an umbrella to escort

Caroline and Harriet to their hack. As they left, they were aware of subdued voices behind them.

"H'mm, there's a bit of income for them, isn't there?" An elderly cousin, his voice carefully neutral, drew his collar about his throat.

"Not from him, but *she*"—carefully, the woman beside him avoided Caroline's name—"gets a little from Richmond."

The first speaker frowned. "I'll say one thing—that girl was the brightest one in her father's congregation, with the sternest upbringing of them all. Too much learning, though! She'll be worrying about women's rights and such, and it will ruin her looks. You'll see."

Back in their shabby frame house on Fourth Street, Harriet made tea, which failed to cheer them as they sat in the living room with its delicately patterned, faded paper. The rain beat monotonously on the window. Hattie turned on the lamp, and its circle of cozy light shut out some of the drabness of the walls. Caroline lifted one of her lined hands as if to shield her cheek from the light, but it was also a familiar habit, a gesture of defense against a world in which she found herself uneasy. Arousing herself to the necessity for some positive plans for the future, Caroline suddenly said:

"You're to finish school, child."

"Mother, we can't afford it." Harriet's protest came spontaneously. "And you know I've never liked it there. I learn more from the things I read outside; they're much more interesting."

"No doubt. . . . Still, your father always wanted you to get a full education. He thought you were the smartest of his children—smarter than any of those others."

"He did?" Hattie asked in delighted surprise.

"Your father didn't say much, but that's the way he felt." Though Hattie wanted to question her mother further, Caroline went on to another matter. "We'll have enough to get along, if we're just careful."

When hadn't they been careful? And that wasn't the word Hattie would use for it. She looked around the small room, at the handsomely carved old sofa and the pair of matching chairs precisely flanking it, set beneath the Holmes family portraits imported from Richmond. They had all been designed for a large-scale Tidewater drawing room. Crowded into too narrow a space, among cheaper pieces, they seemed like ladies on a visit to the deserving poor.

Hattie suppressed a sigh. She knew every curve, every scroll; regularly, she and her mother dusted and polished them. They remained a shrine to Caroline's earlier life, and meanwhile the family ate in the kitchen and saved the best table linen for guests who rarely came.

"You'll be finished with school in two years," Caroline said, "and then, perhaps . . ."

Hattie broke in bitterly. "And then, I suppose I'll be ready to earn my living at teaching?"

"You will not." Caroline could not bring herself to go on and utter her romantic hopes that Hattie would somehow be able to take a place in Philadelphia society. In their present circumstances, it was even more hopeless than it had been before. Afraid that she would lose her composure, Caroline dropped the subject. "Harriet, please get my embroidery, in the library."

As Hattie searched quickly for the embroidery box in the room down the hall, with its rows and rows of theological books and gold-tooled sets of English histories behind leaded glass doors that her father had kept locked, she tried to avoid the sight of the sagging leather chair—her father's chair. The room was still filled with his presence. Sitting there, even toward the end Ezra Ely had dominated the household. A thump of his cane and Caroline had darted to his side. Only on rare occasions did he come into the sitting room to join his guests in singing hymns around the spinet piano in the corner. (Any other music would not be allowed.) Those songs, all so grim, telling of the eternal struggle against temptation, of damnation and punishment. . . . A single error, then eternal loss.

Yet Ezra Ely also believed in repentance, and called his own viewpoint broad-minded. He had laughed when his wife, like most of her friends, who were largely members of her husband's old congregation, lined up books on the library shelves with male authors on one side and lady authors on another, "unless they are married." Once Hattie had heard him chuckle over a shouting preacher of another denomination. "A good man, but he must think God is deaf."

Still, such expressions of wit were rare, and Dr. Ely had many a strict view of his own. Outside of his own writing and the classical education he had prescribed for Hattie, other reading was unfit for a young mind and to Hattie the other reading was the most interesting of all.

But now Hattie was alone, and nobody could stop her. Her errand for her mother rebelliously forgotten, she lit the lamp. From the side drawer of the desk she took a little key on a string, and soon her hands were groping among the heavy volumes. She knew where the novels were hidden—Sir Walter Scott behind St. Thomas Aquinas—but she reached now for a new book she had been forbidden to read only a few days ago. It was by a traveler to eastern Europe and Asia.

Shivering a little in the chill of the room, she sat down in a chair. Her hands riffled the pages until she came to her place: Russia and Ivan the Terrible, the Great Peter, and vast processions toward palaces that towered over the frozen wastes. There were stories of mass murders, of nods that meant death by fire for thousands of men and women. With a shudder, Harriet read passages describing how Peter made his enemies kneel before him and summoned his nobles to assist him in methodically chopping off one head after another.

Now followed more pleasant pages: the ice palaces of the Tsarina Anna, sleigh rides across the ice, and St. Petersburg summers with long white nights, when the sun never set. She studied the illustrations—majestic women in furs with strange high headdresses and oriental sleeves that trailed to the ground. Finally, she read about Catherine, who was the Tsarina over all those white leagues, and over the young men. . . . Hattie stopped herself. These were not things to be read about, much less to be enjoyed. Again she felt a hidden presence, as if the old man still sat over there in his chair, and she closed the book. What did it matter? She'd never see anything like that, anyway. Ice palaces in a book, castles in faded drawings—they were all she knew and all she would ever know.

The small walls of the house seemed to close in. Letting the book slide to the floor, she began to sob in frustration, sorrow, and weariness at the end of the long day.

T W O

A NEWLY ROPED TRUNK STOOD IN FRONT OF THE MIRROR IN THE parlor. Hattie had to bend over it to tie on her spring bonnet. As she struggled with the taffeta of the bow, she thought with satisfaction of her new figured lavender basque, and wished that she could avoid putting her old cape on over it; even the taffeta of her bonnet was beginning to split, but the bunch of velvet violets that she had extravagantly purchased the afternoon before might help. When she had secured them firmly in place on the top of her bonnet, she sighed with relief—while she looked like that, the cape didn't matter; no one would notice the split taffeta. She was young, she was beautiful, she was going on a trip.

She had changed a great deal in the past two years, and most of all, it seemed to her, since Caroline had let her take down her braids and draw back her golden-blond hair into a fashionable knot at the back of her neck. Actually, the change from a striking but awkward girl to a beautiful young woman had been gradual; as she had grown taller, her figure had rounded, her small high breasts had become fuller, and she had learned to carry herself with grace and pride.

She whirled away from the mirror, and the sight of the drab room sobered her gay mood. In the May morning, the frayed upholstery appeared more shabby than ever, her mother's heirlooms more out of place. They wouldn't sell the house or the carved pieces until they knew "how things would turn out." They couldn't turn out a great deal worse than they had in the past two years, Hattie thought. The war, of course, had something to do with it. Philadelphia had lined up more and more firmly with the Union side. Northern feelings had grown stronger

10

with each defeat; the city had become virtually an arsenal, and factories ran day and night. The women, even more violent than the men, favored no dealings with "disloyalists," and since Caroline Ely refused to hide her Confederate sympathies, Hattie and her mother were often snubbed by Dr. Ely's former parishioners. They were not asked to join in canteen work for the Union soldiers and Confederate prisoners who passed through Philadelphia, or to help with bandage-rolling in the parlors of their neighbors.

In fact, the only change in their uneventful daily routine was when they made equally uneventful trips to deliver packages of Bibles and prayer books from the Presbyterian Board of Publications to the Union Volunteer Refreshment Saloon. Hattie supposed that the soldiers would eventually see the Bibles; she never saw the soldiers.

And worst of all, they were poor. They could not pretend to keep up. Going to Miss Dudley's school had been even more humiliating than she had feared. She was occasionally invited home after school with the others, but she was never asked to the formal occasions when the guest list was supervised by the mothers. On the day of Mary Rittenhouse's fifteenth birthday party—a particularly grand occasion, to which she had not received an invitation—she returned home in tears. When Caroline questioned her, she sobbed.

"I might as well be a mulatto."

Caroline rebuked her for this outburst, but the older woman was troubled. Several times after that she spoke of a summer visit to her Holmes connections in Virginia or to others in Baltimore.

"I owe it to you to show you that life. It's so different from this place . . . so different."

Nothing was done about it, however, until one day shortly before her graduation Hattie found Caroline frowning over an unexpected tax bill. It was Hattie who forced the issue.

"Mother, your little property just doesn't bring in enough for the two of us. The war is sending prices up every day. We haven't had fresh meat for over a week. As soon as I finish school . . ."

Caroline cut short whatever indelicate proposal her daughter was going to make. Things would be better, she'd see! And surprisingly enough, Caroline was right. The next week brought a letter from one of the Holmeses who now lived in Parkersburg,

11

in western Virginia. Would Caroline and her daughter like to visit them for a while? To be sure, Miss Holmes wrote, it wouldn't be like old times, especially now that the Yankees had taken over— temporarily, she had added firmly.

And this was the day of the journey to Parkersburg. Things would surely be better there. No matter what changes the war had brought, at least there would be relatives who would welcome them; there would be no more humiliating encounters with the McClellans. It was some satisfaction, Hattie thought, to know that the McClellan family too had suffered humiliation. After General McClellan's great sweep of early victories, there had been a strange period of indecision and defeat, and Lincoln had intervened dramatically to remove the first Northern hero of the war. How quickly everything could change! The South was high in the ascendancy these days, and McClellan waited in the dim background. All at once Hattie felt sorry for him.

There was a knock on the door. Hattie opened it to Madge Morris, her plump schoolmate, who had been closer to her than any of the other girls.

"I'm on my way to the Southwark Refreshment Canteen, to serve the soldiers—the Union ones," she added unnecessarily, squinting nearsightedly and admiringly at Hattie. (Madge needed glasses, but refused to wear them.) "So you're really going?"

"Oh yes," said Hattie, nonchalantly drawing on her small glove. "Thank heaven I've delivered my last pack of Bibles for the Board."

Madge's face showed her disapproval of such frivolity, and her envy of the trip.

"When are you coming back?"

"Never, I hope."

From outside came the sound of marching soldiers, and Madge asked:

"Aren't you afraid to go South right now when the rebels may be invading?" Madge had lowered her voice lest Caroline Ely hear the word "rebel."

"I'd love to see a battle!" Hattie said intensely. "And soldiers. Mother won't even let me go near Independence Square where the recruiting is, and the band plays, and they have lights in the trees; all I know is what the other girls say about the parties for the soldiers. Mother pulls me away if I even see a uniform."

Madge was shocked. "Why, you couldn't talk to them anyway unless you knew their families."

"Oh, couldn't I?" said Hattie. "You wait. Someday, even if I don't know his family, I'll meet a tall, handsome man who waltzes divinely, and reads Sir Walter Scott when he isn't fighting, and if there's any danger, he'll save me. Of course I'll know right away if he is a gentleman," she added.

There was a loud knock on the door and they heard Caroline's hasty step on the stair. The hack had arrived. On the doorstep, Madge kissed Hattie, curtsied to Caroline, and peered wistfully after them as the hack disappeared down the street.

The ride to the station was frustratingly slow. It seemed as if files of soldiers halted them at every street—depleted regiments from New England and New York passing homeward, wounded men stopping over from the battlefields of Chancellorsville and Fredericksburg, and now and then a new regiment on its way South, clean and fresh in new uniforms.

Bad news for the Union was arriving with every wire. Since the terrible tidings from Chancellorsville, the newspapers had been filled with funeral notices, and the wounded were rolling in by the hundreds. Philadelphia itself trembled under the threat of capture.

Their vehicle jerked and stopped again. A cart blocked the street and Hattie saw, hanging over the side, an arm wound in bloody bandages. Their horse grew restive; the hack scraped by the cart and crushed the dark fingers as it passed.

"Oh, take care!" Hattie cried. The driver spat.

"Miss, you could yank that un's arm off—overdue for the ground already!" Sniffing, he spat again against the cart, and the hand, too, as Hattie turned away with a shudder.

In the station waiting room Hattie pushed past soldiers, old men, and loungers to get to the ticket window. Helpless in practical matters, Caroline had taken a place near the platform, leaving her daughter to buy the tickets. As Hattie waited in line, she turned to look over at her mother and found her gaze intercepted by a tall young man who was watching her intently. With a thump of her heart, she saw that he was strikingly handsome and that he wore what seemed to her to be very elegant clothes.

She looked away in confusion, but when she stepped up to the ticket window, she lifted her face in its most fetching profile, with continuing awareness of his stare. Hoping that she sounded dignified, she asked for tickets to Parkersburg, and gave the agent their names when she inquired about checking the trunks. As she left the window, her heart beat harder than ever to find the young man advancing, hat in hand.

"Miss Ely?" His voice was pleasant, and he made a low bow. "Excuse me, I have seen you before with friends of mine, and I have heard that we are to be neighbors, in a way. I'm Calvin Blackford from Parkersburg."

His full dark brows were raised, and his long thumb hooked in his waistcoat. Mr. Blackford was lean—perhaps too lean; the clean-shaven face, a trifle pale, was almost poetic; he had long sideburns, and his eyes were intent.

"Never speak to strangers"—she could hear Caroline's words. Still, Mr. Blackford wasn't actually a stranger. Hesitantly she asked him:

"You've seen me . . . with friends?"

He blushed, his skin coloring down to his flowing stock. "Yes, here and there."

Somehow, Mr. Blackford's discomfort made her feel more at ease. It was flattering to know that he had wanted to talk to her so much that he had lied about his "friends." She smiled at him, and was about to speak when she heard a warning whistle from the train. She turned in alarm to see Caroline beckoning to her from the doorway. With a hasty "Good-by, Mr. Blackford," she hurried toward her mother. If Mr. Blackford said anything in answer, she missed it in her departure.

Caroline remained silent until they had settled themselves on the hard seats in their car, and then, frowning, she inquired:

"Who was that?"

Without having planned it, Hattie's answer was quick and smooth.

"He just thought I was somebody else."

Caroline looked dubious, but was so preoccupied with the details of the trip ahead that she let the matter go. For a few moments, as the car backed and pulled, Hattie kept circumspect watch, hoping she would see Mr. Blackford pass by, or perhaps even come into their car. But when after a time he did not appear, she felt a strange relief. It was too upsetting—she wouldn't know what to say to such a man of the world. . . . But that wistful look . . . surely he needed encouragement, too. She felt a steady pressure of excitement at the pit of her stomach. When would she see him again?

She dreamed of one imaginative encounter after another, and the day went slowly by in the unventilated coach with its odors of dusty plush and ancient tobacco. Men in uniform, dirty and redolent of liquor, lurched by; Hattie and Caroline stared ahead when their bold admiration became too apparent. Then, unexpectedly, a heavily whiskered conductor bent down to Hattie with a large package. "For you, the man says." Without further identifying the sender, the conductor smiled and went off. Hattie looked up inquiringly, and after a moment's hesitation she tore off the wrapping to find a basket of fresh pears, peaches, and apples—luxuries, in this year of deprivation.

"Oh, Mother—look!" she exclaimed.

With greater restraint, Caroline searched for a card, and found none.

"We can't accept it," she announced.

"We already have."

"I won't touch it."

"Should we throw it away—in wartime?"

Reluctantly, Caroline accepted an apple and Hattie settled back, hoping that her mother would not hear the pounding of her heart. It was from Mr. Blackford, of course. What a romantic, wonderful thing to do! And what would he do next? Now she glanced up every time the door opened, but there was no Calvin Blackford. Her impatience increased. Caroline dozed and Hattie walked to the water bucket at the end of the car. There, through the glass, she saw him standing on the outer platform. His face brightened as he recognized her, and he opened the door for her. After a quick look behind her, she joined him.

Outside, with the rattle of wheels in her ears, she could barely hear his words. When the train roared around a curve, she swung against him, and as he reached up to steady her, his hand was briefly around her waist. He shouted:

"I've waited for hours—eating cinders!" Though his words were teasing, his eager expression frightened her a little. Self-consciously, she began to brush some of the cinder fragments from her hair. Suddenly she saw his expression change. "Your mother's coming. Introduce me."

The explanation was less difficult than Hattie had expected.

"Mother, I just remembered, I did meet Mr. Blackford—with Madge. He was sorry he didn't have a card with him to present his compliments when he sent us the fruit."

Her words sounded feeble in her own ears, and she was surprised that Caroline, after a moment's hesitation, accepted the introduction. As the three turned back to go into the car, Hattie's eyes met Cal Blackford's. She looked away quickly. Although she had refused to acknowledge his conspiratorial glance, the two small misrepresentations had brought them closer together. Facing them on the seat opposite, Mr. Blackford spoke of Parkersburg:

"Been away for years, ma'am, and I'm not sure the Holmes ladies would remember me." His face crinkled in a smile. "They're hot rebels." At the hateful last words, Hattie could almost feel the tensing of her mother's shoulders, but Cal Blackford blurted on. "The war's not going well now, you know. They're talking of burning bridges to keep the enemy out of Philadelphia. If only Lincoln had held hands off and let McClellan stay. You'll see, though—Little Mac's going to run for President yet and take Abe's place."

For the first time, Hattie noticed that Mr. Blackford's voice lacked something of the soft Virginia inflection. He must have been away a long time. In the nervous silence that followed, her mother asked directly:

"You're in the war, sir?"

Calvin Blackford's ears reddened. "No, ma'am—my chest." He added: "I'm a clerk and telegrapher, though, and I'm training for the Military Telegraphic Corps. That's civilian, but directly under the War Department. You ladies know, of course, that the railroads have an important part in this war—first time such a thing ever happened. If I make it, I will be intercepting and decoding messages . . . secret work."

Union or not, Mr. Blackford was in the middle of excitement, with plenty of opportunity to be heroic. In Hattie's view, he had proved himself. Involuntarily she asked:

"It must mean traveling so much. . . . Do you like traveling, Mr. Blackford?"

"Of course," he said hastily.

Later, thinking over this hour, she would understand that to Cal Blackford, travel meant the route from Sandusky to Centralia. Meanwhile, despite her mother's silence, Hattie's soft voice went on:

"After the war is over, I want to see a lot of new places." Her eyes begged him to assure her that she would. As he listened with a smile, she clasped her hands together. "I'd like to go to some of those Continental restaurants that have coffee mixed with chocolate, and . . . hear music . . . and ride in a barouche . . . and most of all, see the Prince of Wales!"

Cal Blackford laughed indulgently. "And what's wrong with American men?"

At the personal note in his voice, Mrs. Ely rose abruptly. Such indelicate talk! Her daughter might not know that Queen Victoria's oldest son was already famous for his taste in American women, but she was sure this stranger did.

"Good-by, young man," she said, inclining her head, and Mr. Blackford, who had risen hastily as she rose, could only withdraw. At the end of the car, he made a gesture of parting, which served further to enrage Caroline Ely. "A very pushing person, and common. That suit—practically a river gambler's costume."

"H'mm." Hattie thought it best to be noncommittal, but her spirits were buoyant. Mr. Blackford must lead a fascinating life, much more interesting than anything she'd known, with important things happening all around him. Caroline's voice broke in.

"You'll meet some fine boys in Parkersburg—young Southerners. Our class of people, and I wouldn't be surprised . . ." Delicately, she shrugged, and Hattie smiled.

"Mother, we'll wait until they ask me." She leaned back, dreamily preoccupied with the young man at hand.

When they stepped down from the train the next morning, after a long uncomfortable night during which they had slept but little, they were met by the Holmes cousins. The three thin, gray-brown women, Miss Lucy, Miss Martha, and Miss Ellen, were lined up in a row, and when they nodded to Hattie and her mother they looked like a trio of hesitant sparrows. Their dark skirts and starched white shirtwaists were identical; their faded hair was drawn tightly up to the tops of their heads.

As they gave dutiful pecks, they looked at Caroline in commiseration. She had aged, alas! and showed no trace, certainly, of the rumored Northern prosperity. But it was on Hattie that they turned full inspection. Her face was smudged with coal dust and dark shadows of exhaustion lay under her eyes. Then she smiled, and her appearance was transformed. What an extraordinary complexion—magnolia-like, Miss Martha thought. They had associated that rare fresh pink only with Southern women, and were partly dazzled, partly taken aback by the brilliance of her eyes, so large and dark. If Hattie had thought them sparrows, they in turn felt as if a bird of paradise had dropped among them.

"That's certainly a beautiful costume," said Miss Lucy, and though the words were complimentary, the tone appeared quizzical.

"It's two years old, most of it," Hattie explained. "I had the basque added." She was about to say "like the French model in Godey's," but she realized that this might not be a recommendation for her cousins.

"Harriet must take after her father." Miss Lucy Holmes, eldest of the three, spoke as if in judgment, and on that note they were led to the carriage.

THREE

Two days later, sitting in the Holmeses' side arbor with a book of poems open in her lap, Hattie enjoyed the slow sleepiness of the afternoon, the droning hum of insects, the fall of yellow rose petals. Drowsing there, she forgot briefly the unpainted side of the gray house, the shabby wicker chairs, and her sense of shock and despair when she had first seen the run-down box of a place. Though she had not expected anything more than a simple home, nothing had prepared her for this dour cottage.

Since then, she had learned more about the almost Spartan gentility of the Holmeses, or more specifically, the primness of their place and their ways. Their parlor was seldom opened—so that the faded paper would not fade more; all the shutters were closed with the dark, because it would not be proper for the passers-by to see in. Whatever went on here, it would be proper. And the monotony was worse; there was nothing to do, and nothing happened.

Hattie and Caroline and the sisters remained at home and met no one except a few yet more elderly Holmes relatives. Hattie still knew nothing of the town. When they had driven the short distance from the station to the house, Parkersburg had seemed a crowded, busy place. Situated on the river, and with the new Northwestern Virginia Railroad passing through, the town had a thriving air. It was exciting, and she wanted to see more of it. But most of all she wanted to see Mr. Blackford. Twice yesterday she had started to go for a walk and Miss Lucy had said quickly:

"Not alone, dear, it wouldn't be nice, especially with all those

19

soldiers about—Union soldiers." If she insisted, of course one of them would accompany her. Hattie had stayed at home.

Soon after they had arrived, Hattie had mentioned Mr. Blackford.

"A typical Yankee, even though some of his people are from around here," Miss Martha said, glancing sharply at her young cousin, and Miss Lucy added:

"We don't speak. This place is along the border, with a good many settlers from Ohio and Pennsylvania—not like the *real* Virginia. That's certainly why they let the North take over." Her tight lips made clear her regret that chance had taken them so far into the uncouth West.

Sitting in the arbor, Hattie sighed and her eyes went from the roses to the book open on her lap. Tennyson . . . she repeated the lines under her breath—

> "O tell her, brief is life but love is long,
> And brief the sun of summer in the North,
> And brief the moon of beauty in the South."

She thought they were so appropriate that tears came into her eyes. Calvin . . . What a cold, Puritanical name for a romantic young man.

She was so absorbed in her reverie that she was startled by a heavy footstep behind her.

"Here, miss." It was Asta, the Negro maid; she and Hattie had made friends immediately. "Letter just come."

Asta's look of intrigue showed that she already understood something of the situation. Hattie ripped open the note and read the few words:

"I tried to see you three or four times. Couldn't you come to the station today, soon? Yours, Cal."

The pedestrian phrasing disappointed her; it had none of the elegance she had imagined. And then there was the suggestion that she go to him—certainly unromantic. Still, he couldn't call here, could he? . . . She wasn't going to be caged! She went into the house and upstairs to her room, where she took off her wide-brimmed garden bonnet and put on her best one with the violets—he had first admired her in that. She kept on her old white embroidered dress because she didn't want to look too

20

dressed-up, and besides, it *was* becoming! With a hasty look in the mirror of the marble-topped washstand, she saw that rebellion and excitement had heightened her color and made her eyes sparkle. As she dabbed a bit of Caroline's lavender water in the hollow of her throat, she heard her mother calling her name. Pulse thumping, she set down the wicker-bound flask and darted down the steep stairs and to the street.

The depot was not too far away and she retraced the course of the carriage ride without much trouble; but as she approached the station, a new alarm tightened inside her. How would she ever be able to find Cal in this crowded place, with what seemed hundreds of strange men and women bustling in and out? At the door of the station, she halted and was about to turn around and retreat when she saw Cal smiling at her. He was working at a telegraph key, an eyeshade cocked jauntily up from his forehead, and over the rat-tat-tat of the instrument his lips moved. "Just a moment." He looked leaner than she remembered, and tired; but seeing again the dark hair, the gray eyes, she felt with a return of her first excitement that he was the handsomest man she had ever seen.

Now Cal threw off his eyeshade, pushed back his chair, and walked eagerly toward her. Her first shyness returned, and he also was obviously a little ill at ease.

"Well, good afternoon, Miss Ely. . . ."

To her surprise Hattie heard herself saying:

"Oh, Mr. Blackford, I've so wanted to see the town, and I'm not allowed to go alone. . . . If you have time, perhaps . . ."

Relieved by her resourcefulness, he bowed gallantly, presented his arm, and they left the station together.

They promenaded slowly through the town, seeing nothing but each other's faces. An hour later, having carefully avoided the street where the Holmeses lived, they returned to the station. This time they stood withdrawn from the crowd in front of the wide door of the cool dark baggage room. A freight train was approaching, and as it ground slowly past, it sent a blast of smoke about them.

"Here." He took her inside, away from the noise and smoke, and in the darkness his protective arm tightened. He drew her close and kissed her. Her mouth stayed tight and cool and frightened. The flowered bonnet dropped off, and the hand behind her

21

pressed until she gave a small cry and drew back. Both of them gasped, but when he pulled her close to him again she lifted her face to rest against his. His lips moved along her cheek and found her mouth. This time the kiss was long and warm, and when at last he raised his head, he was incoherent.

"Hattie . . . darling, you're . . . Good God!" Startled, she stepped away from him, and he caught her hands. "When can I see you again?"

"I don't know." Her voice trembled. "I'll let you know."

Slippers tapping sharply on the sidewalk, she hurried home, frightened by Cal's fervor. What she had done was sinful, and she'd regret it! Then, with a rush of rebellion, she thought only of those last minutes and wanted to be back again.

At dinner that evening, Hattie, still flushed, let her fingers caress the soft tablecloth, the crested forks and knives, relics of earlier, more opulent Holmes days. The sisters spoke, as usual, of the Holmes family, tracing down remote connections, de-lighted, also as usual, when they located a new relationship or ripped away a pretender. Then slowly she grew aware of tension in the glances around the table, and a certain tightness about her mother's mouth.

"Grandma was barely eighteen when she married," Miss Martha, the middle sister, said. "A fine Virginia boy, a cousin. No outside elements."

At this, as if the matter had been prearranged, Miss Lucy, the eldest and sternest, turned to Hattie.

"Harriet, we've been thinking of having a reception for your mother and you. People we've known ever since we came. Our kind."

They meant that nobody like Mr. Blackford need be expected, and now she was certain that the sisters had learned about the afternoon's meeting. And she told herself she didn't care at all that they had.

No one mentioned Cal Blackford in the days that followed, yet Hattie was almost never left alone; someone was always hovering within a few feet of her. The reception would be near the end of the week, and the whole house was involved in preparation. A party at the Holmeses was never a simple matter. With wartime scarcities, the problem of assembling ingredients and substitutes for Asta's cakes, punch, and coffee, and for decorations, created an almost frenzied atmosphere.

There would be no dancing. So much for Hattie's visions of balls by candlelight and troops of eligible young men waiting to claim her as a partner.

From Cal there was no word, and as the week passed with no opportunity to leave the house, Hattie became desperate. Finally, with preparations at a height on the late afternoon of the appointed day, her guardians' vigilance relaxed, and Hattie was sent to the arbor to pick roses for the table. Everyone else was at the back of the house, working over last details. Without stopping this time to change her garden bonnet, she hurried down the street.

Cal joined her at once at the door of the baggage room. Taking her hand, he kept his eyes on the clock as he spoke swiftly:

"Hattie, thank God you're here—they wouldn't let me in when I came to see you." Then he added something that was more disturbing. "I'm expecting word any minute; they're sending me to another railroad office—tonight or tomorrow. A place several hundred miles along the line toward Philadelphia." His voice took on a new urgency. "Could you come with me?"

Before she could answer, someone called out his name. "I'm coming, damn it." Then to Hattie:

"I've got to go—they're moving ammunition through. I'll get some message to you." He kissed her quickly and ran back to the telegrapher's desk.

Go with him . . . then he wanted to marry her! Oh, she would, she would! But what about her mother and the Holmeses? Good heavens—what time was it? She felt an inner tumult of such violence as she hurried home that she was afraid she would burst into tears on the street.

She found Caroline in black evening attire, waiting anxiously on the porch.

"Harriet, people will be coming any minute. Where have you been? I certainly thought you'd have more consideration!"

Whatever else Caroline had to add could wait. She helped Hattie into her crinoline, knotting the strings in her haste, dropped over her head the shot yellow taffeta gown they had remade from one of Caroline's, and brought her hastily down to the brightly lit parlor. They were just in time to join the Holmes sisters in a small reception line and greet several women in their fifties, then two mothers accompanied by their daughters. Hattie tried to smile as she faced the curious glances, the long appraisals. Of course, she murmured breathlessly, she knew of the Treleavens. Was Mrs. Brownlee a cousin of the Brownlees of Atlanta or the ones in Nashville?

From the hall came masculine voices. Now at last she would meet some of the "suitable" men her mother had talked about. Through the doorway slipped an apple-faced individual, his eyes like raisins in the wrinkled skin. "My," he rumbled, "I never expected such a . . ." He stopped, and Hattie realized that the lady in plum satin behind him was his wife. The couple made way for a pair of boys who giggled while one struggled with his cuff and the other pressed at his stiff collar.

If only Cal, with his dark hair and Byronic look, would appear in the doorway! When would she get his message? Another group of women thrust forward, then a tired fellow in his fifties, and two more elderly men, one hard of hearing. These were the last arrivals.

Now the small reception line broke up and Hattie found herself piloted from one tiresome little group of people to another by the watchful Miss Lucy. Would it never be done?

It was Asta who brought the evening to an end. The maid shoved open the parlor door with a wide flourish; obviously she had introduced some reinforcing element into the punch she had sampled in the kitchen. Pressing through the crowd, she put out her hand and almost shouted:

"A note fo' you, miss, and you know who f'om!" With a laugh like a friendly cackle she added, "Young gen'man waitin' on the street now."

The guests exchanged glances, then pretended they had heard nothing amiss. But one by one they started to leave. "Such a nice party, Miss Holmes." "I enjoyed meeting you, Miss Ely." The smiles were set. Hattie was vaguely conscious of her mother's embarrassment, but she thought only of the note in her hand. How soon could she read it?

Finally the last guest had gone, and Miss Martha said sternly: "I think we're due an explanation, miss."

Hardly hearing her, Hattie opened the letter. It read:

"I'm leaving tonight, 11:30 train. Will you?" She folded it back in her hand and looked up.

"Whatever he's said"—Miss Martha was growing angrier—"we told him to leave the front of our house." Her small black eyes snapped. "Think of the family's reputation. You're part Holmes, even if you don't act like it. You act like one of those women your fine father liked to write about. And if you think that young man will marry you, you're mistaken. We know his kind. But the way you've behaved, I don't suppose you care whether you're married or not!"

Hattie heard the sharp intake of her mother's breath, and then Caroline Ely came quietly forward.

"So that's how you really feel about Harriet and my husband," she said to Miss Martha. Her hand went to her face in the familiar protective gesture, and suddenly dropped. "We'll leave tonight."

"Now there's no need for that," Miss Ellen intervened. "Let Harriet behave like other girls of good background . . ."

"That's enough." This was a Caroline that her daughter had never known. "Asta, please send for a carriage to be here in an hour."

Taking Hattie's arm, she guided her proudly up the stairs to their room. There Caroline cried, and Hattie desperately searched for ways to tell of the afternoon's incident; but the habitual reticence between them could not be easily broken down. Caroline wiped her eyes.

"We know where we stand, anyway. We'll go home to Philadelphia, and we'll manage."

Yet as they started to pack their clothes, Hattie was thinking that they couldn't live in Philadelphia on their meager income. The thought of Philadelphia made her heart sink. They were going back to the place she despised, to the place they had left hardly a week ago in the happy belief that perhaps they need never return.

In her preoccupation with her mother, she had completely forgotten Cal Blackford, but suddenly she remembered. Their train would be the same that he was taking. As if her mother read something of her mind, Caroline put down a dress she was folding and looked at her firmly.

"And I don't want you to see that man again, ever. Or talk about him."

She had risen loyally to her daughter's defense, yet she would go no further. A sad-faced Asta knocked; the carriage was waiting. Downstairs, Caroline said a cold good-by to the Holmeses, who ignored Hattie completely.

Sick anxiety filled Hattie as they reached the station and she saw no sign of Cal. They boarded the train in silence. Caroline stared ahead, depression already settling on her. In both of them the unspoken question was insistent: How would things be the day after tomorrow, when they reached Philadelphia again? Finally her mother's head dropped, but Hattie stayed wretchedly awake.

Hours later, when she could bear it no longer, she walked to the end of the car. On the platform, she saw him beckoning as he had before. In a moment she stood beside him. Breaking into tears of relief, she flung her arms around him. He held her firmly.

"I've got to get off in an hour, at the next station. Please come with me."

Her eyes searched his face; he looked more tragically Byron-esque than ever, and the gray eyes were pleading. One thought made her hesitate.

"But . . . but can you get a minister at this time of night?"

If Cal paused, it was for only a moment. "Yes, I think so." His hand tightened over hers. "Just get off and then we'll find out. Hurry back to your seat and get your cape."

Her mother was still dozing. Could Cal really get a minister this time of night? If she didn't go with him now, would she ever see him again? The thought was like a hand on her heart. The train slid to a stop and Caroline awoke. Hattie said tentatively:

"Mother, we'll be here half an hour. I'll go get some sandwiches."

"If you want," Caroline said, too tired to protest. Hattie lingered a little, and to Caroline's sleepy surprise, bent down and kissed her mother's cheek. With an inaudible "Good-by," she went away.

Cal was standing on the platform. "You'll have to wait here," he said.

"I'll wait." Her smile was trusting.

He hesitated. "The minister's house is some way off—over the tracks."

Fifteen minutes passed, twenty. As Hattie stood back from the

26

crowd, her ears caught the agitated clicking of the telegraph key in the corner. It underlined the tenseness of the minutes in a way that the sedate tick of the station clock could not. She heard running steps. It was Cal, propelling a man with uncombed hair and one gallus hanging below the edge of his black coat. The minister, smoothing his hair and adjusting his clothing, began to object.

"Sir, such a public place!"

Resourcefully Cal guided them into the railed-off telegrapher's office. Preparing to protest again, the minister recognized Hattie's unmistakable look of breeding and warmed to the unconscious appeal of her tense face:

"We are assembled . . ." As he began, a crowd pressed at the rail to gape; close behind her Hattie heard the whispers, and then, over it all, the insistent click of the telegraph keys, telling of the war's changes, death, and disaster.

In the middle of the ceremony, with a grinding of wheels, a chuff-chuff of steam, the train pulled out, leaving her behind.

". . . pronounce you man and wife." Hattie turned as Cal's kiss brushed her nose. The minister shook hands, pocketed his fee, and shouldered his way through the onlookers. A soldier applauded, and the crowd joined in.

Harriet Blackford said to her husband:

"I must send a wire ahead to Mother so she'll get it at the next stop."

"Sure. . . . She'll get it before she even misses you! We'll find some place for tonight and then be on our way ourselves tomorrow. I'm under orders." Suddenly he grinned. "We've gone to enough trouble to make it legal." And she began to ask herself what, after all, she knew about this man.

An hour later, in the boardinghouse room with its streaked walls, bare wooden floor, and curtainless windows, Cal spoke cheerfully. "Neat, eh?" His words, Hattie realized, were entirely without irony.

From the distance echoed the long wail of a train whistle—a sound that before this had not seemed like a wail, but had stirred her to dreams of travel, the start of adventure. Tonight, frightened and desolate, she began to cry.

"What's the matter, baby?" Cal had taken off his coat and, reaching into his bag, he brought out a bottle. "Toast to the bride and groom. This will make you feel better." As he bent toward

27

her in the glare of the overhead gaslight, his skin looked unhealthily pale, almost chalky.

"All right." She tried to smile, and sipped at the raw whisky. It was the first time she had tasted it, and it made her choke. She turned her face away, and when she had recovered, she saw Cal standing by the bed, his clothes nearly off. She looked up helplessly at the garish light overhead. "Aren't we going to put it out?"

"Not for a while. . . . Let me help you out of that first" Surely he meant to be kind . . .

FOUR

One evening early in the spring of 1865, Dr. Rawley Morris of Philadelphia, on a short trip down the Ohio River to Cincinnati, settled heavily in his seat on the deck of the side-wheeler *Wild Waggoner*. As he did so, he felt the pressure of a hand on his arm. He looked up in surprise that changed to admiration when he saw the vivid blonde girl who stood by his side. Her dark silk dress was a little shabby, but the lace jabot at her throat and the ruffles at her wrists were immaculately white.

"Don't you remember me, Dr. Morris? Hattie Ely, Mrs. Cal Blackford. You used to come to see Father when I thought you were the two tallest men in the world!"

He struggled to his feet, his face lighting with recognition.

"I should have known you, child, but it's been so long."

He had noticed her a few minutes earlier as the loveliest of a group of young women who had come, chattering and laughing, aboard the river boat. Dr. Morris studied the smiling face with the wide red lips and the dark eyes whose color seemed so remarkable against the light frame of her hair. How beautiful she had grown, and how poised! She could not be much older than eighteen, yet no girl of her age that he knew had such an air. He was about to invite her to join him when a young man, glass in hand, emerged from a near-by cabin.

"Hattie, party's started!"

"I'll be along later." She dismissed him in a voice that reminded Dr. Morris of her mother's Southern huskiness when she had first come to Philadelphia. "Do sit down, Doctor. May I talk with you? I see so few people from Philadelphia."

He pulled up a chair for her and settled himself again. "I'd heard you were married, Hattie."

She sat erect and stiffly in her chair. "Yes, to a Virginian." She went on so rapidly that he missed some of her words. "He's doing very exciting work in the Military Telegraphic Corps. We can't talk much about that, as you understand; it's a secret. Cal's on an assignment now. I'm traveling to meet him by boat with some of the other wives." Hattie had been glancing brightly about her, but now she stopped smiling.

"You do think the war is nearly over, don't you, Doctor? I don't see how the South—how all of us—can stand it much longer." Her hand gripped the arm of her chair. It seemed oddly fragile under the fall of lace, and he wondered if she had been ill. Then, to his surprise, she said abruptly, "Doctor, how's my mother?" The low voice wavered. "I haven't seen her since my marriage."

Dr. Morris had heard something about an estrangement, though he could recall none of the details. He replied discreetly: "She was in good health when I last talked to her."

"Did she say anything about me?"

"She said that your letters sounded as if you were doing well and she was glad for you." For a moment he thought that Hattie Blackford would cry. Instead, she stood up, and her smile was brilliant again.

"Thank you, Doctor," she said. "Thank you. I must go now."

After she left, the Doctor sat alone until he went to his cabin. Somehow troubled by the encounter, he lay awake, and for a time he thought he heard shrill laughter and the rumble of men's voices from the cabins down the deck; then he slept. It was past midnight when he was awakened by a staccato pounding at his door.

"Doctor, it's Hattie. Let me in, please!"

Drawing on his robe, he hurried to the door. She stood there, swaying a little, her blond hair disheveled around her face, a frantic and appealing look in her eyes. "My dear!" he drew her hastily inside his cabin.

Hattie started to sob.

"Oh, Doctor, I'm afraid . . . the water . . . If I hadn't had your door to knock on, I might have . . . might have thrown myself into the river."

He urged her into a chair, and spoke soothingly as he fumbled in his bag for a sedative. After she had swallowed it, she seemed

30

calmer, and thanked him. When she talked again her words were cold and hopeless.

"Doctor, I lied to you. Everything's wrong. My marriage—it was a mistake from the beginning. He's weak and . . . and careless, and lately he hasn't even been able to hold his job." Her voice grew bitter. "I'm going to him now because he's sick. . . . I think he's drinking himself to death."

"My dear!" Dr. Morris was shocked, but she felt his sympathy and spoke more quietly.

"We went back to Parkersburg a few months after our marriage, and my cousins refused to see me, sent word I'd disgraced them. I didn't know anybody in town; the only one that would come to see me was the Holmeses' colored girl, Asta. We'd talk for hours; if they'd known it, they might have dismissed her. When I did see people, it was Cal's friends, people like—you saw." The mild drug was making her drowsy. "Then Cal traveled, and I felt like something in a cage. I was alone when our baby was born."

"Where is the child, my dear?" the Doctor asked softly.

"He died the day after he was born," she said.

And though he had not meant to interfere, her helplessness, the despair in her voice, moved him to say:

"Hattie, why don't you go back to Philadelphia? I'll tell your mother the real facts. It's been kind of you not to worry her, but . . ."

"No," Hattie said quickly. "Don't fret about me, I won't do anything like this again." She forced open her heavy eyelids, and rose.

As she went away she did not appear to hear the rest of his earnest words, and in the morning the chambermaid brought the Doctor a message: Mrs. Blackford had left the boat early, and wanted to thank him for his interest.

That was the story brought by Dr. Morris to a circle of Mrs. Ely's friends. When he had finished, he shook his head.

"Poor child, it really isn't her fault."

"It certainly is," said one member of Dr. Ely's old church on Buttonwood Street. "Nobody's forgotten how she behaved—an elopement, and with a railroad clerk!"

"She's headstrong, and forward. I'm inclined to think she deserves anything that happens to her," said another good lady.

"Poor *Caroline*," was the general decision.

Rumors followed, but this was all that anyone in Philadelphia knew definitely of Harriet Ely Blackford for nearly eight months, when the word arrived that Cal Blackford had coughed himself to death, and she was on her way home.

Waiting at the window of her chill bedroom—though the war was over, wood was still scarce and high—Caroline held to the fraying lace curtains and promised God that she would do everything she could to help the girl as her father would have done. Hattie had written to ask if she could stay with her, and Caroline had replied at once. Now if only Hattie would show a chastened spirit it would be so much easier to guide her.

A carriage stopped in front of the house and Caroline dropped her hand, yet continued to stare through the lace design. At her first glimpse of the slim young woman who carried herself with such graceful assurance, she felt her old feeling of helplessness return. This wasn't the Hattie she had known, who had left her that night on the train—the sixteen-year-old girl who had been defiant but over whom she had felt, however mistakenly, that she had some control. The bell jangled. Caroline said a quick prayer and went downstairs.

The girl in the doorway was no longer composed, but pale and young and frightened, and Caroline saw the shabbiness of the black veil, the cheap cloth of the mourning dress. "Child!" Caroline took her daughter in her arms. Hattie had known so much trouble in these past few years—death all around her in the war sections, and then her own baby and husband! Why, she herself was still a baby . . .

Hattie clung to her mother for a moment and then, no longer disdainful of what she saw, looked about her at the same old carpet, the Holmes portraits, the old furniture crowded against the wall. Beyond, in the dining room, she could see the well-set table, the family silver and linen, so seldom brought out. She went in, touched the edge of one of the chairs, and found herself in tears.

Caroline led her to the table, and as they ate they talked quietly, happily. Caroline told her about Madge, who was engaged to be married, and about the McClellans—General George had found return to civilian life difficult and had taken his family to Europe.

She did not mention Cal Blackford, nor reproach Hattie for her elopement, and Hattie felt grateful; she would not have to speak of those grim last years and confess the release that had come with his death. She was enjoying her favorite pudding, which Caroline had lovingly prepared, when she realized that her mother's tone had changed.

"Hattie, things will be all right. People will accept you when you show you feel differently"—Caroline had trouble finding the tactful words—"that you realize your mistakes." Before Hattie could protest, Caroline went on: "You can join the Ladies' Aid at the church, and go with me to prayer meeting. I'd like you to call with me on Mrs. Sharon and the other members of the Missionary Board. We meet three times a week." She hesitated. "And I hope you can help with the embroidery I'm doing. I'm selling it. Only to a few special people, my friends; they always said I did it so beautifully. Of course it doesn't bring in much money— but it helps, and I like to keep occupied."

Hattie pushed back her chair and got up. "Mother, you know that won't provide for both of us," she said tersely, "and I didn't come home to turn your genteel poverty into genteel starvation!" Her voice deepened in anger. "Cal left me nothing at all, and I'm going to find a job. A lot of new businesses are starting up, and there's speculation and fresh capital everywhere."

Caroline remained silent, torn between futile protest and relief. But when Hattie went on to say she had heard before she came home that young women were being employed as clerks at the Federal Mint, Caroline cried out:

"Work for the Northern government? What would my friends say—and our cousins?"

"If it's a choice between helping you embroider in a freezing room when we can't afford enough wood, and hurting your friends' feelings, I'll just have to hurt them. As for our cousins . . . !" She left her bitterness unsaid.

How like her father Hattie suddenly seemed. At Caroline's frightened look, Hattie relented.

"Come on, Mother, you've had a hard day, and I'm here to care for you." She reached for the lamp and led her mother toward the stairs.

A little later, Hattie stood alone in her cold room, aware only that it appeared much smaller and that she felt exhausted. She had returned to the place from which she had twice tried to escape; now all she wanted was to survive.

Caroline's friends, ever curious, could discern no difficulties at the Ely household. Hattie found a clerical post at the Mint, and Caroline said that she worked hard and came home very tired. Sometimes her mother shook her head as she saw the girl's tired face in the morning; it was still pale and drawn in the gaslight when Hattie arrived home after dark. The good ladies, noting Hattie's drab attire and her air of constraint, nodded to one another with satisfaction. Their prayers for her were being answered.

Caroline had additional worries; things were going badly for most of her family and old connections. The South suffered in these broken days; from Parkersburg the Holmeses humbled themselves to write of biting want, and from Atlanta, Memphis, a half-dozen other places, she heard stories of trouble that grew worse after the ending of the war rather than better.

In Philadelphia, the Unionists were celebrating their success. What a harvest of ills their victory had brought the city! Every day saw new corruption and revelry, scandalous social affairs, parties at the hotels that went on far into the night. And the names that people mentioned! Names once too disreputable to be whispered. What would Dr. Ely be saying were he here now?

But one night Caroline forgot all such general concerns. Hattie did not come home at her usual hour of six. Caroline kept her dinner hot, but eight o'clock came, then nine and ten, and Hattie had not returned. In the sitting room, which they were able to keep a little warmer than the bedrooms, Caroline bent over her sewing. At last she heard the sound of wheels in the street. Hurrying to the window, she saw a shiny victoria halt and her daughter alight on the arm of a tall, florid man who was dressed in the height of fashion in a long, tightly fitted light coat, and carried a gray top hat in his hand. Caroline opened the door.

"Mother, this is Mr. George Madison."

Caroline stood in frigid silence as Mr. Madison bowed. His quick blue eyes scanned the older woman's set face, and he made his adieus brief. When the door closed behind him, Caroline remained silent.

Hattie's face was flushed for the first time since she had come home, and she looked warmly alive. She clasped her hands and spun about in a remembered dance step.

"Harriet!" Caroline finally forced herself to speak. "You're never to be seen again, unchaperoned, with a man like that."

"I met him at the Mint." Hattie's dark eyes were no longer lusterless; they had a bright new fire. "He was kind, and I don't know what you mean by 'a man like that.' You can't call him a Yankee. He's from Texas, and served under General Lee in Virginia."

Caroline's voice became shrill. "Don't forget your father's words—'the first step in licentiousness . . .'"

Hattie spoke in quick perversity. "Not all of Father's women in the almshouse died there! Some repented and got married. I've just had the finest meal I ever tasted—I brought home some fruit for you—and I'll repent being across the table from a handsome man at my leisure!"

"Hattie, I know you've had a lot of discouragement," Caroline pleaded, "but your good name—it's all you have."

Hattie shook her head. "If you'll allow an expression I learned at the Mint, that's not negotiable currency! I intend to go out with Mr. Madison as often as he asks me."

Caroline cried out, "You know, of course, that such a man won't suggest marriage to a girl without money!"

"Mother," Hattie said as if to a small child, "I hope it won't be necessary to marry every man I find good company."

No more was said, but when boxes of roses began to arrive the tension increased, and when, at last, happening to see Hattie writing a note to Mr. Madison, Caroline remonstrated again, her daughter spoke in a new tone. It was gentle, yet decisive.

"If this distresses you so much," she said, "I think I'd better take a place of my own."

That week Hattie moved to a flat in the unfashionable quarter north of Broad Street, and Caroline's friends exchanged scandalized reports. A young woman living by herself away from her family—it branded her as lost. Thereafter, except for the few conventional words they spoke when Hattie made a brief monthly call to bring her a check, Caroline acquired most of her information about her daughter from rumors that grew increasingly more alarming.

35

When it was whispered among the Presbyterian ladies that young Mrs. Blackford had gone to the much talked-about summer resort of Long Branch, even the most charitably inclined no longer prayed for her. The war profiteers were throwing their money around like paper at such "fashionable" watering spots, where the favored ones parading on the sands hardly bothered to touch the water, but "danced and gambled the night through." And it was said that Mrs. Blackford's costumes were equal to any.

Where did Mrs. Blackford get the means for such trips? And for her wardrobe? Word spread that she had given up her place at the Mint.

One evening she was recognized as one of a festive party at the Academy of Music in the box of John Robin, the long-legged, saturnine attorney of local celebrity. That same spring, gossip told how young Mr. Cabot from Massachusetts, admiring her from a distance, said he had heard she was a half-sister of the McClellans and inquired innocently if he would meet her at that night's reception. He was quickly enlightened, but one of the women added that Mr. Cabot still gave every indication that he was going to call on the woman.

Later that year Philadelphia had a new name to mull over when Mrs. Blackford's escort for several evenings was a Philadelphia artist who had inherited a fortune; and meanwhile Mr. George Madison of Texas made frequent appearances. As one of the town's sportsmen put it, they'd all have to admit that the lady's range was considerable. She came forth in even finer costumes, richer carriages, yet there was a certain element of mystery; nobody could point to any single individual as her protector. . . .

Rumors became still more extravagant. Some whispered about a breach-of-promise suit, at least a threatened one, against a man, or perhaps two of them. Those who claimed to be informed said that such matters were settled out of court, and handsomely, in Mrs. Blackford's favor. But no one seemed to be certain of any of these things.

Then, shockingly not only to the Presbyterian ladies but even more to the fashionable families led by the "other Elys," Hattie Blackford moved into the heart of enemy territory. She took up residence in a mansion facing the fashionable Rittenhouse Square. It was a place of many rooms, imported paintings, and period furnishings built by a war-rich butcher who had recently committed suicide when his profits proved no key to the society to which he had aspired. Along the sunny square, with its air of settled serenity, not a single matron would leave a card, or would speak when the "most fascinating woman in Philadelphia," bright head held high, perfectly gowned and hatted, passed them at their door. Mrs. Blackford, unlike the butcher, did not seem to notice the omission.

Who made it all possible? There were certain Philadelphians who contended that at least some of her means, if not all, came from gambling. Like other houses of the day, they said, Mrs. Blackford's simply provided an opportunity for men of good standing to try their luck under congenial (and also discreet) circumstances.

At one time the whole town was talking of her "Chinese bowl," an idea, it was said, that she had imported from Paris. In the corner of her wide drawing room, among its brocaded sofas and gold chairs placed casually along the walls, was a porcelain dish overflowing with silver dollars. If anyone's funds ran out, he was free to dip into it. No attempt was made to watch over exact amounts; within the next few days the borrower replaced the money, usually with a gift for the generous hostess.

Thursday night at Mrs. Blackford's—the expression meant something to the Philadelphia of 1868! Yet the establishment on Rittenhouse Square was more than a place at which one tried his luck; it became known as a center of bright parties, a salon, a residence of gaiety and good talk. More and more the adventurous, the bohemian (the word was now being used), sought her out. Here they heard urbane conversation, met flavorsome strangers; here, too, they heard good music, and some contended that it was the only private house in town in which one could be sure the music would be first-rate.

After a time, to the further amazement of the moralists, certain young women of good family appeared at Mrs. Blackford's. Later, when her fame had become international instead of local, newspapers, quoting old citizens, were emphatic on the point. The young women were warned explicitly, and they were talked about; nevertheless a number of them still were seen there.

What was the explanation of Mrs. Blackford's appeal? She was beautiful, yet Philadelphia had other beautiful women. Stories of her odd fascination drifted about. As one young clubman told another:

"She's amazing. She gets what you're trying to say—like that." He snapped his fingers. "She'll look up from under that fringe of dark lashes, repeat what you just said, phrasing it better than you did, tell you how clever you are to have said it, and by God, you believe it!"

By now, too, Philadelphia heard a great deal about Mrs. Blackford's wit. She read French books, and poetry from England, and she made easy use of both. Once the well-entrenched Mrs. Montgomery, who had known Dr. Ely in his early days, observed with a sniff that Hattie was no better than one of her father's famous strumpets. Hearing this, Mrs. Blackford shrugged and said something that only readers of the poet Mr. John Keats would understand—that Mrs. Montgomery was a *"beldame sans merci."*

A contemporary journalist later described the Mrs. Blackford of this period: "A woman of extraordinary beauty . . . hair in great profusion and an imperial sort of forehead, broad, open, and white as ivory. Her dark eyes flashed under her long lashes . . . aglow with wit and kindness." The word "kind" must have made the Presbyterian ladies sniff, but it is there still in the old newspaper, next to the column warning young people against her, as if she were not herself still in her early twenties.

In these years she had her effect on the city's styles; women not only repeated her bon mots but also copied her hair modes, the long ringlets dripping from a high comb that she wore in the evening, or the way she sometimes pulled her hair down simply to a bright knot at the back of her head. In time she started a trend in costume; she began to wear white everywhere, in all seasons. The unimpressed frowned at the inappropriateness of the color. Was she trying to mock her betters?

One evening early in the spring of 1869 Hattie Blackford was waiting for George Madison to come to dinner. A glance about the upstairs sitting room told her that everything was in order— flowers on the pair of tables at the window, the flicker of candles in their holders, the brocaded curtains drawn against the late dusk. How different from the dark parlor of her youth! But her face clouded as she thought of her mother's favorite room, and again she wondered if Caroline would ever greet her or accept anything from her with understanding instead of cold suspicion. Catching a glimpse of herself in the elaborate gilt-framed mirror above the marble mantel she looked sadly into the reflected eyes, so dark beneath the white forehead and the golden hair wreathed with Parma violets. There were many more violets in small silver bowls about the room. George Madison had been generous with her. Though almost nobody in Philadelphia would believe it, he had been the only one.

She had learned more and more during these two years. George Madison had brought her the Chinese bowl, had provided the background for a new education in worldliness—taught her a great deal about food and wines, introduced her to the fashionable shops, and encouraged her to develop a natural talent for expressing herself in her dress. With a smile she thought of his sometimes bluff manner and his booming voice, of his habit of waving to her across the room whenever he came in or left, and of his jokes (often repeated) about his holdings in the Louisiana-Texas marshes.

She moved to the window and looked out, thinking she heard his carriage. A few moments later he came into the room.

"George, you're a little late," she said, without censure.

The tall man with the shock of light hair falling across his forehead kissed her hand, then her lips, and, settling into a comfortable brocaded chair, reached for his cigars in an inlaid box. He did not speak, and after she had rung for his brandy and soda, she sat down by him.

"Well, George, what is it?"

"Nothing." A minute later, however, he was pacing the floor, glass in hand. "And you?"

He lifted the thick, irregular brows, wrinkling his forehead. He looked all at once like a worried boy, but she knew that he wanted to pass over his own concerns, at least for the moment. She clasped her hands in a nervous gesture.

"Somewhat disturbed, I'll confess. My old friend Madge, from school, walked past me today—and kept on walking."

"That's the penalty of being seen with rascals like me," he said.

Her reply had a mocking note. "Yes, you're the most notorious man in Philadelphia, and I'm the most notorious woman. I think we owe it to society to get married!"

Hattie was not certain what answer she expected; the one she received, however, was a shock. George Madison put his cigar down and told her, without preamble, that next week's papers would announce his engagement to Miss Newell of Baltimore. She rose, turned away from him, and went to the window, as if to look down at the square. Finally she turned, and shrugged.

"It had to happen someday, didn't it?"

He took a step forward. "You know it wouldn't have if you'd ever let me know you wanted marriage."

The corners of her mouth curved up a little in a smile, and she looked directly at him.

"George, even if I had?"

Still more uncomfortable, he remained on his feet while she sank into a small gold chair by the window. Before he had time to speak, she went on.

"I'm tired, George, just tired." A memory returned to her. "My father once explained the Latin roots of the word 'transgressor' to me. *Trans*, across, *gredior*, flock—across the flock. Not simply sinning, but going another way from the others. And the way of the transgressor is hard!"

George came over to put his arm around her shoulders. For a minute or so she allowed it to remain, then she rose.

"As if I ever worry nowadays about the flock, except to separate the *chic* from the *gauche!*"

He laughed, feeling relieved. "My dear, you're the wittiest woman I've ever known."

Her anger came suddenly. "I've had to be; when a woman gives up the support of conventions, she has to make her own. But . . . right now I don't think I can do it any longer." She put her hand to her cheek; it was almost Caroline's gesture. How lonely and how precarious her position had become. The city was too powerful for her. It had, after all, defeated her. "I've got to get away from Philadelphia, George, to New York, or Paris—anywhere."

Still more relieved, though he had known she would not make it difficult for him to break away, he said:

"I've been to Paris, Hattie, and you'd like it. Society's free there, really free. To the Parisians music and good talk and such things are important—not simply food for scandal, as they are here. You'll meet amusing people, and they don't call the women

40

strumpets over there!" After a moment he added, "I know several Parisians, and I can . . ."

As he talked on she seemed hardly to be listening. Late that evening in her unlighted room she stood alone, a pale figure in her dressing gown of white silk, staring again at the square, where the fresh leaves showed under the hard light of the gas standards. So it was settled. Slowly her depression left her. As it had many times before, the prospect of a journey or a change stimulated her. She thought of the day when she had looked at herself in the mirror in her mother's sitting room, pleased with the cheap velvet violets on her bonnet and hopeful of the future. Her face was wry; how naïve she had been then, and how foolish!

Yet even now, in spite of everything that had happened, her hopes were not altogether different from those of that younger girl. The violets were real now, grown in the hothouse of the best florist in town, and she still loved them. Perhaps she would never find the man she had dreamed of then, but without forming it into words, she knew that she would never stop looking until she did.

FIVE

UNDER THE SIGN "SALLE DES BAGGAGES," HATTIE BLACKFORD WAITED impatiently as the officials made their slow inspection. Tapping her toe, she looked up to see a Frenchman leaning on a counter and appraising her as if she were an item of merchandise. When she turned her back to him, she saw another, who stood leaning on his cane for a more leisurely evaluation. She flushed, but a certain amusement lightened her embarrassment—so this was what Paris was like, even at six o'clock in the morning!

She heard one of them say *belle*, and knew that meant "beautiful." But Hattie had already decided that the French she had learned at Miss Dudley's school and from reading was not adequate; that she must find a teacher at once to improve her accent and her ease of speech.

When her trunks were finally removed to the gray stone entranceway, she met new difficulty. Through a cluster of grumbling men and women she saw a cab and tried to attract the driver's attention. When he ignored her, she ran up to him. Barely bending his head, he told her, "*Loué, madame.*" He indicated the blue flag to show that the cab was engaged. She went up to another, a third and fourth; all were *loués*. The spring morning was already warm; in dismay she felt her face grow hot, and tears started to her eyes.

"*Eh, ma'mselle!*" The shrill feminine voice, rather like a child's, came from close by. A ripe-faced, smiling girl of irregular yet pronounced beauty, dressed in magnificently fashionable attire—soft brown silk with gold trimmings and a hat of deceptive simplicity—was smiling at her. Diamonds sparkled at the plump throat, in the ears, and on the fingers. Beside this resplendent in-

42

dividual, Hattie felt suddenly that her wine taffeta basque, which had been almost ahead of the fashion in Philadelphia, was conservative to the point of being dowdy.

Despite the sophistication of her costume, the stranger had a look of bland innocence. Her lightly curled red hair had been shorn almost like a boy's. Also, Hattie thought, her French was rather odd. Who could this remarkable individual be? Now the girl spoke again.

"Couldn't I *help?*"

"You're very kind," Hattie replied. "I think my hotel's only a little way from here."

"Ai, dearie! I *thought* you weren't one of these Frenchies."

Good will beamed from the round pink face.

"Come along; my carriage is waiting. Oh, I'm Cora Pearl!"

She seemed to be somewhat disappointed that Hattie did not recognize the name. Gratefully following her, Hattie realized that a growing crowd clearly *did* place Miss Pearl. It gathered around them as they came to a resplendent equipage. The horses were fine specimens, curried to a gloss; the carriage, silver-trimmed, had satin seats draped in lace.

Cora Pearl, ignoring her admirers, shoved her guest expertly in, allowed the driver to arrange their wide skirts, asked Hattie the name of her hotel, and directed him to stop there.

"I arrived *behind* you just now," she sighed. "A week at Biarritz, and I was *crazy* to get back to Paris!" She made a mischievous face, then asked, "You *know* anyone in this city, lovey?" (Cora emphasized some word in nearly every sentence.)

Hattie hesitated. George Madison had given her the name of one man in particular; she had not planned to use it so soon, if at all. But now she felt the need of establishing some definite identity.

"I was told to see Monsieur Jeanmarie."

Obviously this gave Miss Pearl a clue to the question that puzzled her. "Oh yes." Her round blue eyes were innocent. "I haven't *met* him, but he's certainly *wealthy*. I've heard, though, that he's spending the season in the *South*. Oh, we're here." Miss Pearl waved her jeweled hand. "When you're settled, come *see* me. Wednesday's my at-home day, one o'clock *on*. On the Champs; *anybody* will tell you."

The artless voice ended with a touch of amusement, as if the

43

speaker all at once perceived a joke. Hattie was momentarily nettled, but Cora Pearl had been very kind, and she bowed gratefully and thanked her.

She found that her room in the hotel, though small and with characterless furniture, was more expensive than she had anticipated. She felt a little frightened and very much alone, and when the maid came in to help her unpack, she could not resist asking in her halting French if the girl knew of Cora Pearl.

"Madame does not jest? Everybody knows . . . They say half the men of the Court are hers, or would like to be. The most beautiful legs in Paris. And the finest carriage."

Hattie dismissed her. She had understood enough of the answer; Alexandre Dumas fils' had catalogued these women of the glittering Second Empire: "ladies of rank, actresses, and courtesans of elite place," and "those of good birth who have thrown over at least some of the restraints." Dumas had called them "demimondaines"—those of the half-world. That, she supposed, was the way she herself would be classified if she joined the Parisian world.

On her way downstairs for breakfast, a memory came to her, and with her croissants she asked for half coffee, half hot chocolate. How shocked her mother had been that day on the train! . . . Poor Caroline. . . . Hattie had gone to see her before leaving Philadelphia, and they had kissed, yet the reconciliation had not been so complete as she had hoped.

She made a little face at her first taste; the second left her undecided, but after that she drank with gaiety, beginning to savor along with the new brew the atmosphere of the large, well-appointed dining room. She felt a growing excitement. This was really the capital of the world, and she was ready to find out about it, on her own. Perhaps she might call on Miss Pearl, after all. There'd be none to whisper here; it wasn't Philadelphia. But first she would explore the city for herself.

And she must not forget that French teacher. She went to the desk to ask about one; a really good man was recommended at once. He would come the next morning.

That evening, in a hired carriage (she had dressed in her favorite white and dined too early in the hotel restaurant, which at that hour had been as deserted as at breakfast time), she watched the lights go on in one park after another. From a bridge she traced the river, and then she saw the Tuileries, a many-turreted mass against the disappearing clouds. It flamed with light and she thought of the stories that were told of the Empress Eugénie, her perfumed processions and fantastic tableaux-games. From a doorway she heard a strain of music, and her driver bent over in friendly fashion.

"The American lady might be interested. Just going in that door. The Prince—the Prince of Wales."

Leaning forward, she made out a portly man of thirty or so, Germanic-looking with his blondish sideburns. He was directing a broad smile at a lady who suggested light opera rather than the halls of Sandringham. Her majestically billowing skirts had five tiers, and silver ornaments twined over her black locks.

Well, it was the closest *she'd* ever be to royalty. And Hattie remembered for the second time how she had told Cal that she wanted to taste the coffee-chocolate mixture and look at the Prince of Wales.

"Madame's hotel. *Merci,* madame." The night was early, and the stars hung close over the trees; at the front of the hotel was an open-air café with lines of tables facing the street. As the waiter led her to a table she became aware, not unpleasantly, that her appearance—in fitted white broadcloth, a white wreath around her head—had created a stir. She was accustomed to admiration, but it was reassuring to find it here too.

Sipping her vermouth, she settled back to watch the passers-by: the flower-sellers with fresh blossoms and dirty faces; boulevardiers with stovepipe hats, long-tailed coats, and goatees trained to a tapering point. Against a line of sloping trees that seemed painted against the blue evening, the open carriages rolled by, conveying couples or perhaps a single woman, her skirts flowing over the sides, headdress blending into the pattern of the lining. The early summer of Paris. . . . It was not hard to see why the world would want to come to it.

"Madame." The waiter put down another vermouth.

"I didn't ask for this."

By way of answer he put down a card. "The gentleman with the yellow gloves. He prays that Madame accept."

With a shake of her head, she put down some coins and left, but she could not resist the temptation to look toward the table

45

that the waiter had indicated. The gentleman with the yellow gloves had hair of silky white; she would have put his age at seventy-five. This was no part of her dream! Upstairs she sat alone at her window for a long time, hearing the sound of a pair of violins, rising and falling in the blue night.

The next morning the French lessons began, and it was soon apparent that it would not be long before "Mrs. Blackford with her keen mind and supple tongue" would be speaking French with ease—"with a slight accent to be sure" but one which Parisians, especially the men, would find attractive.

By the time Wednesday arrived, Hattie had had her fill of solitary sight-seeing. And Wednesday was Cora Pearl's day at home. Why not? The driver knew the address at once, but as the carriage stopped Hattie thought for a moment that he had made a mistake. The residence was of ornate stone, with glass-and-iron portals flanked by tall lights. The rewards of Cora's world were more lavish than she had imagined.

The doors swung open to reveal a tiny black boy in scarlet turban and white loincloth. No less surprised than she, he was preparing to close the door in her face when from inside they heard Cora's baby voice, shrieking in her atrocious French:

"*Bien, Toucoutte.* Let 'er in, let 'er *in!*"

Hattie stepped into a vast silent interior from which the day was nearly shut out, a circular foyer heavy with Eastern hangings; several Louis XIII chairs rose from the dimness. All was elaborate, rich in color and ornament, yet, unlike its owner, correct in every line and detail. Beyond, opened a long parlor revealing red velvets, monumental sofas and sideboards, with one wall dominated by a pale tapestry. It, too, was empty; as she went through it Hattie caught the movement of a pair of discreet servants at a distance.

Something touched her foot, and Hattie jumped. It was a most unusual cat, its white fur dyed a bright pink. From yet another chamber she now heard voices.

"*Entrez!*" Again it was Cora's unmistakable French. "*S'il vous* please."

Hattie paused on the threshold. The sunlight blazed into this room through a set of great paneled windows. Still, she could make out only the backs of a seated semicircle of men, most of them elderly. They leaned forward in intent postures, several supporting themselves on their walking sticks. On the floor beside each man lay a shining tall hat, gloves tossed precisely over the rim.

Then she saw a flash of pink. Moving closer, she could see over their white heads. There was Cora, stretched full-length on a sofa, arms languidly behind her head, and entirely nude. Hattie drew back. But Cora cried:

"Hattie, come *over!* We're nearly finished our salon, anyway."

Cora stood up on the striped satin divan, yawning and stretching her hands high in the air; the Negro boy darted forward with an almost transparent silk covering that she slipped over her shoulders. In it Cora's nakedness looked more wanton than before.

"Good-by, messieurs." She dismissed them as if they were servants, then, as if it were an afterthought, introduced the men casually to Hattie. Her face a bright red, Hattie acknowledged the confused greetings. Senators, professors, doctors, each with his hat in one hand, gloves in the other. All France seemed represented here, except the clergy. They scrutinized her with interest, and several were about to speak when Cora waved toward the door. Humbly they left.

Cora descended from the couch, and taking Hattie's hand, led her through a gold-hung boudoir to the black-and-gold bath chamber at the side.

"Dearie, I got to 'urry," Cora said. "This one's waiting, and those Hungarians are *anxious*." The thought of his anxiety seemed to please her, and she moved more slowly.

As Cora slid into her onyx bath, Hattie, recovering from her first shock, noted admiringly the soft curve of Cora's hips. But those celebrated legs were no better than her own! Running her soapy fingers caressingly over her throat, Cora smiled.

"You *know*, Hattie, I like you. You going to take an *apartment?* I can help find one."

Hattie was touched. Cora's was the first warm interest she had met in a long time. And Cora had nothing to gain through her friendship.

"I think I'll get accustomed to the city before I decide." Her voice sounded almost prim.

Cora went on: "Lovey, I'm going to the *theater* Saturday, supper afterward. There'll be people there it will do you *good* to meet."

Though Hattie was curious about it all, this was a quicker plunge than she had expected. Then, because she could think of nothing else to say, because she was bewildered, she agreed.

"Well, yes, I'll come."

"*Bien.*" Cora stepped out of the water. The turbaned boy, Toucoutte, appeared with two towels, and while Cora rubbed arms and breasts, he carefully dried her legs. Backing away, Hattie left her in a fragrant mist.

Saturday evening, Hattie dressed carefully for the theater in a low-shouldered satin gown. The green panels against the white cloth were outlined with embroidered green and gold leaves, and in her hair she had fixed ivy leaves in a style she had noticed the day before in a shop window on the Rue de la Paix. She would do, yet she would need many more costumes like this. In Philadelphia her few French imports had been enough; here they would be lost among richer, more extravagant wardrobes.

Downstairs Cora's silver-trimmed carriage was waiting; the footman opened the door.

" 'Urry—we'll miss the *best* part, before the curtain goes up!" Cora cried out. She was dressed in silver cloth and white ostrich feathers. She signaled the driver and they drove quickly down the boulevard, following the evening lights that stretched into the haze of distance. "The gentlemen will join us later," Cora explained, leading Hattie through the foyer of the theater.

As they entered Cora's violet-lined box, Hattie saw hundreds of faces turn toward them. Her face flushed, but after the flurry caused by their entrance had subsided, she felt less on display, and looked about, enchanted by the blaze of lights, the mingled perfumes, the glint of silks and design of lace. Behind her feathered fan Cora indicated some of the personages.

"The Count de Persignac, a *gay* dog, that. Went through two fortunes, his *own* and his *wife's*, and now he's faithful to her again because he can't *afford* anybody else."

A little later Cora pointed out a woman who looked like a courtesan in a bright-red satin dress cut to reveal almost naked breasts. But Cora identified her as one of the more staid Princesses of the Court.

"I know all about '*er*," she said, grinning. "We have the same *dressmaker;* once she liked one of my dresses, and we exchanged patterns."

A moment afterward Cora pointed to two sisters, a blonde and a brunette, who, she said, shared an apartment; a gallant who called on one was always expected to pay tribute to the other.

"So their income *doubled!*" When Hattie did not smile, Cora was amused. "Hattie, you're so *ladylike!*" She nodded in another direction. "Rossignol. She sang here, and had five lovers at once, and not one suspected any of the others!"

Then Cora grew shrewder. "The stage, my girl, is a *wonderful* way up the social ladder." She named eight actresses who had married into nobility. "Still, don't *try* it unless you've got more than looks, Hattie. I *did,* and they 'ooted me off!"

Hattie laughed. "I never will," she said. "I'm much too fond of the theater to deprive myself of the pleasure of being in the audience."

At last the lights dimmed. It was a comedy, *Fanny Lear,* by the sprightly librettists Halévy and Meilhac, and Hattie was promptly absorbed in the adventures of the sailor's daughter who received a grand inheritance, then went off to Paris to buy a marquis for a husband and win a place among the aristocrats. She sighed when Fanny Lear admitted, "I wasn't born to have the virtues of the poor, but those of the rich!"

The virtues of the rich, the well-placed. She was still thoughtful when the curtain fell, and Cora hurried her out to join the others at the Maison Dorée. Inside the restaurant redolent of wines, rich sauces, and spiced game, they proceeded to a private salon in which two or three other women sat at a table with a dozen men.

"Mademoiselle Le Blanc. . . . Mademoiselle Guimond." Cora called out the names of the girls, who acknowledged Hattie's presence warily. She had scant chance to heed most of the men, for her dinner partner, a gray-haired, aristocratically lean man in his fifties, immediately captured her attention. He asked a great many questions.

"Your name?" "You're really an American?" Presently he inquired, "And what's the news from the United States?"

Her black eyes sparkling, she answered:

"I couldn't say. When I was there what interested me most was the latest word from Paris!"

"Then I shall tell you," he said, smiling. The man had charm, and an air of command that Hattie found disturbing. She asked about his own background, but received evasive answers; she learned only that he was the Duke of Bodenbach, here on a visit.

The heavily sauced dishes came and went, each with its wine. By the time coffee was served the conversation around them was growing shrill, overemphatic; down the table two men started to quarrel about Cora. Under the scores of candles the room was suddenly overwarm; Hattie noticed that the panes of the windows had misted.

"May I take you home?" Bodenbach inquired, and gratefully she accepted. At her door he kissed her hand. "Will you dine with me tomorrow?"

She answered cautiously, "I'm not sure I'll be free; may I send you a note?"

"Please make it yes, and let me show you Paris. You can reach me at the Jockey Club." He bowed.

Hattie was attracted to him, but as she undressed, her indecision increased. She could not go to sleep, and when she did she dreamed of her father—not as the abstracted old man who had seemed to ignore her, but as the young, vibrant minister. Sentences that he had once addressed to the Magdalenes of New York poured into her ears. Yet his eyes were warm and magnetic, and she felt a wild happiness. Then his voice changed to supplication:

"Go home, go home to the lost purity of your youth." And at that she turned from him and wept.

"How can I go home? There is no one there who loves me."

Hattie woke, crying in actuality. The lights of the city outside her window were dimmed, and the few that remained bright seemed far off and alien. Her sobbing went on until the sky began to lighten, when she fell asleep only to wake with a start. It was near the hour when Cora was to call for her to take her driving in the Bois.

She rose exhausted and depressed, but the gaiety of the chambermaid who hooked her into her dress, and the bright afternoon, made her dream seem far off. "*Les songes ne sont que les mensonges*"—dreams were only lies, and Cora Pearl's chestnut horses waited below.

A few minutes after she joined Cora, she forgot her dream completely.

"The afternoon *parade!*" Cora said happily.

Along the tree-bordered Champs-Elysées they were in a close procession of calèches, victorias, open carriages, each filled with women. Sometimes the carriages were accompanied by dashingly uniformed men on horseback. From beyond the trees came band music, to blend with the steady whir of wheels. On the sidewalks men raised their headgear; women bowed and their bell-shaped skirts swayed, tilting now and then to reveal the cage below, the white-silk stockings and buttoned black-kid boots of the mode. High feminine cries reached them, and the hearty laughter of officers. Cora nodded to members of the Jockey Club, government officials, a Zouave with flashing, baggy trousers, and members of the Cent Gardes, the Emperor's own regiment, each man at least six feet high, in blue tunic, white breeches, and helmet topped with red plumes. Then unexpectedly Cora grasped her arm.

"The *Empress!*"

Hattie had only a glimpse of a tall, finely molded figure in warm purple, a woman with chestnut hair. The Empress Eugénie! Yet as her carriage disappeared Hattie wondered aloud:

"How would a stranger tell the Empress from almost any one of the demimondaines?"

Cora laughed. "Haven't you *heard* about the visiting Russian at the Satory races? He asked, 'Who are all the *women?*' and they told him, 'The *gay* ladies.' He wanted to know, 'Where are the respectable ones?' And they answered, 'There are *none* left.'"

Hattie smiled. "I certainly couldn't tell them apart at the theater last night."

Cora was reminded of something else.

"You were taken with the *Fanny Lear* last night. A *nice* name, and yours has no *dash*, dearie. Why don't you try *that* one, before someone else does?"

"Change my name?"

Cora was amused. "Did you think my *real* name was Cora Pearl?"

"Why, yes."

"Well, I don't tell this to just *anyone*, and you mustn't *repeat* it—but my real name is Emma Crouch."

Hattie couldn't help laughing aloud, as Cora had intended her to, but she felt a little sorry for her. Despite the change of name, Cora had not been able to shed her cockney past. Was anyone ever able to discard a background with a name? . . . But why

51

not try? . . . The zest of the hour and the scene made her reckless.

"Fanny Lear," she repeated. . . . "Why not?"

"Your *nom de plume!*" Cora waved her hand.

"No, my *nom de guerre.*"

Years later Hattie Blackford would recall that as the moment when she made her decision; from then on she would be part of this world. She had a curious sensation of relief. As Cora signaled to the driver to turn back, she asked:

"Did you *like* Bodenbach? I've got a feeling that man's somebody to be *careful* with."

Cora's somewhat patronizing attitude nettled Hattie.

"Oh, I don't think so at all. He's certainly charming—and different from any man I've ever met."

Cora patted her hand. "If ever you have *trouble* with one of 'em, come to me. The thing to remember is that you've got your *choice* here—anything you really want. You can keep some men on your leash *forever* and never have to give anything but a *smile* if you feel like it."

All the way home Hattie continued to think of Bodenbach with increasing warmth. She repeated to herself his words of the night before. "Please make it yes," he had said, and the memory of his oddly accented voice stirred her. The first thing she saw when she got to her room was a note on her dressing table, propped up against a little black-velvet box. She opened the note eagerly. "May I hope it will be supper tonight?" it read. The velvet box held a small diamond brooch. With quick decision she went to the escritoire. After she had signed her own name to her note of acceptance, she added "Fanny Lear."

A month later Hattie waited uneasily for the Duke of Bodenbach. It was to be his final visit; these past weeks had gone by quickly. Her dreams had been even more short-lived. At their first supper he had seemed to respond to her warmth, but perhaps she had been too eager. He had remained elegantly correct in his courtesies. He had taken her to a series of private suppers; he liked music as much as she did, and he had arranged for several quartets to play in their upstairs dining salons. Yet, though he had spent a great deal of his time with her, they had rarely gone out in public.

52

He had told her that Bodenbach was not his real name, that he was a member of a small royal house in Central Europe, one who must watch appearances. And she had accepted the situation. Tonight would be their farewell before he went to the Austrian baths. He had hinted that his rewards to those close to him were generally royal, too, but the diamond brooch had been his only recognition of the unconcealed fact that she was a stranger in Paris whose funds were going rapidly.

He was late. At the desk, she took up her journal, in which she had begun to make irregular entries, most of them epigrammatic observations on her new life. This time she wrote: "It is odd how the same character trait is called by different names at different ages. At fifteen lack of knowledge of the world is 'innocence,' at twenty it is 'naïveté,' and from then on, it is 'stupidity!' I don't wish to be stupid."

Hattie glanced at the clock; he had been due an hour earlier. There was a knock on the door and she opened it to find not Bodenbach, but a hotel attendant with a package.

"The Duke was sorry he was not able to see you tonight, madame. He left this for you."

In the package was a batch of strange certificates, English stocks. No—American, a petroleum company from Pennsylvania. She had heard that sharpers cheated Europeans with such worthless paper! Clipped to one of the certificates was a note.

"Madame Lear: My son has run into gambling debts, which unfortunately prevent me from favoring you as of course you deserve. However, the enclosed may prove some measure of my gratitude for our friendship; you will understand better than I what value they represent."

Cora had been right; he'd made a fool of her, and with what suavity! In spite of all the fine words she had just written, she had been so naïve, so innocent, so stupid! What would she do now? Letting the certificates drop to the floor, Hattie sat down at her desk again, put her head on her arms, and cried.

The next morning Cora Pearl, sitting on her famous couch intent on gilding her toenails, looked up as Hattie came in.

"Honey, what *is* it?"

Through fresh tears, Hattie told her what had happened.

"I can't go home . . . but I'll have to move from the hotel," she ended miserably.

"Don't be *foolish*. Several men have been *asking* about you, and you've got to keep up appearances, or how will you ever meet new people?" Barefooted, Cora padded across the room and unlocked a drawer.

"I don't want to meet new people."

But Cora was shoving banknotes into her hand. "*Here*, a loan. Now let's make sure that damned stock's *really* no good; maybe they need petroleum for medicine or something. You know a businessman you trust?"

"You know I don't know anyone," Hattie said dismally.

Cora persisted. "An *American* back *home?*"

George Madison! Of course. She could write to him at his office . . .

"Good." Cora gave a final touch to her toes. "Offer 'im *part*, if 'e finds a way to cash in. But send one certificate at a time; trust 'im just that much." She got up and stretched. "You're coming with *me* tonight, lovely, and from now on ask me what you want to know. Ask *first*."

Cora was in Hattie's room at the hotel several weeks later when George Madison's reply arrived.

"Must've used the *fastest* mailboat." Cora puffed at her tiny cigarette. "What's 'e say?"

Hattie read:

"Hattie darling! . . . Where did you get it? Send the rest, right off. It's a gold mine; the oil came in only two or three months ago, and everybody's wild about it here. Enclosed find a check on the Moulton bank for the ten-share certificate, minus the percentage you so generously . . ."

Snatching the check, Cora figured. "You got *nineteen* more. God, it's wonderful! But don't forget, still *one* at a time!"

Hattie just sat there, the letter in her hand, tears in her eyes.

"Lovey, the only thing *you* have to cry about is if the market goes down before you *cash* 'em. Right now, we're going to fix you all over." Cora's delight was unrestrained at the prospect of the fascinating shopping ahead.

A few weeks later, Hattie paused for a moment with her purple-gloved hand on a carved white doorknob. Then she opened the door and crossed the marble hallway; with pride she looked up at the white alabaster staircase, swirling to the third floor. The stairway was the real reason she had bought the small mansion on the Boulevard Malesherbes. The finest stair in Paris, the agent had said—with that new conceit, bright-green ivy, growing from boxes below and twining tightly along the reeded banister.

She had had the walls in the drawing room painted a soft white. Italian cabinets, picture frames, and rugs were of the same creamy shade, and sofas and chairs had been finished in white satin. Finding the house cavernous and gloomy, Hattie had added something of white in every room. Cora approved. "Your *trademark*, chérie!"

Hattie had dismissed the former staff, and today she was to interview an applicant for housekeeper. If she proved satisfactory, Hattie could move into her own house the next day. Her new life was beginning well. Today she had received a letter from her mother, who though reproachful had at last agreed to accept money from her.

The bell sounded, and Hattie admitted a brisk middle-aged woman in dusty black, pencil-thin, gaunt-jawed, with a sharp nose, who looked down at Hattie from under a potlike gray hat that matched her hair. Yet the eyes, of an uncertain shade, were kind, and they asked to be liked.

"They call me Joséphine," she said. "Joséphine Arnault, from Brittany."

She looked harsh, Hattie thought, and yet there was something winning in this face. "Tell me about yourself," she suggested when she had led the way back to the little sitting room off the hall and they were both seated. Joséphine sat forward in her chair.

"I have worked most of my life, madame. My husband died years ago. I have been with"—she named three families of the lesser nobility—"then Madame Albonne."

Hattie had heard of the well-known actress of a decade back. "Where is she now?"

"In Père-la-Chaise, madame, quiet at last. I straightened her poor limbs."

Hattie liked the woman's way of speaking; and, having served an actress, she would probably not gossip behind her back. Then she saw that Joséphine's glance had gone to the ivy-green stairway. "Is it real, madame?"

The Breton's almost wistful admiration decided her. When final arrangements were being made, Joséphine asked:

"Could I have a whole day off every week, please?" and went on hastily: "Ah, not a lover. My little girl, at my cousin's. *Merci, merci!*"

Hattie smiled at her as they made plans for Joséphine to start the next day. "I hope we'll be together a long time," she said.

Cora's carriage was at the door; she had come to take Hattie to Monsieur Worth's for a fitting, and a dressmaker was one of the few Parisians who could not be kept waiting.

Cora had just come from a visit to Renée, the most fashionable of the many popular spiritualists of the day. "She predicted a *castle* in Italy, and a brown-eyed Duke," she told Hattie as they drove off. "Why don't *you* go to see her?"

"I can't think of anything, even a castle, that would lure me from Paris. And I don't believe any more in tall, dark men."

Cora reproved her. "*Everybody's* seeing mediums. Grand Duke Constantine, the *Tsar's* brother, came here with his wife, and they're *crazy* over a Scotch one—even took him back and the Tsar had him as his *guest.*" Cora giggled. "Those Russian boyars. They may be only lesser nobility but there's nothing *madder*, or more friendly, if they *want* to be, and they're all *over* Paris. But I don't have to tell *you*. Goodenough is fascinated with you."

Hattie shrugged. "Goodenough is like all the rest of them; he's fascinated by Americans—he talks politics most of the time. Thank goodness, he's interested in the theater, too. But all the Russians I've met are fun."

"*Fun!* That's the trouble with you . . . I've been *thinking* . . . I've never seen you in *love*, dearie. Really in love. Doesn't *anybody* mean something to you?"

Flushing, Hattie shook her head, and Cora tapped her arm.

"One of them *will*, yet. Then *watch* yourself, my girl."

Hattie looked off into the trees, shimmering in the Indian summer day.

"Isn't the city beautiful today?"

Putting up her fringed parasol, she glanced about her, savoring the September afternoon of Paris in the enchanted year of 1869. She felt no premonition of what lay ahead for her beloved city— or for herself.

SIX

AT THE TOP OF HER ALABASTER STAIRS HATTIE, DRESSED IN MONSIEUR
Worth's latest creation of lace and billowing white chiffon, was
ready to receive at her usual fortnightly reception. The musicians
in the drawing room behind her were already tuning their instru-
ments. She felt a faint beginning tension and excitement, as she
did so often while waiting for the curtain to go up at the theater.
As a matter of fact, she was exhilarated most of the time in this
magical spring. Though she drank very little, it seemed to her that
she, along with everyone else, never quite recovered from the
gaiety of one night's champagne before the corks flew to the
next night's painted ceilings.

Hattie's receptions, which would have been considered lavish
indeed in Philadelphia, were really only small parties, in compari-
son with the elaborate masquerades and balls given nightly by the
nobility and their wealthy hangers-on. But in their "informal"
way her salons were as crowded by the intellectuals of the day as
anyone else's in Paris. Cora's men, both at her wildly improper
receptions and at her more public parties, were members of the
Jockey Club or Le Cercle Impérial—government officials, generals, and noblemen. Hattie's admirers were more apt to come from
the crowd of artists and men of the world who called themselves
Les Mirlitons. Among lesser artists and writers, and younger sons,
there were Isabey, the painter, Gounod, Boulanger, the Prince
de Polignac, even the great Wagner.

Waiting for the first guests to arrive, Hattie paced slowly back
and forth, the stiff white lace of the bottom ruffle of her skirt
sweeping the shining white stone of the floor. At twenty-four,
looking with her soft chignon like one of Monsieur Isabey's ele-

gant blonde miniatures—about to receive guests who called her tenderly "the delicious American," and possessively "our brilliant Fanny Lear"—she was no longer Philadelphia's "scandalous Mrs. Blackford," but a part of the city of Paris, of its gaiety and laissez faire and luxury. She smoothed the white-kid gloves that only Privat, the English glovemaker, could make so that the oval of the fingernail was outlined, and smiled as the front door swung open below and the first of her guests was announced.

The Comte de Lagrené—a writer for the largest newspaper of the day, *La Presse* . . . Mademoiselle Adèle Remy, gentlest of the glittering girls, greatly admired by the Emperor . . . and yes, behind her, as usual, the slim elegant figure of Monsieur Dumas, author of those brilliantly revealing lines about Parisian society. Now that she had become a part of the world he loved so well, he was bowing before Hattie with the familiarity of one who knew and admired her, and he lingered a moment to speak to her.

More guests swirled up the stair toward Hattie—the bright ribbons decorating white shirt fronts, the gold lace and epaulets of the military, the shining flower-trimmed heads of the women, all flashing together in color that delighted her. Dumas, standing just behind her, caught her mood.

"What does this stairway remind you of, Madame Lear—all this glittering company coming up this insubstantial stair? Like a child's picture of Heaven! And you an angel on a billowing white cloud at the top—a cloud no doubt carefully designed by Worth for that very impression."

Hattie laughed. "The heavenly metaphor goes on. Monsieur Worth assured me he had put his soul in this dress." She paused. "Who would have thought he valued his soul so highly?"

"Our wicked American!" Dumas said appreciatively. . . . "But I want to talk to you seriously. I've asked a friend of mine, a young journalist, to come along tonight. He is actually a financial genius; the Emperor consults him constantly about his investments. But he's shy, and needs to be about a bit more. I thought your Tuesday evening would be one of the best introductions to the lighter side of Paris—sufficiently intelligent so he won't be frightened," he finished teasingly.

Hattie smiled at him. "That's even a nicer compliment than your first one." She added, "I'll look out for your protégé," as the butler announced "Monsieur Guernet."

58

"Ah, here he is," said Dumas. "I'll present him, and we'll go in to Mademoiselle Remy."

The gentle-faced, lightly bearded young man who bowed before her did appear a trifle nervous. As Hattie smiled with special welcome, he blushed, and she was touched.

She did not see him again until later on in the evening. He had joined Monsieur Mérimée, the old writer, who was one of Hattie's favorites, even though his presence did mean that Cora had refused to come. Monsieur Mérimée had said publicly that Mademoiselle Pearl had the taste of a chimney sweep, and now they came on alternate occasions. If Cora had been there tonight she would have frowned as she saw Hattie approach Monsieur Mérimée and the unimportant young man whose only distinction was a dangerous one—finance, Dumas had said; and Cora had warned her against two things, the stage and the bourse.

She inclined a receptive ear to Monsieur Mérimée, who was chuckling over a child's remark that he claimed to have overheard: "Your papa works for a living. Mine's a Senator."

To Hattie's surprise a bitter light came into the blue eyes of the timid Monsieur Guernet.

"That's a wise child. These politicians . . . We're in for trouble."

"You mean all this war gossip?" Hattie asked him directly.

The young man frowned. "More than gossip, madame. But the real story is complicated and tiresome, and would bore you, I'm afraid."

Some men assumed that a woman was automatically a fool, thought Hattie, and she left them abruptly, but she wondered about his remark. Rumors of dissension between France and Germany had been current for some time. Bismarck had started the trouble over the succession to the Spanish throne and France's hotheaded Prime Minister had done nothing to prevent the rift from widening. Members of the Chamber of Deputies talked furiously of Prussian insults, yet none appeared sure what the hostilities, if any, would be about.

At supper, Hattie was monopolized by a heavy-faced count from Belgium whose flowers had arrived almost hourly since he had met her a week ago. Across the table, young Guernet was deep in conversation with Dumas and the young journalist, the Comte de Lagrené. After brandy had been served, the Belgian, in an attempt to impress his hostess with his financial shrewdness, leaned toward Guernet:

"You're not right about that stock, young man. I already have a large profit from it."

Guernet replied coldly, "There'll be fortunes made, but not in that."

Fearing a situation, Hattie intervened. "They're playing waltzes again," she told André Guernet, "and must I ask *you?*"

He danced well, yet he held himself away from her with a faint but unmistakable reserve. He hardly seemed like a Parisian at all. A little piqued, Hattie was determined that he should at least know that she was no fool. Under her questioning, Guernet admitted that he wrote regular economic pieces. Well, yes, it was true; the Emperor had received him once or twice to talk over finance.

"Oh, I myself never invest," he said. "I'm naturally an observer, not a participant."

"Indeed, in everything?" He grew red at her smile, and she changed the subject by reverting to his remarks at the table. "If I wanted to . . . buy stocks, tell me what you'd advise."

He named one. "I'll know better in a few weeks; I'll let you know."

Hattie had no intention of trying the market, yet this talk had interested her, and so had the restrained young man. When the dance was over and she discovered that the Belgian had stormed off, she was relieved. For all his rumored wealth and high position, the man was a pig in black trousers. She thought how Cora would scold her for neglecting her "chances" and for even thinking about the bourse.

Cora would be pleased, however, to hear the next day that Prince Jérome Bonaparte had appeared very late—and alone, without his friend, the famous Julia Barucci, obviously with the hope of seeing Cora. Disappointed and morose, he had stayed only a few minutes. He liked his women beautiful, non-intellectual, and frankly on the market. And Hattie herself could provide only the first essential. For all her gaiety, she too, like André, had been actually a fascinated onlooker rather than a participant. This was not unusual. Many of the more fastidious demimondaines conducted their liaisons like a series of marriages, with intensity and faithfulness, and these relationships frequently did end in marriage.

Adèle Courtois, the beautiful mistress of a Danish nobleman, put the case in more practical terms. She had drawled to Hattie on one occasion that the life of a real courtesan was quite beyond her strength, let alone inclination.

"Such a life requires two digestions and the strength of four seamstresses!"

Fortunately, Bodenbach's stock had netted Hattie so much money that she needed no "protector." Unhappily, he had also left her in no mood to try romance hastily again. She had accepted the attentions of one or two insistent suitors but rejected their offers of a definite alliance. Later, perhaps; not for the present . . . She waited with a kind of inner boredom for someone to come who would be able to conquer her inertia. In the meantime, she was delighted with the surface charm and ease of her life. She could afford to wait for the right man, and to enjoy herself while she waited.

The last guest had left. Her bedroom was lighted, a warm milk drink ready; on the chair lay a copy of *Madame Bovary*, open. Had Joséphine been reading it?

"Yes. Poor lady!"

Joséphine was taking an ever larger role in Hattie's life. The Breton had located other servants, organized her establishment; she took messages with minute accuracy. Daily she searched the floors to make sure that Hattie had dropped no earrings as she often did; nightly she scoured wastebaskets for missing notes. Her mistress enjoyed these services; it was good to be looked after in this way.

Joséphine haggled well—food, scarves, shoes; if Joséphine went along for a purchase, prices dropped automatically. "Except for me, madame, you might be in the poorhouse," she lectured, and Hattie agreed. She had never learned providence. Yet Joséphine also had the gift of silence; she would sit beside Hattie by the hour, her proximity a comfort, and she could listen as well. Though she indicated her opinion of this or that caller, she did not press it and she was no sniffing Puritan—her reaction to *Madame Bovary* proved that!

This evening, after Hattie was settled in the Valenciennes-lace-trimmed bed, Joséphine hesitated a moment.

61

"Clothilde—my daughter—has sent you something, madame—if you are not too tired?"

She disappeared and was back in a moment with a tiny white poodle in her arms. The little dog whined as if in supplication; the piquant nose sniffed, and the dark eyes entreated. Hattie held out her arms. What a wise and enchanting little creature—and what a pleasant ending to her happy evening! While the poodle licked at her throat she hunted for a name. She had it. "I shall call you Alexandre Dumas—*grand-fils*," she said with amusement. The third Alexandre barked excitedly, as if in approval.

With Joséphine and little Alexandre at her side, Hattie rode regularly along the boulevards. On their return one day they found the promised note from André Guernet. It gave a list of stocks he considered good, though as he pointed out, no stock was absolutely certain.

"What do you think?" she asked Joséphine.

"I don't believe in throwing money into the Seine."

Hattie smiled at her vehemence, but the Breton's caution made her hesitate.

The next morning, however, new excitement hastened her decision. As she was brushing her hair, she heard a boy shouting in the street. She leaned from the window and caught words repeated again and again: "*La guerre! La guerre!*"

So it had really come at last, after all the expectation, the talk, the tension in the air. Behind the boy ran others, screaming, "*A Berlin! A Berlin!*" On to Berlin. . . . She repeated the words. To her own astonishment, she felt an outpouring of delight. Paris was her city now, and Paris was leading France against the barbarian enemy! When Joséphine scurried in weeping, she took the maid in her arms. After a few minutes she pulled away. "Help me dress."

An hour later, she pushed open the door of André's office. He spoke quietly; his very lack of insistence decided her. Stocks had been lucky for her before, with the "Duke of Bodenbach," hadn't they? The French were to fight the Prussians, and she believed in their victory. . . .

When she left, the young man stared after her, and stood for a time, inconspicuously, at the door to watch her as she turned back, smiling, to wave. Her little yellow straw hat—the fashionable *paille blonde*—was so near the color of her hair that he could hardly tell where the curve of the hat ended and the curl of the hair began, and what a delectable color the silk parasol cast on that white skin! André went back to his desk, but he worked no more that day.

A few afternoons later he called to take her to see the Emperor review the troops—those first, fresh, excited troops for the front. When the soldiers pounded past, flags waving majestically against the skies, Hattie ripped off her flowers to fling them after them, as women were doing all around her. It was glorious, this surging might of the people.

"On to Berlin!" she cried, and she saw that André too was strongly moved. When he continued silent, she caught his hand. "In three weeks we'll be there, with the Germans on their knees!"

To her surprise he gave her an enigmatic look. "I hope we have French maps ready, too, in case of retreat." At once he regretted his remark. "Oh, it's only that we're so confident, and so unprepared. But I'm probably wrong. Anyway, your investments are all right."

André puzzled her. Was he somewhat afraid of her, or was he constrained by his background, and hers? Peculiarly, he never called her Fanny Lear, as most people now did. When she asked why, he looked away.

"I prefer Hattie. The other's—oh, artificial, and you're not that way."

She was much more disturbed than she would have believed by the news he brought when he called a week later. She was in her small sitting room studying one of the first war bulletins when the maid admitted him. Without a preliminary remark, André dropped into a white chair and announced in a flat voice:

"Hattie, I'm enlisting. I think we'll win in the end, but every man in France is going to be badly needed." Before she could say anything, he handed her an envelope. "It seemed like a good time to sell your stock. It's turned out rather well."

She held the envelope in her hand, thinking only of his leaving; then, realizing that he had told her in just this way so that there would be no discussion or emotion, she opened it. In sudden happy disbelief, she ran through the contents and found that he had increased her investment by nearly a third. With a delighted cry, she kissed him, and his fair skin crimsoned.

"Why, André—the innocence of you!"

Both laughed, and both were disconcerted. Alexandre bounded in barking, and André made an excuse to go. When they met again he was uniformed and besabered, and she felt touched at the sight of the brave young figure; most of the men she knew would not be in the fighting. But, again respecting his reticence, she talked of other matters. She had decided to try the market a second time with a bigger transaction.

"Unless everything's lost, I'd consider it as good as before." As he drew on his gloves, she saw that his hands shook. "Hattie!" he said abruptly. His breath came quickly. "Hattie, if I come back, would you leave this"—his glance went around the room, to the hangings and the marble—"and marry me?"

His light eyes searched her face, but he did not touch her. What could she say? The swift declaration found her unprepared. She did not want to hurt him, and if she had suspected that he would speak before he left, she would have had a tactful answer ready— if there was one! And it was an answer that would have been hard to give in any case. She had a growing affection and appreciation for him, and she did not want to lose him as a friend. She shook her head, slowly and sadly.

"Thank you, André. Right now I don't think so, and I don't really think you'll know until later. . . . Let's just go on as we were."

He did not urge her, but he looked back at her sadly as he went through the entranceway. After he had left, she went to her room and cried. Tears were suddenly easy again, and Hattie felt with an odd presentiment that all the deprivation of her childhood—inextricably tied up with war days—might come back.

It was early in September, only a month after the beginning of the tinsel-gay war. Some of the glitter had already deserted Paris. Military wagons roared through the outskirts, and the lights were going off. The city shuddered and fell silent as successive days brought worse and worse news. "Always the Germans—! *Sales bêtes!*" Joséphine's wirelike frame quivered in hate.

One day she walked in, cheeks pallid, with a muttered account of incredible losses at Sedan—whole regiments, France's choicest soldiers, ground down in the churning advance. And the Emperor had been taken prisoner by the Prussians.

A few days later Eugénie fled the city before the Paris mob. The imperial cancan was over.

Hattie was not one of those who joined the gaiety in the streets when the Third Republic was declared. The Court as a symbol of the world in which she had so secure a place was gone forever and she could not believe that wearing tricolor rosettes to celebrate the new Government of National Defense would turn back the inexorable Prussian advance. The stock market had crashed with the Empire, and how much of her own fortune would be retrieved she did not know. She wished desperately for André's counsel, but she had not even heard whether he was still alive. She could only wait in a daze, with the rest of her friends in Paris, although some were reacting simply and primitively with flight. . . .

The rich were deserting the capital, fleeing in any vehicle that offered itself. At the same time the streets were crowded with traffic going in another direction. As the enemy marched steadily closer, thousands of country people moved into Paris with their cattle, camping in the squares.

On the fourth or fifth day of her paralyzed indecision, Hattie was at a window in her sitting room watching a van being loaded next door. She became aware that a stoop-shouldered, unshaven young man in uniform was dragging himself up her own steps.

She had opened the door before she saw who he was. "André!" she cried, putting her arms around him to keep him from falling. She called to Joséphine to bring brandy. After he had swallowed it, he gasped:

"Hattie, you've got to go. It's worse than people know; I barely reached my regiment before we turned back. We were so far from ready—no guns, no real plans." Then he said bitterly: "One general even telegraphed Paris; he'd got separated from his own forces, and wanted to know where they were! We're burning bridges, throwing up earthworks, but nothing stops them. Paris will be under siege in a few days."

Hattie protested: "But they'll organize new armies; France won't let this happen. And maybe England will come in and help us." She didn't have the slightest idea whether she was uttering wisdom or naïveté—but who knew the difference now? All decisions in Paris were emotional, and so was hers. "I'll stay," she announced.

In spite of his insistence that she leave, André looked pleased. If she were going to stay, he had good news for her. The new government had declared a moratorium on rents and debts until the war was over.

"At least your creditors won't be driving you into the street, and there'll be enough saved for yourself and Joséphine. The other servants will have to go. But what will you do?"

She felt a wonderful freedom as she replied:

"I'll join the Théâtre Français ambulance and do what I can. They'll need everyone they can get." She turned to Joséphine. "But you, chérie, and Clothilde—you should leave for Brittany now!"

"I sent Clothilde back two days ago. My place is here," Joséphine said. Then, in a rare gesture, she took her mistress's hand and kissed it.

SEVEN

A MONTH HAD GONE BY. IT WAS THE END OF OCTOBER, AND THE SIEGE of Paris had been under way since the third week in September. On brief leave from constant duty in the lines outside the city, André walked past the Théâtre Français. Just ahead of him, a small figure in black uniform with the armband of the ambulance women hurried out of the door. She had a familiar look, and when the blond head turned, he ran to catch up with her.

"In the name of the Lord, Hattie, why aren't you home packing? Don't you realize what's happening? The siege is tightening; Americans and British nationals will be allowed safe passage through the lines on the twenty-seventh only, and that's day after tomorrow!"

"Because I'm not going to leave Paris; I just can't." And she told him of that afternoon's performance at the theater—Corneille in modern dress—while three dead soldiers lay in the greenroom, which had been turned into a hospital. "That's why I'm staying."

She had never looked lovelier to André, despite the severity of her uniform-like dark dress. He could not bring himself to urge her to leave.

"And you," she asked, "how long will you be here? Can you come to dinner later?"

"I was on my way to beg an invitation now." He laughed. "I have an errand to attend to, but tell Joséphine to expect me at eight."

Her natural gaiety returned. "If your 'errand' is a romantic one, the flowers I'd prefer would be cauliflowers. Joséphine and I even have to hide poor Alexandre; they've opened a Boucherie Canine et Féline a block from the house. It's the one unpatriotic thing I do—and Joséphine helps me! People are getting quite epicurean about their taste in dogs: bulldog is coarse and tasteless, spaniel is quite good, rather like lamb, but poodle is the best of all!"

"My dear Hattie, I didn't realize it was as bad as that inside the city. I'll make a quick trip back to the country and see what I can bring for supper."

He brought the most luxurious present of all, a carp from the Seine, and also the coveted cauliflower, done up like a nosegay with a lace bow. Joséphine opened their best white wine, and served them. It was a happy occasion.

"If Metz and Strasbourg can hold out under siege," Hattie said, lifting her glass to André, "why not the most gallant city in France? . . ."

But this was the last supper of the kind she was to have for a long time. Metz fell on the twenty-seventh—the day she had scorned to pass through the lines of Paris along with most of her frightened compatriots. The terrible news came in bits and pieces as the papers doled out the story of the tragedy, reluctantly. At Metz 6,000 officers and 173,000 men had been forced by starvation to surrender. . . . More German armies, released by this, would be upon them.

By the end of November there was no beef at all left in Paris. Thanksgiving Day morning, Joséphine came in with a new dish for breakfast. Hattie looked at the dark gamy flesh on the tiny platter and left it untouched, feeling a little ill. The Breton grew stern.

"Madame, even the sewers are being scoured for rats, to sell at three francs apiece. The delicate folk are beginning to starve. You want to live?" Hattie picked up her fork.

Today her fingers were blue. She huddled under the blankets until the last minute; it was so cold in the echoing white rooms, whose unsalable luxury taunted her. As if nature were on the German side, the winter was one of the worst in years. Wine froze in casks; the lines of fine trees, once the delight of the "new plan" for Paris, the most beautiful city of the world, were being hacked down for firewood. All Paris was now without light. Once Hattie had waked after noon and retired with dawn; now she got up at six and went to bed with the dark.

The day at the Théâtre Français ambulance went grimly. Fear

was openly expressed that the Germans would soon make good their threat to bombard the beleaguered capital. There had been another desperate sortie in an effort to break through the enemy's ring, and it had failed. As ceaseless carts carrying the wounded clattered up to the theater Hattie was in constant fear that the next one would bring André, wounded—or worse. For weeks they had no word from him.

In the evening, after work, Joséphine met her and they walked back together. The boulevard rides had ended; both Hattie's and Cora's horses had been taken by the government. As their steps sounded over the altered streets, Hattie thought of the quip once current in Paris that "Cora Pearl had driven her lovers less kindly than she had her horses."

Finding themselves near Cora's house, they knocked. The black Toucoutte, trembling under an overcoat tied with rope, opened the door for them and led them to Cora, who greeted them with a cry.

"Come into the *icebox!*" Chattering on, Cora had all the news of their friends, as always. Morosely she ticked them off. "*Him?* Ran away the first week! . . . Marie, she's on the corner, waiting for anybody that comes along. But *some* of the girls"—Cora's mouth twisted—"they're keeping fat and warm, slipping in and out with *information* for Bismarck. Pretty, eh?"

Hattie shook her head and Joséphine looked fierce and muttered, "*Cochons!*"

"You will stay to supper?" Cora went on, "It *doesn't* come from the Germans, but Toucoutte was *lucky* at market today. He stole part of the trunk of that *elephant* from the Jardin des Plantes, *right* out from under Prince de Brimont's nose."

She tried to look disappointed when Hattie said that though she was desolated not to stay and share the new delicacy, it was getting dark and she and Joséphine had another errand before they went home.

"We go quite often to send letters to Clothilde by the balloons. Of course we have no way of knowing whether they reach her."

It was getting dark as Hattie and Joséphine hurried through the unlit streets to the only place in Paris where light was allowed— down by the gasworks close to the railroad tracks. There, balloons with mail took off nightly, although they were at the mercy of the winds, and came down frequently into the German lines, where the aeronaut was held prisoner and the mail destroyed. On the other hand, a strong quixotic wind might carry a balloon as far beyond the besieging armies as Denmark before it came to rest. This mail service was just a little more reliable than entrusting a message to a bottle and throwing it into the Seine with the hope that it would be picked up in the country.

The usual excited crowd surrounded the circle of light made by the headlights of several locomotives. People now went to see the departure of the balloon as they had once gone to the theater. The balloon in the center was nearly ready to leave. Joséphine hurried to the attendant at the side and gave him her expensive message—ten centimes for a letter under three ounces. Hattie looked up. Above her head the balloon was billowing and swelling in the dark sky; the light around the basket on the ground seemed a frail and tenuous bit of life in the shadowy city. It was perilous to come there, and perilous to find one's way home afterward. The city of light had shrunk to this brilliant circle. Tonight all was soon ready, and at the sharp command *"Laissez aller!"* the ropes to the heavy sandbags on the ground were cut, and the balloon was gone—swiftly, for a cold wind had come up.

Hattie shivered as she and Joséphine left the warmth of the crowd to pick their careful way home. The next morning she woke with a bad cold, which turned worse because she insisted on going as usual to the theater ambulance. Then one morning early in January, as she and Joséphine sipped their pale imitation of coffee, a heavy explosion sounded from the distance. Hattie dropped her cup, but neither spoke. There was no need for words; the bombardment had begun.

Ten days later, walking from the hospital to an early evening engagement, Hattie stopped on the heights of the Trocadéro, to watch the artillery and shell fire over Paris. It was dangerous, yes; at times she shuddered when a blast came close and crashed into the street. But like the courage of the Parisians she admired, her own courage was tempered with persistent humor.

"The show's over for the day!" a workman shouted. Hattie applauded with the rest of the observers, and went on her way. She smiled too as she passed the display in an ironic jeweler's window. Magnificently arranged on cotton, there lay a single egg—the most expensive thing in Paris. She wished she could take it with her.

She was to have early supper at a restaurant near Auteuil. There they would dine on *paté des rats, consommé de chien à la Bismarck!* The restaurant was within dangerous shell range, and after the proprietor had stopped up several shell holes in his walls he had rechristened it "Le Rendezvous des Obus." It was also the rendezvous for such men in Hattie's circle as had remained in Paris; some of them were in the National Guard; a few of them, like Edmond de Goncourt, did nothing but keep their own private journals of what was going on (hoping for later publication). It seemed to Hattie that they all shared theatrical delight in being there to report on one of the greatest dramas in history.

Hattie's note from Dumas, asking her to the supper, had complained that he never found her in since she had been working at the ambulance, and threatened to come to see her there. "I shall come at the first ray of sunshine. It will remind me of the color of your hair." It was the only color she had nowadays, thought Hattie a bit grimly. And she had grown so thin that Joséphine worked long hours taking in her dresses.

At supper, there was great teasing over a new weapon of defense mentioned in *La Presse.* It was for Parisian women should the city fall to the German officers—a glove armed at the tip of the index finger with a tiny glass vial containing prussic acid; the smallest scratch would be fatal.

"They call it," said Dumas with some amusement, "the finger of God. You had better get yourself one at once, Madame Lear. What German officer would resist you?"

Hattie wrinkled her small nose at him. "Any woman with so few resources as to need protection like that will be in no need of it!" The drawn faces around her relaxed in laughter. But it was short, for disaster lay close to the surface; thousands were dying in the night and the dead were being thrown into the trenches because it was impossible to bury them otherwise. . . . How much longer?

The next week brought the answer. On January 19, the news flashed along the streets: "Negotiations" had started with the Prussians. Men and women wept on the street corners. The war was over—and Paris was lost. On the same day, a black-lined envelope arrived at Hattie's house. André had been killed in the last sortie outside the walls.

She felt crushed in despair and complete physical exhaustion, and that night she had one of her old nightmares. She dreamed of her father again. Young Dr. Ely, the evangelist, whose face now seemed to be also the face of André, was lecturing her sternly; he would leave her to her evil life . . . her sins had brought her to this pass. . . . She woke abruptly, crying aloud with a feeling of loss and terror, and Joséphine came in to massage her brow until she fell asleep again.

Always, it seemed, Joséphine stood firmly between her mistress and the immediate impact of disaster. It was Joséphine who faced the frowning men who paid an unannounced call on a bleak day several weeks later. The new National Government in Versailles that had succeeded the Parisian Government of National Defense had lifted the moratorium on debts. Hundreds of thousands of Parisians were forced out of their homes, and Madame Lear's rent was long overdue.

Holding Alexandre tightly in her arms, Hattie watched as they strode about, touching pale sofas and fringed curtains. Cora, having heard the news, pushed past the guard in time to hear the ultimatum: "Just a trunkful of things, nothing more." She spat out a variety of insults in pungent French-English, and ran up to help Hattie and Joséphine. She herself had been dispossessed a few days before.

Their last sight as they left the house was the withered remains of the ivy that had once twisted along the banister of the alabaster stairway; long ago it had died of the cold. On the street the three women stared bleakly at the closed front door, and then Hattie cried:

"I left half my jewels!"

Joséphine stopped her with a whisper. "Not so loud, madame! They're here, in my waist."

Cora threw out her hands. "Where'll you go? I'd offer you a place, but I'm living in *one* room now."

Hattie sobbed. "Joséphine, where?" Resourceful as always, it was Joséphine who acted now. She knew of a rooming house that came within their reduced means: Rue Saint-Jacques—not too far away. Later she went with Hattie to the pawnbroker and bargained cannily for her.

"Everything's got to last," the Breton warned. "There's worse ahead, madame."

All during the month of March they shivered with cold. Some food had come into the city at the end of the siege, but who could buy it? Hattie's jewels went for outrageously small sums. (To the end, however, Hattie would keep the Bodenbach brooch, her luck token. The luck had hardly lasted, but she would not give it up!) Joséphine had disposed of the more salable parts of her mistress's wardrobe, though taking care to keep at least three or four of the most elaborate costumes against the day when she might use them again.

While these small acts of preservation took up much of their energy, the apathy that had come over Hattie on hearing of André's death had lifted a little. She began to want to see someone who could talk intelligently of what was happening. She knew only that the new National Government was strongly suspicious of the present government of the city of Paris. Her beloved city had borne the brunt of the war, but now was not consulted on new laws or about the proposed peace treaty with its unheard-of indemnity, its humiliating conditions of occupation. The new National Government distrusted the traditionally radical city of Paris; there was even talk of making Versailles the capital.

But who was there left for Hattie to talk with? Those of the leisured class whom she had known had left either before the siege or immediately after it; none returned to the cold, strife-ridden city. And at the beginning of April, Joséphine's dark premonition was justified. The National Government sent troops to force their way into Paris and subdue the city government, now calling itself the Commune. Another siege! The German Army of Occupation looked on ironically. Black reports spread of impending clashes between elements of Commune and anti-Commune within the city. One morning as Joséphine worked over the meager fire, they heard the sound of rapid steps up the narrow stairs leading to their door and Cora Pearl burst in.

"It's the Revolution again—fighting and shooting!"

For hours the three stayed inside, peering through a window crack at the fighting in the street below, hearing the whine of snipers' bullets. Horrified, they watched an old woman who lay for hours on the street; none dared approach the body.

"There's more danger than when the Germans were shelling," Joséphine muttered.

Through April and May, spasmodic conflict continued. On May 21 the National troops poured into the city and Frenchman fought against Frenchman in seven days of bloody rage. The

Opéra was captured, the Ministry of War, and Cora brought word that buildings were being set afire. Then came the terrifying whisper: "The Tuileries!"

They went up to the roof. Looking down over Paris they could see crowds running, and the vast building of the Tuileries ablaze, flames shooting out of the roof, remnants of wood flying through the air. Cora pointed.

"They've soaked furniture in *petrol,* and there's tar everywhere, and *gunpowder!*"

They heard a crash; a section collapsed, and the historic cupola broke away. Everywhere they looked new fires broke out. There was no way to escape the holocaust. All they could do was hope the fire would not reach their quarter. The Porte Saint-Martin, the Church of Saint Eustache, were burning. Flames were sweeping up the Rue Royale, the Rue de Rivoli. The Palais Royal and the Hôtel de Ville were immense red braziers. From beyond the city's gates, cannon blasted at stricken Paris. A crisscross of gunfire kept up in the streets. The city was destroying itself, in rage and hatred.

"Quick!" Hattie pulled Joséphine and Cora to one side. As she stumbled, tearing the skin from her knees, the chimney crashed, showering them with powdered brick. With dawn the three climbed down from the roof. Hattie lay down on her narrow iron bed, too dispirited even to stroke Alexandre, who had leaped up to curl at her feet. She pulled her thin coat more tightly about her neck. Would Paris ever come to life again?

Paris was leaden, broken, but by June the last of the fighters for the Commune had been hunted down, shot to death. The city tried to count the thousands of its dead. Bit by bit Hattie got news of men she had known. Some had left the city in the very beginning, before the German siege, and had never returned. Some had been shot as hostages by the Commune. Some had been capriciously deported to tropical penal colonies by the new government, which condemned men hastily without due trial. . . . No one knew what had happened to others. The Comte de Miranda —gone back to Spain? . . . The Comte Feuilhade de Chauvin— killed in the war? . . . The Marquis de Vivens—fled to England?

Now it seemed that of all that glittering circle she alone watched an exhausted Paris begin the dreary task of rebuilding. A fright-

74

ening debt piled over it, and France sank from its once high rank among the nations. The desperate summer ended, and with fall the buildings were icy again, the future even grayer than before.

Hattie did not see Cora for some time, but early one morning in mid-October Hattie and Joséphine had an unexpected visit from her.

"My dears, I decided it *last* night!" She ran her hand through her hair, and Hattie saw that it had been freshly tinted. "A new friend made an *offer,* and I'm leaving." Sitting on the edge of Hattie's bed, she caught her shoulder. "Girlie, it's what *you've* got to do—get away."

Tears came into Hattie's dark eyes. "I don't have anywhere to go."

"I *didn't* mean *America,*" Cora said. "I've been *thinking* about you. There's just one place that's *lively* as ever, and richer, too." She nudged Hattie. "*Russia.* They say they *like* foreign women in their capital; anyway, *nothing* could be colder than this town today. Try it, lovey!"

Hattie looked at her hopelessly. How could she go to Russia, and with what, even if she wanted to?

But Cora had opened her purse. "I set *this* aside for you last night." When she held out a handful of crisp notes, Hattie began to sob. She was still crying as Cora started to the door. "My English friend is *waiting,* and you know how Englishmen are!" Over her shoulder she called back: "Maybe I'll write, but you know I'm not too good at *that.*"

Hattie lay still for a while, wondering if she would ever see Cora again. Then, with a sudden movement, she sat up. Even with a new rich friend this gift must have meant a sacrifice to Cora, and the numbers on the notes were not small! She would use the money. Acting quickly, before she could think better of it, she went to the American Embassy to inquire about her passport. The long period of hopeless apathy had ended. She sent Joséphine from one pawnbroker to another to redeem a few of the jewels and furs she had thought she would never wear again. Her voice had regained its vibrancy as she ordered:

"Buy milk and eggs and good meat; we'll have to fatten up a little. And bring a piece of liver for Alexandre for once. He will need strength, too. And go to the Demoiselles Noël and see if they still have the face cream in porcelain jars—get a big one."

As she thrust her hands into the scented cream that night and worked it slowly into her face and throat, she studied herself critically in the cracked mirror. She had pinned her hair up carelessly on top of her head; some of the shine seemed to have gone from it, but the curls were as soft as ever and it was still a bright contrast to her dark eyes and lashes. Her face was, of course, too thin; but she knew it would not be long before she looked her best again. She would spend every spare hour before the mirror or in bed sleeping, making up for the ravages of the past few months.

The next day she and Joséphine began to refurbish her dresses and by the end of the week, though the American Embassy had appeared dubious about her passport at first, she had succeeded in wheedling it from the clerks. Then with departure imminent, Joséphine unexpectedly confessed her real feeling.

"Madame, Russia—just the thought of that place frightens me. The winter, and the people!"

"Joséphine, I thought you were as glad as I to leave Paris."

"Leave Paris, yes, madame—but the Russians! I know them, madame!"

Hattie delayed their departure from one day to another, hoping that Joséphine's obstinacy would pass. But when her maid's persistent practical questions as to where they would go and what they would do began to undermine Hattie's own faith in the adventure, she decided she would not wait any longer. Impulsively she took the final step alone, leaving a scrawled note for Joséphine: She was going on the three o'clock train from the Embarcadère du Nord; Joséphine must follow, meeting her in Cologne.

With Alexandre in a basket at her feet, she rode sadly down the boulevard. A handful of yellowed leaves rustled against the window of the carriage, and she turned away. She preferred to remember that other Paris; someday, if she could manage it, she would be back. She promised it to herself.

EIGHT

HATTIE RESTED HER HEAD AGAINST THE BACK OF THE STIFF HIGH SEAT in the old railway compartment and closed her eyes. She was tired from endlessly watching endless snow as the train plowed its way through Germany toward the Russian border. Though it was still only early November, it seemed like midwinter. Joséphine, who had joined her mistress at Cologne, sat opposite, uncomplaining, although her lips were blue with the chill in the compartment. Only Alexandre's little black nose was visible as he wiggled back into the blankets on Hattie's lap.

Despite the discomfort of the journey, Hattie was happy as she had not been in months, and Joséphine grudgingly admitted to herself that the change was already doing her mistress good. Under Madame Lear's small fur toque with its tight veil, her face was serene and soft, almost like a child's. She was smiling a little, and Joséphine guessed that she was not asleep, but thinking of something pleasant.

Hattie's thoughts were not as pleasant as they were exciting. She was remembering fragments from her childhood reading about Russia—St. Petersburg was the capital city created in icy, marsh-bound wastes by the savage determination of Peter the Great. It was Russia's "Window to Europe," its westernmost center, the crowning work of the man who brought education to the Russian Empire, covered it with new wealth, made it a part of the world. He had fought those at home who wanted to build a wall against the West—he'd fought his own son when he had disagreed with his father and had ordered him tortured to death. But all that was past. The present Tsar had freed the serfs, had opened the courts, and allowed the people freedom of speech. Nothing remained now of the old savage Russia but the grandeur, the gold spires, and the thousand refinements of the wealthiest Court in Europe. . . .

Hattie must have slept a little, because she was startled when the brakes screeched and the train slowed to a halt. It must be Wirballen. She sat up and looked eagerly out the window. Russia lay just beyond the border settlement.

There was a quiet rapping at the door, and in response to her *"Entrez"* two lean men in uniform entered, bowed, said something she did not understand, then pulled her two trunks and Joséphine's small one into the center of the compartment.

"What is it?" Hattie got up and went toward them. One of them said something unintelligible and held out his hand, obviously asking for the keys. When she handed them over, they bowed as politely as before, then went ahead with what seemed like a routine customs inspection except that they drew out all papers and books and piled them carefully on the floor. One of them even bent down to look under the seat and found Hattie's latest magazine to add to the pile. After the trunks, they went through Joséphine's small handbag and Hattie's jewel case with equal care.

"What are you doing?" Hattie's voice was angry.

The two men bowed again, and one spoke quietly, though not less unintelligibly than the first one had. They then scooped up their pile of books and papers and left. Joséphine closed the trunks and snapped them tight. A moment later Hattie realized that they had taken her diary, but she had neglected it in the past unhappy year—they would get little for their pains. . . . She would begin a new diary with her new life. A new life, she thought ironically, that was itself starting without very great encouragement for the expression of private opinion.

Almost as soon as the gendarmes had left, a red-haired man with a beard like a bush, and wearing a grotesquely padded suit with long skirts, thrust his head in the door and indicated that they must get out. Their trunks were still in the center of the compartment. Hattie finally made him realize that they would not leave the compartment without their luggage. He blew a whistle and six more porters with swinging skirts came in—three more than were needed. The trunks disappeared in their midst, and Hattie and Joséphine followed across a wind-swept snowy passageway to a

78

gray waiting room. There every one of the six helpers held out his hand. They looked disappointed when she tipped them, and left without bowing.

It was only a few minutes later that she discovered that one of her own trunks was missing—the one that contained her toilet articles, her chignons, and her evening costumes. Thrusting Alexandre into Joséphine's arms, she ran back to the train, only to have the way barred by the bearded porter, who pretended not to understand her frantic questioning. He shrugged his massive shoulders and pointed to a gendarme standing near by. But she got no more satisfaction from him, although he did speak a little French. Perhaps "they" would know inside the station.

Inside, Joséphine was being questioned by an alert blond man with humorous eyes. He knew a few words of five or six languages, including English, and he promised to "watch" for the trunk. Then he asked for their passports.

"When will we be able to leave?" Hattie asked.

"We have to await orders." He scratched a word on the papers, put them in a portfolio, and started to walk away from her.

"What does that mean? Whose orders?" The man grew less pleasant; obviously a traveler should not ask questions. She decided to bluff. "I demand to know why we are being held. My friends in Russia will hear of this!"

He hesitated, then said in a low voice: "Not properly visaed. We must send to our consul at Königsberg for instructions."

At that moment they heard a clanging of bells and the long whistle of a locomotive—the train was leaving for St. Petersburg without them.

"There are rooms upstairs," the official said. "I advise you to take one right now." As if embarrassed at overstepping his function, he turned away.

They saw nothing else to do but follow his advice. The best chamber was moderately neat—a plain unheated cubicle with a white iron basin and a narrow bed that she and Joséphine must share. There was no mirror, no water pitcher. If she only had her missing toilet articles! She put on a brave face for Joséphine.

"A woman on a journey without her powder is like a soldier in the field without *his*," she said attempting a smile. Joséphine sat grimly silent.

Alexandre was shivering, and Joséphine tucked him into his

shawl and went off to hunt warm water. Much later she returned with a few cupfuls in a chipped enameled pitcher, and they took turns in washing. Feeling somewhat better, they were about to go down to the station restaurant when suddenly the poodle started to quiver in a strange way. His bright eyes glazed, and in spite of their frantic ministrations, in a few minutes he died of convulsions in Hattie's arms.

"Poor little Alexandre!" Hattie said, sobbing. He had endured all the hardships so bravely; what would she do without him? But when she looked over at Joséphine, she saw that her maid was completely overwhelmed. "It is a bad omen, madame—to have lived through the siege and the coldest days in Paris, only to die at the Russian border. We must turn back, madame, before it is too late!"

It was Hattie who wrapped the stiff small body in her best silk scarf and called the station attendant, gave him the little bundle, and asked him to dispose of it. She made Joséphine lie down, and found some smelling salts in her handbag.

There was little air in the room, for the single window was sealed against the cold. It was so grime-covered with the smoke of passing trains that Hattie could see nothing through it. Experimenting with the catch, she discovered a pane that could be opened inward, but the rush of freezing wind made her close it after only a minute's quick look at what lay outdoors.

All around the station stretched a wide white waste, a plain of unrelieved snow. Then, far to one side she had made out a pavilion-like building painted bright green, and with a blue dome dotted with golden stars. In her unhappy mood, the bright dome attracted her. Throwing on her fur-lined cape, she went downstairs and pushed her way through snow above her ankles to the street leading to the building, which she was now sure was a church.

On the threshold she stopped, blinking at the general dimness, the austere walls, and the rich altar before her. As she watched, it seemed to grow larger, more heavily ornamented. There were no seats; in a Russian church only the sick or crippled might sit. Before the altar rose a tall screen, intricately painted; moving closer, she made out patterns that glowed in golds, reds, and purples, shining with many jewels.

When her eyes grew accustomed to the half-dark, she saw that a peasant woman was kneeling near her, her head covered with a

80

bright shawl. After a moment's uncertainty, Hattie knelt beside her. She did not formulate her prayer, but when she rose to her feet she felt new courage and a new sense of peace. The woman beside her had risen too, and looked at Hattie with a tentative smile. Hattie smiled back warmly. Impulsively she held out her hand. But the Russian woman lowered her eyes and hurried past Hattie to the door.

Though it was hardly four o'clock, dark was falling, and with it a gray mist. At the station, a second officer, with eyes of hard brown, was waiting for her with the officer who had taken their passports. Both of them began to question her. Had she declared everything? What were her beliefs? Did she know university people? What had she done during the Commune in Paris? She thought of the way they had confiscated her books, of the old frightening stories of travelers who disappeared, leaving no trace. This new officer must be an agent of the secret police. She protested:

"I know very little about politics, messieurs."

She smiled at them, her dark eyes appealing, and their questions suddenly became more personal. Where had she lived in Paris? Was it true that the trees along the Champs-Elysées had been cut down? She must understand that this was only routine questioning.

One of them relaxed still further. "Do you know anyone in St. Petersburg? General Trepov?"

"I never heard of Trepov, but I know others." Hopefully she mentioned a few names, and they shook their heads. Suddenly she brightened—that amiable one from the theater—"Goodenough?"

"There is no name like that in Russian, madame."

"But I thought he was so well known in the theater." She stopped, troubled.

The theater? Suddenly both of them cried out a name. "Ghedeonov!" Hattie looked bewildered, and the brown-eyed one explained. "Stepan Ghedeonov, director of His Majesty's Theater. Madame is an actress, then?"

"Yes, an actress—my stage name is Fanny Lear."

At two the next morning, a gendarme knocked at Hattie's door. Her sleep was so deep and exhausted that the knocking was repeated several times before she woke. The gendarme almost purred.

81

"A telegram from General Trepov of the police, a special order —you may go on to St. Petersburg."

Years later, Hattie was to write in her memoirs: "and so I entered Russia, as I was to leave it, by special order of General Trepov, chief of police."

N I N E

THE TRAIN SPED ACROSS THE SNOWY PLAINS EASTWARD FROM THE border. As the whistle sighed through the morning, Hattie put her hands inside her muff to hide their trembling. At last they were approaching St. Petersburg. For hours she had been pressing her face to the window, peering at the snow-covered plains, snow broken only by an occasional hut that seemed to have been dropped into the soft whiteness. In rare moments, when the sun shone, the snow glittered, but even under the gray skies it had a light of its own.

The train was slowing to a stop, and she stood up impatiently as Joséphine gathered their small cases together. They climbed down into a confusion of luggage and officials. The wind tore about Hattie in a way she had never known; the cold bit at lips and eyes. Twice again she and Joséphine had to show their papers; twice the wind almost pulled them out of their fingers.

On their departure the now obsequious gendarmes had recommended the fashionable Hôtel de France. Hattie's eye caught the name in gilt on the cap of a driver standing by a decrepit carriage. Joséphine protested:

"Is that the right name, madame?"

"Yes, I remember it," Hattie replied, pushing the maid in ahead of her, "and I'm sure this coach remembers Catherine the Great!"

St. Petersburg was a city of wide streets and grand plazas, of wooden houses and stone mansions. They passed long empty spaces out of which loomed onionlike domes, all golden and blue, masses of pillared palaces, then store windows ashine with light. Hattie turned to Joséphine.

"Peter the Great built this almost overnight. A hundred thousand people died to do it."

"I can believe it, madame." Joséphine put up her hand to protect her throat against the damp cold.

Inside the hotel, however, even Joséphine's spirits improved. They were ushered into a comfortable suite. The tile stove was warm; lamps were brought in to dispel the murkiness of the dark day. A hot bath was made ready, and Hattie emerged from it relaxed and hungry. The midday meal was brought into their room, and it was excellent, particularly the crisp bread, and Hattie told the waiter so, in French:

"The best bread I've ever eaten." He replied haltingly, in the same tongue, that most of Petersburg's bread was made by German bakers. "I'd heard so," she said, nodding. "Didn't the Tsar order it that way, to keep the Russian ones from poisoning him?"

He withdrew in astonishment, and Hattie cautioned herself that she must not make light of such things. The meal over, she wrote several letters to the Russians of her acquaintance, the first one, of course, to Ghedeonov at His Majesty's Theater, and sent them by a hotel porter. He went off smiling, full of assurances that the gentlemen were well known in the capital and he would have no difficulty in finding them.

Almost before the door closed behind him, Hattie was in the luxurious bed with a satin coverlet tucked around her. By the time she woke, evening had come and Joséphine had word for her.

"That stupid fellow said he could find only one of those men, and here's his answer."

Hattie sat up eagerly. Prince Golitsyn had answered:

"Make yourself beautiful. I will wait upon you at your hotel at midnight."

Tonight! And her other trunk had not been heard of since it had disappeared at Wirballen. Joséphine's look was tragic. What would Madame do without her best dresses, and her chignons, to say nothing of powder and rouge? The maid at the hotel provided the last two items, and Joséphine's spirits revived. Hastily rummaging through Hattie's one trunk, she found a simple black silk dress and a tight sleeveless jacket of pale rose.

"Those will pass," Hattie said, "and I'll be unfashionable—my own hair will have to do by itself!"

When the Prince appeared punctually at midnight, his first look of admiration reassured her. She had only a dim recollection of a day they had both been guests at a garden party in Paris, but he was much as she had remembered him—a man in his late fifties, pleasant and polished. As he kissed her hand, it was chiefly the memory of the gaiety of the last time she had seen him that made her give him her best smile.

Downstairs in the snow waited a sleigh that Prince Golitsyn called a troika. The muffled driver was perched precariously on a high seat behind the three nervous horses. A footman wrapped them in fur robes, and the horses bounded forward into the wind.

"We are going to the Restaurant Vert," the Prince told her. "It is on one of the islands across the bridge. I was able to get word to a few friends, and they are anxious to meet the first American"—he hesitated only a moment—"girl to come to St. Petersburg."

He obviously considered it a personal accomplishment to be the first to present her. Holding her hand tightly under the bearskin robe, he beamed at her fondly. She had heard that a few British women of her element had established themselves here. Were there no other Americans? As they raced over long bridges, past gleaming buildings, her nervousness began to grow. The troika stopped and they alighted. They ascended some stairs. A door was flung open by a lackey and they passed through a small blue-walled room into an enormous salon of black and gold, where about twenty men were all talking at once.

She heard the clink of spurs against chairs and stiff boots, caught the glint of medals, shoulder knots, and epaulets, as every man rose and faced her. Heels clicked, spurs tinkled as officer after officer came up for presentation. Counts, barons, princes . . . and she the only woman. There had been nothing like this in Paris. But the faces were old, wrinkled, gray-bearded. This was not the *jeunesse dorée*, but the *vieillesse argentée*—silvered old age, not gilded youth. A little dizzy with the sudden warmth, dazzled and self-conscious, she smiled mechanically, her heart pounding. A glass of vodka was thrust into her hand; someone locked her fingers around it. "Zakuski!" Prince Golitsyn, holding a wide plate, taught her the name of the rich hors d'œuvre.

Slowly her composure returned. These were good-humored men, with the ease and grace of the friendly Russians that she had known in Paris. All of them, she discovered, spoke French, and when she asked about the uniforms and decorations, the *vieillesse argentée* leaned toward her, amused and pleased.

"What's an order of Stanislav?" she asked, dark eyes alert. "How can you tell the Vladimir?" She learned quickly the differences between hussars and Chevalier Guards, dragoons and lancers. Already, one of the officers assured her, Madame Lear knew the military classes better than most Russians.

But when she was sufficiently relaxed to tell of the way her other notes had miscarried that afternoon, Prince Golitsyn shrugged.

"Those men were probably transferred to the provinces. Aren't you happy with us?" He pretended to be hurt.

"Oh, I am."

"That calls for champagne." Over the wine followed compliments and toasts and then a General bowed low. "I'll teach you to drink *na ty.*"

The custom, it developed, was for people who wished to address one another with the fond *ty* (thou) instead of the formal *vy* (you). Arms were linked, the toast drunk, and kisses exchanged on both cheeks. She and the General executed the rite to loud applause, and the Prince called out:

"My turn, but we'll do it the right way. Three kisses, two on the cheek and the third on the mouth!"

He demonstrated, and to her slight dismay, all nineteen others followed. It was seven in the morning when the party ended.

With Prince Golitsyn, she was standing in front of the restaurant in the gold-gray dawn when she heard a striding footstep behind her on the walk. She turned to see an imposing man, mustachioed, and with an air of easy command. Head high, he went by without a side glance, though the Prince saluted. A little drunk, Golitsyn poured out his resentment in an indiscreet flow.

"That scoundrel—as dangerous a man as there is in Russia. A traitor, a revolutionary, plotting to get the Tsar's throne, and nobody does a thing to stop him when he works against his own brother." Hattie came to startled attention. "Who is it?"

"Constantine, the Grand Duke." As if realizing he had been careless, the Prince stopped.

Wasn't Constantine the one who came so often to Paris to amuse himself and to patronize the Scotch spiritualist? A revolutionary?

As they drove back in the troika, the Prince seemed to forget the episode. Close together under the fur robes, they glided along an elegant street. "Millionaya Street," he told her, "because it cost so much and the millionaires live on it." Then they were speeding along the frozen Neva itself—the river that stayed frozen seven months of the year. Just ahead was a frowning mass—the Fortress of St. Peter and St. Paul, "where we bury our Tsars, and keep our prisoners—keep them well." She shuddered at the implications in that low voice. The sun hit the top of a lean shaft that towered like a golden lance against the clouds, and lines from Bayard Taylor's poem "The Neva" that she had learned by heart as a child came to her mind.

> "The river-arms, dividing, hurry forth;
> And Peter's fortress-spire,
> A slender lance of fire,
> Still sparkles back the splendor of the North."

How much had happened to her on this first day! She was so exhilarated when she got home that she sat down to begin her new diary. The words she wrote were exuberantly poetic as she described the city and its tradition, ending with her feeling about the Neva and Peter the Great. . . . "Nothing troubles Tsar Peter's sleep . . . spring and autumn the river hurls its waves against the stone wall with which he subjugated the Neva to his will. And in wintertime, as now, the river encloses itself in a tracery of ice, and thus guards Peter's eternal sleep."

From that first evening, the days raced by like troikas over the ice—dinners, parties, suppers, with the Prince and his set. Two weeks passed before he confessed with a grin:

"You've wondered about those men you wrote to? The messenger happened to come to me first. I didn't want competition, so I gave him a few rubles and he handed all the letters to me." His bland face wrinkled in merriment like a little boy's.

She pretended to be flattered, but she was secretly very much annoyed. Must she remain a captive of the older generation? She could not hurt his feelings by writing her younger acquaintances now.

Her sense of isolation increased. Knowing only a little Russian, she studied it by the hour, but she found the hotel servants shy and distrustful, even with her new phrases. They seemed almost afraid to talk to her. She remembered the gentle-faced woman of the border church. Would she ever break down the barrier?

She had also discovered that her French magazines and novels had to be inspected (by whom she never learned) before she received them. Newspapers arrived with whole articles cut out. At one of the few magazine stands, she asked for a mildly satirical English journal and the proprietor looked blank.

"We don't carry that kind."

"What kind?"

"It is not allowed," he whispered, and then turned away as if alarmed.

There was no one among the elegant graybeards to whom she could tell her feelings. Then without warning a message came, by scented note: "We're strangers in a strange land; we speak the same language—we should be friends." Wouldn't Madame Lear join a sleighing party that night? The name signed to the note was Mabel Grey, and Hattie placed it at once as that of the most famous "foreign" woman then in favor in the capital. Cora had told her about the beautiful London shopgirl who, it was rumored, had enjoyed the friendship of one of Queen Victoria's younger sons, then run off to Russia with a wealthy boyar.

Hattie accepted Mabel Grey's invitation. It was a friendly overture, and she need not keep up the relationship if it turned out badly. She was ready that evening when the bell rang.

"My dear Madame Lear!" Mabel Grey's voice was warm, and astonishingly cultivated. She was no longer very young; her mouth had a tired look, but the eyes, deep and almost green, were haunting. The nose had a tilt, in a kind of mutiny against the intent face. Here stood a complex woman, observant, sharply intelligent, and clearly ready to be generous. As they caught one another's hands, Madame Grey exclaimed, "You're as lovely as they said." The eyes were direct and flattering.

"They didn't do you justice," Hattie answered. She looked at Mabel's deep-gold dress, and the small ribbons of the same shade with which the dark hair was tied; Mabel Grey eyed with appreciation the soft white net that Hattie had chosen to wear that night.

"You have what some of the Court women lack—the discipline to keep off the last ornament," Mabel said, and reached up to her own ears. "A lesson for me," she added, and dropped the gold pendants into her purse.

The young gentlemen, gathered that evening in the private salon of a fashionable restaurant to meet the beautiful American, were blond and pink-faced, strong-framed. No wonder Prince Golitsyn and his friends wanted to keep her away from them! When they were presented to her, Hattie suppressed an impulse to laugh— each was a connection, a son or a nephew, one certainly a grandson, of the men she had already met!

Champagne, oranges, and ices were on every table. Guests ate or made believe they ate, but mostly they drank. The young men addressed Hattie in French, German, or English. She astonished and delighted them by answering with some of her newly acquired Russian.

Toward midnight, troikas came to drive them to Dorrot's, where they would hear the gypsies sing. Through the deep snow, brilliant in the light of a full moon, they skimmed along too quickly for speech. The young men shouted and sang as the sleighs rushed into the night. The runners sent a light powder into their faces, and now and then bits of ice darted past them. Hattie was transported. This was a childhood dream come true.

Three sets of doors guarded Dorrot's against the cold. As the innermost one swung open, palm trees and tropical plants of delicate exotic color spread before them. It was a restaurant in a hothouse. Chinese lanterns hung here and there in the green, and heavy gas jets glimmered among brilliant flowers.

As they settled down in the grand salon for a midnight supper, double doors opened to an adjoining room. Before them sat a semicircle of women, with a half-dozen men behind them, all glossyhaired, swarthy, dressed in loose, violent-hued costumes. In the hard light the deep-set eyes looked out shrewdly.

"Ai!" A woman's cry made her jump; the men's voices joined in a melody that was untamed, barbaric. A man unlike the others, tawny-headed, his skin very white, leaped forward; with a violent stroke of his guitar he began a plunging rhythm. Now Hattie could make out some of the words:

> "The peasant lives for his Tsar,
>   Chief of his body and soul;
>   If he would die for the Tsar
>   His heart makes him face iron, flood, flame . . ."

A woman jumped up, and another, and the men leaped to join in a free-swinging dance.

The Russian youths swayed with the music; one laughed in a kind of intoxication, and another cried softly, his head buried in his arms. The tempo grew faster, the garishly lighted room ever warmer. The heat of the dancing bodies reached them, and this seemed only to stir the listeners to more abandoned movement. As the gypsies swept about the room, crying softly, several onlookers rose, to shout approval. One pulled off a ring and tossed it to the performers; another, a stickpin.

All at once, Hattie found herself on her feet. Taking an impulsive step forward, she threw out her diamond brooch, the "good-luck" token from the Duke of Bodenbach. A gypsy caught it in mid-air and bowed from the waist. As Hattie sank back, she knew that Mabel's eyes were on her in wonder. With sudden sanity she wondered why she had done it. Whatever Joséphine might say, she'd deserve it! But she didn't care. A diamond brooch . . . her father's gold pencil . . . When the time came for giving, one gave.

From that night on she was part of the *jeunesse dorée* of St. Petersburg. Her diary recorded one gay occasion after another. On one rare quiet evening when she dined early and alone with one of the young Princes, he planned the most prodigal party of all. She and Mabel were to go to Tsarskoe Selo, the Tsar's village near Petersburg, where a famous regiment of the Imperial Guard was stationed. One of the senior officers had offered to place his own mansion at their disposal.

As she and Mabel boarded the late afternoon train on the appointed day, Hattie found the Englishwoman in a more sober mood than usual.

"Fanny, I hope you'll be careful," she said, sighing. "It's so easy to make a mistake here—and so hard to keep it secret. To keep anything secret."

"What do you mean?"

"The secret police, of course." Mabel was a little surprised by her companion's innocence. "They spy on everybody, even on themselves. They have files on practically everyone you know. On us, of course. They probably know all about this party—and knew about it even before we were asked! They just keep track quietly."

"But even on the nobility—on people close to the Tsar?" Hattie realized as soon as she said it that her question was naïve, and she got the answer she expected.

"On them most of all! Of course there are some things everybody knows about the royal family, even about the Tsar himself—his second family is in pretty plain view; that Princess he helped educate and then made his mistress. At night the Tsarina and her children are supposed to hear the children of the other family as they run across the floors overhead. . . . And the Tsar's brother, Constantine, the one with the peculiar wife—he's had his ballerina for years, too. And Nikki, Constantine's eldest son—the one that breaks up restaurants, Nikki—even for a Romanov, my God!"

Hattie was fascinated, but the short ride ended too soon to ask more. The Colonel of the regiment himself met them at the station, and conducted them to the resplendent mansion, where they hurried to dress for dinner. All their young friends were there as well as the older officers, and as usual she and Mabel were the only women. Against the scarlet of the uniforms, Hattie's white satin stood out with all the effect she could wish.

Dessert was served to the accompaniment of music and singing. The singers were soldiers from the Prince's squadron, giants of prodigious physique. Their songs were of love for the fatherland, of the heroic traditions of the regiment, and of the wonders of the Caucasus, where the regiment had been stationed. Suddenly, at a signal from the leader, the singing stopped. The soldiers, smiling broadly, seized their Colonel and tossed him into the air again and again, each time catching him before he could hit the floor.

The man next to Hattie laughed at her surprise, and explained: "Just another Russian way of showing affection!"

The Colonel, hot and smiling, beamed as he was toasted in tribute to his stamina. Then came the young Prince's turn, next the other officers'; then unexpectedly they turned to Mabel. She put up her hand firmly.

"No, I've told you before. No." After some hesitation, the men moved toward Hattie. Why not?

She made herself relax as she was thrown in the air with a swirl of lace petticoats, then caught in their upraised arms. As she later wrote in her diary: "They repeated this outlandish exercise several times, and in dismay I thought of the dire effect it might have on my digestion." But when they set her down, breathless and dizzy, she had her reward. The whole company saluted her.

She had barely caught her breath when the troikas were announced for a moonlight ride to the park and palace of Pavlovsk. "It belongs to Constantine, the Tsar's brother, you understand," the young Prince explained. "We cannot enter the palace itself, but it is permitted to ride through the park."

For an hour they rode along winding alleys of ice, past the sweeping grace of snow-laden trees. Hattie called out in admiration as they crossed tiny bridges with finely wrought grills that stretched across frozen ponds, and drove slowly past the massive columns and ornamented roof of the palace itself. "A thousand cultivated acres over there where the gardens begin." Such sweeping expanses, such luxury for a single family—no, a branch of a family. And these were only some of the exterior trappings. Inside? Few knew about that. The outer splendor must be enough.

The Prince pointed to a dark wooded stretch.

"That's the stag park. Belongs to Constantine's son, Nikki." After a moment's hesitation, he bent low to whisper: "You may hear a lot more about that branch of the family, Fanny Lear, if things work out. Constantine's one of the few hopes for a better country." The young Prince suddenly checked himself. His outburst made her think of Prince Golitsyn, who had so hated Constantine. This was the other side of the coin, then, and there were others beside herself who felt that if Russia had left the dark autocratic days behind it, it might be slipping back again.

To her dismay, she discovered that for her companions the night had barely begun. The next meal finished at eight in the morning, and another long sleigh ride was proposed. "The sun won't let us sleep anyway."

"But I've been awake for more than twenty-four hours!" Her protest was weak, yet as they protested in turn at her "frailty" she fell asleep in the satin chair where she sat.

Later in the day, she still dozed while she sat opposite Mabel in the train. Mabel was obviously very tired, but wide-awake. After a few prefatory remarks she said:

"Wasn't Constantine's palace marvelous? Funny how the Tsar keeps him in luxury when they really disagree so." She looked intently at Hattie.

Hattie thought of the drunken confidence of the young officer, but decided to take the advice Mabel herself had given her the day before. She realized that she almost never knew just what Mabel was thinking. How different from the forthright Cora Pearl! Hattie thought drowsily of Paris and longingly of the lace bed in her old room on the Boulevard Malesherbes—and fell asleep again.

Back at the hotel at last, she knew as soon as Joséphine opened the door that something was wrong. Inside the room stood a flint-faced man. He was not in uniform, but he carried himself with unmistakable authority.

"I'll talk to the lady alone," he said, nodding toward Joséphine, who left the room with a parting look of deep suspicion. Before Hattie could speak, her visitor moved toward her. "Madame Lear, this is a call of"—he paused—"discretion. Some of your activities have interested us. Permit me to congratulate you on the many friends you have made in so short a time." The smile that followed had no humor.

"And who are 'we'?"

The man shrugged. "I don't represent anybody. But you must have heard of General Trepov and"—again he paused with an extra significance—"Count Shuvalov." He had made his point; by now she knew that though Trepov was head of the powerful Petersburg police, Shuvalov directed the whole secret machinery of the state.

"So"—the smile came and went—"some of us wondered if you wouldn't like to assist the government, which has been, after all, kind to you. It is simply that you would listen to what certain of your gentlemen say on certain subjects, perhaps encourage them to give you the benefit of their thoughts. Other women of your type have done it for us, and my superiors would be grateful."

A revulsion rose within her. Of her type! With dignity, she asked him to be seated, but her reply was brief.

"I'm not familiar with that sort of thing," she began. "I'd be very bad at it. And I know my friends only as friends. Perhaps you'll understand." Her anger was so great that she was completely unafraid, and smiled at him easily.

The man nodded, and got up abruptly. "Well enough, madame. We'll both remember our interview."

Although her next words were in her sweetest tone, they were carefully enunciated. "And you'll tell your superiors—the General and the Count—exactly what I did say, and no more?"

His face grew red. "Allow me to make my own report, and I advise you to say nothing to anybody about this." With these words he slammed the door behind him.

Hattie was suddenly shaking with fatigue and the emotions she had repressed during the short, ominous visit. Joséphine ran in, more distressed than ever.

"Madame, this country, this country!"

TEN

As DECEMBER WENT BY AND CHRISTMAS APPROACHED, HATTIE FOUND the pace of St. Petersburg society more and more strenuous: dinners at six o'clock followed by the theater or the opera, supper parties and balls that often lasted until six or seven in the morning. Her days began at three in the afternoon and with the early winter dusk, she felt as if she had seen no sun for months.

Returning to her suite about five o'clock one Sunday afternoon, she sank onto her bed and lay back exhausted. There was to be a masquerade ball at the opera house that night, but for once she was too worn-out to go.

Joséphine came to draw off her little fur-lined carriage boots, and handed her a letter from America. It was from her mother. Caroline had heard with astonishment that her daughter was now in "that weird, far-off country," and though she remained noncommittal, clearly had her doubts about it. Still, she said, she would "hope for the best," and Hattie should know that she always prayed for her.

In the last paragraph, as usual, Caroline reported the current deaths. Miss Ellen, the youngest Holmes sister, had "passed quietly" in her sleep. Though Hattie had no pleasant memories of any of the Holmeses, she sighed. What a rigid, deprived life poor Miss Ellen had had—and she had probably died thinking of Hattie as a lost soul. Hattie smiled faintly, but the letter had depressed her. She handed it back to Joséphine and turned her face to the pillow.

"Don't call me," she murmured. "Shut the door to the world. I'm going to rest around the clock."

A few hours later she woke with a start. Bells were clanging in the distance, the insistent bells of Petersburg's midnight. She got up and went to the window; the patches of snow on the bulbous church domes gleamed invitingly, the town was covered with white. The traffic moved silently along the wide expanse of the Nevsky Prospekt. St. Petersburg at Christmas time, and the whole town awake!

She knew she would not be able to go back to sleep. Lighting a lamp, she looked for a book to read, and saw her invitation to the ball propped against a vase on the table.

"Shall I?" She tapped the heavy card against her fingers meditatively, slowly. "Shall I?"

Mabel had said, disdainfully: "The affair's lost its éclat. The Tsar himself, and all the Grand Dukes, used to go, but now it's only the boyars. And the women! More and more of the cheaper ones."

But Hattie was curious. She had never been to one of these balls. It was too late to get in touch with any of her friends, and suddenly she was glad. It would be an adventure to go alone. Hattie woke Joséphine. "We're going to the ball after all."

Joséphine protested, but got up, rubbing at her pointed nose. Sleepily, she helped her mistress into a soft white dress and held out the flowing black-silk domino. Hattie adjusted her lace-trimmed black mask. Through it, her eyes sparkled like jet. She had tried a new coiffure—like that of a certain ugly princess she had seen the week before. Her blond hair was piled high in braids at the back of her head, a chain of pearls twisted around it. It gave her a look of Slavic elegance.

The ball was at its height when they reached the opera house. It was difficult to avoid being swept into the crowd that seemed to billow up to the door. She saw no one she knew, although the men in their dress uniforms, carrying headgear with white plumes, wore no masks—a simple black armband was their only gesture to the masquerade. The women were all masked, all dressed in black, but as Hattie looked about her she could place some of them. There were young milliners, haggard sporting women of advanced age, and a flower girl or two—Mabel had been right. About to flee from the scene, she drew back and collided with an attractive guardsman, and as they both broke into apologies she recognized him—a young Prince she had met at the party at Dorrot's. He exclaimed in pleasure at the sound of her voice.

"*L'Américaine!*"

With him were several others of the *jeunesse dorée*, and they drew her in among them before she could protest.

"Madame Lear!" They greeted her with surprise and pleasure.

There was only one stranger in the group, a tall, handsome, fair-haired young guardsman. He stood looking around the room in boredom, and when for a moment his green eyes met Hattie's they were without expression. Folding his arms, he touched his light mustache with a long, careless finger.

The young Prince was offering his arm, and so were others. She took a step backward. "No, I know all of you." She lifted her face to the young guardsman. "But I will take the arm of this man, whom I do not know."

There was a flicker in the deep-set green eyes. The strange guardsman offered his arm and spoke in a low, resonant voice that carried a long distance across the room:

"At your service, madame." As they moved away, he had to bend to talk to her, because he was so tall. "My English is limited, unfortunately." His mouth, large and full, had a sardonic expression.

"It doesn't matter," she said easily. "I know French and I'll talk enough for the two of us!"

But his own French was fluent and he proceeded to do the talking, asking one question after another. How long had she been in St. Petersburg? Had she seen the Tsar? Met any of the Grand Dukes?

He hardly gave her a chance to answer, but when at last his bombardment stopped she laughed.

"Naturally, being a typical American, I'm fascinated by royalty! But also, being a typical American, I don't think I'd feel comfortable with the Russian royal family."

"Why not?" He encouraged her to go on.

"I'm just not used to a ruler's having such absolute power."

After a pause, he asked, "You know who I am?"

She touched him with her fan. "I know that you are young and handsome and a captain of the horse guards—and judging by your shoulder knots, you must be an aide-de-camp to the Tsar."

He looked at her in surprise. "You've learned a great deal!" Then the sardonic expression returned. "Yes, an aide. My father was a Moscow merchant who gave money for the Crimean War,

97

and so the reward. But I have no fortune myself—I've squandered it all on beautiful women."

Hattie smiled up at him. Money or no money, this was an unusually attractive young man. By the standards of the people she knew—by Mabel Grey's rules—he would rank rather low, a merchant's son. But she was finding him more exciting than anyone she'd met in a long time. Was it his air of superb assurance, or his physical force? His shoulders were magnificently built, and he carried his height with graceful ease. She noticed his finely muscled hands with the down of light hair—in the days of Catherine the Great, this young aide's immediate promotion would have been assured!

As they walked on slowly, rhythmically, making several rounds of the hall, the music grew livelier, the room still more crowded. An all-pervading erotic current flowed among the hundreds of bodies, charging the air with nervous longing and anticipation. Suddenly she realized that he was leading her off the floor. "Would you like to sit down?"

There were benches along the wall, but he led her away from them. "Not here, I have a box up there." He gestured upward. His father must have contributed a great deal to the war! At the head of the stairs, a footman in gold braid bowed deeply as he opened the door for them. The box was hung with heavy crimson velvet. Double-headed Romanov eagles were embroidered in gold on the crimson satin chairs. . . . Hattie's hand shook a little as he took it and led her to a small sofa.

"May I smoke?" he asked. When she nodded he took out a cigarette case, and she saw that the same eagle was engraved on the lid. Unconsciously she put her hand to her mask, to hold it in place. "So you've never seen a Grand Duke, Fanny Lear? You can see one now, at your ease, if you'll take off your mask."

"Grand Duke?" Her voice sounded thin.

"Yes. Nicholas Constantinovich." The raillery remained, but now there was a hint of pride.

Nikki, son of Constantine, and the Tsar's nephew. What had she said to him about the Romanovs? She wanted to dart from the sofa and out of the room. As he smiled again, his hand reached out for the ribbon that tied her mask. When she drew back, he asked:

"Are you ugly, perhaps, under that mask? They say you are astonishingly pretty."

At that she laughed, and took off the bit of silk. "Judge for yourself, Your Imperial Highness," she said.

His fervent green eyes, narrowing a little, missed no detail of her appearance: the curving red mouth, the faint hollow under the cheekbones, the high white forehead, the exquisite oval of her face.

For a long minute she returned his scrutiny. His bright chestnut hair was cut short enough to show the fine shape of his head. His forehead was high and open. The thought suddenly occurred to her that they looked, oddly, rather alike. But what was making them look most alike at this moment was the expression she saw in his eyes, and felt in her own. She could not stand the intensity of his gaze, and lowered her glance to his expressive mouth. His mustache was cut short—like the mustache of Peter the Great as she had seen it in portraits. His mouth was strikingly like that of Peter the Great, too—sensuous, but with a hint of harshness to it. Her uneasiness increased. She broke the silence.

"Have you looked enough?"

"Not half enough, Fanny Lear. I don't believe that it would ever be possible to look enough at you."

She flushed. Was his tone still mocking? But as his intent gaze continued, her confidence grew and her gaiety returned, and when he asked, "May we have supper at your hotel?" she forced herself to hesitate.

"I will be delighted to receive Your Imperial Highness, but supper—it's so late. I'm afraid all the attendants at the hotel are in bed."

"Never fear." Rising, he spoke the words as if they were a command. "My aide will bring us something."

As they left the box, Hattie suddenly remembered Joséphine. She found her half asleep in the lobby, and sent her ahead to be sure that their rooms were in order.

As she and the Grand Duke moved toward the entrance, people stepped aside deferentially before them. She noticed for the first time that as he walked with a light, proud step, he held one shoulder slightly higher than the other. Outside the opera house they were surrounded by eager footmen, and at a whistle, a little man bounded around the corner. He was almost certainly a dwarf.

99

His black trousers were tucked into tiny top boots, his red coat was bordered in gold, and he wore a trim fur cloak that swung in the wind.

"Karpych!" the Grand Duke called, and the dwarf swaggered up self-importantly and opened the door of the waiting carriage.

It was a magnificent vehicle, with the same Romanov gold eagle on the door. On the box sat a large and stately coachman, like an oversized statue. Just behind Karpych, a young man waited to follow them into the carriage. "Captain Vorpovsky, my aide-de-camp," Nicholas said. Captain Vorpovsky had jet-black hair, a merry grin, and an eye that appraised as it probed. For a moment Hattie felt uneasy, but the Captain's look was not unkind, and after all, he must have met many others with the Grand Duke.

She sat back against the satin upholstery of the seat. "I am traveling in the eighteenth century!" she thought, and when the carriage halted in front of the Hôtel de France and she alighted leaning on the Grand Duke's arm, she felt like a princess out of the book she had read in Philadelphia.

Joséphine was there to open the door for them. She took their furs, but Hattie made no move to follow her into the bedroom to rearrange her hair or take off her domino. She was watching Nicholas, who immediately started to circle the room, restlessly touching her photographs and little porcelain boxes, reading the titles of her books.

When he came to the plants in the window he touched a finger to some tall green onion stalks and turned to her questioningly. Joséphine had grown them, considering the Russian salads under-flavored, and Hattie kept them in the salon, liking the touch of bright green against the eternal snow outside the window. Now she explained.

"I really prefer onion greens to flowers—you see I use them both for ornament and for salad." As he continued to look puzzled, she added solemnly, "I eat only raw onions and dry bread."

He threw back his head and laughed. "But all they said about you is true—you *are* unusual, you are delightful!"

As he looked at her, Hattie suddenly realized that her hair was disarranged. She lifted both hands to the back of her head. "Don't," he said. "Leave your hair as it is. You have no idea how refreshing it is to meet a woman who isn't continually primping!"

100

Inwardly amused, she obeyed him, but she did take off the black domino, tossing it onto the sofa near the fire. Her simple soft white dress rounded in under her small high breasts, clung to her tiny waist. He drew in his breath, took a step toward her. A knock sounded at the door, and he turned. It was Captain Vorpovsky and the dwarf, bearing several baskets. Joséphine was bowed out of the way. The aide reached out expertly for a small table, set out a cold roast chicken, a bowl of fruit, and several bottles of wine. Then it was discovered that there were no knives, forks, or glasses. The Grand Duke's oath echoed through the room.

"It's all right—we'll use our fingers," Hattie said quickly.

Joséphine whispered: "Madame, I broke my glass today. Yours is the only one left."

Overhearing this, Nicholas chuckled. "We'll make it do between us—improve the wine for me."

When they sat down at the table, Joséphine withdrew. Surely the Captain would leave, as the dwarf already had? But, taking a chair in the corner, he sat there with his arms folded, his bright dark eyes on them unblinkingly, and now and then Hattie had the uneasy feeling that he was making mental notes of all that happened.

The chicken was excellent, the wine, drunk in quick succession from the single glass, of fine vintage. When the meal was finished, the Grand Duke gave a signal and Vorpovsky, after clearing the table, snapped his heels together and made a brisk farewell.

Nicholas drew her down beside him on the sofa.

"I want to talk to you." His tone was peremptory.

"But Your Highness, it's six o'clock in the morning!"

"You must promise me something—on your word of honor."

A little frightened, she replied lightly, "I'm too bohemian to have a word of honor."

"You're right." His voice was solemn. "Spoken words have wings. We'll do more than that."

Before she realized what he was doing, he went over to her desk. Thrusting letters aside, letting several fall to the floor, he found a sheet of paper. After a moment's thought, he wrote rapidly. Back at her side, he handed her the paper and a pen. "Sign it."

The first words made her want to laugh, but her amusement died immediately.

"I swear by all that I hold most sacred never to see or speak to anyone without the permission of my master. I bind myself as a well-born American to remain faithful to this oath and declare myself, body and soul, a slave of Grand Duke Nicholas Constantinovich of Russia."

His hand was on her shoulder, his green eyes almost hypnotic. She started to say something, then stopped. . . . She signed.

He smiled as he thrust the paper in his pocket. "It's a contract. Tonight—that is, today—I'll bring you something to seal it." He lifted her chin and kissed her—the kiss she had been waiting for all evening. But now it was slow and deep, not wild and passionate as it would have been before. Now it was almost like a betrothal kiss. Still holding her, he murmured:

"I loved a woman not long ago, a beautiful one, very much like you. They wouldn't let me marry her—but I shall have you!" Abruptly he got to his feet. "I'll be back at five today." A bow, and he was gone.

Standing motionless where he had left her, Hattie felt dazed. Why had she obeyed this strange, theatrical command? And suddenly she felt that for years she had been lost and alone—and now she would be lost and alone no longer.

She slept until one in the afternoon, and woke remembering everything without the spell of the night before. There was no time for an elaborate toilet. She spoke over her shoulder to Joséphine.

"I'm going to see Miss Grey."

"Her?" Joséphine's heavy brows lifted.

Hattie did not stop to ask Joséphine to explain. "I'll be back around four."

A few minutes later she found Mabel Grey having breakfast in bed. The Englishwoman looked up with vivid interest as Hattie came in saying abruptly:

"Mabel, I need your advice——"

Mabel interrupted her. "I already know what happened at the ball."

She knew, so soon? Hattie sat down slowly, and took the cup of tea Mabel handed to her. Mabel leaned forward, and her voice dropped confidentially.

"My girl, look here. You don't realize what all this means! The Tsar and his brothers, and one or two others at the top—they're all safely settled, with wives and generally women friends as well, permanent ones, princesses or such. But Nikki, he's single, and very eligible." Mabel hunted for words. "You couldn't have hoped to go much higher. And there's the future to think of."

"What do you mean?"

"Don't you understand?" Mabel gave her a sharp look. "There's always been a chance, there still is, that an upset may take place and Constantine will get to be Tsar. If he does, Nikki's his oldest son and might even be Tsar himself one day."

"An upset?"

Mabel jumped up, her long gown trailing behind her. "Look, there's the heir apparent, the Tsar's son, a dull stick of wood; they call him Sasha the Bear. But the talk always pops up that neither young Sasha nor even the Tsar himself belongs on the throne. It's like this. When Alexander, the present Tsar, was born, his father wasn't on the throne. When Constantine came along, the father was! You see, born to the purple when Alexander wasn't. Well, Alexander's there now, but a lot of Russians think Constantine has a stronger claim and may make it good in time. The Tsar's getting on in years, and Constantine's only forty-five. He's head of the navy now, and head of the State Council. He was viceroy of Poland for a while, and he practically ran the Tsar's commission that freed the serfs. They say the more power he gets, the more he wants. His daughter's Queen of Greece, and that's made him still more ambitious, I suppose."

Forgetting to be cautious, Hattie said, "But I've heard Constantine's practically a revolutionary, and stirs up trouble when he can."

Mabel gave her a shrewd glance. "If he is, it's trouble that would help get him on the throne. He'd like a revolution, certainly—in his own direction!"

"Then whether the Tsar trusts them or not, the police must be watching everything Constantine and Nikki do," Hattie said.

"Everything." The Englishwoman's wide gray eyes held hers. "That will include you, too." What did Hattie read in those eyes —concern for her, or a touch of jealousy?

Mabel's tone took on an affectionate indulgence. "Of course Nikki's been spoiled from the beginning—no control at all. The mother's a fool, even a little potty, they claim, with her spiritualism and all that. Idolizes Nikki and then sits down and cries when he gets into trouble." She went on: "And then there was that German cousin of his he wanted to marry. . . . She was a princess of Hanover, but of course the Greek Orthodox Church won't allow first cousins to marry—or it may have been only that the girl wanted somebody else. Right afterward she married her father's aide, and that made Nikki even more unhappy."

Mabel sighed. "Since then he's gone wilder than ever—parties that last for days—and that big room in the restaurant, his special room with thick cushions over the walls and ceiling, to keep the sounds in! It got so that even Count Shuvalov heard too much about it and gave orders; if the fellow let the room to Nikki again, he'd regret it. A Grand Duke on one side and Shuvalov on the other—the restaurant owner was frantic! But Shuvalov is more powerful than ever, and everybody thought the Tsar himself had given orders. So Nikki lost. And now . . ." Mabel opened her hands.

For a long time Hattie sat there, her fingers clasped tightly in her lap. It wasn't an appealing story; some of it was frightening. And yet Mabel knew a great deal about St. Petersburg below the surface. Even discounting a little jealousy, she would not lie.

Hattie looked at the clock and her pulse pounded in her temple. He was due at her hotel within an hour. She stood up quickly, and caught at her cape. Her fingers trembled in her haste to fasten it, and her good-by to Mabel Grey was brief.

ELEVEN

THEY SAT TOGETHER IN THE DARKENED ROOM, THEIR ONLY LIGHT the irregular play of the fire on wall and ceiling from the door of the tile stove. The shifting flames, the sounds of the coals as they settled inside, gave an additional intimacy; as his hand rested on hers, she felt happily isolated from all the world. He had brought her a pretty little pearl bracelet with a chain ending in a turquoise heart that had a padlock with a key.

"I will have your initials and the date inscribed, if you like."

"Put my initials on the heart and yours on the key, Your Highness."

He had taken her in his arms. "Not Your Highness—Nicholas—" he murmured, "and not Nicholas, but Nikki."

Now as they sat together he sang to her, in a low voice. She did not understand the words, but she knew it was a love song. Suddenly he stopped singing and gathered her to him. She lifted her face for his kiss.

"Nikki—say it," he whispered.

"Nikki," she repeated, dreamily, gratefully. He lifted her in his arms and carried her toward the other room. As her head fell back over his sleeve, her loosened hair tumbled down in a golden swirl. Afterward he lay beside her, stroking her hair tenderly . . . "my adorable blonde . . . *je n'aime que les blondes*, my Fanny Lear!"

He took her to cafés and restaurants, each time to a private room, and each time she was conscious of the stir as they arrived, the whispering that broke out as soon as they had gone by. Hattie wrote notes to all her friends; she was sorry, but she could not see them again. Sorry! She was delighted.

Late one afternoon, Joséphine went to the door to find little Karpych looking more important than ever in immaculate white trousers, red coat, and tall hat. Approaching Hattie, he bowed, then broke into a monologue in high-pitched Russian, with many gestures, and handed her a note.

"K. will bring you," she read. "We will dine at the Marble Palace."

Hattie showed the note to Joséphine. Her maid's eyes widened. "Madame, would he take you there, with the family?"

"I don't know, Joséphine—I don't know." Hattie was half trembling as she dressed.

In the carriage, she found trouble in breathing the cold air. Could it be possible that the Grand Duke Constantine would *not* object to their love affair? But under his own roof! Thank the Lord Nikki's mother was at their palace at Pavlovsk. And then, along the avenue above the snow-powdered tops of the firs, she recognized the Marble Palace—the Grand Duke Constantine's residence at the capital. A gateway opened and they swept through, the bells tinkling over the still air. They rode swiftly past the ornamental main entrance to a small door at the side.

Nikki's welcoming words were defiantly loud in the echoing hall. With a slight air of bravado, he led her through one immense room after another. Afterward she remembered countless Persian rugs, and hunting trophies along the paneled walls—stags' horns of frightening size.

At last, in a little room that looked more lived in than the rest, he helped her out of her cloak. "My library and smoking room," he said. Above the shelves of books in heavy leather bindings, paintings covered the walls. He pointed to an imposing oil of a voluptuous goddess. "Bryulov's 'Venus.' . . . And here *she* is," he said, turning Hattie by the shoulders to face a portrait hanging on the opposite wall. It was that of a tall blonde, a delicate-faced girl in full Court dress.

"Who is it?" she asked.

"Princess Frederika, of course."

She stood silent.

"Isn't your resemblance remarkable?"

106

It actually was. Hattie was somewhat flattered, but miserably jealous.

"Well, what do you think?" he demanded irritably.

She made herself speak. "If I can be anything to you that she should have been, I will."

He said nothing, and she still stared at the portrait, afraid to turn and see his face. But somehow she understood that he was pleased, and she felt relief. She had passed the first small crisis. When would the next one come?

Karpych provided a happy interruption. "Dinner, Your Highness."

The tablecloth and napkins, of fine linen, bore the imperial arms; the silver was heavy yet of simple design, its only decorations the Romanov crown and the initials C. N. Five servants stood ready to serve them at the small glittering table. Two were former sailors, transferred by Constantine from his Navy to his private service, Nikki told her. On the breast of the older one, a weatherbeaten, taciturn man, brass medals jingled heavily. Apparently he was allowed liberties, for he stared at her from under iron-gray eyebrows, and then addressed his master in sonorous Russian.

A tall Circassian of almost yellow skin in a velvet uniform of gold and crimson, with a dagger at his belt, stood behind Nikki, and a sleepy-looking fellow in a flamboyant costume that she did not recognize placed thick soup before them.

At her question, Nikki smiled. "A Cossack. One of my tutors used to dress that way. Once a party of us went to Leipzig, and he got so drunk with schnapps that he collapsed. I hired a booth at the fair, exhibited him as a 'real dead Cossack,' for money, and shouted for the crowd in front of the tent! He was so dignified— he was furious when he woke up, and he made a lot of trouble. But Papa enjoyed it and sided with me."

Hattie was amused but wondered a little nervously whether any of the listening servants understood French. She felt distinctly as if they were quietly watching and passing judgment on her. As the heavy courses progressed, she hoped her lack of appetite for the strange and rather tasteless food was not noticeable. But Nikki noticed everything about her.

"Our cooks here are all French, you know," he said, almost defensively.

107

"Then I shall be even more at home." She smiled sweetly, but thought privately that working in Russia had spoiled their touch. The wines made up for the flat dishes; there were several and each one was more delicate.

"This last one's from the Hungarian cellars—our cousin Emperor Francis Joseph." Nikki was so insistent that she taste every one of them that her head felt light and swimming at the end of the meal. He helped her to her feet, laughing. "There's a peculiar law of nature in my wines. Other vintages operate to send corks upward, mine to hold *you* down."

He led her through more rooms of the vast palace and she grew bewildered; so many statues and paintings, more and more guns and daggers hanging from the walls. Casually he pointed to two paintings by Greuze. She ran toward them to look at them more closely in the dim light.

"'La malédiction' and 'Le repentir.' Oh, if it were only daytime! Why don't you light them better?"

"You must come back in the daytime," he said, then added hesitantly, "someday." They were both suddenly conscious of the silent space around them. Hattie's hand clung to his, and they moved on.

"Where did you learn these things?" he asked. "I must confess to you when I first went to your suite, I was already in love with you and afraid that at any minute I would find evidence you were just like every other woman of your world. Now I realize that you know more than any woman at Court."

She smiled. "Is it so wonderful to you that a woman should know things?"

"Why, yes." His frankness had a disarming note. "But not only that—you're *interested* in such things. Most women have minds, I suppose, but they don't want to use them."

They came again to Nikki's small study and library, from which opened his bedroom and bathroom—the most luxurious bathroom Hattie had ever seen. It was cavernous, and decorated lavishly in Oriental style. Hattie ran her fingers over the veined marble of the walls above the bath and the pools, and tried out the soft ottomans beside them. Arms folded, Nikki watched her, his eyes beginning to burn in the intent way they had when he was really absorbed in her. "You won't leave the palace tonight?" His question was almost a command.

108

"If you wish." She made him an ironic curtsy, but lost her balance and fell laughing onto one of the velvet sofas. He took a quick step toward her as if to help her to her feet, but sank down beside her instead.

They slept late. Breakfast was served at two in the afternoon on a low marble table between two couches. They had barely begun when a bell rang sharply from a few rooms away. Putting down his coffee cup, Nikki listened intently. It sounded again and he sprang to his feet.

"Father's coming. Hide! Hurry!"

Looking frantically about her, Hattie saw no closets in the smooth paneled walls, but the large medieval bed, canopied and curtained, stood a few feet away and she jumped into it and pulled the curtains. Nikki hurried out to greet Constantine, and she could hear their voices in the anteroom. Their steps approached; now she knew they were standing near the door of the bedroom itself. Nikki's voice was raised slightly in nervousness. She realized with horror that Constantine was discussing the bed, and she lifted her head to listen.

"I've heard about your new purchases—especially this bed." The voice was urbane. "You paid a lot. Let me see if it's really an antique."

"Oh, but really there's nothing to see, Father." Nikki's alarm was too evident. Steps sounded in the room itself and the heavier ones came up to the bed.

"Nevertheless——" Without warning, the curtains were parted and Constantine thrust his head in. Hattie felt his curious gaze one second before she drew back, shutting her own eyes in an agony of embarrassment, and snatching up a small pillow to hold it before her face. Constantine withdrew with pretended discretion, and the curtains fell back into place.

"Ah!" His rich voice reached her; it was triumphant. "I can't quite see in there. Who is she?"

"Well—I——" Nikki stammered. "She's—a lady who came to ask for funds for charity. She lost her head when you came, and tried to hide."

"So." The note of amusement grew stronger. "Is she pretty?" Nikki was whispering. "No, old and ugly."

"I think you're quite mistaken, my boy." Then the voice rose.

"Nikki, this must be the American I've heard about." (As if it had just occurred to him! Hattie thought angrily.) "Let me see her."

Her heart beat more heavily than ever as Nikki answered: "No, Father. Not here, please."

There was a long silence. "Not here." Constantine repeated his son's phrase, and without humor. As their steps went away, she realized that Constantine's last words had been very stern indeed. Miserably, self-consciously, she climbed out of the fatal bed. Nikki's defiant protestations did not soothe her feeling of indignity or lessen her realization that he too was far more upset than he pretended. Grave-faced for once, Karpych appeared to take her home. The tinkle of the sleigh bells rose mournfully in her ears as they drove away.

Joséphine ran to her, tears in her eyes. "Madame, I was afraid you were hurt or something had happened!" Hattie, already saddened, cried with her maid. She had forgotten to send Joséphine a message; as she wept into Joséphine's own linen handkerchief she told herself she could be sure of at least one friend in Russia.

"That Miss Grey's been looking for you, twice." Joséphine's sharp nose went up in a dislike stronger than she had heretofore disclosed.

"If she comes again, tell her I'm still not in." Hattie could not face Mabel today.

There was no word from Nikki. By late afternoon of the next day Hattie was frantic. Would they ever be allowed to see each other again? Constantine's power grew more and more ominous in her mind. That air of elegant amusement, then the cold withdrawal! Why should he punish Nikki for taking her to the palace? Everybody knew about his own ballet dancer.

But the knock she had been hoping for came, and a moment later Joséphine entered the bedroom with a broad smile. "From the Grand Duke, madame," she said, handing her a dark package. Ripping it open, Hattie discovered a flat leather box. In it was a necklace of rubies, each perfect stone encircled in gold. As she lifted the magnificent jewels, a card dropped out. "Be ready for a trip tonight, at nine."

Tears of relief were in her eyes when Joséphine came in again. "Miss Grey—Are you in?"

110

She could face the world now! As Mabel embraced her, Hattie apologized.

"I've been out of sorts for a day or two."

"You're better now—good news?" Mabel spoke swiftly, and too late Hattie saw that she had left the rubies on her dressing table. She regretted it more when Mabel reached for them. "Really good news!"

Leaving out a great deal of detail, Hattie described what had happened. Before she finished, Mabel interrupted softly, with an inflection that sounded almost amused, "Oh, I know you met his father—in bed."

Hattie felt a new sense of wary alarm. "How did you know that?"

Mabel shrugged her fur-clad shoulders. "There aren't many secrets here. I told you that, my dear."

Hattie was furiously annoyed with herself as she blushed. To think of that scene elaborated, giggled at—the curtains, the pillow before her face! And Mabel was obviously enjoying it. Hastily, Hattie suggested tea, and shortly afterward she managed to bring the visit to an end. As Mabel left, she said, "Maybe you ought to go back to bed again, Fanny." There was venom in the words, but Hattie ignored it.

Nikki came that night, happily, boyishly, and kissed her as though he would never stop. "Papa's come around," he told her. "I think he may even be a bit proud of me; everybody says what a beauty you are."

Her fears of the other night seemed silly and schoolgirlish. She thanked him for the ruby necklace.

"I wanted to wear it tonight—but your card said to get ready for a trip."

"To our palace at Pavlovsk—two hours and a half by troika."

"Pavlovsk! But isn't that where your mother is?"

"It's so big she'll never know you're there—and I want you to see it. It's the finest palace in the world!" He grinned at her. "Should you eat a little first, before we start out? You don't like our Romanov food; you may die of hunger."

She glanced up at him. "Or from meeting your mother!"

"Darling, don't worry—she's not like Constantine; probably

111

hasn't even heard about us. She's preoccupied with her own ill-health in a wing that's almost a mile away!"

Three powerful horses stamped impatiently on the hard-packed snow below, smoke blowing from their nostrils. Captain Vorpovsky was waiting for them. The footmen wrapped them all heavily in extra fur blankets. It would be a bitter ride in the open sleigh.

They had hardly got under way before the wind cut into Hattie's face like a set of knives. At the outskirts of St. Petersburg, the lights went out one by one around them; they plunged through the moonless night over a plain of snow. Dimly, on each side, mountains of ice seemed to rise. There was an occasional glimmer of light; otherwise it was all darkness and the echoing iciness of deep winter. Hattie moved as close to Nikki as she could under the fur robe. "It can't be colder than this in Lapland," she quavered. He murmured an answer and drew her closer to him, but when she spoke again there was only silence. Nikki and the Captain had both gone to sleep.

The night was eerie, disturbing. She remembered stories of wolves that prowled through St. Petersburg's outskirts, racing after sleighs. To save themselves, leaders of riding parties were supposed to throw one member, then another, to the animals. She shivered, but her humor reasserted itself. The Captain was one of Nikki's oldest friends; if the issue developed, which would Nikki drop first? Then all at once she thought of tales about riders who dozed off and froze to death.

How cold Nikki felt at her side! To her relief, a light appeared ahead, and when she shook Nikki, he grumbled and woke. Other lights came from a huge building seen only dimly until they were actually upon it, and then the sleigh drew up under a porte-cochere where a sentinel presented arms when they appeared. A bell rang. They had arrived at Pavlovsk.

As she took off her numerous wraps in the well-warmed hall, Nikki excused himself.

"I must go see Mother for a minute." He turned to Vorpovsky. "Viktor, see that my lady is comfortable."

The young Captain moved solicitously about, ordering cups of steaming tea, telling her about the palace. "This is Nikki's favorite, the one he's always liked best. It has so much of his family's history connected with it." She stared in awe at the long stretches of dark wood broken now and then by pale statuary gleaming in the distant recesses.

Nikki returned, rubbing his hands, just as the servants wheeled in tables bearing steaming casseroles. The food was a surprise, as delicate as the Petersburg fare had been gross. Nikki and Viktor chuckled over her appreciation.

Nikki began the meal with a toast of welcome to her, and went on talking quickly, at his wildest and wittiest. As she looked about the big room she could understand one reason for the gaiety that contrasted so with his mood at the Marble Palace. This place was more colorful, less restrained. It had an air of ease that the formal city palace could never offer. She herself, however, was slightly oppressed by the great full-length portraits that stared down so sternly at her. They were studies in deep reds and ivories and fading blues against backgrounds of dim brown that slipped into black. Harsh dark eyes scrutinized her, under powdered wigs that looked out of place above the barbaric faces; the big-chested men demanded that all bow before them, even now. Nikki identified several: "The great Peter . . . also Tsar Paul, the mad one, who built Pavlovsk in the eighteenth century, and his mother Catherine, that old sinner."

Two o'clock sounded, and she jumped. Eighteen or twenty clocks, all around them, began to strike—low notes and high, tinkling notes and booming ones, a carillon of mixed melody. Captain Viktor withdrew discreetly, and Nikki led her down the hall. On the way he stopped before a cupboard.

"That set of blue Sèvres—a present to Tsar Paul and his wife from Louis XVI and Marie Antoinette. The initials of the four, interlaced, see? The set can never be reproduced, because the mold was smashed after these were made." He paused. "Of the four monarchs, only Paul's wife, my great-grandmother, died a natural death. Louis and Marie Antoinette were guillotined, and Paul was strangled to death."

When Hattie shuddered, Nikki seemed pleased and proud. "Yes, in his bedroom, by his generals, with the scheming of his son. My great-uncle Alexander I—the one that conquered Napoleon. Ah, I love this place! Now the bedroom, with Mad Paul's bed."

Was this where they were to sleep? Apparently it was. Her dressing case had been set on a low stand. The room was dark,

113

oppressive, dominated by towering tapestries. The bed had a canopy like a black cloud.

A little later, Nikki explained: "Paul bought this bed in France; he slept in it the night he was strangled. . . . Oh, my dear, it didn't happen in the bed itself!" He drew back soothingly. "He jumped out as soon as he realized what was going on. He was hiding behind a screen over there when they caught him and finished him. It wasn't in this room either—they just brought the furnishings to this palace after the place where it really happened was made into an engineering school."

"But why do you choose this room?" Hattie was still a little indignant, but he spoke on, ruminatively, almost to himself.

"He wasn't always crazy, you know. At first he was ruled by everything good and true; a great deal of temper, and zeal, nothing more. It was his mother who drove him mad. Catherine the Wicked . . ." His voice took on a harsher note. "He once said that if he had a dog and his mother thought he loved it, she would drown it. When a plain soldier came to tell him that she was seriously ill, he had him promoted to captain. At each stopping place on his way, as he found her condition had turned worse he raised the news-bearer's rank. When finally one told him she was dead, he made him a general!"

Hattie shuddered. Peter had murdered his own son, Catherine had schemed to kill her husband, Paul had met a hideous death. Imperial power and blood! Only in the past generation or so had there been a transfer of imperial authority without such blood-letting. Could there be another break in the line of inheritance from the present Tsar, with Constantine's help or without it?

Then from the dark Nikki spoke, musingly. "It's still not easy to hold the throne. They've tried to kill the Tsar several times in recent years, and missed him by only a little . . ."

She turned with a question. "Nikki . . ."

He smothered it with his mouth, and she was glad that he had.

She woke later. A single candle burned below an ikon in the corner, throwing faint light into the blackness of the chamber. There was a sound like a step—no, a cracking in the floor—and she stifled a scream. For a moment she had been sure someone was walking across the haunted chamber.

Then she heard a groan. She sat upright, terror in her throat.

114

Another groan, and a muffled cry: *"God help me!"* It was a man's agonized appeal; it was Nikki, tossing helplessly beside her. She shook him; he cried again, then woke fully.

"What is it, Nikki? What is it?" She reached out to comfort him. He caught her hand. After a moment he told her:

"It's my dream—the same dream that comes to me over and over. I've been accused of some awful crime, and condemned. They take me to the Winter Palace, between two rows of my own soldiers. I can hear my mother begging the Tsar to save me.

"He is upset; he embraces me, but then he says that he has to condemn me. They tie my hands, blindfold me, and my own regiment lifts its guns. I was born under an evil star. . . . I've always known I have bad times ahead of me!" His fingers trembled in hers; he was like a frightened child.

"What could happen to a Grand Duke," she said, "and why wouldn't the Tsar save you, his own nephew?"

He spoke slowly. "I've always thought the Tsar was my friend. Still . . ."

She tried to shake off the spell. "*'Les songes ne sont que mensonges!'* The French say it, 'Dreams are only lies.'" At last he dozed, but now she lay awake beside him, remembering her own recurrent nightmares. Were they too only lies?

In the morning, as they sipped chocolate together, she felt a new bond between them. In the daylight the chamber was still imposing, but the colors were brighter, less ominous. She began to like it; at least there were no portraits of that German princess!

How serene this country place seemed with the snowy landscape spread before the tall windows, and how far removed from Petersburg's intrigues! As she dressed, her mood brightened further. The furnishings and bronzes in eighteenth-century French style . . . the newer Empire pieces . . . the whole palace enchanted her this morning. She touched the porcelains and delftware on the long tables with red porphyry tops. Divans were covered in brocade with embroidered golden birds, in clear relief, yet how old. Generations had been needed to accumulate all this. . . . Nikki's mother was somewhere beyond this wing of the building.

Hattie joined Nikki in a many-windowed dining hall. He had begun to drink before breakfast. His tunic, loose at the throat, had fallen open. She saw that his chest, covered with thick blond hair, was really too thin, and that his skin was very pale. Casually she moved the brandy decanter away from him before she sat down.

"Why did you do that?" he shouted.

"Because it's time to eat." The second crisis she had been fearing had come. Fortunately, at that moment the dwarf Karpych came in with several dishes. As he placed them on the table she spoke to him in a low voice.

"What are we to have?" Grinning, Karpych used some of his new French words to explain. Smoked fish, two casserole mixtures. She stopped him. "Also bring us"—she thought a minute—"some eggs, milk, and fruit. And some plain cutlets."

Puzzled, Karpych withdrew, while Nikki glowered at her. She tried to explain to him. "But Nikki, you're so thin. These things are delicious, but they're not really nourishing. . . ."

Nikki pushed back his chair with a crash. His face was set in surly lines. "Who are you, a silly little American girl, to tell me what to eat!"

"Nikki, just look at yourself in the mirror."

It was a mistake. With a curse, he turned toward her, hand raised. As his denunciations rang about her, her own temper cracked. She jumped up and slapped him across the mouth. He was livid, trembling.

"You dare to hit a Romanov!"

"You're not a Romanov to me!" She began to cry. "You're the man I love, and when you forget yourself, I've got to bring you to your senses."

For a moment, she thought he would knock her to the floor. Instead he turned and stormed out. She dried her eyes and tried to look unconcerned when Karpych and two helpers arranged the double sets of dishes. Then the door opened and Nikki came back into the room. His face was still red, but he had an abashed, uncertain look. Did a Romanov know how to say he was sorry?

In silence he took her hand and drew her down beside him at the table. He wavered between the palace dishes and the plainer fare that she had ordered. With a smile she reached out, cut part of the meat, and held it out to him. They laughed together, and the meal went well. When they had finished, the implied apology came.

116

"Fanny Lear, it's too bad you weren't one of my teachers!" He leaned over and kissed her. "You're the only one that really cares for me, the only one that can help me."

Her eyes filled with tears, and he reached for her hand. "My wife, my little wife."

If only she were his wife; if they could be together without the constant threat of separation! If she could go with him to pay her morning respects to his mother and have Constantine be proud of her beauty as his daughter-in-law.

Was it really an impossible dream? On the wall hung a picture of the Tsarina Catherine I in her regal robes. She had been an outsider, too, a peasant even . . . And Hattie . . . Her mother's proud words came to her . . . "You have good blood from both sides, my dear, from the Holmeses and the Elys . . ." "My little wife." She felt that she was Nikki's wife more than she had ever been Cal Blackford's.

Nikki's hand over hers was warm. She turned her palm upward, and felt their pulses throbbing together.

"I am beginning to understand him." Hattie wrote in her diary a few weeks later. "He is too often overexcited, irritable, violent, haughty. But at the same time he sees through everything. And he is good, affectionate, and so protective toward everybody near him, beginning with me and down to the last dog belonging to him."

She closed the little book with a feeling of satisfaction. She would have liked to go on recording hundreds of details that made up the present richness of her life, but she expected Nikki at any moment. When he came, in one of his gayest moods, he was bearing a florist box.

When she opened it, a strange hothouse flower trembled to her touch. "Nikki, how beautiful! What is it?"

He shrugged. "Some kind of imported thing from Borneo, with a peculiar name. See what's under it."

It was a white card proclaiming her ownership of a special box at the opera. "Take your maid with you," he ordered. "I won't be able to come along every time, but I'll join you whenever I can. In any case, you must wear all your jewelry. Leave it at the American Legation betweentimes."

She went to hear *Il Trovatore* the very next night. The curtain

117

was just going up when she entered the box. As she let her ermine cape fall back from her bare shoulders and her ruby necklace caught the light from the stage, she saw the glitter of moving opera glasses turning toward her. And a few minutes later not a person in the audience made a pretense of watching the performance, for Nikki had come in, bowed, kissed her hand, and taken his seat beside her.

In the adjoining box, an aging countess, whose husband found his interests elsewhere, turned a sharp look on them, then shifted her chair to face in another direction. Hattie's black eyes were on the stage, her pearl-wreathed blond head held just a little higher than usual. She was with the man who meant more to her than everything else in the world. Let them look.

Back in the hotel, Nikki stared moodily into the fire. "With you there beside me tonight," he said, "I couldn't help thinking about other men who have wives and families. . . . I've never had a real family life; we've never been anything but a collection of people living in monuments!"

He got up and paced savagely around the room. "My father! Papa wants everybody to like him—admire him, that is. The great gentleman, the goodhearted hero to rich and poor. He can be as common as a kitchen-cleaner when he wants to be, and then when he leaves the kitchen-cleaners, a boulevardier of boulevardiers." He summed it up. "The truth is, Papa has only two real interests in life: his political ambition and his ballerina."

He stopped his restless pacing and came back to stand in front of her. "God knows about my younger brothers—I don't. One likes horses, the other one poetry. We don't meet often." He sighed and sat down again. "Now my sister Olga is a sweet girl— my favorite, if I have one. Takes after Papa in some ways, though; she's practically married to her Navy. She's an admiral. . . . But she looks like Mother." His face softened when he spoke of the Grand Duchess Alexandra—whom he sometimes called by the family's affectionate nickname of Sanni, instead of Mother. "Sanni's German, you know. She's always been a beauty, so she's been spoiled by everybody except Papa. If only she wouldn't go on the way she does about those damned ghosts of hers, spirits and table-tapping and healers. She's even had Papa going with her to the mediums. Once she brought one to the palace, a very pretty girl, and Papa 'mesmerized' her until she got pregnant.

118

The Tsar sent orders that the girl had to be sent out of the country for a 'cure,' and she was."

Hattie laughed, but he went on with vehement bitterness. "Certainly I never had any kind of real training, even education. Only the talk of fakers and tricksters. One day they assured me I was brilliant; then they let me know I was a fool. I had dozens of tutors, and only one or two were any good. The rest—stupid and rotten, or crafty and scheming, and most of them dirty Germans."

Yet his mother was German and he himself half German! He seemed to hate himself as well as his family tonight. Hattie looked at the clock.

"Nikki, aren't you expected at the reception at Court?"

"Let them wait," he said stubbornly. "All I'll do is think about you and how soon I can come back. This one's for the heir apparent anyway—Sasha the Bear!"

She spoke gently. "Is it wise to offend him by being late?"

"That lout! It's just an accident that he's heir apparent, you know; some even call him a murderer. His older brother was in line, a fine boy, not a blundering fool like Sasha. . . . Sasha was always wrestling, knocking people and things about. One day he rolled his brother on the grass in some kind of surprise trick and hurt him—just playing. They didn't realize how serious it was; when he died, Sasha stepped into his shoes."

"What a terrible thing to have hanging over him!" She exclaimed.

"It doesn't prey on Sasha! Not that some things don't!" He told her of the time Sasha had come to Pavlovsk for a visit. At the table, careless as usual, he had upset a large wineglass with much splattering. Constantine, annoyed, had called out, "Look at the ox they sent us from Petersburg!" "Sasha's never forgotten," said Nikki. "I think he really hates Papa—and me into the bargain. He's got a political excuse, anyway. He didn't like the idea of Papa's helping to free the serfs. Sasha holds the old view. He's too stupid to understand the necessity for a new one."

Hattie could say nothing. If only Nikki were more diplomatic, less open in his rebellious dislikes. This talk was dangerous. To her silent relief, he decided to leave for the reception.

Hattie watched from the window as his sleigh went down the street. He was like a boy, changeable, confused, and above all, despite all his outward show, unsure of himself. How typical of

119

him, she realized now, was that curious "document" he had made her sign. It meant nothing, and yet Nikki clung to things like that. She thought of something she had written in her journal: "The love I have for him is a mixture of the love one has for a child, for a lover, and for a protector."

He needed her also in practical affairs. He knew nothing whatever about money. Prodigal in large matters, he could be miserly about small ones. She saw him make scenes with Karpych over five-ruble expenses, then squander thousands of rubles on a whim. Generally he carried no money; after the usual Romanov custom, when he made purchases he simply left his initials with the merchant and the bills went to his account at the palace. What room that left for padded accounts! As a boy he had been allowed small monthly amounts; then abruptly at twenty-one his whole fortune opened before him with a tremendous annual allowance at his disposal. Once he confided gaily to her:

"At first I thought I'd never be able to spend it. Now, long before the year's over it's all gone."

The old scrimping days of her childhood, which she never remembered unless she had to, came back to her, and she exclaimed in horror:

"But can't you do something to keep people from cheating you?"

"I suppose so." He was clearly unconcerned. Was this what they called Slavic lethargy?

So many times he said, "Let it go, my dear. Next week." He began things firmly, brilliantly, then ended by doing nothing. There was the matter of eating the right food; unless she kept constant watch he paid no attention to it. She managed to make him rest—sleep regular hours—by pleading fatigue herself. She could always play upon his solicitude for her.

But he liked to tease her, too. One night, his great length stretched out comfortably on her sofa, he drawled:

"Do you know who sent me a note today? Stéphanie, the young general's wife." When she made no reply, he went on: "They write me innocent letters, these wives, and then they receive me half-dressed—letting their robes fall casually to here," and he made a circular line low on his chest. "Each one is Potiphar's wife—but I am a Joseph," he added hastily, seeing by the tense look in her face that he had gone too far. He caught her

120

face roughly between his hands. "Do you think I would want them when I have you? And they dare to talk against you! They who pretend to be so virtuous. Actually they're more corrupt than the lowest streetwalker." He kissed her forehead, and reached into his pocket. "Judge them by their letters," he said, tossing over crumpled notes, "and burn them for me when you're through."

And when Hattie met the scornful ladies afterward, in the theater, or out driving, her smile was genuine. She knew more about them than they knew about her. . . . She had their letters, and their Grand Duke too.

TWELVE

THE LONG WINTER WAS GRADUALLY LIGHTENING. ALL AT ONCE THE Northern spring burst upon them with a preliminary bluster of rain and wind; then, almost overnight, the trees were washed in bright green, and the bushes seemed to explode in reds and yellows. They watched the green come most brilliantly at Pavlovsk; then sometimes, despite his father, they strolled in the formal gardens of the Marble Palace. It seemed to Hattie that Nikki walked more and more openly with her down the streets and into the cafés. With carriage top lowered, he rode at her side along Nevsky Prospekt.

"If it matters," he told her one day, "they're all talking about us."

"Do you mind?" she asked.

"Why should I?"

As if to prove his words, the day before Easter he brought her a ticket assuring her a good place at the Cathedral of St. Isaac for the midnight Mass that the Tsar and his Court would attend.

"I'll be with the family, but Karpych will call for you in my carriage. All the women are to wear white—which will not be hard for you, my love! Every woman from Court will be there— I won't have you left out."

She blushed with pleasure, then said, thoughtfully, "Of course I would like to go, but why does the whole Court feel so——?"

He interrupted her caustically. "Because religious mysticism is now the rage. It all swims around Dostoevsky."

She raised her eyebrows, and he elaborated, "He was once a revolutionary—actually taken before a firing squad and reprieved at the last minute, but after ten cold years in Siberia, he's back with a brand of religion that's very fashionable at Court. Whatever he once believed politically, he's against it now. Sasha loves him . . . I know, darling, he writes beautifully, but our real writer is Tolstoy . . ."

This was revealing—the aristocratic, rebellious Count Tolstoy a hero of Nikki's—the man whose constant cry for justice had made him unpopular with most of the nobility. There was another reason, too, why Nikki's partisanship was interesting. Tolstoy's brothers had both defiantly married women from the lower middle classes.

Nikki completed his final directions to her. "Karpych will wait outside the Cathedral to take you home."

When she entered the richly ornamented building with its bulbous domes that shone in the moonlight, it was dark except for a few flickering points of candlelight. All was silent; even the scraping of feet ended as the hour approached. At the front, about the jeweled screens that shielded the altar, she detected a slight movement. Out of the dark came deep voices, unaccompanied, in an organlike surge of sound that began softly, then grew deeper, more sonorous.

One by one, more candles were lighted; as the surroundings brightened, she saw hundreds of women in their pale dresses, and men in black and gold and scarlet, against the luminous walls. From his many likenesses, she recognized the Tsar, in white with jeweled decorations. He stood a little apart from the others, a heavy-set man with thick mustache and whiskers; authority and dignity in an almost palpable aura around him. Yet Hattie was close enough to see that his bright blue eyes seemed cold. She remembered Nikki's dream in which his uncle rejected him. She looked at him intently. Did she only imagine that she read uncertainty, a hint of indecision that grew out of weariness?

She gave a start as a deep voice, that of the heavy-bearded Metropolitan with his gleaming miter, addressed the throng:

"Christ is risen!"

From everywhere came the response:

"He is risen indeed."

It was a high moment; she held her breath. Then everyone began to kiss everyone else—the customary three kisses on cheeks and lips. She watched, hoping to catch a glimpse of Nikki, but he was hidden in the press around the Tsar.

123

The Tsar, too, as head of the Church must receive the ceremonial kisses on this day. She watched him unbend. He even smiled.

The next day Hattie had her own share of Easter kisses. Like most of St. Petersburg, she held open house. Nikki arrived first with Captain Vorpovsky. He greeted her solemnly: "Christ is risen!" She replied in her best Russian. They exchanged the three kisses, and he presented her with a wide basket of rare fruits. Later Karpych, the fat coachman, and servants from the hotel brought in flowers, and for each of them she had a large porcelain egg filled with coins. For all her guests, Hattie had a surprise.

"An American drink," she told them as she ladled out an aromatic eggnog.

The Russians came back repeatedly for more. When they all left around midnight, one guest remained, an elderly count curled up on the rug, his eggnog glass in his hand. They were unable to wake him, so Nikki assigned young Captain Vorpovsky to share the floor with him for the night. He was making sure that nobody would gossip over the incident. He was proud of the whispering that linked his name with Fanny Lear's, but fiercely jealous of her honor.

Easter that year was followed almost immediately by summer. For a time Hattie luxuriated in the warmth, so welcome after the biting cold. But within a month she was wiping perspiration from her arms and face. She had never known such heat. Nikki reassured her. Nobody stayed in the city during the summer. He had ordered a summer house made ready for her at Pavlovsk. It was one of a number of luxurious little dachas, most of them Imperial households, that lay only a few miles eastward from the Tsar's own palace at Tsarskoe Selo.

"I've made a few changes for you," he told her when they arrived at the rambling painted frame house. They were standing at the end of a long double line of enormous pink rosebushes. "I ordered these transplanted for you a month ago."

She thanked him with her eyes as they walked together along the cool passage between the roses. It led to a new wonder. Hattie ran forward to a miniature summerhouse, a thing of feminine

124

caprice, all mirrors and ivy and climbing roses. She looked back at Nikki in delight. "The Pavilion of Roses," he told her. "Catherine the Second ordered it copied after something of Madame Pompadour's." How different from the heavy magnificence of the Romanov palaces. . . .

"I like this best of all," she exclaimed.

During the weeks that followed, they spent hours there, with Viktor hovering in the distance to warn if others approached.

Sometimes they remained in the pavilion until two or three o'clock in the morning. It was the season of "white nights" when darkness almost never fell but a soft twilight continued until the coming of the new day. And when she sat at Nikki's side with the pale light all about them, Hattie felt that they were in a new and magic world that would never end.

Even in the bright sunshine, the dreamlike quality persisted. In her stable, the grooms watched over two cream-colored ponies and a fine Arab horse. When they strolled along the lakes in the great park of Constantine's palace, boatmen appeared to take them gliding over the smooth cool surfaces.

On one of the dreamy summer days, as they stood beside the largest of the artificial lakes Nikki told her that the walks in the vast park covered a hundred miles. "Papa thought he'd make an impression on the public, so he's opened most of the park to them; even the farm attached to the palace is there for inspection; it's the fashionable thing to eat black bread and drink milk there in the afternoon."

Hattie fanned herself in the heat: "I'd like some cold milk this minute. Is it far from here?"

"Only over the next hill. . . ."

Tranquilly they wandered through a thicket of ash and birch and elm, and crossed a sun-splashed lawn with the warm smell of half-raked hay. Ahead began a series of low hills on which stood summer villas with terraced gardens, and always more roses. The farm stood in a hollow, looking neat and trim, its buildings like little wooden German toys.

As they sat in the gratefully cool courtyard, they heard a confusion of high voices, and in strolled a trio of elegant Court women in flowing pastoral dress. Effusively they bowed to Nikki; elaborately they ignored his companion.

The wife of a Colonel of the Guards beckoned to Nikki coquettishly. With a word of excuse, he left Hattie sitting alone at the little table; then across the short space she heard a lightly reproving voice, which the woman did not bother to lower.

"Ah, Your Imperial Highness, how can you compromise yourself with such a person?"

Hattie did not pretend to look unconcerned. She stared straight at them, her eyes at their blackest beneath the shadow of her flowered hat. Anger tightened Nikki's face.

"Madame," he said, bowing stiffly, "I must deprive myself of the pleasure of talking further with you." Wheeling abruptly, he returned to offer his arm to Hattie and lead her past the startled ladies. Outside the courtyard, he drew a deep breath. "Little wife," he said, "it won't always be this way."

He had chosen to fight for her publicly—and for the second time he had used the word "wife." The countryside looked greener, more glowing, to her eyes.

The day was drawing near when Nikki would have to join the summer maneuvers of the Imperial Guard under the direct command of the Imperial Commander-in-Chief, the Tsar himself, at near-by Krasnoye Selo.

"I'll have my own cottage there, with the other officers," Nikki explained, "but women are forbidden in the camp at any time— you'll have to stay in Pavlovsk, my darling." Hattie looked so dismayed that he was delighted. "Thank you, my dear." Suddenly he caught at her hands. "Why not?" he almost shouted. "Errand boys can come and go, and you'll be one—a *kazachok*, my sweet little American!"

Within a few minutes, Vorpovsky produced small trousers, bulky jacket, and cap. Laughingly Hattie tried them on.

"Nobody will guess I'm not a boy, will they?"

"I will, my angel," Nikki said, "and that will be enough."

Joséphine clicked her tongue. "Madame, it's unnatural, it isn't right." This only added to Hattie's feeling of rebellious excitement. Nervously at first, then more confidently, she moved in and out of the camp. Nikki and Captain Viktor, who behaved as if he thought it a comic-opera conspiracy, gave her envelopes and small packages to make the device more realistic in case she were questioned. Viktor would help her to the top of the grandducal equipage—a perch that befitted a young valet, and terrified

126

Hattie. Sometimes she thought people looked at her oddly, but she decided it was only her imagination.

Reaching Nikki's cottage, she would change into her own clothes and they would be alone. They grew increasingly more daring, until one day they heard a commanding voice outside the window. "Nicholas, home?"

"His Majesty!" Nikki rose, looking desperately around the room. Hattie, remembering those hard blue eyes at the Easter service, scrambled up the little ladder staircase at the back of the room to the low-ceilinged cottage attic. There she lay with her ear to the floor, trying to make out what they were saying. She could not distinguish the words, but the murmuring tones beneath her sounded amicable enough. There was a long silence, and finally she crept down. Nikki greeted her with a burst of laughter. "Darling, you look so funny—like a frightened yellow kitten." Funny! But her relief was as great as his.

They decided that these escapades were too dangerous and that he should take the risk himself of trying to leave camp when he could. Usually that was only for a few hours, but sometimes he stayed with her boldly for several days.

Stealing away from camp one week end, he took her to Strelna, another palace belonging to Nikki's mother, the Grand Duchess Sanni. These Romanov palaces, the Imperial family history, had a romantic fascination for Hattie. "It's the law of antithesis, a thirst for the unknown," she wrote in her journal, "and for me love is the unifying thing that closes the distances."

The great house stood in a ring of giant flower beds and ancient linden trees. As they went through the halls, Nikki told her stories of the family tapestries, of the jewelry and other objets d'arts on the little tables. In one of the large bedrooms, Nikki's eyes went to an enormous canopied bed. He gave her an impish look. "Let's try it out," he suggested, and in a gust of pagan happiness, they did.

Another time, they journeyed to Peterhof, the palace of Peter the Great, with its riotous grandeur of fountains and statues. The stone house rose high above a promontory, and Baltic waves beat endlessly on the marble walls at the shore.

"Peter always had a vision of the sea," Nikki said. "It was the only way he thought the Western world could come to Russia. And," he added, for once without mockery, "my father feels the same way." How strange and complex Nikki's relationship with Constantine was.

Inside the palace, they found things much as the sovereign had left them. Nikki pointed. "His shoes." Hattie looked over at the little satin ones beside them. They must have been hers, Catherine the First's, the mistress whom he had made his wife and his Tsarina. Nikki could think of the Tsar; her thoughts were of this woman that he had chosen.

This was their last excursion of the summer. The war maneuvers were approaching their strenuous climax, and Nikki could come only infrequently to the dacha at Pavlovsk. He would arrive white-faced, exhausted, with perspiration plastering his short hair to his head. Though he protested, she made him rest, and he spent most of his brief leaves in the pavilion, his head on her lap while she read to him or massaged his forehead and temples until he fell asleep. Each time he left clear-eyed and refreshed.

"I think you've saved my life," he said to her once as he stood up to go. He took her roughly in his arms. "You won't ever leave me, will you?"

It was nearly time for camp to break up. At any time, a surprise signal would boom out announcing the final day-long grand review. When the call came, it was on one of Nikki's rare nights at the dacha. The sound of the cannon cut through Hattie's dreams. Waking Nikki from his exhausted sleep, she handed him his clothes and his sword; in an astonishingly few minutes he was dressed and gone. Presently she would follow. Women of the Court were allowed to watch the final parade, and there would be so many that she could go unnoticed in the general excitement.

By midmorning the parade was at its height. For hours the hussars and dragoons, lancers and grenadiers, swept by to the deep-throated songs of the soldiers and the martial music of their bands. Horses reared, and the women applauded and waved. Hattie saw Nikki, at the head of his regiment, then lost sight of him in the clouds of dust. He would be looking for her too, she knew, but how would he be able to see through this choking screen?

She returned to the dacha in the early afternoon and changed into a cool white linen dressing gown. She was brushing her

128

long hair when he came abruptly into her bedroom. He moved menacingly toward her.

"Where were you today?" His mouth was tight. "Sneaking around with someone else behind my back?"

Hattie's hand stopped in midair. Then a sense of outrage overwhelmed her, and she sent the ivory-backed brush whirling toward him. He caught it, snatched up the matching brush on the dressing table, and threw both of them out of the window. They faced each other in fury.

"I'm going to lock you in," he said. "I'll make sure it won't happen again."

She hardly realized what he was saying before she heard the door slam behind him and the key turn in the lock. Pacing up and down the little bedroom in angry tears, she heard the rumble of cavalry, a gay regimental march fading away. Did he really think he could make her his slave? How could she escape? She couldn't jump from the second-story window. She couldn't let the servants, not even Joséphine, know of her humiliation. But as she looked down for what seemed the thirtieth time, a stable boy passed by, and she called to him that she had locked herself in by accident. Would he bring up all the keys he could find and try them on her door? Soon, to her relief, she heard a grating of the lock, and finally the door was open. Her ponies were waiting in the stable. She had the boy harness them to her open carriage, and drove swiftly toward Krasnoye Selo.

She met a stream of returning vehicles. She was too late. The review had ended and the crowd was going back to Pavlovsk. Suddenly her heart beat faster. She saw a familiar coat of arms. Nikki's carriage was approaching, and he was with his mother. Hattie had a quick impression of an amiable face, composed and vacant. The Grand Duchess Sanni showed the ease and serenity of her life. Hattie did not look at Nikki as their carriages passed, and she could not tell whether he had seen her or not. Her anger was fading. She wanted only to be back with him when he returned to the dacha. She tried to turn her ponies around, but the lane was narrow, and crowded with carriages going both ways. It was more than an hour before she was able to get back. By that time her dejection was complete.

As she reined in the ponies, Viktor darted out to meet her.

129

"Madame, come right away. He's sick—it happened just after he got here."

Jumping out of the carriage, she threw the reins to him and ran into the house. Nikki lay unconscious on the couch. His face was flushed, and he breathed with difficulty. The servants stood around in paralyzed helplessness.

"Bring cold water, hot plasters, brandy. Quickly!"

She tried one thing after another. It was fully half an hour before he opened feverish eyes. "You're back!" He clutched at her hand. "I saw you and wanted to call out, but Mother was with me. When I didn't find you here I thought you'd left me—I've been nearly crazy. Never leave me again!"

Her misery ended in happy tears. "No, no," she said, sobbing. "I couldn't leave you again."

"We've been too long in this place, don't you think?" Nikki said when he felt completely recovered. Casually, as if he were suggesting a day's excursion, he added: "Let's go abroad—to the south: Vienna, Italy, Greece, even Egypt, perhaps." Within an hour, it was decided.

Back in St. Petersburg, a few days later, Hattie was helping Joséphine pack when Karpych came in with a gnomelike grin that almost cut his face in half. In his hands, balanced like a delicate toy, was a long black case. On the lid, stamped in gold, was one magic word: "Fabergé" . . . the Court jeweler, celebrated for the exquisite perfection of his work. A collar of pearls lay on white satin, and as Hattie looked at it, she realized that here was a creation that would rival any of the Romanov treasures. She fastened it around her throat. Joséphine was startled out of her laconic calm.

"Oh, madame, madame, it's fit for a queen! How the Grand Duke adores you!"

But Hattie sat silent. She was recalling Nikki's story of a certain count who was in the habit of provoking the Tsar's fury so that he would benefit from the royal repentance. Rage followed by fabulous, guilty generosity. It was a beautiful necklace, but the price had been too high. There must be no more scenes.

THIRTEEN

As Joséphine watched, Hattie traced the route on the map:

"Vienna, Rome, Athens—we'll be in Cairo by the time it's really cold."

"Not Paris, madame?" It was as much as Joséphine would permit herself to say, yet Hattie knew she was disappointed. Her daughter, Clothilde, was in Paris now, working for a milliner in the Rue de la Paix.

"I'm afraid not," said Hattie, but she added kindly. "Perhaps though, the Grand Duke will decide to stop there on our way back from Egypt."

"Ah well"—Joséphine's tone was resigned—"at least it will be a change. Perhaps I will get used to this country someday, but I think it will take a long time."

"Isn't there anyone here——" Hattie hesitated. "Don't you know any of the girls at the hotel, or the men?"

Joséphine's pointed nose rose in disdain. "None that one would associate with, madame. They are not to be trusted and they try to question me about you." As if this were a subject on which she had already said too much, Joséphine excused herself to finish their packing.

Calling the staff who had served her, Hattie thanked them and gave a gift to each. None of them seemed to be anything but faithful, and affectionate, servitors. One woman was even in tears. "Good lady. Good lady." Hattie was touched. There were not many in the world who would call her that.

She and Joséphine took the noon train to Cracow. Nikki had suggested at first that it might be more discreet for them to leave a few days ahead of him, but at the last minute, unable to bear

131

the idea of so long a separation, he arranged to take a train only a few hours after theirs. They would meet in Poland and go on from there together—to Vienna first, because the doctor had recommended it for Nikki's health.

"From what I've heard," Hattie observed, "most people would recommend Vienna as a place to cultivate *poor* health!"

"Oh," Nikki said, laughing, "we're not actually going to stay in Vienna—we'll go there, of course, but as a concession to my doctor we're staying in Friedrichsruhe. It's an international resort not far from Vienna, but quiet."

They settled in the Archduke Karl Hotel in the little town built around a park of shadowed footwalks and carriage lanes. For a while it seemed that their privacy would be undisturbed, but the first time they strolled through the park a tall horseman hailed them eagerly and dismounted.

"Your Highness and Madame!"

Hattie was puzzled for a moment; then she recognized the robust blond officer. His name was Gagarin—Prince Georgi Gagarin, a pleasant, somewhat shy fellow whom she had met once or twice with Nikki at the theater. She smiled as he kissed her hand. "What a happy surprise for us!"

But the Grand Duke did not share her pleasure. He nodded curtly and did not suggest that they meet again. "We might as well be in Petersburg," he fumed as he led Hattie off.

A little later, however, as they continued their promenade, she saw that Nikki was enjoying the attention she attracted. People did not know him here, and if they noticed him at all it was because he was with her. As they strolled by the outdoor cafés men lowered their wineglasses and stared. She had never looked more beautiful. Though she had lost weight through the summer and dark shadows lay under her eyes, there was a radiance to her face—almost a touch of fever. Her heavy golden hair drawn back in soft loops framed and delicately defined her face.

Nikki was at his most adoring. Passing through streets in which no one bowed low, he behaved more and more like an ordinary young man in love. He seldom showed his morbid melancholy these days. Even when letters came from St. Petersburg, his gay absorption in her persisted. One of the letters would have amused him in any case, and he read it aloud to Hattie.

"This will interest you particularly, my darling. My cousin Alexis is in America now; he's creating a real stir. They've even named a mountain peak for him in the West. They say he went on a buffalo hunt with the Indians, but decided that he preferred to chase one of the Indian maidens. Then he came back and fell in love with a blonde actress, a Miss Lydia Thompson. Have you ever heard of her? She's in a new play called *Bluebeard*. He showered her with gifts and followed her on tour to a place called New Orleans. You'll know where that is, I'm sure. They say the town will never be the same again! It was just before a kind of folk festival at Mardi Gras—like the one in France, I suppose. It seems that Alexis grew bored with Lydia and took to an actress there called Lotta Crabtree!" Nikki grinned, "This New Orleans won't forget the Romanovs!"

"But I thought Alexis was very much in love with Alexandra Joukovsky."

Nikki looked surprised. "He is! But the family doesn't approve. That's why he was sent on this trip. Still, naturally when he sees a pretty face, he admires it."

Hattie felt a momentary pang. But what did it matter? She had no doubt of Nikki's love.

A few afternoons later Hattie decided to go for a walk in the park. Nikki had left the hotel, pleading an errand early in the afternoon, and the day was too beautiful to stay inside. A band was playing among the trees in the distance as she sauntered from one leafy path to another. Rounding a corner, she caught a glimpse of a couple sitting on a bench half hidden by the shrubbery. There was something familiar about the man's back and she paused. When he got to his feet, she saw, with a sudden intake of her breath, that it was Nikki. She heard him say, "At five o'clock, then," as he raised the girl's hand to his lips.

Hattie turned and almost ran back down the path. Trembling and half-sick, she returned to the hotel. By the time he arrived, whistling gaily, her misery had turned to fury.

"I saw you in the park this afternoon! I heard you, heard you——" she stammered.

They had a terrible scene. He accused her of spying on him, and his voice rose to a shout.

"Don't you know that people who eavesdrop never hear anything pleasant?"

To her horror she wept. She hated herself for her piteous protestations. How could he do this to her after all she had done for him!

"I tell you I simply met the girl by accident."

"And will meet her at five by accident, I suppose?"

Nikki looked at the clock on the little marble table beside her. It was a quarter to five. "Yes," he said, "I must hurry."

"Hurry now—and you need never come back."

He stood still and his face grew very pale. Then he slapped her. The sound of the blow appalled them both.

She shrank back against the wall. "The final argument of a man in the wrong!"

He looked at her in shame and hatred. "This is enough. I can endure this no longer. Karpych will pack up my things and bring them to the Imperial Hotel. It's over now, all over."

When the door slammed, the sound was like another blow. She was frantic. She could not stay in the room and watch his things moved away. She called to Joséphine to pack her own.

She had no idea where they could go—she had no money at all and she knew no one in Friedrichsruhe—but she continued her preparations. She wrote a series of notes to Nikki, one harsher than the other, and tore them all to pieces. None of them would do. She remembered her own wise words written before she could imagine herself in such a state: "Nothing can stop a man who wants to leave a woman—not prayers, or love, or hatred— except perhaps three words: 'Well, then go.' But these words must be said resolutely while showing him to the door." At least her note could be cold and calm.

There was a knock on the door, and she ran to open it.

"Nikki! Nikki!" she cried.

But it was only Prince Gagarin, who stood there looking at her in surprise.

"You have a note from him?" she demanded.

"From His Highness?" His confusion was evident. He was just passing by and thought he would pay his respects. Was something the matter? Too upset to be discreet, Hattie told him what had happened.

The Prince was warmly sympathetic. "His Royal Highness is only a foolish boy," he said. "He is incapable of appreciating

134

you." And suddenly, to her surprise, he took her hand and was kissing it over and over again.

"Listen, Fanny Lear, listen." Breathlessly, he was telling her how he had watched her in St. Petersburg, how he had wanted her yet hadn't dared go near her. He pleaded with her. "But now you are free—come away with me! I promise you I'll make you happy."

This was not the timid man who had treated her so deferentially in St. Petersburg. He was urgent and commanding. If she had searched all Friedrichsruhe she could not have found anyone better able to protect her in her frantic misery. She drew a deep breath.

"Can we leave tonight?"

"Of course!" He kissed her hand. "Have your maid get ready. We will take the seven-o'clock train to Vienna. I will stop by for you."

Joséphine looked at the stranger resentfully. When he had left, Hattie turned on her angrily. Was Joséphine more loyal to Nikki than to her? Couldn't she see this was a crisis in which they had no choice? She urged the maid to hurry, and she herself paced up and down slowly, wringing her hands. If she did not hear from Nikki by six . . . but he would not call at six . . . he would be with that woman. With fevered energy, she swept her toilet articles off the dressing table into her little case and roused the hotel staff to frantic activity.

They were ready and waiting by the time Gagarin arrived. Without hesitation, Hattie preceded him into the carriage, pushing the reluctant Joséphine ahead of her. But when they reached the platform and she saw the train waiting, heard the puff of its steam, and saw Joséphine entering the compartment, she was suddenly appalled by the realization that the step she was about to take would be irretrievable. She turned to the Prince hysterically.

"I'm sorry—I can't go with you! I can't go on this train."

People were looking at them. Gagarin strengthened his grip on her arm and brought his face very close to hers. "Come," he said in a low voice. Despite herself she responded to his strained smile. Her own voice lowered.

"Let me go, please. I can't decide it all so soon—I can't leave Nikki."

"Your maid and your baggage are already on the train," he said inexorably.

Tears started to stream down her face. With unexpected physical strength she held back. "I don't love you, I don't even know you. Let me go, or I'll make a scene."

He released his grip on her arm, seemingly acquiescent. "I understand that you don't love me. It makes no difference. I have loved you for a year, maybe longer. Now I have the good luck to hold you, and I won't let you go."

He picked her up and carried her into the compartment as the train pulled out of the station.

Prince Gagarin was outwardly a shy man, but when he acted it was with the accumulation of all his strength. He took no chances. With arms folded, he sat opposite her, keeping a steady eye on her white face. Her eyes were closed and she seemed ill.

Joséphine's slate-gray eyes, however, had never been more watchful. The ride was short, and when they reached Vienna they drove directly to a hotel where rooms had been made ready for them. Joséphine listened from her chamber next to Hattie's. She heard Gagarin's voice. He was calling her mistress a fool.

"The man left *you!*" he shouted, and Joséphine thought that she heard Madame crying. Then she heard quick footsteps, there was a silence, and the Prince's voice came from Madame's door. "Tomorrow we'll see. Meanwhile you will stay here." To Joséphine's relief, the door closed and his steps went down the hall.

Next morning, her mistress listlessly refused the coffee Joséphine brought her and asked only not to be disturbed until noon. It was Joséphine who overheard Prince Gagarin's low-voiced instructions to the valet. A compartment was to be ordered on the train to St. Petersburg, a closed carriage was to drive them to the station, and the greatest care was to be taken that no one knew of this. And if a certain Grand Duke or anyone coming from him should ask questions, Prince Gagarin was traveling alone. Joséphine also heard the valet's reply.

"I understand, Your Highness. There was a disturbance in the hotel early this morning, around three o'clock—someone claiming to be from a Grand Duke Nicholas, demanding to know the whereabouts of a Madame Lear. He was quite troublesome."

Joséphine spoke softly outside Hattie's door. "Are you awake, madame? Madame, I must talk to you; it is of great importance."

A little later, composed and bright eyed, Hattie received the Prince. She acquiesced agreeably to his plans. She was to wear the widow's weeds he would provide for her, and leave by a back stairway to the hotel with Joséphine.

"It seems a little dramatic," he said apologetically, "but I think it's necessary."

She agreed. "We don't want Nikki to cause trouble."

He wondered fleetingly at the change in her and how she knew that Nikki might try to stop them. But her complaisance was very moving. He melted into further confidence.

"Of course when we get back to Russia, he won't be able to do anything at all. The Imperial family are definitely against you."

"They are?" The effect of his words on Hattie was obvious, and the Prince looked at her suspiciously. So there was something behind her amiability, after all!

As Hattie had hoped, there was trouble at Cracow, near the border. Prince Gagarin conferred with officials, sent telegrams, conferred again. Finally he came to her distraught.

"Your visa is not in order, it seems."

"Perhaps we should give up the idea of Russia," she said tentatively.

He looked sharply at her. "Affairs of my own demand that I return immediately."

She went on in a sweet, hesitant manner: "Then perhaps I could wait for you here while you attend to them. Or you could join me later. In a more pleasant place, Paris perhaps?"

It was not too difficult to persuade him. He was still suspicious of her, but there seemed to be no other way. Reluctantly he bade her a solemn farewell. Even more reluctantly he gave her money for her stay in Paris.

"Be sure to let me know at once where you will be. I will join you in six weeks at the latest."

Despite their air of command, his words were anxious. Hattie felt a little ashamed of herself. He was really very much in love with her. And in spite of his aggressiveness, he might never hurt her as Nikki had. If she were wise, she really would write to him and give up this wild hope that once she got to Paris, Nikki would find her. . . . .

The rising excitement of fall was in the air of Paris. Many of the buildings had been restored, the restaurants along the Champs-Elysées were crowded again, the promenades bright. But it was all savorless to Hattie. The music sounded out of tune, the cafés seemed tawdry. She thought only of St. Petersburg, the long sweep of the Nevsky Prospekt, the hills of snow, the ring of the runners as the sleigh swung over the frozen river. She remembered none of the bitter moments, only the wild, live ones that now made Paris overcivilized and dull.

But for Joséphine it was a happy homecoming. Although she hesitated to leave her mistress alone, Hattie sent her off for frequent visits with Clothilde or with other relatives from Brittany who had settled in the city. Joséphine refused to make these visits long ones; there was always the unspoken fear that though Hattie had not written to Prince Gagarin, he would find her, always the hope that word would come from the Grand Duke.

And then one noon Viktor Vorpovsky stood in the doorway, smiling, but ill at ease. In silence he handed Hattie a crested envelope. Her face encouraged him.

"Madame Lear, I have looked everywhere! Even in England. His Highness told me not to come back without you—and now we must leave at once!"

Why had Nikki not come himself? She hesitated a second, the letter in her hand. His voice became pleading.

"Please. The only reason I am here is because he cannot be. He is sick at Friedrichsruhe."

At that she hesitated no longer but tore open the letter.

"Madame, I cannot endure the thought that you have forgotten me, that your last impression was unfavorable.

"My behavior has often made you suffer badly; I don't know how you put up with it as long as you did. Let me explain my outbursts of rage, the reason I said good-by. The fact is that I love you with all my soul, and—God knows why—I was sometimes ashamed of it and thought it unworthy of a man. I built in my mind the ideal of an attachment lasting until death. This is not a caprice; these are my sacred feelings. I've been in love before; other women caused me only tears, you gave me eight months of happiness.

"Question your heart. If you find there even a small spark of love, give me another chance to take you into my arms. Let me call you again, if only once, my beloved Fanny Lear. Only you can bring me rest again. Don't refuse this prayer. Yours, all yours.

                                                                "Nikki"

Tears were in her eyes as she finished reading.

And yet on the way to Friedrichsruhe she was fearful of the future. Vorpovsky, happy at the success of his mission, was in a talkative mood, but she grew more silent as the journey drew near its end. She felt an odd foreboding. There would be more crises, perhaps even another separation. Once again she remembered Gagarin's hint that the Court was hostile.

The train was pulling into the station. She sat listlessly in her place while Viktor and Joséphine collected the luggage. Then through the window she saw Nikki on the platform. At the sight of his eager face all her pent-up longing returned.

A moment later she was in his arms. "Well," he murmured, "well." It was all he could say, and she could not speak at all. In the carriage she regained her composure.

"Don't you want to kiss me?" she asked. At that, he began to kiss her so violently that she cried out, "Nikki, I'm suffocating!"

"I won't let you go until you promise never to go away again," he said between kisses.

"I don't think I can stay more than three days," she said teasingly.

He released her. "Before I'd lose you a second time I'd kill you —and myself too."

She felt a quick moment of terror, then, strangely, a kind of exultation. Whatever the future might bring, this was her destiny.

"I couldn't ever leave you again," she whispered.

The next evening they went to a German performance of *La Traviata*. Though the story lost a great deal of its flavor in the Teutonic setting, Hattie still found it touching. Nikki, however, left the box abruptly toward the end of the act in which Camille was separated from her lover. Hattie found him a moment later in the anteroom, in tears. He looked up at her.

"It will happen this way for us, I am sure of it. They will break us apart and I shall be helpless to stop them."

She quieted him. "No, Nikki, not if we don't let them do it." She repeated the phrase he had used to her: "Never fear."

He raised his head.

"How I have needed you, my darling. I'll need you always after this. Now I can achieve things I never could before. I know it. I'll make you proud of me. They think I'm a fool, the people in St. Petersburg—and what have I ever done to make them think otherwise?" His voice took on new energy. "I'll demand a chance to show them. You'll see."

But as they left the opera house she was thoughtful. "Never fear," she had said. Yet her own fears were coming back, and that night she dreamed that she had lost him again and, as she had seen him so often, her father stood before her, a terrifying figure of wrath . . .

With Joséphine and Vorpovsky in attendance they resumed their interrupted trip. The next stop was Munich, and there important mail from St. Petersburg awaited them. Over breakfast Nikki frowned as he read a letter from Constantine.

"We are to have four more traveling companions," he said. "The Tsar has decided that we must travel with more dignity and decorum." He shrugged. "We'll get used to it. Could be worse."

Was it possible that Gagarin had been wrong? And Hattie wondered what sort of entourage the Imperial family considered "suitable."

She did not have long to wonder. The new arrivals presented themselves the next evening at dinner. The chief of the entourage was a short, stout old Russian-German doctor, grotesquely bulging, with gold glasses, gold cane, the coat of a Don Juan, and a high hat perched atop a bulletlike bald head. Despite his fat, he attempted a narrow waist (unquestionably with the aid of a corset) that cut his body into two ridiculous spheres. His white hands were ornamented with a pair of enormous diamonds. He was forever putting on and taking off his gloves—to show off his hands, or his diamonds, or both, Hattie decided.

Next in importance came an ancient of seventy-five, very nearsighted, tremulous, ever busy. As they all took their places at the table he worked hard to show his usefulness, throwing out superfluous orders in a squeaky voice: "Good butter, now, waiter! And His Highness will have two kinds of bread, mind you!"

The third was a clean-shaven man with a scholarly air and a vein-threaded nose that indicated his taste for liquor. Nikki whispered that this was a retired admiral from the Ukraine who had been one of his favorite tutors.

Last was a tiny, dark fellow, as old as the rest. Sharp-featured and worrisome, he was the possessor of a long waxed-linen bag that was never far from him. As he sat at his place he reached in for several gold sovereigns and a big book, in which he made an entry.

"He takes it all to bed with him," Nikki whispered. "He's my treasurer, one of my crosses. When I was a boy he fished me out of a pond and the Tsar rewarded him for life."

They were all most respectful to Nikki; the white-faced German doctor had a thick servility as he bowed, beamed, almost genuflected. Hattie tried to talk to him, but his yellowish eyes, half lost in circles of fat, looked at her as if she were a gaudy and dangerous insect under the miscroscope of his heavy lenses. She turned to the dark little treasurer, to find him grumbling already about expenses, especially those of the railroads.

"Too democratic," he fretted. "Ought to carry His Imperial Highness free."

"Why?" she asked innocently.

His reply was a belligerent squeak. "For the simple honor of having him in their cars!"

This was going to be a charming experience. But she did not allow herself to lose her composure, even when she found that two of the entourage had their own servants and that her trunks were swallowed up in the twenty-seven others they had to take with them.

The fat doctor, it developed, had brought two dogs with him. When he gave Joséphine a peremptory order to watch them, she refused flatly. The doctor came to Nikki, twitching in rage.

"That French peasant ignores me!"

Nikki shrugged. "If a lady doesn't like you, not even the Tsar can make her change her mind." Still quivering, the doctor withdrew.

Meanwhile Joséphine was fretting over the awkwardness and the waste of the entourage. "When I think of the useless bills . . ." but she spent most of her time thinking up new snubs for the German doctor.

So they started out for Italy—a grotesque mountain of bags, two yelping dogs, the half-blind helper, who had to be assisted in and out, and finally the trembling treasurer, announcing constantly that they were spending too much.

From Rome they went to Caserta, then to Bologna, overwhelming the hotels where they stopped. In Bologna the panicky hotel manager, unused to Grand Dukes, could think of nothing better than to put a great bed in his reading room for the two of them, crowding the rest in down the hall. She and Nikki were there in the morning when a pair of pinched Englishwomen found the door unlocked and entered to look for their London *Times*. Speechless on the threshold, the ladies looked outraged, and somewhat intrigued.

"You explain," Nikki muttered sleepily. "Your English is better."

"No," Hattie murmured. "You're a man, and you'll frighten them out faster. We should have locked the door."

She smothered her laughter in the pillow as Nikki explained to the ladies, who retreated, now more charmed than outraged.

Later, evading the doctor, the admiral, the treasurer, the dogs, and the others, she and Nikki went about the town like truants. Inside the ancient gates they visited the market place, noisy with farmers, organ grinders, herb-sellers, and charlatan dentists. Nikki drew her into an arcade lined with small shops, some displaying crude gimcracks, others fine paintings, and statuary.

"Look at this! . . . Don't you like that?" His eyes were bright. Rubbing his chin, he began to price things. Then he was ordering. "This porcelain, and that big vase." A moment later: "Those statues, both of them, and could you get me several more?"

He did not ask the price, and Hattie knew the merchants were adding heavily to their usual figures. Then she noticed that he was growing careless, calling for cheap objects, ugly pieces.

"Darling," she whispered, "a lot of this is worthless."

He hardly heeded. "Yes? Then we'll sell it later." And he drew her to the next shop.

Now he was buying everything, big, little, good, regrettable. It would require heavy cars to transport this stuff to Russia, and how much of it was worth the effort? After several attempts she managed, to the fury of the merchants, to lead him away. His eyes still shone, and he talked of other things he must acquire.

Later she would remember this day in the Italian arcade, the pleasant winter day that held no hint of the things that were in store for them.

FOURTEEN

Nikki dashed in one day, tossing his hat onto a rattan chair.

"Madame," he cried, "we are sailing tonight for Corfu to see my sister Olga."

"We . . . ?"

His smile became uncertain. "Of course. It's a beautiful trip."

From Brindisi, early on a summer evening, a steamer took them to Corfu, through a world in which sea and sky merged about them. They stood on deck until late that night, watching the glittering of thousands of stars close over their heads and the other thousands reflected in the black water. Before six the next morning they were on deck again to see the sun rise boldly in the sky. As they came within sight of the island of Corfu, its rays stained the beach with pink and touched a salmon line to the top of the abrupt hills, the walls overhung with orange and olive trees.

A Russian man-of-war was in the crowded harbor—a frigate—awaiting their arrival. As they cruised into the bay, there was a rasp of trumpets and a small boat left the side of the frigate. Watching the little boat come nearer, they could see that it was filled with military and naval officers, all in Russian uniform except for one tall man with insignia that Hattie did not recognize.

"The King of Greece!" An excited whisper ran around the boat. On the frigate, Nikki's own flag was run up. Hattie's pulse quickened. She turned to Nikki in excitement, but he had been drawn aside by the fat doctor, whose manner had suddenly become less unctuous. Nikki looked pale and distracted. She heard his words clearly: "In that case I won't go ashore. She comes with me or I stay."

The doctor waved his pale hands. "Tremendous scandal. The Court will be furious."

Nikki went below, his head down as if in brooding thought. When he appeared on deck again he wore the uniform of the Tsar's aide-de-camp, and by now the King's boat was nearing the steamer to the accompaniment of booming salutes.

"Come with me, madame." The doctor stood at her side.

Without looking at Nikki, she accepted the doctor's arm. Almost roughly, he led her down to her stateroom. There she watched through the porthole as other warships from Russia, England, France, Italy, and Germany crowded about the frigate, their flags waving in the breeze. She saw Nikki and the King in the boat as it went toward the shore. Bands struck up; on the Russian frigate, sailors spread themselves up the rigging, one hand holding to a mast or rope, the other at stiff salute.

The boat drew farther away and the figures grew smaller. There was a spyglass on the table and Hattie picked it up to watch the scene on shore. From a semicircle of uniforms and bright women's costumes, she saw a tall young woman come forward to embrace Nikki. Then the crowd pushed in and hid them from Hattie's view. The breeze brought the tinny echo of a band. Sighing, Hattie sank back in her chair.

It was noon before Nikki returned. "I've got to be with my sister and the King for a few days in their villa," he told her gently. "I'm afraid you will all have to go back to Brindisi. Viktor will look after you, my darling—and I'll join you as soon as I can. Never fear."

She managed to smile at his old byword, and that afternoon the boat took them from the shore of Corfu. Through the following day she stayed in her hotel room at Brindisi, looking out over the blue waters, watching for the ship that might bring him back. Again, her fears were upon her, and her doubts.

Restless that evening after she had dismissed Joséphine, Hattie tried to read. It was impossible. Through the window she could see cool moonlight flooding the terrace below. At one of the little tables a man sat alone and she saw it was Captain Vorpovsky. She went downstairs and joined him. He rose and greeted her with a flourish. "Pray be seated." He had been drinking more than usual, and for a moment she regretted that she had come. But almost at once he began to speak of Nikki.

145

"Madame Lear, may I thank you? You are a good influence for my friend—the best he has ever had. It is a hard thing to be brought up by contesting tutors in an atmosphere of great intrigue." He sighed. "Things might have been different, so different." Looking about to make sure they were alone, he lowered his voice. "Things might still be different for Nikki, and for Russia as well."

What an odd note in his voice! . . .

"You understand," he said, as if certain she would, "that if a change ever comes, and if the Grand Duke Constantine takes his rightful place . . . the Grand Duke stands for another kind of Russia." The Captain's voice was almost a whisper. "You may have heard how Tsar Alexander began his rule by giving the people new rights. His brother was closest to him then, urging him, helping him. But lately the Tsar has wavered, and other men at the Court have been turning him to the old way, the way of gun and club. Sometimes he may not know what they are doing in his name, how much they are taking back what he gave. But whether he knows it or not, we are facing away from the future and back to the past!"

She had never seen him so moved; she had thought him only a frivolous, careless boy. Viktor's words tumbled out.

"Russia is at a crossroads, madame. If things go on as they have, God help us! If it is to be the Grand Duke Constantine's way, good years are ahead. . . ." He stared moodily at the floor.

She herself was stirred; these were things she had hardly dared say even in her own mind. "You mean—a revolution?"

His head jerked up. "Oh no, not at all. The Grand Duke's way would prevent revolution. Give justice, grant people their rights, and they will not rise to quarrel for them. Now autocracy rules, and conformity, with policemen in charge. Trepov and Shuvalov, a proper pair! One day we may have to pay for such mistakes in blood. You watch, madame!"

"Does Nikki understand this?" she asked cautiously.

"Some, but not all." The Captain was sober now. "His father sees it, but will he act? I don't know if he really can; nobody does. . . ." His voice trailed off, and he retreated into some inner melancholy. He said no more, and Hattie slipped away. It was a long time before she slept.

Vorpovsky had not really answered her questions about Nikki. The following day, discreetly, she tried to bring up the subject

again. But he gazed at her blankly. "I don't understand, madame
. . ." The bulging doctor was standing near by, one white hand
on his hip. She caught Vorpovsky's hidden imploring look—
please, she must never reveal what he had said. Nor would she—to
anyone but Nikki himself, when he returned.

When he finally appeared late that night she was so relieved
and happy to see him that it did not even occur to her to mention
Viktor's outburst until the next morning. He made a grimace.

"Viktor? A fine boy—a real idealist and a dreamer. He wor-
ships Papa, but he is a little unpractical, I'm afraid."

She was relieved at his answer. But something more concrete
was troubling her; Joséphine had come to her the day before.

"Madame, every night now, that fat doctor spends hours at his
desk and then the little monkey fellow goes out to dispatch the
letter. . . . Where to? The manager found out for me. Petersburg, the Tsar's palace."

Nikki's face showed hot anger, but not surprise. "I've suspected
it all along. They were sent to spy on us, and also"—he looked
somewhat ashamed—"to prevent scandal." For the first time he
spoke frankly. "The Tsar heard about our quarrel. He wants no
incidents that could be talked about outside Russia, and Papa has
written asking me to be discreet."

"But—they didn't say you couldn't see me?"

"No, no! We'll have to watch, though, and be careful." She felt
a curious relief. What he had told her was only what she had
sensed all along and now at last it was open between them.

When Nikki suggested a trip to Naples, she welcomed it, if
only to help them both to forget the insecurity in which they
lived. There her spirits improved, and Nikki's even more than hers.

Their hotel was an ancient palace facing the sea; they could hear
it always, outside the tall mullioned windows. "Sometimes," Hattie
recorded in her journal, "the sound of the waves is low and
caressing—like the murmur of a young woman in love. At other
times, the crash of the waves can almost frighten us, and it
sounds like the shrieking accusation of an irritated wife. . . . N.
is full of the most frenzied activity. He agrees with me that he has
probably discovered the secret of perpetual motion. Every day
we go somewhere, but always in the evening we come back to
this enchanted place, to the Neapolitan songs outside our window—to the moonlight on the sea beneath."

They went to Sorrento and took a winding road up the mountain. When they found it obstructed by rocks, Nikki insisted that they climb down and proceed on little donkeys. His legs were so long that his feet nearly touched the ground, and Hattie wrote: "We nearly died of laughter, trying to manage our unmanageable mounts. N. looked so much like Don Quixote that I prayed there would be no windmills on the way. When I told him so, he called me 'Dulcinea' the rest of the afternoon." That was the evening they saw the tarantella danced in the court of their hotel, "by two hideous women," Hattie wrote, "and two handsome men. In spite of this contrast, or perhaps because of it, this spectacle fascinated us."

They went to Pompeii, climbed Vesuvius, visited the Sibylline Cave, until finally Hattie would go no farther, and announced that she herself would stay in Naples for the next few days. This proved to be nearly as strenuous. Nikki dragged her to all the museums and art galleries in the city. He had heard of a certain sculptor, Solari, and insisted that they go to his studio. He revealed the purpose of the visit almost immediately.

"Do you notice Madame Lear's resemblance to Pauline, Napoleon's sister, as Canova did her?" he asked Solari. "Will you make my lady's statue reclining, like Pauline?"

The swarthy Solari looked admiringly at Hattie. He saw no such similarity; Hattie's beauty was her own. "An astonishing likeness," he vowed. "That would be"—he searched Nikki's face—"fifty thousand francs."

"Can you start at once?"

"I'll need plaster molds of the lady's body."

Nikki nodded. Hattie had an impulse to protest. The famous statue was almost entirely nude. But they gave her no time.

"The body must be cast in two parts, madame, the front and then the back. We can do the front today."

She was hurried behind a screen, where an attendant rubbed grease on her "thoroughly," as Solari had instructed. The sculptor cleared his throat. "Madame, I am ready."

An hour later she was lying stiff, unable to move, her legs stretched before her, her arms numb, perspiration slipping into her eyes and mouth as the plaster hardened. At last, prodding at her, Solari announced that this much was finished, and reaching out gingerly, he cracked large segments from her legs and throat. The next day she returned for the second part of the process, which she found even more unpleasant. Then followed days of posing while the sculptor peered and labored.

Nikki insisted that the whole entourage, including Joséphine and Vorpovsky, be present at the unveiling. Hattie stood in an agony of self-consciousness as their eyes passed over the astonishing replica of her own body. The doctor stood back in frigid disapproval; by contrast the nearsighted assistant bent low scarcely an inch from the figure, his nose almost touching the marble.

There was no question but that it was a superb reproduction. The glowing marble was almost flesh-toned, the figure voluptuous in every detail.

"It does you full justice," Nikki declared, "and that makes it perfect. There will be no more exquisite work of art in all Russia!"

In higher spirits than ever, Nikki set out to collect more works of art: bronzes, terracottas, curios of jade or porphyry, busts of medieval princes. The simian treasurer sweated helplessly as he signed order after order against Nikki's personal funds, over which he had no control. At last the doctor also protested. Nikki gave him a scornful smile.

"You telegraph home about everything; why don't you try it with this?"

"I will, Your Imperial Highness!"

When the answer arrived that the Grand Duke's expenditures were not a matter of Court concern, Nikki roared happily and the doctor's jowls rippled with anger. In the morning Nikki was off an hour earlier than usual, and Hattie had to accompany him.

"I'm buying it all for you," he told her with an excited smile.

She, too, could no longer contain herself. "What will I do with it all? Only a palace would hold it. Nikki, you must stop." Nikki gnawed his lip in a rare effort at self-control, and this time he did stop.

The doctor was writing more and more messages. Joséphine, still vigilant, reported that the various important-looking individuals who came to see him were special couriers from Petersburg.

One afternoon as Hattie entered Nikki's room she heard the doctor's voice: "The Tsar's troops are advancing in Central Asia, adding new provinces." His tone became dramatic: ". . . Striking

149

at the treacherous Turkomans of Khiva, the forces captured——"

So this was it. She had read only a little of the far-off punitive expeditions against the Khivans who were molesting nomad tribes allied to Russia. It had not seemed important.

At sight of her, the doctor's face showed such guilt that she grew more suspicious than ever. Nikki was staring at the doctor, his green eyes distended with excitement. He spoke in a low, fervent voice.

"It was Tsar Peter who first tried to take Khiva. They massacred his men."

The doctor spoke again. "When you come back with victory and the Cross of St. George—after that, who knows?"

Rising abruptly, he saluted Nikki and walked past Hattie without glancing at her. She touched Nikki's shoulder and he looked at her in surprise.

"What is it?"

"Nothing." She shook her head. She had reached the door before he caught her arm.

"Dearest, it may be the chance of my life, the one thing I need most to prove myself to them."

"Nikki, don't you see?—this is a scheme. That's what the doctor was sent along to do—to get you away from me."

Nikki looked at her steadily. "Perhaps," he said, "but the situation has become serious only in the last few days. The Khivans have taken fifty Russian prisoners. And I am the only member of the Imperial family trained to lead the Tsar's troops. Neither my brothers nor my cousins were graduated from the Imperial Academy for the General Staff. And they're still giving me the chance I've been hoping for." She could say no more. His look became tender. "And you know, my dearest, the absence can't do what they plan."

It was only a few days later that orders came from St. Petersburg. He was to return immediately, and report without delay to his commander-in-chief, the Tsar of All the Russias.

As Hattie and Joséphine searched once again for the lumbering old carriage of the Hôtel France, the wind whipped sharp fine snow in their faces. After the sun-dappled plazas of Italy the change was almost symbolic.

In the familiar rooms that she had left so happily many months before, Hattie gave way to her despair. Slow tears rolled down her face as she went through the motions of taking off her furs and changing to the white-velvet robe she used to wear for Nikki when he came to see her in the old happy evenings. Joséphine, brushing out her mistress's long hair, quietly set a little glass of brandy on the dressing table in front of her.

"I've ordered fresh white roses, madame, and tea brought when the Grand Duke comes." Hattie covered the hand on her shoulder with her own and looked up gratefully. She laughed a little through the persistent tears.

"Can you think of a way to fix my eyes so that he won't know I've been crying?"

"Ice—an ice pack, madame," said Joséphine capably. "I can fix it in a few minutes."

Her hair was shining and her eyes brilliant when Nikki came in. Although he brightened at the sight of her, she could see that he was exhausted. He told her his news immediately. The brisk confidence he had shown at the station when an honor guard turned out to meet him was gone.

"I'm to help lead the expedition against the Khan. I leave in a few weeks."

At the anguish in her face, he said: "Oh my dear, you don't understand; they're to leave you alone, and when I come back we'll be together. I had a hard time making them agree."

When he came back! "How long will you be gone?"

"Four, five months or so, I suppose. It will be a lifetime, but we will have to wait." Her eyes filled with tears again. His fingers under her chin raised her white face; his own expression had so much pain that she tried to smile.

"Nikki, whom did you see?"

"Papa"—he stopped—"and the Tsar. . . . When I saw Papa he handed me a long report from the secret police. Count Shuvalov and General Trepov had sent to France and America and got— information about you."

Poor Nikki, to see it all in black and white without an understanding of what really happened, the way it had come about. . . . Nikki took her hands.

"I told them I knew all about those other years, about Gagarin too, and I didn't want to hear any more about it. . . . Papa pounded his desk, said I might need a mistress for my health, but I

151

shouldn't have displayed you all over Europe. Claimed it was immodest." Nikki grinned.

"I told him, 'If it is, it's in the Romanov tradition. Did Tsar Peter, or Anna, Elizabeth, and Catherine, ever do anything but make a show of their love? And your own grandfather Paul, and your father, and your brother the Tsar himself.' I started to say more, but he stopped me. I was getting too close to home. Of course when I saw the Tsar it was another matter. I told him as politely as I could that I regretted the trouble I had caused but that I could not give you up. I would do whatever they asked except that."

Hattie's face was radiant. She could bear the spying, the separation, anything, as long as he felt and spoke like that. Then Nikki told her something that would have devastated her had she heard it first.

"They want me to marry some princess or other." At the look on her face he held up his hands. "Don't. Don't. I said nothing at all to that. Let them look around. I won't marry her, no matter what happens."

It seemed, in the little time they had left together, that Nikki had never been so generous, so loving. He behaved too as if he had won the right to be with her openly until he went away.

"I have a surprise for you," he said shortly before Christmas. "Come along."

They drove straight to Millionnaya Street. Before a tall, newly finished apartment building the coachman halted. Nikki led her into an ornate marble entrance hall.

"Just a moment," he said, pushing open a door. "Wait here." He closed the door behind him. Then a second later he threw it open with a flourish. "Madame, you may enter."

An enormous Christmas tree gleaming with candles stood in the center of a spacious salon. Heavy white-brocade curtains were drawn across the high windows. Inlaid tables of pale wood were piled with packages bearing her name.

"This is your own apartment," Nikki said. "I want to think of you here while I'm away. Look out the window," he said, smiling. When she parted the white brocade and looked out, Nikki's carriage was gone and in its place stood a pair of glossy dapple-gray horses harnessed to a shining sleigh. "Your anniversary present!" he said. "Do you remember?"

152

She had remembered, of course, that they had met just a year ago at the masquerade ball; that he did, left her so touched she could not speak.

Just then the door opened and Joséphine came in beaming, calling directions to the men who were bringing their hastily packed trunks. Laughing and crying at once, Hattie ran past her out into the hallway and down the steps to the sidewalk. As she stood there breathless in front of the sleigh, Nikki came up behind her and put his hands on her shoulders.

A bearded, raw-faced man bowed before her. "Fyodor," he announced. "My lady's coachman."

Passers-by stopped to watch. All at once Karpych appeared on the scene, officiously shooing them away.

"What are *you* doing here?" Nikki called in mock severity.

"I had to show Fyodor the way," the little man said, grinning.

Next morning the story was whispered all over town. By three o'clock Mabel Grey was at Hattie's door. The Englishwoman swept in past Joséphine, holding out her arms. Heavy furs hung from her shoulders.

"Hattie, what a place! I would never have thought—ah well!" Her smile was bright. "I've missed you." She hesitated, then said with emphasis, "We all have."

She dropped into a chair near a gilt-framed mirror. Looking into it, Mabel touched at her tilted nose. "Dear, you've certainly got that boy on a chain. It must have been hard to manage, at that. You know, I hear some of the revolutionists are getting out a pamphlet about it." This time there was no mistaking the resentment in the gray eyes. "Whatever made the Tsar give way to Nikki like this?" she asked abruptly.

Hattie kept her voice quiet. "I wasn't there."

The lines in Mabel's face were suddenly accentuated. Her voice sharpened. "Have you thought what you'll do when Nikki's away?"

"It isn't a problem," said Hattie. "I'll stay here and wait for him." Was Mabel fishing for information, or offering a suggestion?

"Alone? You could have a pleasanter time in Paris." Then she came to the point. "Fanny, some of us wonder if you'd—well, agree to an understanding, a certain reimbursement—if you'd leave Russia."

So that was it. But who was it Mabel was representing? The Tsar was a man of his word. The police? Whoever employed her, she must have been at this sort of thing for a long time. Hattie's face grew hot; she rose and held open the door. "No, I would not agree to any understanding, to any reimbursement—and I shall leave Russia only when I choose. I shall not be home if you call again."

Mabel drew on her furs. "Don't be so high and mighty, Fanny Lear! You're closer to trouble, real trouble, than you've ever been in your life!"

The Grand Duchess Sanni was ill in Nice and Nikki had been summoned to his mother's bedside to say farewell before he left for the army. The letter Hattie held was dated January 29, 1873.

"My dear little wife, I have been received with open arms, but like a lost one who is about to be rescued. Well, I am lost, lost within you—a delightful state, provided I don't lose you! That's all I ask. So long as I have you I feel capable of great deeds. But if misfortune comes, if to save me, as they say, we must separate, you can be sure that I shall no longer be a Grand Duke. I'll kill myself or escape to America with you. The first suggestion is cowardly, but the second would give me the chance to see you always."

He had never sounded more desperate. Could this be a solution, nonetheless? They might at least be free in the United States to live as they wished. America for a Romanov? The provincial pretensions of the East would bore him, but he loved open plains. Texas, where George Madison had made his fortune, or the unsettled West? She picked the letter up again.

"Mother suffers much and I try to distract her, but she keeps on bringing up the subject of my marriage. They have already prepared a letter that I'm to write from Khiva to the Tsar. . . . I kiss you so strongly that you will have to rest for an hour to recover."

She did not smile at his last extravagant words.

The clouds hung sullenly over the frozen Neva as their sleigh skimmed along the dark ice. It was Nikki's last day in St. Petersburg. By an old custom he was to bow before the tombs of his ancestors in the Church of the Fortress of Sts. Peter and Paul.

They entered the grim, gray, prisonlike building. Along austere halls, they passed through chamber after chamber to the central room in which white-marble sepulchers gleamed in the half-light. Silently, his face impassive, Nikki knelt before each in turn, his lips moving in a prayer, his fingers making the sign of the cross. Awe-struck and silent, Hattie walked slowly by his side, remaining standing while he paused and prayed. Before one tomb, unexpectedly, he turned to her.

"This is Tsar Paul's. Come."

She knelt beside him, and again before the resting place of his grandfather, Nicholas I, and finally before that of Peter the Great, where they stayed for endless solemn minutes.

Then Nikki drew her up, embraced her, and fastened around her neck a thin gold chain with a cross hanging from it.

"I was given this when I was here as a boy, at Peter's tomb. He is my protector. Now he will be yours as well. Promise me that you will never forget me."

With white lips she whispered: "I promise."

This was the real moment of their parting. . . . Back in her apartment, he took scissors and cut a curl of her hair for the locket that hung on his breast. "I don't want your picture." He tried to smile. "I know you by heart. . . . God keep you safe for me!"

He kissed her once solemnly; again, quickly, desperately. Then he was gone. He was dining with his father alone that night, and she could not go to the station in the morning. She stood still for a moment, then swayed forward. Joséphine tried to catch her in her arms but she sank, crying, to the floor. She felt as though she could not stop crying until he returned.

FIFTEEN

At first daily, and then weekly, Nikki's telegrams and letters had come.

"As the train was taking me away, my father and the guards lifted their hats to make the sign of the cross, as is their custom. It seemed to me that I was being buried. . . . I wonder if a woman can love me enough not to forget me during an absence of six months. God grant that it be so."

"Moscow: At the Kremlin for a few hours; a state luncheon with the governor general. All my thought, all my sentiments, with you."

"Orenburg in the Cossack steppes: Already made seven hundred and sixty versts by sleigh. Soon the telegraph wires end. Telegraph me; I will carry your message as a talisman through the war."

She had wired, of course, and he replied:

"You are my only true friend. Happy as rarely in my life. A prince of the blood is too little for you; you need a hero of whose power you will be proud. And you will be so."

Then the last letter:

"Write if you need anything. If it's possible it will be done; if impossible, it will be done. . . . We have crossed the Urals. We are in Asia. Good-by, Fanny Lear; good-by, my country. The farther my body moves from you, the nearer my soul comes to you."

156

Ten days had passed without fresh word from him. From now on, riders would have to carry his messages across the sands for hundreds of miles before they sighted the telegraph poles at far-off Orsk. Every day the new coachman drove her to the post office; several times she argued with the clerks. No, there was nothing. Were they keeping his letters from her; or was he sick, or dead? But he had warned her that the distances were long, very long.

Joséphine was her only companion. Shortly after Nikki had left she received a delicate note from a member of the *jeunesse dorée;* then another pointed inquiry came from one of the silver-haired gentlemen. She ignored all of them. But one day she became aware of attention of another kind—attention that could not be ignored. Joséphine told her that she had observed strangers standing across the street, seeming to be casual but always watching the apartment. And one afternoon, approaching her door, Hattie found a man hovering near by.

"This is Madame Petrovich's?" he asked. She was angry enough to make an indiscreet reply.

"You know very well it is not."

Had he been planning a secret search? Anxiously she called Joséphine and told her that thereafter they must make certain that one of them was always at home. It was the ever practical Breton who answered:

"Madame, is it safe to leave your things here at all? Your jewels and the Grand Duke's letters—someday we will wake up and find them all gone."

Hattie was used to Joséphine's warnings, but this time she took her seriously. She remembered what Nikki had said when he had ordered her to wear all her jewels to the opera. "Between performances leave them at the American Legation." She had not bothered then, but now she packed most of her valuables in a leather box and summoned the coachman.

She and Nikki had met the secretary of the Legation one night at a restaurant. Schuyler, his name was, Mr. Eugene Schuyler . . . very proud of his Patroon Dutch family background, she had heard. He was in his early thirties, not bad-looking, but he seemed precise and professorial. She had been told that he had a thorough knowledge of Russian, had even translated Turgenev's *Fathers and Sons.* Businessmen or politicians who came here as Ministers

157

knowing little of the place, and caring less, could not have got along without him.

At the Legation, Mr. Schuyler's blue eyes blinked in surprise when he saw her.

"Yes, Mrs. Blackford."

He knew her real name, then; he too had probably received a long report about her. She managed a tentative smile. "I'm not disturbing you?" There was a pause and now Mr. Schuyler gave an almost imperceptible shake of his head, saying nothing. She took a deep breath. "Mr. Schuyler, I must confess that I have come to you because I am worried. I am alone here, and I'm afraid that my property is not safe in my apartment."

"This property"—he cleared his throat as if anxious to avoid entanglement—"it *is* yours?"

"Of course it is." She looked back so steadfastly that his gaze dropped. "Will you accept it?"

"It isn't customary."

"I understand that you have done it in the case of other Americans."

Schuyler's eyebrows lifted. "Well, we could manage for a time —but only for a time." Restraining her resentment, she rose and thanked him sweetly. He tried to make brief amends. "You've been traveling, I understand. I'm leaving soon for the Turkestan steppes." He spoke in clipped, precise tones. "I'm going to refute the claims that human slavery doesn't exist there by buying and bringing back a slave."

As she put on her gloves, she could not resist the temptation to ask: "A girl slave?"

Mr. Schuyler's face became dark red. "No, I mean . . . no." The Legation's butler passed through with a bouquet of hot-house sweet peas and Schuyler turned to her as if an explanation were necessary. "For the supper table tonight."

Her curiosity was aroused. "You prefer them to roses?"

"I'm having roast beef. Certain foods require certain flowers."

Hattie looked with inward amusement at the prim tight face, the well-modeled ears and prominent eyes. As if reading her thoughts, Mr. Schuyler drew back. But after all, he had agreed to let her leave her box. She thanked him warmly again and left, hoping that she had at least tempered his hostility.

On the way home it began to snow, and Fyodor made miserably slow progress through the streets. An ornate droshky passed her. In it, half reclining on the cushions, lounged the aging Princess Magda, one of the women who had written Nikki, inviting him to her rooms. Magda had been a Baltic peasant's daughter; by a series of marriages, each one higher than the last, she had reached the nobility, where her promiscuous affairs had become an open scandal.

The Princess looked now, as usual, half-drunk. Her clothes were rumpled and untidy. Beside her sat a pretty, vapid young man. All Petersburg saw that, day after day, and yet the woman was one of the inner Court circle!

At Nikki's insistence, a new helper for Joséphine had been added to the household.

Plump young Katya had only recently arrived from the country, and she was pink, light-haired, and pug-nosed, with a disposition of smiling earnestness. She opened the door for Hattie.

"Oh, madame . . . madame, would you mind?" Even though she was due time for herself, Katya hesitated to ask for it. "My friend is waiting. May I go?"

"Of course," Hattie said. From the window she made out a young man standing at the corner. He was sallow-skinned, heavily mustached, as glum-looking as Katya was bright. "Is that the one?" Hattie asked.

Katya's round cheeks reddened. "Yes, madame, a university student. He works so hard, and worries so—about the world, and Russia especially." Already some universities were shut down for fear of revolutionary doctrines.

"Is he interested in economic affairs?" Hattie ventured.

"Yes. Too much so." Katya did not smile.

"He needn't wait for you out there," Hattie said warmly. "Ask him in."

The response was unexpected. "Oh, he wouldn't come." As if she realized that she had said the wrong thing, Katya covered her mouth. Her round eyes showed her dismay. "I mean he doesn't like fine living and white-satin sofas. And, begging your pardon, Anton doesn't hold with royalty. Any kind!"

Then, in a flurry of confusion and confidence Katya added: "Oh, madame, it's not so easy for me with Anton. I love Petersburg, the sights, and being here with you—the excitement and

159

all—and I want to marry Anton. He wants it, too, I think, but it's his family. They don't think well of somebody from a village, like me. Anton's against all such—such 'barriers.' And yet he can't go as far as he wants with things—yet." Hattie patted Katya's arm. It was a problem she well understood. With a self-conscious smile, Katya apologized, bowed to her, and disappeared.

"Poor little girl," Hattie murmured. But a second later she forgot Katya's concerns, for Joséphine was hurrying through the door.

"A letter, madame. At last a letter."

In her haste to open it Hattie almost tore it in half. Holding the ripped sheet together, she read eagerly. . . . As Nikki moved more deeply into the East, the people of the isolated tribes were pouring out to meet him, with honor guards and ceremoniously presented salvers of bread and salt. He told how hundreds milled about, gaping, pushing to touch his sleeve. It was not often that a Romanov came to these far-off areas. "It is only in seeing all this that you can understand the power of the Tsar. It is the people."

She read on. He wrote of the mounted Turkomans awaiting them, daggers in their teeth, among the blue distances of Asia.

"Yet another thought excites me, the thought of seeing my ravishing one in the oriental costume I will bring her, her arms langorously behind her. I belong to you like a child, a slave."

The letter sharpened her loneliness. She went to bed early, only to shift restlessly back and forth. When she finally slept, her old frightening dreams returned, and mingling with them new dreams in which the secret police trailed her like wolves through a moonless night. Mr. Schuyler of the Legation was in her dreams now, too, but she could not tell whether he was helping or hindering her. He was bearded, and his carefully tended fingers were pressed primly together in a judicial manner, as her father had once pressed his—holding her fate in the balance.

Waking the next morning, she was shocked when she looked in her ivory hand mirror. Her face was chalk-white, her dark eyebrows drawn together in anxiety. How much longer could she stand it here in this atmosphere of suspicion and suspense! A little later Joséphine found her at the window in an agony of tears, and again it was Joséphine who helped her reach a decision.

160

"Madame, we should go to Paris. We can wait there just as well as here."

Nikki had written in his last letter:

"I can understand how dreary the city must seem to you alone. But if you leave, go on only short trips. The idea of coming back unexpectedly and not finding you haunts me. Go to Vienna if you like, for the Exposition, but don't stay away long."

If she could go to Vienna Hattie thought she could certainly go a little farther to Paris; it would take him weeks to return, and she could come back to Russia in a few days at the first hint that he was on his way home. She could not tell him that it was not only dreary but dangerous to stay in St. Petersburg. It was a hard letter to write, but she made its tone light and gay and loving, giving no hint of her desperation.

She started the message on the long route toward Nikki and sent Joséphine to retrieve her belongings from the American Legation. Giving the keys to Katya and bidding her take charge in their absence, they arranged to leave that same night. As Hattie locked the apartment on the Millionnaya, her hand slowly tightened on the key. She had not considered it before. Would she have trouble returning? She turned the key in the lock. She had managed it once; she could manage it again.

On the train, in sudden relief from anxiety, she thought warmly of Paris: the boulevards, the little restaurants, the journals, the theater life. This time, like the last, she would be without Nikki, but it would be different. This time, she knew they would come together again. When she reached the Gare du Nord her heart was almost gay for the first time since Nikki had left. They found a pleasant apartment on a side street; she would need to keep up no appearances.

The faithful Katya lost no time in forwarding Nikki's letters. Within a few days, Joséphine came in with the first, written several weeks before. She read the beginning and the end first to savor his love before she read the main part of the letter. "My dearest, my prettiest, my sweetest," he began, and ended: "I think of you, I live for you. Love me as much as I love you, that is all I ask. Yours till death, Nikki." The reference to death disturbed her. She went back hastily to the beginning of the letter. He had

161

been given command of the advance guard of one of the four columns soon to converge on Khiva, the largest and most important of them. He was to put up the fort that would serve as a base for the final expedition, and he had been chosen to do this in recognition of his services.

He went on to write of the mud-caked streets and bazaars, ill-smelling but packed with goods. He had bought her curiously patterned silks of Kokand, deep-red carpets from Turkmenistan, dark-chiseled silver of Bukhara, all of them for "our apartment." They were being sent back by camel caravan.

He pictured the scenes along the march into the heart of Asia. In from the steppes swept men of a dozen peoples, armed to the teeth: Kirghizes with their slant eyes, dark Turkomans, Bukharians, Kokanders, Uzbeks of a bitter ferocity. All were deadly enemies of the Khivans. Meanwhile other natives drove in their animals, horses and camels by the hundreds, for sale to the expedition. The horses were "very little and very ugly, but strong, and they can go several days without eating, which is very important."

A week later a letter told briefly of the next stage of the march. With solemn ritual the priests had blessed flags and soldiers as they moved steadily forward. But this letter was more about themselves. Apprehensive again, he confided: "My mind is tormented. I imagine certain people are going to court you and that with your passion for the theater and gaiety you will be led away. . . . I am sure that if I were in their place I would succeed." Then he told her that he was under a doctor's care with fever, but added lightly: "How unfortunate to be a descendant of conquerors and not have their temperament!" There it was again, that old feeling of inability to cope with his tasks. Impulsively she reached for her pen and wrote a long letter reassuring him, insisting, too, that he watch his health as much as was possible.

The next letter did not allay her concern. They had crossed an important river over the ice. It was now six degrees below zero with a north wind. The sands had a heavy chill and often men sank into them to their knees. "Several of our soldiers are dangerously sick; some of the camels have died of fatigue." For ten days they had seen nothing but desert; a north wind had whipped up a wind storm that lasted five hours. But Nikki thought of the

162

treacherous March winds at home, and with great concern he wrote:

"Take care of yourself, my dearest. Dress warmly, always wear your fur cloak. Petersburg can be dangerous in the spring. There is more reason to think that if death separates us, it should be through me. But I get such forebodings about your safety. Without you my life is like a soulless machine that has no reason to function."

His words troubled her. He was still thinking of her in the St. Petersburg apartment. What would he say when her letter arrived?

When it did, he was less distressed than she had feared. He was so relieved to hear from her at all.

"After four weeks of waiting I savored your letter with a passion difficult to describe. Rather like that of the prisoner who is suddenly given liberty to see his loved ones once more, although such a one is luckier than I am. . . . It is, oddly, less painful to think of you in Paris than it is to think of you among people and places I know, but without me. Only come back as soon as I give you word, for we must not be separated a minute longer than is necessary."

He went on to tell her of the campaign. His letters were long and filled with technical military details and political observations on the tribes they dealt with. He observed:

"It is wonderful to think that all this interests you as much as it does me, not only because the things I tell you concern me, but because you are interested in everything—extraordinary wife!"

Then all at once he wrote: "Thousands of the enemy are assembling." He had driven his men to complete the new fort.

"For two days and nights one hundred and fifty men worked in shifts to finish it. Nomads rode in for miles to watch the flag being hoisted slowly into the sky. As cannon pounded, two eagles were spotted at a vast height over the banner, almost motionless against the clouds. The soldiers shouted madly at the good omen and I ordered another salvo."

From this outpost, Nikki was able to lead his force toward the hazardous red sands. Water became a more and more terrible problem. He wrote of the parched wastes, the arid vistas. And yet if water were ever brought to the area, it would bloom in magnificent fertility. Someday he would do such a thing, he told her. But meanwhile the enemy had been striking ahead of them. Coming upon the infrequent wells, they found them filled with earth and filth. When they dragged bottom they brought up carasses of rotting dogs. Also, they must guard constantly lest the wells be poisoned.

Once a scout brought news of ducks in a marsh, and Nikki took his Cossacks along for a hunt. Night surprised them far from camp; losing their way, they circled helplessly for hours. "We might have fallen prisoners, or died of hunger, for it is not easy to get food in the desert," he explained.

"I should like to know what would have happened to us if they had captured us! The Asians are masters of agonizing tortures. I have heard they sometimes use sharp knives to slice off all the skin, very slowly—sometimes hours in the process—while the tribe watches, and sometimes victims are set loose in the desert after their fingers and toes have been chopped away."

They were about to cross a river, the legendary Oxus crossed by Alexander the Great. It was obvious that Nikki, for the first time in his life, had begun to sense his new power. Some of it made him excited and happy—

"At twenty-three I have two colonels under me. I sign myself Chief of the Advance Guard, Aide-de-Camp of His Majesty the Tsar, Captain of the General Staff."

Some of it made him thoughtful. His training in the Imperial Military Academy had not prepared him for the power of a commander in battle.

"I have the right to charge any man in my detachment, even to have him shot, under military regulations. When I signed the first order against a deserter I was more disturbed than I wanted anyone to see."

164

He ended the letter on a somber note.

"I wish that when you are dying, someday, you will say, 'How I loved Nikki; I never loved anyone more.' You know that this is true of me—that I care nothing for life itself and that I value only you in this false world."

But his postscript made her smile.

"You don't need to put stamps on your letters; they go free if addressed to a member of the Imperial family. Economy!"

Late May had come to Paris, with its scent of blooms and lulling winds against her window. In earlier days she would have ridden in the park with Joséphine. Now she would not leave the apartment because there had been no news for several weeks. At any time the letter might come telling of actual battle. In his last note he had said that the Russians had taken positions for a grand offensive but rumors had reached them that the enemy planned a surprise attack, before it could be launched.

She felt as if her real life were led with him; it was almost as if the objects in the room about her, the city itself, were faintly out of focus. Instead of the Seine, she saw the Oxus, the hurrying Parisians on the street below took on a dark Asiatic cast.

Newspapers gave belated and distorted news; besides, they could hardly be expected to report whether Nikki had or had not nearly starved to death, or been wounded. Surely they would report if he were killed . . . but why didn't she hear from him? She wrote in her journal on one particular afternoon in this waiting period: "It must seem very strange, but I think that Nikki has a magnetic force that touches me no matter what distance away from me he is. When I am about to receive a letter from him I feel an agitation I am not able to suppress. I feel his presence to such a point that if suddenly I should see him come into this very room I would not be in the least astonished. In my impatience I plague both Joséphine and the clerk at the post office when these premonitions come over me, demanding every fifteen minutes whether something has come for me. I am sure this annoys and bores them both, and they will be as relieved as I when the letter comes."

She had barely finished writing when, as she had expected, Joséphine came in with the letter. But the calm she had written of deserted her. She trembled so that her maid had to slit it open and tell her what was in the first sentence.

The Russians had suddenly been surrounded on all sides. Hattie snatched the letter from Joséphine.

"Imagine three thousand cavalrymen on magnificent horses, guns and sabers in their hands, tall black skin caps on their heads."

The rival forces had faced one another; stealthily one section of the Russians started to break through, made headway, and then

"the enemy concentrated his strength upon us. The bravest of them galloped within four paces of us, shooting as they half-circled. We shot back. I saw several fall dead or wounded, and horses dragging them off. They must be given credit; they never leave their wounded behind, but ride swiftly up and lift them to their saddles directly under our fire. I have seen so many dead, theirs and ours. It was a horrible sight."

Shells had fallen around him; the earth spattered up in geysers of dust. His doctor's horse had dropped, sending the rider crashing to the ground. Animals were dying all about them, sometimes silently, again with agonized breathing. The enemy was losing, re-treating. The General sent orders to Nikki and his men. "I raised my saber, giving the signal," Nikki wrote, "and then I noticed that the Cossacks were bowing and crossing themselves and it came to me that this was the most dangerous moment of my life." He had led his Cossacks in a dash to the river, shooting as they went.

Along the stream they surprised a heavy boatload of Khivans trying to cross. From the boat on the opposite bank the enemy fired. Nikki ordered the Cossacks to blast at the vessel. Their guns found quick targets, and the Khivans fell, drowning before their eyes. A force of four hundred cavalry—the last of the native offen-sive—swept down against Nikki's men, but were driven back.

His troops had won the decisive battle for General Kaufmann. Now they must push toward Khiva, and accept the surrender of the Khan himself. The next battle—that of the peace terms—would be fought by diplomacy.

The desert ended; villages appeared among the fields, and square-built houses along the twisted streets tempted the soldiers. And then, Nikki wrote, he saw the fabled city itself, beyond a slim belt of graceful trees. The Khan's capital rose high in the air with its painted minarets, its stately domes of mosques and palaces, their tiles glittering in the sun. Walls of dried clay opened before them, then long avenues of mulberry trees, leading to plazas, the holy buildings, and the harems.

There, on a sultry day of June 1873, the Khan of Khiva stood before the General's emissary, the Grand Duke Nicholas.

"I stared at the great Khan; his large eyes looked forth imploringly beneath a low, perspiring forehead. His black beard quivered, his mouth opened with nervous jerks. The chin, in contradiction to the massive upper face and figure, showed that of his father's many sons this was the least fitted for the throne he had received."

The Khan had bowed low; through many interpreters he expressed eternal gratitude to the Romanovs for sparing his life and continuing him in his palace. (Khiva would still be "independent," with the Tsar's troops as "advisers" on the scene. They were turning back his kingdom, his women, and his pretty young boys, with whom he was supposed to amuse himself.) But now the Khan asked: Could he be certain that after the Tsar's nephew left, the others would not kill him? "To this unregal speech, I replied with comforting assurance." For Nikki it was an important moment, but then he wrote: "As I stood there saying farewell, I began to think of a blonde girl in Paris." His last lines swam before her eyes:

"I am leaving in a day or two, my dearest. Get out a map, and be sure you understand my directions. We must both travel thousands of miles, but I have planned it so that we will meet at the first possible moment.

"You must go to Berlin, then Warsaw, into Russia to the town of Nijni Novgorod; then down the Volga by boat to the far southern city of Samara."

Meanwhile he would be racing by camel, by wagon, by boat and train, toward their reunion.

"Joséphine Joséphine!" Hattie was laughing and sobbing, and called out five or six directions at once. Had she ever thought she would be so happy to leave Paris!

SIXTEEN

THE DOCK WAS HOT AND CROWDED. HATTIE AND JOSÉPHINE, WAITING to take the Volga steamer, had been standing nearly two hours in the sun. The boat was being made ready but no one had yet been allowed on board. At the end of the dock, a flat, narrow barge floated low in the water. Suddenly the desultory conversation about them changed to a low muttering and a woman beside her cried out as a ragged file of men and women shuffled onto the dock in chains.

"Siberia," a man mumbled beneath his breath, and he crossed himself. The muttering grew more distinct. These people were being transported for "political" offenses—suspected revolutionary interests, dangerous tendencies, or because they had displeased this or that official. After the narrow barge had been towed down the Volga, they would be marched for hundreds of miles across the steppes, then over the Urals. "They have thousands of miles to go . . ."

A woman prisoner in her late sixties, white hair falling over her face, stumbled, and one of the guards raised a threatening whip. How many of the prisoners were women; a peasant girl with the face of a blonde angel; a woman who must be her mother, whose only sign of terror was a slight jerking movement of her throat; a girl, almost a child, far gone in pregnancy.

Hattie felt Joséphine take her arm. "Don't watch them, madame." But she could not turn away. The barge bumped at the bank; a dozen new guards ran up and began to shove the men and woman toward the steep incline down to the vessel. Some did not move fast enough. When an old man slipped, a thick hand grabbed his collar and threw him forward. A girl fainted, and others half lifted, half pushed her ahead.

Some of the prisoners showed no emotion, but in the eyes of the onlookers she read warm sympathy, and a touch of fear. There but for God's grace went any one of them. Slowly the barge slid from the dock. Under the eyes of the guards, the victims stood at the metal screens that kept them from escape, staring at the bank. Hattie would never forget the despair in the white faces, growing smaller and smaller as the barge moved away.

New shouts rose on the dock, and rousing from her preoccupation with the tragic scene, Hattie discovered that their steamer was ready. They pushed up the gangplank in a confused mass of people, and looked helplessly about to find the captain. A gentle-voiced merchant pointed him out. The captain, a gruff, red-faced fellow, blinked amiably at Hattie, then shrugged.

"Eh, they didn't tell you at the office? Not a single cabin left, first or second class."

She hesitated; she was in no mood to ask for special attention after what she had just seen. He looked at her, slim and pale in her black taffeta, the maid behind her. Ordinarily, he didn't like aristocrats—they could take their chances with the rest of them— but this was a very pretty one, and she wasn't taking out her annoyance on him or trying to bribe him when he had no space to give.

"You take my cabin, madame. I'll move in with the first mate."

She protested only weakly, then thanked him with relief. Even though she was used to having men go to special trouble for her, this was particularly touching. Yet nearly all the people in this country were kind, once the first shell of suspicion broke away— all except, say, some of the Court, the ultra-privileged, and the ultra-suspicious.

The captain's cabin, bare and stifling, was hardly big enough for her trunks; yet they had privacy, and for that she and Joséphine were grateful. After much delay, the steamer moved forward, but relief from the heat did not come. There was not the slightest breeze as they glided past low, green banks in endless succession, and the flies thickened on the walls. For a time, she stared out of the little porthole at the melancholy river, Mother Volga, with its sandy banks and solitary trees. Nikki was somewhere ahead—

but how far off it must be! She felt as if she were crossing the earth to be with him.

Joséphine, pushing the flies away with a brusque hand, touched Hattie's arm. "Madame, can we go out in the air?"

On the top deck they found crowds of men, women, and children sitting about at random; below, on the third-class deck, the congestion was worse, families sprawling, swarming, in an unbroken mass. Neither roof nor awning shielded them. Children's cries and the adults' doleful songs rose in a chaos of sound.

On the upper deck some had brought tea, sugar, and other provisions, and were having small picnics among themselves. Hattie's appearance created a stir. In the babble of comment as she and Joséphine moved to the rail, she caught references to her strange white skin and yellow hair. A stout woman approached warily, tried a remark about the heat, and cried her astonishment when Hattie answered in Russian. She called her sister, and a thin young man who was with her. All three talked at once.

Other Russians crowded about; as always, she found them ready to tell their life histories and curious about hers. She answered their questions vaguely—"I'm from New York on my way to Samara as a governess." Several officers' wives said that they were meeting their husbands on their return from Khiva. She recognized the names they mentioned of places, battles, and tribes, but she merely nodded.

The talk around her helped to distract Hattie from the slowness of the trip, but it began to seem interminable. The flies came and went in clusters, and sometimes they had to fight swarms of mosquitoes from the mud flats. At night, she was restless and dreamed uneasily. The exiles to Siberia moved in a miserable file before her eyes again. The blonde peasant girl seemed to be crying, though no sound issued from her lips. Then Hattie herself became that girl, half-dying in a blizzard-like fury of wind. Waking, she found that it was only a hard rain against the side of the vessel, but her terror remained. Gloomy thoughts about Nikki came to her. Suppose he had been delayed, or had met with a mishap; he had told her only that some emissary would arrange their meeting. But the cool of the rain and the steady, reassuring throb of the engines taking her toward Samara with every revolution at last soothed her into sleep again.

When the rain finally stopped the next afternoon, and they

170

went on deck, it was to find that the river had gradually widened and deepened, and the green hills were looming higher. They were approaching Kazan, the old-time Tatar capital, where the boat was to dock for several hours. Restless and impatient at the delay, Hattie went ashore. Women in veils and flowing robes fixed their limpid black eyes on her unveiled face in childlike curiosity. To her amusement, she began to feel uncomfortably exposed, and she returned to pace the upper deck of the steamer.

New passengers were thronging the boat. Presently a shy servant girl touched Hattie's arm. "My lady—would—like to meet you," she stammered, indicating an ancient woman holding court in a shady corner of the deck. Although she had just boarded the boat, all her belongings were about her in a rigid arrangement, as if this had been her rightful place for days. With a broad smile, she beckoned, and after a moment's hesitation, Hattie approached. The woman rose with some difficulty, patted down the yellow crepe dress that hung in many folds, and made an imperious gesture that cleared a space beside her.

"My dear," she cried, "you're the most beautiful young lady I've ever seen! What are you, English? . . . American! I've never known an American. Are you all so beautiful?"

The yellow-brown eyes glittered with an almost serpentine brightness, yet the mouth, cut by long, vertical lines, indicated warm interest and kindness. Hattie sat down beside her, and the old woman went on with much vivacity, waving her hands, shrugging, blinking her eyes.

"I'm very rich, you understand, from Saratov. I've got a lot of relatives everywhere. I travel all the year around to keep them from poisoning me for my property!" She gave a high cackle. "Summers I sail up and down the Volga; winters I spend on trains between cities. My relatives . . ." She grimaced. "But those that are no kin, they're very good to me. Everybody knows me."

She spoke the truth. At every stop new passengers came up to kiss the old one's hand. When Hattie started to leave, her new friend took her arm. "Please, my dear. I have never seen anyone like you." She continued to introduce Hattie to the friends who flocked around her.

"You're practically a queen," Hattie said to her—"Queen of the Volga."

The old woman was delighted. "You're good to me. Yes, be

good to me. It will bring you luck. I hope you're superstitious; it's fine to be superstitious!"

When Hattie's Russian failed, they turned to French. "I haven't used it in thirty years," the Queen explained. "My second husband didn't understand it, and thought I would use it to be unfaithful, so he forbade me to speak it." The wrinkled face contracted. "Husbands! They're crazy and wonderful too, eh?" Her bony elbow nudged Hattie, and her high screech rang out over the river.

They were due in Samara the next morning. That night again Hattie tried unsuccessfully to sleep, the throb of the engines pounding in her ears, a heavy undertone to the quickened beat of her own heart. She finally dozed for about an hour, but woke sharply at four o'clock. They were not due until six, and everything was packed, but she got up to dress. By the swaying lamp she struggled with the fresh white-lace collar Joséphine had guarded since they left Paris. In the captain's tiny cracked mirror her face looked as fresh as if she had slept for hours. Her eyes were black with excitement.

At last, as dawn streaked the sky, the boat's engines stopped. They were gliding into the dock at Samara. Everyone on the steamer was awake; the Queen of the Volga, on her campstool throne, summoned Hattie again. The pale lips drew together.

"Would it be too much for you to embrace this shriveled creature? A kiss from lips so fresh—I think it would give me new life!"

Hattie put her arms about the old woman's neck. The Queen caught her with an almost convulsive delight. When she released her, she said softly, in parting, "May God return your prince and may you be forever happy with him!" The faces around were turned to her, and Hattie, shocked by the fact that they knew who she was, still felt gratefully that they were friendly and sympathetic. But the gangplank was being lowered, and Hattie turned from the smiling faces around her, looking down eagerly into the crowd waiting on the dock. There was no sign of Nikki, or of a uniformed emissary.

A few minutes later, she and Joséphine stood forlornly in the midst of their baggage, looking about them. A soldier pushed authoritatively through the crowd toward them—and there was a letter in his hand. He bowed before Hattie. "Madame Lear?" She

172

nodded and he presented the letter to her. Careless of the inquisitive onlookers, she tore it open.

"Samara, July 6, 1873: At last, after five months, I will see you again. It still seems impossible, but your telegrams and letters prove I am not dreaming. The soldier who bears this letter will indicate the way to the hotel. Take Room No. 16. I have reserved Number 18, and will be there as soon after you arrive as I can.

"Only God knows how happy I am. It is hard for me to bear, even to understand, this happiness. You were right when you wrote that I had become a stronger man. If even this long absence did not really part us, nothing can. . . . Still a few more minutes, dear friend of my soul. . . ."

Though everyone was watching, she could not hold back her tears. The soldier helped them into a carriage. The passage over the uneven cobblestones was swift and bumpy, but she paid no heed. Her hands tightened over the letter as if she were touching Nikki himself.

Hastily, Joséphine unpacked, arranged her mistress's hair, and left her alone in the room. Drawing up the blinds at the window, Hattie looked down into the dazzling heat and movement of the street, listening and watching.

From the distance came a vague hubbub, which grew louder as people pushed forward toward the hotel. They were surrounding a group of men in uniform. She heard his name before she saw him. Above the din of the street the cry was clear again and again —"Our Duke! Nicholas Constantinovich!" After all these months, to hear his name for the first time shouted in the streets! . . . Exultantly, she repeated under her breath—"Nicholas! Nicholas!" Then she saw him, a tall figure in a green uniform. How brown he was, how bleached and bright his hair—and how well he looked! He was staring up at the hotel as if searching for her window, and she longed to lean out and call to him.

She thought he would never reach the door of the hotel. The crowd was increasing by the second. People were breaking through the small guard around him to try to kiss his hand; an old woman embraced his leg. Even after he had entered the door, the crowd remained below, still cheering.

At last she heard his familiar springing step in the next room. A french door leading to a balcony a few feet from her window opened, and Nikki appeared. She could have leaned forward and touched his sleeve. As he faced the crowd, he looked in the direction of her window for a moment, as though he sensed her presence. Her eyes traced the familiar face, the high forehead, the full lips, the cleft chin—and then she heard his voice.

"I thank you in the name of the Tsar." He spoke for a few minutes of the Russian victories, saluted, smiled, and waved acknowledgment to the crescendo of shouting at the end. Finally he stepped back and through the wall she heard the french door close. Only murmurs came from the crowd below, straggling away. Now she heard the well-loved voice through the connecting door between their rooms, "Fanny . . . open the door."

The door was locked and she had no key. She told him so, sobbing with impatience, and heard his oath and an order to Viktor. She pressed her body against the door, telling herself he was there, a few inches from her. He must be doing the same thing, for his low voice seemed very near.

"You missed me?"

"I still miss you!"

She heard Viktor's voice, the lock turned, and Nikki caught her against him. One passionate kiss, and then he pushed her away from him, to look at her hungrily. "Dearest, dearest, dearest." His words were feverish.

He lifted her in his arms and carried her to the long sofa by the window. She clung to him, burying her face against his chest. He stroked her hair, murmuring tenderly, and finally she drew back to look at him.

"Darling, you're so brown—almost black. I've never seen you so handsome. But you *are* a little thin."

"I've never felt better!" He thumped his chest, and she touched the breast of his tunic.

"You'll soon be wearing the Cross of St. George."

He nodded. "They haven't given it to me yet, but they will."

His green eyes looked at her softly. "You should have been with me on the balcony. Everything successful that I have done and will do is because of you. Actually, it would be more to the point if you stood there alone than if I did! But we'll have to

174

keep you in hiding until I see the Tsar. Then things will be different. Never fear! . . . Then will you marry me, Fanny Lear . . . little Hattie Ely?"

"I have been your wife since I first saw you. But oh, Nikki, Nikki, to be always together! Will they really let us?"

"I'll insist—I can now. It's got to be that way.

She believed him. In sudden exaltation, and for the first time, she believed him completely. This was another Nikki, self-assured, certain of himself. There was much more that she wanted to ask, much more to tell, but as he bent over her there was no time for words.

As they traveled toward St. Petersburg, it was more and more apparent that Nikki's fame had spread. At every railroad station, troops lined up for his inspection; the local nobility came to greet him, with the clergy in silver chasubles, and military officials in gold braid. In some towns small arches of triumph, flower-ornamented, awaited him, and merchants had hung out flags and ceremonial rugs. Hattie stayed in seclusion, but although she could not share his triumphs in person, they seemed like her own. Her only impatience came when he had to stay through endless banquets and receptions, and could not openly cut them short to return to her. But they did not have much longer to wait, not much longer.

They reached Petersburg in mid-July. Faithful Katya was waiting at the apartment on Millionnaya, and its windows had been thrown open to what air there was stirring.

"Home," Nikki murmured as he stood beside Hattie at the window. "This is still my home."

The stifling capital had been deserted by the Court and the Tsar was at his military quarters in Vilno. He would send for Nikki presently. This was an ominous delay. Nikki had expected to be received and rewarded immediately.

Petersburg was too warm for them to wait there comfortably, and since the Grand Duchess Sanni was still abroad they could go to the green restfulness of the summer palace at Pavlovsk.

Karpych went ahead to prepare the staff. When he met them at the door, he had a welcoming gift for his master's lady. From behind his back he brought out a gaily painted tin box filled with fruit cakes, and presented it to her, talking so fast that Nikki had to translate. "He had one of the best cooks make them for you . . . from one of his mother's old recipes . . . he says they are good-luck cakes."

Again they walked along the terraced gardens and followed the shadowed paths; they even rode out to the little rose pavilion. But Nikki was tense, waiting for word from the Tsar. The command came when they had been there a week.

"I leave tonight for Vilno," Nikki said. "I'll let you know when you're to follow—probably day after tomorrow. By that time I will have made my report, he will have presented my reward—and I will have told him what I consider the only real reward!" His tone was defiant rather than confident, and Hattie kissed him good-by with special tenderness.

But she would not let the flash of apprehension she had felt disturb her. Exploring the scarlet magnificence of the palace rooms, remembering still, with a little shudder, her fright on her first evening there, she ordered flowers to brighten the long halls and picked a large bouquet of white roses to place under Tsar Peter's portrait.

When Nikki's note came, there was nothing in it but the time of the train she and Joséphine were to take—and his love. When their train pulled into the Vilno station, Karpych's familiar clown's face smiled at them from the platform. At that moment, a high wind tossed stray papers through the air, and a burst of rain splattered against the glass.

"This way, madame." Pulling his coat about his ears, the dwarf hurried them to a closed carriage. Inside, Hattie shook the water off her skirts. The full strength of the rain beat on the roof as she called up:

"Karpych, where's your master?"

The window in the roof opened and the dwarf's head appeared. He said nothing, but pressed his finger to his lips. Hattie felt a twinge of alarm, which increased when they drew up at the side entrance of a magnificent old building. A servant helped her alight, and she and Joséphine followed him to a salon decorated in yellow and cluttered with antique furnishings. Karpych, having attended to the carriage, announced that Nikki would be delayed a few minutes. . . . Tea had been ordered for them.

"It will be served, madame, on that table over there—the very one where Tsar Alexander sat to plan his retreat to Moscow, and where Napoleon sat the next day to trace his maps for his drive on Russia. Both of them were in a hurry. They left the inkwells and pens." He puffed out his lips, "You're in the old palace of the Lithuanian Grand Dukes."

His chatter failed to divert her. She tapped her fingers on the famous table uneasily until she heard a noise at the door.

"Nikki!" She jumped up to meet him. But he did not take her in his arms. He came forward with a strange smile.

"My love," he began gravely, "I have bad news for us." He sat down beside her. "The Tsar was furious. He really wanted me to stay months longer in Asia, because he hoped I'd forget you. In fact, he's swearing at the General for letting me go." Nikki's face grew bitter. In the gloom of the room his tan looked yellow. "He had reports about the demonstrations on the way home—he claimed I had ordered them. . . . He didn't care to hear about the campaign at all—and of course there was no medal." The pulse in his temple had begun to throb. "He talked mostly about us. He reminded me of the letter I was supposed to write, saying that I would marry the German princess."

Nikki's calm was deserting him. He sprang to his feet and looked down at her tensely. "I told him that I would never write the letter, that you were going to be my wife." He stopped. The memory of the Tsar's outburst was not pleasant. "But I think it still would not have gone so badly if the heir apparent had not come in. Sasha claimed I was plotting with the revolutionists to kill him, and the Tsar too, and then take over with my father." Nikki's voice filled the salon. "Nobody has ever talked to me like that. Nobody!" He paused. "But Sasha really went too far, and the Tsar quieted him and told us both to go. Now I'm supposed to await further orders."

In the long silence that followed, Hattie's eyes left Nikki's face. She looked down at the cup in her hand, then at the yellow hangings of the room, the rain outside the french doors. The rain was growing worse. The winds rattled the tall glass doors, and low thunder sounded around the horizon. Orders, Nikki had said. What orders? She looked back at him, still in silence. Nikki's eyes met hers.

"I'm not going to wait to find out!" Jumping up, he took her by the hands and drew her to her feet. "We're leaving town on

177

the next train. In this weather it will be easy to get out without being seen. Come!"

"Leaving? . . . Where can we go?"

"The border!" His face was white. "We'll get to Vienna and find a priest. After that, let them try to do something."

Hattie hardly knew what was happening as Nikki wrapped her cloak around her and pushed her out of the door, shouting to Karpych. In the carriage, Nikki bent forward, hands clenched between his knees. "The seven o'clock train is sometimes late. It had better be late today." He checked himself nervously. "But not too late. We can't stay in the station long."

It was past seven already. Hattie found her own hands tightly clenched. Let them make it, oh, let them get there in time! She was suddenly alive with hope and fear. All around them was the fall of water, blotting out the town; the wind shook the doors of the carriage. As they neared the station, vehicles blocked the road in a long line. They heard a locomotive whistle, close ahead.

"This way!" Nikki took her hand and pulled her after him out of the carriage. Karpych and Joséphine stumbled out, snatching at their hand luggage. As they all ran into the station, she heard the final call for the train. Nikki darted ahead and helped her up the step of the last car. Joséphine jumped after them, and Karpych began to pile on their light bags. The train was moving slowly away. The dwarf threw on the final bag and leaped after it.

The train had gathered full speed by the time their car reached the end of the platform. Nikki pointed behind them. "Look!" A gendarme was running after the train. He looked up at their faces in the back window of the car incredulously, then turned and started to race back through the rain, hunching his shoulders. Hattie laughed in nervous relief.

"It isn't over yet," Nikki cautioned. "They know you're with me now, and they may telegraph ahead."

At the border they shifted their bags and boxes with trembling hands, and Nikki spoke imperiously to the officials. "We're in a hurry. Don't take hours at it." Two of them riffled through their passports, then called another. Would he come out with a telegram in his hand? But the border agent lifted his head and nodded. A few minutes later they were outside Russia, speeding toward the freedom of Europe.

178

SEVENTEEN

THE STOUT RUSSIAN PRIEST WITH THE CIRCULAR BUSHY BLACK BEARD
listened impassively to Nikki. His fingers folded over his stomach,
moved slowly, then rested. He looked troubled.

"Your Imperial Highness forgets that I am attached to the
Embassy here in Vienna under His Majesty's orders. You understand what would happen to me if I performed such a ceremony."

"Nothing would happen." Nikki spoke scornfully, then added,
not altogether reassuringly: "Show more courage! Yes, the Tsar
would be angry at first; then, when he realized it was over and
done, the whole thing would be dropped. He would never disturb the sanctity of a legal marriage!"

The priest's expression was stubbornly unwilling, and Nikki
went on desperately: "Suppose the worst happens? I'll make you
independent for life. I have a fortune of my own, some of it in
foreign banks. My wife and I would travel in Europe, America;
you could follow us. They could only unfrock you." The priest's
mouth moved in horror, and they knew it was hopeless. Nikki
caught the man's arm. "If you won't help, at least don't turn
against us! Not a word of this."

"Not a word, Your Imperial Highness." The frightened man
was gone.

Dispiritedly, Nikki returned to her, and she took his hand.
"Would you think of being married by a minister?" she asked. He
nodded, reluctantly; they had no choice. He went downstairs, and
when he returned, his voice was confident. "The hotel clerk's
sending for somebody from the Town Hall to see about it immediately."

Hattie's eyes shared his delight. Within the hour there was a

179

knock, and Nikki admitted a lean factotum whose bows were abject. A white rabbit might have appeared magically in his hands at any minute.

"Count Herder?" The stranger addressed Nikki by the name he had used when he registered. "You wish my services?"

"We want to be married—tonight, if possible."

"May I see your birth certificates?"

"You may not. I'll show them to the clergyman when you bring him."

Again that subservient bow, and then a significant glance. "It will be a little difficult. Our laws are strict."

"I know. Let's make it less difficult." Nikki tossed out a small but heavy purse.

The man nearly bowed himself in half. "Thank you, Excellency, thank you. I'll do my very best. By noon tomorrow."

They spent an uneasy night, then a morning of increasing tension.

"You remember my dream," Nikki asked, "about the way I was going to be executed and the Tsar refused to save me? I had it again last night."

She could only repeat the consoling French phrase she had once used with him, *"Les songes ne sont que les mensonges."* . . . But it reassured neither of them.

At noon the knock came. The factotum was alone, his expression flustered.

"Begging your pardon, Excellency, all the ministers I have spoken to have doubts."

"Doubts!" Nikki seemed about to throw the fellow to the floor.

The man stepped back and held up a trembling hand. "All they want to know is whether you're really Count Herder. The police are looking for a very important personage—one rather answering your description."

Nikki grabbed him by the collar. "Traitor. You went to them!"

"No, no," the man struggled, "you'll see!"

There was a light tap at the door, which stood ajar into the hall.

"Yes, Nikki, you'll see." From the hall Hattie heard another voice, a cultured one, with a dry tone. She had heard it once before. The Grand Duke Constantine of Russia sauntered into the room.

180

"A pretty mess." Nikki's father sat down comfortably and lit a cigar. "Pretty." He drummed his fingers on the arm of his chair. Hattie felt his eyes pass over her, in hostility yet with a certain curiosity. He had not acknowledged her presence; he simply observed that she was there. His mouth pursed, and his chin jutted out in a gesture of disdain for the couple before him.

"Sit, both of you!" the Grand Duke said in irritation.

Nikki sat down stiffly, as if he were on guard to jump up again at any second. Hattie sank down because her knees would not hold her up any longer. She thought of the last time she had seen Constantine, on that absurd day when he had found her hiding in Nikki's bed. The present encounter had scarcely more dignity.

"So you were going to *marry* her!"

Nikki stared back in defiant silence and Constantine continued in a flat, contemptuous tone. "The Embassy priest went to the Ambassador, of course; and he knew where to reach me, fortunately." He crossed his knees comfortably. "I was visiting your mother in the Bavarian mountains, and didn't I get here very quickly?"

He asked it lightly, as if he expected applause. Nikki remained silent; at the corner of his mouth a muscle twitched. Constantine's eyes went to her again, then to Nikki, and his manner softened a little.

"Your mother's ill; she asks for you all the time. And I have news from the Tsar."

Nikki finally spoke. His voice was low. "What does he say?"

"He was shocked, of course, and hurt. He's had time to recover, though, and he feels less badly. Young Sasha's the furious one. I've never known him to be so concerned." His smile at this showed the first glint of sympathy for his son. He paused. "The Tsar, I gather, feels somewhat sorry for you—and your lady. He understands the depths of your feeling, and he's willing to give you a chance. His orders are for you to come back to Russia and stay there, say seven or eight months, quietly; no attention, no scandal. There's been too much talk already."

"What about Madame Lear?" Nikki's suffering was in his eyes.

His father's face showed no expression at all. "Well, I think she can be with you, if it is done discreetly; but you must try nothing more of this kind."

181

Suddenly Nikki leaned toward his father. "Isn't Cousin Marie going to marry Queen Victoria's son?"

"Yes, early next year. What does that have to do with it?"

"A great deal." Nikki's voice showed a contemptuous desperation. "The Tsar wants us back in Russia because he can't afford a scandal now. It might hurt his daughter's marriage, mightn't it!" His last words were less a question than a cry of accusation.

There was no answer. Constantine adjusted a pearl stickpin in his cravat as if he had not heard. Nikki went on:

"In other words, no trouble in Europe until my fat cousin is safely off with her English dolt."

"Nicholas!" For the first time Constantine was about to lose his control.

Nikki spoke again, almost to himself. "At home they could hush up trouble, but not in Europe . . ." He turned to Hattie deferentially. "Do you want to try it, my dear, and see if they'll keep their word?"

Was he making this gesture before Constantine to prove his respect for her, or did he really want her to decide? Suppose they chose defiance and Europe; what could the Tsar do? Lurid pictures rose before her—kidnapping, dark figures in carriages down the street. Perhaps this was only her feverish imagination, though she had heard stories . . . on the other hand, things might yet work out if they went back and bided their time.

Constantine interjected with a word to Nikki. "The Tsar wants you to visit your poor mother to reassure her. She's really very ill. You may take your lady to the nearest town."

It was his last remark that won Hattie. "If you are willing," she said to Nikki, "I am."

Constantine got to his feet. "Thank you, Madame Lear." He was about to say something more, then, coloring, he turned instead to Nikki. "Another thing, the Tsar thinks it would be a good idea if you'd be more diplomatic with Sasha. He wants you to do your best to win him over. Will you try?"

When Nikki nodded, Constantine brought his heels together, bowed in a direction somewhere between the two of them, and walked quietly out.

In Munich, they had a few hours together before Nikki would have to leave for the hills where the Grand Duchess Sanni had taken a villa. They hired an open carriage and rode about the hot, dusty streets, saying little. They had accepted the compromise because there was nothing else to do, and at first it had seemed so much easier than they had feared that they had been relieved. Now a reaction had set in, and they held hands in a miserable and despairing closeness.

Presently they stopped at an open-air café where a small string orchestra was playing love songs in a corner. As they sat at their table under the trees, the wind swirling dusty leaves around their feet, Nikki said: "I brought you something from Vilno. It was to be your wedding present . . . but I think you'd better have it now."

He brought an old leather box from his pocket. As she took it, she covered the hand holding it for a minute, and looked at him with all her love in her eyes. He freed his hand gently and opened the box for her. Inside was a long double bracelet of diamonds. As he fastened it about her wrist, he said, "It used to belong to the Empress Eugénie."

The shining Empress, riding in the Bois, standing on the balcony with the Emperor as the confident troops below surged "on to Berlin!" The woman whose wrist had been ornamented by these diamonds had known glory, and then disaster, and now slow, dim years in the shadow. . . . Hattie kissed Nikki, and said nothing of her thoughts.

Nikki was back from the visit to his mother in a few days, and when Hattie met him at the station after her own dreary solitary stay in a hotel in the town, his wide smile comforted her immediately.

"Mama's quieted down. I gave her a promise to be good—which is vague enough, God knows. . . . I told her the Tsar doesn't want the matter talked about at all, and she accepted it. She was relieved, I think, because she'd much rather think you didn't exist at all." Nikki hugged Hattie's arm to him and kissed the tip of her nose. "She doesn't know that if you didn't exist, her son wouldn't either."

"But your father said she was so ill . . . ?"

"She has a new doctor," Nikki said, a look of somewhat shamed amusement on his face. "Another spiritualist, the worst of all. When I got there, I found her brooding over Mama like an owl

183

in black silk. Mama refused to send her away, even made me speak German so that her sorceress could follow! Mama's only in this out-of-the-way place because of that woman. It all began a year ago when Mama had trouble sleeping and this Bavarian quack 'cured' her. She wrote back to Mama that it was her mattress and that it must be sent to Bavaria to be 'cleansed.' A special courier took it all the way from Petersburg. He brought it back two weeks later. The woman had picked over the whole mattress and found 'invisible ingredients' that were causing trouble, 'enchanted leaves' that no one else could see. She had said incantations—and Mama slept like a baby. Mama was so impressed that she came to the sorceress, and now the woman lives in luxury; she has half the villa!"

He let out a long breath after his story. "Now, let's see about connections back to Petersburg . . . at least we can see each other every day there. . . ."

When they got back to St. Petersburg, they discovered that the long winter was beginning. The day after their return the sun came out through the clear cold of the first frost. Yet soon after Hattie's arrival she had a curious reminder of the summer and of the South. Katya handed her a letter, much postmarked, in French. It had originally been written in Yalta. She could hardly make out the words—then a phrase stood out—"beautiful American who so brightened our trip." It was from the Volga Queen. Hattie struggled over the letter until she could understand most of it. The old woman said that she thought often of their meeting on the steamer. She wished that she herself could come to Petersburg, but she had relatives there. . . . She wished that Hattie might have everything she hoped for, and that she and her prince would live in happiness at the capital.

Hattie answered her, and thereafter every few weeks brought a letter from some strange point, as the Queen halted in her travels. Nikki, amused and pleased, sent the old woman a leather-bound book with the Romanov crest. A delighted reply came back; she was showing everybody this token of "our Grand Duke and his wonderful lady." In the subtly hostile atmosphere of St. Petersburg, Hattie found herself genuinely looking forward to the touching warmth of the letters.

One evening at the opera she saw Mabel Grey again, but Mabel stared coldly past her. That same evening, on their way out of the opera house Nikki almost collided with a big-framed man whose large, finely carved nose dominated a florid face.

"I beg your pardon," Nikki apologized, turning. Then, "Ah, good evening, Count," he added, a little less pleasantly.

To Hattie's surprise, the other man gave only a curt nod and moved quickly away. Nikki flushed, and Hattie laid a hand on his sleeve. For a moment she was afraid that his anger would break out in the midst of the crowd. When they had stepped across the pavement, she asked:

"Who was it?"

Nikki spoke savagely. "The great Shuvalov, head of the Third Section!" She had had only a quick impression of coldness—and of high breeding. Nikki went on furiously: "How does he dare treat me that way in public! He's been prying into our affairs, mine and Papa's. He's hated Papa for a long time!"

By now Hattie had no reserve about asking Nikki political questions.

"How did it start?"

Reluctantly, Nikki explained. "For one thing, Shuvalov's pro-German, wants an alliance with them. Papa's a Pan-Slav, and he hates the Germans. Then, it's a fundamental difference. When the serfs got more freedom, it was my father's doing. You know how he thinks. Shuvalov and his kind want to shoot down all opposition, and they've been edging closer to the Tsar every day."

She turned the conversation to a less distressing subject. Nikki's moods were uncertain, and he was easily upset, though their own relationship had never been more secure. There were no more scenes, no more accusations. All his high-strung fluctuations came from this new situation. One day he was ready to accept it.— "Well, they seem to be keeping their word." A little later he would be gloomy—"We're fools to let them manage us like this! They're holding their fire now, but it will come."

"What about Sasha?" she asked hesitantly. "Are you getting along better?"

Nikki's look was contemptuous. "We don't even speak."

Softly she said, "You told your father that day you would try."

"That was that day." His tone was willful. A moment later he went on sarcastically: "Anyway, now they can go ahead with that great marriage to Queen Victoria's son."

185

The wedding was to take place in the spring, and after that? Hattie refused to think about it.

In these days Katya talked more and more with Hattie. They seldom mentioned her student sweetheart, Anton, but Katya had collected an amazing amount of the young intellectuals' gossip about the Court. Had Madame Lear heard about the Tsar and his mistress, the Princess Dolgorouky?

"They say he's been getting more and more repentant about her and her children; and the Tsarina, you know, is old and feeble. They claim that once something happens to the Tsarina, he's going to marry the Princess and recognize the children as his, make them legitimate!"

When Hattie repeated the story to Nikki, he said, "Why, yes, I'm sure it's true." But he seemed tranquilly unaffected. She felt sudden puzzled despair. What could happen to one Romanov would be forbidden to another. Politics and morals were so inextricably mixed, and the Romanov moods so wildly unpredictable. There were no certainties; there were only fantastic possibilities. She might as well drop into the Slavic mood of resignation and try to concentrate only on the happiness of being with Nikki from day to day.

She began to notice that Katya was looking unhappy most of the time. Some trouble with her student sweetheart, perhaps; it would be best not to interfere. But finally she spoke to her.

"It's nothing." Katya started to walk away, then turned back to weep. "Oh, madame, it *is* something. Anton!"

"He's left you?"

"Oh no—he's in trouble. They're questioning his friends, and he's afraid they'll all be exiled . . . Siberia."

Katya buried her face in her hands. Hattie thought of that terrible procession to the Volga barge. She stroked Katya's hair. "It's all right, little one. I'll speak to the Grand Duke."

She did speak to him that same evening, but as he listened he shook his head. "My dear, I'd help if I could, but it is a matter of the Third Section, the secret police—and the Tsar lets nobody interfere there. Nobody."

Their evening was spoiled, and when he left for an official supper, Hattie had the unhappy task of telling Katya. To her surprise, Katya was resigned.

186

"I expected it, madame," she said softly. "The Grand Duke is not in favor at Court. We'll just have to wait. But, madame, I won't forget what you tried to do."

It was that same week that Nikki bought a palace. On Tuesday morning he came running to the apartment on Millionnaya. "I've got something I want you to see. Come on." When the sleigh stopped in front of a familiar pink-plastered building on a fashionable avenue, Hattie exclaimed, "Why this is Princess Magda's palace, the Pink Palace. We're not here on a *visit?*"

"Yes," Nikki said, grinning—"a visit to my house. It's mine since this morning. A Grand Duke is expected to have a palace of his own, you know. I heard that old Magda wanted to get rid of this right away—said she had to give her daughter a dowry; everybody knows it's for gambling debts. I got it for a fine price, with a lot of the furnishings thrown in."

Taking Hattie's arm, he escorted her through richly paneled doorways, up a staircase of rose marble, to a white-and-gold ballroom done in Renaissance style. "You like it?" he asked, then led her through another long chamber in the style of Louis XIV; then to a balcony, from which they overlooked a massive hallway and another stair. Before she had had a chance to look at it he dragged her excitedly to one side. "Look, my smoking room. Moorish!" He indicated markings on its wall. "A pity—it was once covered with oriental sabers and daggers; she gambled them away." Then he brightened. "I've ordered a lot of new things, as fine as the others or better."

Bewildered, Hattie had said nothing. For the first time since they entered the palace he noticed her mood and turned to her reassuringly. "Dearest, this will be *our* home. . . . In the meantime you'll be here half the time, and we'll be in my other 'home' on Millionnaya the rest of it." He handed her a small ornamented key of gold and silver. "Your private entrance."

The remark was unfortunate. But she sensed that right now while his wild, unrealistic confidence kept on, he could not guess how she felt about the endless succession of little side doors. She tried to look properly pleased.

In the next room he proudly showed her a great fireplace with metal rings for a dozen people to warm their feet. "And did I tell you about this?"

As she followed him, she thought, "I have a real rival now."

The next day he sent her word by Captain Vorpovsky: she must join him at the Pink Palace. On the way she and Viktor discussed it. Clearly, the Captain shared her feeling about this elaborate acquisition—this pink elephant. "Do you realize it covers a whole city square, the building alone?" he asked, and his handsome face settled in worried lines. They sat in silence.

When they entered the palace, a dozen men were scurrying about, lifting and pulling at heavy packages, opening others—packages from that stream of purchases Nikki had made in Italy. As the Captain looked quizzically about him, Nikki took him by the arm.

"There's lots you haven't seen yet. Come ahead."

He led them up and down several bewildering levels along corridors and curving passages, and Hattie began to grasp the true vastness of the palace—and also its emptiness. Princess Magda had sold whole roomfuls of furniture to meet her debts. A master bedroom with skylights of stained glass had half a set of medieval carved furniture; next to it a dressing room was completely empty except for a few Sèvres ornaments standing on the floor.

Much of what remained was valuable: Gobelin tapestries, Aubusson rugs, cabinets of superb watches and ornaments; next to them stood half-broken chairs. Though the Princess Magda's last husband had been a man of taste, she had gradually let the place fall into neglect, replacing countless original pieces with lesser objects. The floors, Hattie saw, were superbly inlaid. The terrace of an enormous hothouse was exquisitely tiled, yet most of its delicate plants were dead on the vine, and the garden had been abandoned. It was a melancholy sight, and a disturbing one. Viktor turned abruptly and left them. Nikki did not notice.

"Come in here!" He piloted Hattie to a Pompadour boudoir hung in white lace and pink silk. "Think of all the lovers she brought to this place." He threw himself down on the couch, with the vapid gesture of one of the ancient woman's boyish admirers.

Hattie held out her arms to him in mock coquetry, then shook her head. "How many erotic debates took place here!"

"I don't think she ever debated," Nikki said with a grin. One of the workers for the Imperial warehouse bumped in with a picture, apologized, and left. Then, as a door swung open, Hattie saw a long hall, almost the length of the palace, completely bare. "The picture gallery," Nikki said thoughtfully. "I ought to be getting paintings for it." As they watched, the workman hung the picture he had been carrying. It was lost in the empty expanse. "I'm going to buy a lot more tomorrow."

"A lot?" Hattie said casually, feeling inner panic. "Won't it be more exciting to fill it in one at a time? Then you can really develop a collection—find a few painters you want to concentrate on and wait until you can get their work, at a fair price, one at a time."

The suggestion bored him. "That would never end, and I want people to see it complete."

"But there'll be nothing left to improve."

He seemed puzzled for a moment. Then he said carelessly, "I'd sell some and buy more."

"Oh, Nikki."

With that, he gave her a cold glance. "Leave this to me, my dear, and worry about your chiffons."

He had never used such a tone before. She had been able to stop the fantastic purchases in Italy only once. Suddenly tired, she excused herself and returned to her apartment.

There she found tragedy. Joséphine sat on the sofa, and Katya lay sobbing, her head in the Frenchwoman's narrow lap. With a shriek, Katya ran to her.

"Oh, madame, they've taken Anton. They took him from his house." She was crying wildly, but the words came out. "When his mother tried to—just tried to—kiss him good-by, they, they hit her in the face! . . . They said she was trying to give him a message."

Hattie stood still in horror. "But why did this happen?"

Katya had sunk down to the floor. Now she raised her head and said quietly: "They claim he was in a plot to assassinate the Tsar. They'll try to make him talk, but he won't. I'll never see him again. Never again."

Hattie and Joséphine looked at each other over the blond head. There was nothing either of them could say; both knew that she spoke the truth.

EIGHTEEN

For weeks, as Hattie looked on, the men moved in and out of Nikki's Pink Palace.

"You care more about this place than about me," she told him, half smiling.

Patting her cheek, he went on with his arranging and rearranging of the pieces. Then suddenly one afternoon he announced that he was bored. "Let's drop this. We haven't been to the theater in a long time. Let's go tonight! It's something I think you'll like."

He refused to tell her the name of the play, but his air of mystery and importance impressed her with the feeling that it was a special occasion. She wore her most splendid evening dress, her Fabergé collar of pearls, and carried a large white ostrich-feather fan that Nikki had sent her from Nice. Joséphine exclaimed in pride. Her mistress had been only another one of hundreds of elegant women in Paris, but here in the last year she had gone beyond chic, into true distinction. Tonight she looked like a Grand Duchess, and the soft radiance of the pearls, the swirling white of the feathers that she held, actually seemed to dazzle Nikki when he met her. "You'll be the only one there to watch the play!" he said.

When the curtain went up on the first act, Hattie discovered that they were about to see a Russian production of *Fanny Lear*. In the dark she touched Nikki's hand and whispered:

"I don't know whether to kiss you for your thoughtfulness or scold you for being indiscreet."

She was delighted by the first act, but toward the end of the play she began to feel oddly uncomfortable. She heard one of the stage figures tell the heroine:

"You've made the most of your opportunities. And you've never made the mistake of falling in love."

It was Cora Pearl who had told her that she was missing her chances. She could see the childlike face in its shrewd reproach, even now. She realized all at once that she had chosen the name for its sound, but that she had not considered the character of the stage heroine. Henceforth she would call herself Mrs. Blackford in public and keep Fanny Lear as an intimate name, which only Nikki would use. She was thoughtful as the curtain went down.

"Thank you. It's been an enlightening evening."

Descending the great stairway, she caught the glance of Eugene Schuyler, the secretary of the American Legation. He bowed stiffly, and his prim features contracted in a smile. She noticed his companion, a trim, genial-looking man of about fifty—undoubtedly an American, judging by the poor cut of his expensive suit. He was staring at her with marked interest, as if he expected Schuyler to introduce them. As she anticipated, Schuyler did no such thing. Nikki said in her ear:

"The man with Schuyler is the new American Minister, Mr. Jewell." Mr. Jewell looked far more like a human being than his brilliant secretary. She hoped they would meet again. She told Nikki about Schuyler and the sweet peas that must go, unfailingly, with beef. "I've been uncouth for years without knowing it!" he said, laughing, but added: "Still, Schuyler's a good man, I hear. Very dependable and honest."

Nikki had to go on to a Court function, and left her at the Millionnaya apartment. She was startled to find all the lights on in the drawing room. Joséphine and Katya were waiting for her; both were crying.

"Oh, madame, it's Anton!" Katya ran toward her. "They've had him for questioning all this time, and now I've heard what's happened. Siberia, last night, and no chance for anyone to see him."

Hattie put her arms around Katya, and Joséphine went to a little cabinet to get some brandy. "Now, now," she said as she handed it to Katya, "You must try to rest." But Katya could not be still.

"Once one goes to the fortress nobody ever knows. No charge, even. And Anton was innocent. Oh, madame, he was!"

The round blue eyes were passionately earnest. In Hattie's mind a dreadful, unspoken thought arose. Would they question Katya too? Katya seemed to pluck the thought out of the air. She said, almost to herself: "And the guards in that prison—for the women, too—the kind of women guards they have! They use clubs and whips with metal screws on the end. There are some that'll tell people, in a proud way, how many they've crippled."

These stories could hardly be believed, but Hattie took Katya's hands in hers. "Come, we must get you to bed."

In the morning Joséphine came to Hattie with new alarm—Katya had gone. Her bed had been neatly made, and she had taken her clothes. They grew more and more concerned. There was nowhere for them to inquire. They did not even know the name of the faraway village where her parents lived.

But the next day the postman delivered a crudely written note addressed to Hattie. Madame must forgive her; Katya was hiding with friends, and praying that she would not be discovered. Madame must never tell that she received this letter, and she must burn it. Katya hadn't told this the other day, but that same morning she'd heard about Anton a man had come to her with an offer. The police were watching and they knew she was a friend of revolutionaries—a sympathizer. He had told her that nothing would happen to her if she agreed to help him to keep a close watch on Madame Lear and the Grand Duke, listen to everything, and make regular reports.

"But this I could not do. I am going back to my parents in the village. I kiss your hands, and I will remember you always."

The room seemed to move about Hattie as she finished reading. And there was nothing she could do. She felt caught in a tightening and unseen net. She could not go to Nikki; she felt uneasily that he too might be caught in this net . . . with her, with poor Katya!

January was ending, and it was time for the marriage of the Tsar's daughter Marie, and Alfred Duke of Edinburgh, Victoria's second son. The capital filled with German princes, Austrian archdukes, representatives of all the countries in Europe. Palaces were crowded; the guests spilled over into hotels. Cannon boomed, bells pealed, and Russian and British flags waved as the troops marched in elaborate drills through the streets.

Nikki, with the rest of the Court, was called on to play host to

192

the throng at receptions and dinners, midnight suppers, noon breakfasts. Though he groaned over it, he had no choice.

He could sometimes manage to see Hattie only a minute at a time. In one stolen half-hour, he brought her a surprise—a small table, richly inlaid, that he had had since he was a boy.

"It has a secret; you will be the only one who knows beside myself." His sensitive forefinger pressed in a little inlaid mother-of-pearl star. Several inches away from it a hidden mechanism released another piece of inlay and out slid a drawer about ten inches long. "It's from the Marble Palace. I used to hide papers from my tutors there."

"I'll think of you every time I see it. . . . I'll put it here, by my dressing table."

"Thank God the wedding's tomorrow," he said, "and then you'll have me and not just reminders."

"Joséphine heard that at the last ball there is a gallery where one can watch"—she hesitated—"and that outside guests may attend."

He nodded. "Why not? Karpych will come for you tomorrow, and I'll be able to look up and catch a glimpse of you to help me through."

Silence fell between them as they both thought that she ought to be there at his side. After this vital date, they would know.

January 26, 1874, had the flavor of a spring day rather than that of Petersburg's winter. In the evening, when Karpych knocked, Hattie was ready, and he escorted her out to the carriage with a proud grin. They found themselves in a thick flow of vehicles all going in the same direction on the Nevsky Prospekt, past the spires of the cathedral to the Winter Palace.

Leading her through the inevitable side door, Karpych murmured to an attendant and handed him a ticket. She saw that many other women were waiting in the foyer. At a signal, they were all waved up a flight of narrow stairs to the gallery over the columned ballroom. They reached it just at the ceremonial opening of the ball. Bare-shouldered women in feathers and velvets, satins, silks, and ribbons, and men in uniforms or in dark formal dress, were taking their places in two long lines, leaving a broad aisle between them.

A silence fell as the precise stately figure of the Grand Marshal

walked slowly down the center of the double line. Immediately
after him came Alexander, Tsar of All the Russias, a solemn figure
in white, his jeweled medals glittering across his chest. With him
was the Tsarina, looking so pale and frail that Hattie wondered
how she could support the weight of her heavily jeweled attire.
Her gown was of almost incredible magnificence. It was of
cream-colored satin, decorated in pearls, and a jeweled train
stretched far behind her. Her neck, arms, breasts, and waist were
an unbroken glitter of diamonds. She wore a veil that fell from
a diadem decorated with yet more diamonds.

"She's wearing twenty-eight thousand rubles' worth, at least,"
murmured a woman behind Hattie.

As the Tsar and the Tsarina went slowly forward, the women
sank to the ground and the men bowed low. In an unfurling wave
of movement as the Tsar walked by, the red coats, white furs, and
pale flowers flashed in the background of mirrors.

Four men, walking abreast, followed the Tsar. They were
representatives of the Crowns of Russia, England, Denmark, and
Prussia. Nikki had given her the background for the sedate arrangement; it had been a compromise after hot debate over
precedence. Near the head of the line, facing the approaching
procession, Hattie suddenly saw Nikki, slender and distinguished
in his white uniform. He was smiling—his faint mocking smile. As
if he sensed her gaze across the room, he looked up, and their eyes
met for a moment. It was like the moment of their first meeting in
the crowded opera house. The swirling, magnetic atmosphere
around them existed only to emphasize their own private excitement. It seemed a physical effort for him to look away.

Hattie caught whispers behind her and she turned her head to
see the young bride coming in on the arm of her husband. He was
in uniform; her costume was of silver cloth, its train trimmed
with ermine carried by four attendants. But the most resplendent
thing she wore was the lustrous ancestral coronet of diamonds in
which all Grand Duchesses of Russia were married.

Hattie's eyes searched among the watching throng and saw the
awkward figure of the heir apparent near Nikki. A little behind
him was a small, pretty woman whom others were watching also,
the Princess Dolgorouky, mistress of the Tsar. Her costume
was restrained, her look one of quiet dignity as if she understood
that all of them were searching for the smallest sign of arrogance.

194

Every woman there, of course, knew the situation. Was each wondering how it would work out? Perhaps the Tsar himself, or even the young Princess, would die before the pathetic, aging woman who led the line. Hattie's eyes were thoughtful. In the Princess Dolgorouky, she saw herself.

Slow waltz music had begun, and the couples swung about in placid movement; from above she could see the patterns the dancers formed as they moved to the cadences of the music. Small tables were being set in place at the sides of the room and waiters went about with huge silver trays bearing glasses of wine, fruit, and ices. In the center of it all was a wide semicircular table on a raised platform for Tsar and Tsarina, bride and bridegroom, and the most important guests, with their diamond crosses and flashing jeweled decorations. At one side of the ballroom, Hattie saw another figure she had been looking for. There he was, the stocky Prince of Wales. Her mind went back to the first time she had seen him, her first night in Paris, driving along the Champs-Elysées. She remembered thinking then that was as close as she would ever be to royalty. The thought ended ironically; she was still removed, still seeing, not seen.

Nikki returned to her the next evening. The last honor guards had stood at attention; the trains had started away with the last foreign guests. Nikki stretched out on one of her white-satin sofas with a sigh of infinite relief, but he smiled reminiscently.

"Those last parties, the private ones for the princes . . ." He shook his head, and to her surprise he blushed. "I can't tell you everything. But some of it . . ."

He described the bachelor dinner at which a group of workmen dressed as chefs dragged in a set of heavy metal shells. When the presiding officer clapped his hands, the shells slowly opened. In each lay one of the most celebrated dancers in the capital, presented in a style that offered a further novelty. Each girl, chosen for her symmetry, was dressed in a single bud of a rose.

When five waiters arrived, balancing trays with glasses of champagne, one of the gay young princes crept up to the first waiter, lifted his toe, and sent the tray high in the air. As it crashed to the floor, every glass smashed, and the floor was wet with the wine.

"That was only the beginning."

Hattie's eyebrows raised.

"After you the deluge," she said ironically.

Suddenly more than the surface import of her remark came to her mind. What of their own fortunes after this fateful wedding? Nikki's eyes showed that he knew what she was thinking. Catching her hand, he laid it against his cheek, and they looked at each other in silence.

NINETEEN

THEY HAD HOPED FOR SOME WORD FROM THE TSAR ABOUT THEIR
marriage, but none came, and when Nikki finally requested an
audience after several weeks of waiting, it was denied him. There
was nothing they could say in protest; their life was continuing
without Court interference. But would this uncertainty go on
forever? The worst of it for Hattie was that she knew Nikki
would try to spare her any indications of trouble in the air, and she
could tell only from the heightened gaiety and nervousness of his
behavior that there must be something wrong. Still she could not
question him directly.

He had not yet moved into the Pink Palace, but was busy
"finishing" it. He would not allow her to go into the conservatory,
and kept the huge doors closed tight. She could hear workmen
moving about within, the sounds of their activity muted by the
heavily curtained glass doors. At the end of February, he finally
let her see.

"And now, madame . . ." He waved his hand like a circus
entrepreneur as he threw open the glass doors, watching her
profile eagerly, hoping for surprise and delight. She showed
both.

The transformation was hard to believe; in place of half-ruined
bushes and plants, she saw a blooming garden. He had quadrupled
the space. New expanses of green reached beyond the formal patterns of roses in front of her; she caught a glimpse of a tiled grotto
on one side of the room, and in the center, small rows of orange
trees stood in a square of feathery green trellises, around a
hidden enclosure. She heard birds chirping somewhere. Pushing
aside a palm branch, she took a few steps into the steamy, sweet-

smelling warmth and saw an enormous cage. Birds in flaming reds and greens and yellows darted about in it; one flew toward her squawking, so that she drew back. The scale of the whole transformation appalled her.

"Wait!" Nikki said excitedly, turning a switch in a panel beside the door.

A pair of fountains at her right began to play, and in the center of each a gas jet flared brightly so that small rainbows played about the falling water. Between the fountains was a pool bordered in white marble where rainbow tropical fish swam lazily to and fro.

He led her enthusiastically down the white-pebbled pathway. "Now you must see this grotto." He showed her a stone-lined cavern with a waterfall trickling at the back. At one side of the falls, dimly lighted, stood a figure of Leda; on the other side, Venus and Adonis gleamed whitely in the soft air.

"You haven't seen the best," he said, leading the way to the center of the vast, glass-enclosed garden, past the row of orange trees, to the screen of feathery growth. He raised the leafy branches so that she could look into the green recess. In the center was another statue, its warm marble glowing from the light of small gas jets hidden in the potted plants surrounding it. It was the naked statue of herself. She saw suddenly that this was the center of the whole room; fountains and grottoes, pools and aviary, all flashed around it. In this lush setting, the figure seemed shockingly voluptuous. He looked at her in triumph.

"Nikki," she began; then her voice dropped. "I've never seen anything like it."

When they returned to the marble front hall a servant whispered that there was someone to see His Highness. A swarthy Italian stood in one of the drawing rooms, an object, obviously a canvas, under his arm.

"I forgot," Nikki whispered. "You'd better stay here. I'll join you presently."

Several minutes after their low-voiced conversation had begun, she hovered near the door of the room and glanced in. Nikki looked annoyed, but only for a second.

"Come in," he said. "I'm in fine luck this week. I'm getting hold of a Greuze, a Van Dyke, and this one—a Rubens!"

Her eyes went from the picture to the face of the dealer; in it she read cupidity and a touch of wariness. She lifted the portrait and held it off at arm's length. She knew little of Rubens, but she remembered talk she had heard in Paris.

"This certainly doesn't look like a Rubens. The flesh tones are so dead. . . . Don't you think you'd better get another opinion on it?"

Her knees were trembling. The dealer's high-pitched and belligerent interruption was a relief.

"I didn't say it was a Rubens! I told His Imperial Highness that it was of the school of Rubens."

She handed the picture back to the dealer and turned to Nikki. "It was your impression from him that it was an original Rubens, wasn't it?"

Nikki's face grew uncertain. "I think so."

"Nikki, it's a Rubens or it isn't. You were going to pay this dealer on the basis that it was. And Van Dyke and Greuze, you said." She faced the dealer. "Are those too of their schools?"

The dealer threw out his hands. "Madame, it is often hard . . . If the Grand Duke misunderstood . . ."

Nikki broke in, enraged. "You trickster! Take these fakes with you!"

"You'll be more careful?" Hattie asked as the man hurried away.

"All right, love, all right. Don't crow."

But every day the procession of merchants continued.

"The art dealers are now bringing objects on trial," Viktor told her, "and he forgets to return them." He shook his head. "So he'll pay for it all in the end."

Yet Nikki had sent back a number of his earlier acquisitions, she reminded Viktor. He still looked dejected and said: "Nikki isn't getting his money back, exactly. He just throws the stuff together, and no matter what he paid originally, they give him very little. He doesn't seem to notice, or care. He never knows how much anything costs when he buys it, because he just initials the bill; then when it comes time to get rubles back for it, he really worries."

She went along the next time Nikki took a dealer through the palace, hurrying him from one room to another with his long-legged stride. Picking up one object, Nikki carried it around for awhile, then set it down. Then he picked up other things indiscriminately. "I'll sell that and that and those over there." Some had cost enormous sums. The dealer gave him a packet of notes, but Hattie saw that they had ridiculously low numbers.

She was afraid to intervene again, and remained silent until Viktor pointed out a cheap statue of no conceivable value.

"He paid more for that than they gave him for that set of Chinese ivories."

An hour later she asked Nikki why he had sold the ivories. Was the statue really worth more than they were?

His eyebrows went up. "You are an authority on ivories and statuary?"

Her anxiety made her desperate. Ignoring his sarcastic tone, she asked simply:

"Is your income, whatever its size, large enough for this madness?"

Nikki's green eyes flashed. "Madness!" Then he bowed his head. "You're right," he muttered, "I've got to take hold of myself."

When she touched her hand to his, it felt burning with fever, and she insisted that they go back to the Millionnaya apartment. There he lay down willingly enough, and he went to sleep almost immediately under the touch of her hands on his forehead. When he woke, he turned restlessly as if he did not know where he was, muttering to himself:

"No! No! I won't let them! . . . Fanny, help me!" She tightened her arms around him and his eyes came to her face in recognition and gratitude. "My dearest . . ." But after only a few minutes of calm, he rose and insisted on leaving for the Marble Palace.

He became more and more self-absorbed and distracted.

"What *is* it?" she asked Viktor, but he had no answer.

Spring arrived prematurely in March, covering the parks and borders of Petersburg with a gay, frail blossoming. Then it changed back to raw and slushy days; winter had returned.

Hattie fell ill with a severe cold in her chest. She could not seem to shake it off. It was like the one she had contracted in Paris at the end of the siege, and Joséphine was worried. Nikki behaved as though she were going to die. He insisted on dispatching one of his own doctors to her. The doctor nodded sagely, prescribed expensive medicine, and did her no good at all.

Lent passed, and Easter dawned. Hattie was well enough to go again to the midnight service, but this time it failed to stir her; her mood matched Nikki's in distraction and gloom. The figure of the Tsar in the midst of his adoring subjects filled her with such resentment and anxiety that she left the service early. She returned to the apartment, where Nikki, who had apparently been affected in much the same way, joined her shortly afterward. Pacing up and down the long white room, he suddenly asked her:

"Do you still keep your papers and jewels at the American Legation?"

"No. I did that only when I was in Petersburg alone, while you were in Khiva. Why?"

"Oh, I don't know," he faltered. "It might be safer if you did."

He did not press the point, and she let it pass, thinking it was only part of his nervous unrest. A week later he came hurriedly into her apartment. His eyes barely met hers as he spoke.

"Darling, I feel trouble—in my bones."

"Nikki, has anything happened?"

"No, but I feel it," he repeated. His hands shook as he drew two documents from his tunic and handed one of them to her. "This is for you."

She read it with a sense of growing unreality. In it Nikki promised solemnly that should they be separated, he would give her five thousand rubles a year for life; in case of his death, he pledged himself to leave her a hundred thousand rubles. She protested.

"Nikki, I've never wanted anything like this . . . Separation, . . . death! What are you thinking of?"

He took the paper out of her hand and gave her the other one, saying only, "Read this, too." She found it a complicated version of the other. In this one he agreed to pay her various sums a month, whether or not they separated; it was full of conditions and sliding scales that she did not understand, and which, actually, seemed wildly confused. Before she could question him, he handed her a third paper and asked her to sign it. It was a letter of exchange on her bank for 10,000 rubles.

"I need it," he said in a low voice. "You won't deny me this?"

She had it to give him, of course. He had been generous in keeping up her account, and she had rarely needed to use it; yet the note was the most frightening evidence of his disturbance that she had seen. She signed it, but her fingers were trembling. He almost snatched it from her hand, kissed her on the forehead, and said:

"Someday you'll understand why I need this money. It is for

you, dear—for us, if everything fails." He laid a mysterious finger on his lips and left her.

Alone, she re-examined the papers and put them aside. After a moment she remembered the secret section in the little desk; miraculously, she also remembered the exact tiny mother-of-pearl star to press. The hidden drawer came out, and she put the documents away. At least, if Nikki asked for them, she would be able to find them, and in the meantime no one else would see how strangely his mind was working.

The next day he was back again, beating on her door in mid-morning. When a startled Joséphine let him in, he pushed past her into Hattie's bedroom. Hattie sat up, her hair tumbling down over her shoulders, her heart thudding rapidly. He stood before her, swaying a little.

"Dearest, please take your valuables to your Legation today—everything. They may search here at any hour."

She did not know whether this was his imagination, part of his overwrought and uncertain state, or whether it was really true. In either case, her answer would be the same.

"Certainly, Nikki, at once."

She got out of bed and put on her velvet robe. He continued, in a strange, tense manner:

"Get your jewels ready, and my letters, and all your papers. I'll help you do it, right now."

She thrust her feet into slippers, ran to the door, and called Joséphine to bring her several painted tin boxes in which Nikki had once brought her candy. When Nikki went into the next room to get a heavy cord, she drew the new documents out of the secret section of the desk. As she did so, she impulsively substituted for them some of his letters from the pile on the table. She added her journal, and closed the drawer.

After they had finished the packing, Nikki seemed to feel better.

"Fanny, this trouble may yet blow over," he said. "Listen carefully. If it does, in a week or so you take this all from the Legation and leave Russia as quickly and quietly as you can. I'll follow you."

"Leave Russia!"

"If you are allowed." His eyes held hers. "They may arrest you."

"In God's name, Nikki, what's happened?"

He went on, distractedly: "But it may be too late. Siberia for both of us."

She cried out: "Siberia! What are you talking about—Siberia, for what?"

"It doesn't matter for what! Once they've made up their minds to it, there wouldn't have to be an excuse." He looked at her, his face as tortured as his words. "Oh, you've done nothing at all; but they could blame you, make it look . . ." He faltered. "They haven't said it yet, but I'll tell them you're not to blame when they question me again." His hands snapped nervously at his side.

"God help us, Nikki—tell me what this is! They questioned you? About what?"

For a moment he stared at her as if she too were an enemy; and then he sank onto her bed, his head in his hands. His muffled words were evasive.

"Shuvalov and his police. They're trying to make a scandal." A cold finger touched her heart. Shuvalov, who hated Nikki and his father! Nikki raised his head, looked at her despairingly, and said:

"Somebody's stolen diamonds from my mother, and they're· investigating. They're even hinting that it's poor Viktor."

"But that's ridiculous. Viktor would never do a thing like that."

Nikki's voice was firm. "No, he wouldn't, and he didn't. . . . I . . . I can't tell you any more."

She went over and knelt beside him. She smoothed back the hair that fell into his eyes.

"Nikki, maybe it isn't as bad as you think." She pressed away the lines at the corners of his eyes. "Just rest for a while." He lay back on the sofa as she drew the curtains, and they were close together in the dim room. She lit the tile stove, leaving its door partly open to dispel the late afternoon chill. On the white ceiling, the flames played irregularly, and she felt a false security. They were alone, shut in from the hostile nation, the resentful Court. It had been this way—a dim room, the reflection of the flames on the wall, when they were first together, soon after their meeting at the ball.

She thought he was asleep, but he reached out a hand for her as she sat beside him.

"No matter how things turn out, you love me?"

"I'll always love you."

"Forgive me for the way I've hurt you."

"How have you hurt me, dearest?" She was crying. "If you ever did in the past, I was the one that was impatient and angry and brought it on."

He reached into his pocket and brought out a silk handkerchief, carefully knotted several times. In the center of it was a plain gold ring.

"Look, Fanny, I bought this in Vilno last summer. I thought I'd have it engraved with the date of our wedding. Now I know that they will never let us marry—in Russia." He rose, and drew her up beside him. They kissed, and he put the ring on the second finger of her left hand, saying, as if it were a ceremony: "With this I marry my wife of the left hand—the only wife I'll ever have."

The wedding ring was worn on the right hand in Russia. To those about them, one on the left hand would not mean a great deal. But to the two of them—she was his wife now. Whatever happened would be less hard to bear.

Suddenly his speech was clear, and logical. "This trouble brewing may blow over. I can't tell you what it's all about—you'll just have to trust me. All I can say now is that they will do anything to keep us from marrying, or to keep me from following you out of the country and taking you to America. We should never have come back—we were fools to trust them when we came back from Vienna! But if all goes well, we'll be able to get out together; still, if I should be arrested, you must promise to leave the country immediately—immediately! Schuyler will see to it that your rights as an American citizen are insisted upon at the border." He paused, then added with slow emphasis: "Don't try to figure out what you think is best for me, or for us. Just do as I say."

She felt an obedience that she had never truly felt before. "I will do everything. I promise."

"One more thing," he said. "There's a special performance at the Alexander Theater tonight, *Perichole*. . . . Papa and I will be in the family box. Be sure to go in yours, for my sake. There's so much talk, I want you to be there, to keep up appearances. Perhaps if we hold our heads high, we'll be able to ride this out." His eyes turned to her appealingly. "And just to see you across the theater will make it easier for me. I'll come back here after the theater, probably a little after midnight. You promise you'll go?"

She felt weak and exhausted, but she said again, "I promise, Nikki."

He left almost at once. She drew aside the curtains to watch him. Carrying one shoulder a little higher than the other, he crossed the sidewalk slowly to his carriage. She felt a chill of premonition. Could this be the last time he would ever walk out of her apartment?

There was just time to take the boxes to the Legation before she had to dress for the evening. As she drew on her fur-lined gloves, her eyes went with pride to the plain ring on her finger. "Wife of the left hand . . ." Yes, she was his wife. She didn't understand half of this, but she would do as he had directed.

She ran quickly up the Legation steps. At the door she stopped a minute before she knocked, to control herself. She did not want to seem frightened, as if she had come to beg. The new Minister, Mr. Jewell, had looked good-humored, understanding; might it be better to ask for him? No, she might run the risk of offending the sensitive Mr. Schuyler.

Schuyler was polite, as usual. "Yes, Mrs. Blackford? What can we do for you?"

He saw the boxes in her arms. He knew perfectly well! She said casually:

"Just some papers and jewels. You know how Russian servants are, always prying. You and Mr. Jewell wouldn't mind keeping them in your vault?"

His eyes were wary. "I believe we kept these things for you before, and I told you at the time that the service could only be temporary. You ought to get a box at a private banker's; you can well afford it." She ignored the barb in his last phrase, and said nothing. Her silence had the effect she wished. Schuyler looked uneasy, then sighed. "Still, of course we'll do it, since you're an American citizen—or so it seems."

Or so it seemed! Did he mean that the Legation might not be obliged to protect her; that he wasn't sure whether, living as she did, she could claim the rights of an American citizen?

"You Puritan!" she thought in rage. But she forced herself to smile. "Thank you." Mr. Schuyler wanted to get away. She gave him a pleading, earnest look and said again. "Thank you, Mr. Schuyler. Please thank Mr. Jewell for me as well."

When she got back to the apartment, Joséphine's expression told her that there had been no further word from Nikki. There was a letter for her, however, in handwriting she did not recognize; but she knew the address. It was one of the places where the Queen of the Volga usually stopped. A friend had forwarded it. What a relief to hear from her! Foolish as it was, Hattie could not put aside the notion that the "Queen" would bring her good fortune, as she had claimed she would.

Yet this time the handwriting on the envelope continued in the letter itself. The Queen had died two weeks before, and Hattie was one of a list of friends she had wanted notified. The note ended mysteriously. She had been in considerable agony at the end, and was certain that she had been poisoned. The friend herself wondered. Some people wanted an investigation, but the relatives would not allow it; now they were dividing her estate.

Hattie put her hand over her eyes. Death always disturbed her, and today it overwhelmed her. Had the Queen's suspicions, which had seemed only a strange quirk of character, been based on facts? Her thoughts, never very far away from Nikki, now went back to him. Was there genuine and terrible trouble behind his recent feverish distress, or was he growing ill? Both might be true.

She heard the sound of a footstep and looked up in apprehension. It was only Joséphine, bringing some tea. Hattie thanked her, but could not seem to sit quietly. She rose and paced around the room. As she stood at the window, she saw two men across the street. When her hand moved the curtain, they separated, but only for a few feet—and they did not leave the square. Joséphine's voice broke in.

"Now, madame, it's time we got ready for tonight."

Hattie nodded and went into the bedroom; she sat down at the dressing table and Joséphine took her place behind her and started to unpin her hair.

"Something frightful is going to happen." Hattie spoke her thoughts. "I can feel it."

"That's foolish," said Joséphine, trying to quiet her. But as Hattie held up her arms to receive the folds of her silk dress she

206

saw Joséphine's face behind her in the mirror; it was drawn with anxiety, like her own.

Tonight Hattie could not appear looking so white and strained. She touched rouge delicately on her cheekbones and dusted powder over it. Her jewels were all at the Legation, and Joséphine silently handed her a small gold brooch Hattie had once given her. It matched the only other piece of jewelry she was wearing, the plain gold ring from Nikki.

Never had so many people gaped at her; never had they pointed so openly. She clenched her hands in the white-velvet muff she carried, and set her lips in a smile. Mabel Grey sat near by, and, oddly, for the first time in months there was no hostility in her gaze. She darted nervous little looks in Hattie's direction—almost sympathetic looks, but they were not acknowledged. If Mabel had only been beside her, Hattie might have fallen crying into her arms.

Then, across the theater, she saw Nikki and his father come in. But where was Viktor?

Nikki's face looked oddly yellow. Once, as he rose in the box to shift to another chair, his father's hand helped him for a moment, and she realized that he had been drinking. . . . Miserably, she made herself smile; her lips ached with the effort. The figures on the stage moved without meaning or purpose. Finally the lights went on at the end of the last act. Across the heads, Nikki made a slight signal to her; as his father rose, Nikki's fingers dropped, and he followed Constantine slowly out of their box. Hattie hastened home to be ready for him.

When Joséphine and the new maid had set out a light supper on the table before the fire, she dismissed them. A glass in her hand, she swirled the wine in it absently as she planned the speech she would make to him when he came in. He must clear up this miserable mystery, and tell her how she could help him. She could be of so much more help if she knew exactly what the trouble was. But then she put down the glass and sank into her chair; whatever Nikki wished, she would fit herself to his mood. She couldn't make his burden worse by demands or questions.

Midnight had passed, and she expected him at any second. She waited, hands folded in her lap. The building was silent; outside she heard the carriages approach, rumble by, then disappear into the distance. Each time one approached she bent forward—was that the sound of his horses? No, she'd have known at once.

It was long after one o'clock. Something must have happened; no, she mustn't let this disturb her. Perhaps his father had detained him? Two-thirty, then three o'clock. Still dressed, still waiting, Hattie paced the floor. When four o'clock came, she could stand it no longer. Wrapping herself in her furs, she took the key to Nikki's wing of his father's palace and went quietly out the door. The Marble Palace stood a few blocks away. It was silly to rouse Fyodor at this time of night—and it would take more time. She started to walk rapidly. If Shuvalov's men were watching, they did so from the darkness of some doorway. There seemed to be no one in sight.

Her own footsteps, echoing sharply in the silent streets, made her quicken her pace as if she were fleeing from the sound. Dawn had broken, sending a pale, pink light over the brick and wooden fronts of the buildings. As she crossed the bridge, the sun suddenly touched all the roofs ahead of her with a yellow glow.

Reaching the palace, she found the door under the porte-cochere open. She went through to the familiar entrance of the Renaissance hall. The door was locked. Her key turned and the lock clicked, but the door remained fastened. It was bolted from the inside. Her hand shook, and the key slipped and fell to the stone floor with a small, contained clatter. Only yesterday she would have knocked at the door, pounding until it was opened. This morning she feared that even the small sound of the key would bring men running toward her. She cast a last look, almost imploring, at the locked door. Then, silently, she retreated. Outside, she saw one of the servants sleepily preparing to sweep out the hall. He peered blankly at her.

"Where is His Imperial Highness?" she asked.

"They took him away, an hour ago. The police."

In the brightening light, his face looked as frightened as her own.

"Where?"

"They didn't say. Wouldn't let anybody talk to him, anybody at all."

In the brilliant dawn, her world was collapsing around her.

TWENTY

THE IMMEDIATE EVENTS LEADING UP TO NIKKI'S ARREST HAD BEGUN only a week ago. Much later Hattie was able to piece together the facts behind Nikki's terrible anxiety.

A week earlier, on a sunny April morning, one of the oldest ladies in waiting at Constantine's Marble Palace had happened to pass the Grand Duchess's boudoir. Nikki's mother had gone on another of her periodic trips to her Bavarian quack, and the noble-woman always made a casual daily inspection, primarily to make sure that the servants dusted properly.

She was about to turn away when a shutter blew open. Light entered in a long slanting beam, directed like a pointing finger at a large ikon near the canopied bed. There was something odd about it. Stepping closer, the noblewoman cried out. Someone had roughly pried two great diamonds from the center. Twisting her hands in fright, the lady in waiting ran out of the room. The ikon had a special significance. The last Tsar had presented it to Nikki's mother; few possessions had more meaning for her.

Breathlessly, the noblewoman presented herself before the Grand Duke. Constantine questioned her. Who had access to the Grand Duchess's room? Only two or three ladies in waiting who had not accompanied her, and two of the chief servants. It was not likely that it was any of them, though of course they would be questioned.

Word spread about the Court. The Tsar gave orders to notify General Trepov of the capital police and Count Shuvalov of the secret police. Uniformed men and others in plain dress appeared at the Marble Palace and stayed there for several days and nights.

Two mornings after the discovery of the theft, General Trepov was in the Tsar's study making one of his frequent reports when Constantine entered. Perhaps it was the mere sight of the man whom he did not like, perhaps it was the state of the Grand Duke's nerves, that made him cry out in irritation to the Tsar:

"Fine police you have! They can't even trace a clumsy theft, or the clumsier thieves either!"

Trepov sat up straighter. "Sire," he said, turning stolidly to the Tsar, "I have only followed your directions not to call too much attention to this affair."

"True." The Tsar nodded impassively.

With a quick sidelong glance at Constantine, General Trepov went on: "Still, if Your Majesty ordered me to find the stones and the thief, *without counting the cost*"—he paused—"we should settle it very soon."

The Tsar twirled a pen in mid-air, abstractedly. "Go ahead." He did not look at his brother.

Trepov bowed himself out, and Constantine looked after him sharply, but he had other more important things on his mind, and he settled down to talk about the appropriations for his Navy.

The next day, at a Court reception, Constantine joined a circle of men to find his old enemy Shuvalov among them. He listened as Shuvalov made pointed remarks on a delicate subject.

"Certainly . . ." Shuvalov's big, handsome nose twitched, "certainly, Russia has 'democrats' in high places. They want equality for all—provided they themselves keep their palaces and privileges."

There was an awkward silence. The four other men eyed each other. At last Constantine spoke, his eyes intent on his opponent.

"Yes, and others like 'authority' so much that they don't mind letting Germans run Russia!"

Simultaneously each one of the other men began a different topic of conversation, and in the ensuing babble Constantine and Shuvalov continued to glare at one another until the group broke up. At that, Constantine, turning away, called out in heavy German:

"Farewell, Herr Baron."

Behind him, the Count retorted in Polish:

"Farewell, Polish knight."

This was a cutting reference to Constantine's disastrous experience as Viceroy of Poland, which had hurt his influence at Court. It was a daring rejoinder, even for Count Shuvalov, and the Grand Duke stopped short, his face crimson. Then, controlling himself, he continued on his way.

Behind him, Shuvalov allowed himself to smile. As he smoothed the gray hair around his bald pate, he seemed to be contemplating a new, more challenging prospect. Leaving the reception a few minutes later, he gave a firm direction to his coachman; arriving at the Fortress of Sts. Peter and Paul, he went upstairs at a bound. The case of the diamonds stolen from the Marble Palace was growing more and more interesting.

An hour later, a high police officer, elegantly attired, left Count Shuvalov's office and walked briskly through a rear corridor. He knocked firmly at a locked door, and after a few minutes' waiting while an invisible process of identification went on, he was admitted. In that cramped, windowless room, for more than twelve hours two assistants had been interrogating Captain Viktor Vorpovsky, aide-de-camp of the Grand Duke Nicholas.

The room was smoky; as he entered, the fastidious officer lifted his hand to his nose at the reek of tobacco and the stench of the young man's sweat. The others rose immediately in greeting. "Good afternoon, Colonel." The officer seated himself and signaled for them to continue.

The Captain was in distress. He had been placed on a low, narrow bench, only a few inches across; after several hours he had complained of his discomfort, but there had been no change. He had been out late the night before. He had slept only an hour when Shuvalov's representatives had taken him from his bed. No one, including Nikki, knew where he was, or why. Also, for some reason that he could not understand, and against which he had protested vainly, they had stripped him. He sat now with his hands limply at his sides, his eyes looking intently up at the circle of his questioners.

One of the heavily booted men moved suddenly closer, and the Captain winced as a metal toe pressed against his bare foot.

"A half-hour ago you said you had never seen the ikon! Just now your words were"—he looked back at the paper in his hand—"'the big ikon by the bed.' How did you know where it was?"

The Captain's chest rose and fell; against his left breast his heart seemed to beat heavily. "I don't know." His voice was weak.

"You must have said it." His head dropped, and he murmured, "If I could have a cigarette, or a little vodka or water?" He had had nothing to eat or drink since they had taken him. No attention was paid to his appeal.

"Nobody said anything about an ikon that was by the bed!" The questioner reached over as if he were dealing with a child; he caught at the black, sweat-dampened hair and pulled the Captain's head back until his face turned to the light.

"Now we'll start over, and don't look away." The questioner moved closer. "Again now, Captain."

The Captain gave a low groan. His hands lifted from his sides, but they were pinned down by another officer, and now the hold on his hair tightened.

"I . . . I don't know."

Then, without warning, the young man vomited violently, spewing over the man before him. The questioner, cursing, released his hold on the Captain's head and stepped back to wipe his shirt. The highest-ranking official felt that it was time to interpose. He gave a weary sigh.

"We're getting nowhere. Why don't you leave me alone with this young man?" His tone was resigned, almost friendly, and Viktor, hunched forward, looked up with something like hope. "Clean up this mess." The Colonel snapped his fingers, and the others quickly brought damp cloths. While he waited, the Colonel went on, his voice gentle, "You and I can settle this between us, can't we?"

Viktor stared at him in silence, and nodded almost imperceptibly. Again the Colonel spoke.

"Young man, since you're in custody"—he hesitated—"and we're alone, you'll understand that they'll put back the handcuffs?"

"I don't care." The Captain swallowed. If he had protested, it would not have mattered.

The Colonel made a gesture, and then, to the Captain's surprise, the cuffs were snapped over his hands before and not behind him; swiftly his hands were pulled above his head, his body pivoted to a reclining position on the bench. The cuffs over his head were attached to the heavy base of the near-by stove, and other cuffs were clamped about his ankles and attached to the bottom of the bench. The Captain found himself bent in an arch, his arms and legs lower than his torso; he could hardly move, and already the blood was rushing to his face, which was hanging toward the floor.

With an effort, he managed to strain his head upward. The other men had gone out. He was alone in the room with the Colonel, who had walked over to the tile stove behind his head. The fire had almost gone out, though the room had remained warm. The Colonel removed his white gloves, reached over for several heavy pieces of coal, tossed them in, and used the poker to stir them. The response was immediate; a breath of new heat washed into the small room. Holding his head up in increasing strain, Viktor saw that the Colonel did not withdraw the poker, but thrust it deeper into the stove.

Then, sighing, the Colonel shifted a chair to a place close by his prisoner's knees. The Captain craned his neck in a spasmodic movement, staring in silence at the other man.

"Captain," the Colonel began, and his voice showed a hint of emotion, "this is a very distasteful business. You will, I trust, understand my feelings as a gentleman. Nevertheless, I think I should tell you that this is an important matter to us. And despite the friendship of one or two people, you hardly occupy a high place in Petersburg. In fact"—his voice sharpened—"we have reason to suspect that your loyalty to these people interferes with your proper patriotic duty to your Tsar and your country. You could hardly cause a great deal of excitement if you protested after this little session of ours. Providing you were in a position to protest."

The Colonel waited but Viktor was silent.

"Captain"—the voice softened—"you're something of a favorite with the ladies, aren't you? I gather you still want the . . . capacity for that enjoyment?"

From his tightened throat, Viktor cried out: "Please, Colonel . . . please! I have nothing to tell—how could I?" His head fell back in exhaustion.

"We'll wait"—the inquisitor glanced at his watch—"fifteen minutes."

In the stillness, a clock on the wall began to tick in their ears. Tentatively, Viktor tried to shift on the bench; the Colonel's leg was in the way and remained there. The Colonel lit a cigar. The scratch of the match, so close to his flesh, made Viktor jump. By now the sides of the stove were beginning to glow, and both

213

men were perspiring heavily. From the hair on his chest, small currents of water ran along the Captain's throat and over his hanging head. His forehead, close to the stove, was fiery red. The Colonel sighed again. Viktor's head lifted slowly, and both of them looked at the clock. They had five minutes left. At last the police officer spoke:

"I said we could settle this reasonably. Don't you think we could, Captain?"

The young man made a vague guttural sound. The muscles of his arms and legs were strained; he could not work himself free. The veins in his darkening neck swelled with the effort; then he subsided. The Colonel got to his feet, but only to throw off his coat; he kept on his spotless gloves. The eyes of the two men met. With a shrug, as if of regret, the Colonel moved toward the stove. Slowly the Captain's head lifted; the veins of his neck stood out again, and this time the head did not fall back.

Delicately, as if he were lifting an ice at a Court party, the Colonel drew out the glowing poker, its prongs red-hot. He spat and there was a hiss. The police officer returned to his chair, the implement in his hands like a rapier. Viktor's voice rose to a shriek.

"I won't . . . I won't!"

The Colonel waited for the heaving stomach to quiet.

"Still, as I was asking you, would you choose to give up the happy hours we were talking about? Would you? *Well?*"

As yet he had not thrust forward the poker; but already his victim could feel a dull heat on the upper part of his legs. The Captain's head sank slowly, then jerked again with a contorted gesture; the tendons of his leg twisted. As a slight burning smell filled the room, he let out a high, wild screech and thrust his body up with so convulsive an effort that his head dashed back violently on the floor. The Colonel sank back in his chair. He got up and went to the door. He opened it and beckoned to the waiting attendants.

"A glass of water! I think our Captain is ready to listen to reason."

After the water had been poured, gently, over the face that was hanging slightly awry toward the floor, they waited until the head moved. A slow whimper started, like that of a puppy.

"Captain?" The Colonel leaned over. "Captain?"

"Yes?"

"I have put the poker back in the stove. It will be ready again in a minute or two . . ."

"All right!" Viktor's voice rose as if he were shouting to a hundred tormentors. "All right, I'll say it the way you want!" He begged: "Unfasten me, let my head up, won't you?"

"Talk first." The Colonel snapped his fingers. "Take this down over there. Now, His Imperial Highness Nicholas Constantinovich himself broke those stones out of the ikon, didn't he?"

"Yes."

"Tell the whole story. And hurry!"

"His Imperial Highness called me on Tuesday a week ago," Viktor began, starting to sob as he spoke. He continued with difficulty: "In his hands he held two diamonds and several other stones that I had seen in the big ikon by his mother's bed. His instructions were . . . were for me . . . to take them to Paris and deposit them in his vault there."

He was silent and the Colonel leaned forward. "Why didn't you make the trip?"

The chest rose and fell, and the face, by now almost purple, lifted. "I argued with him. Suddenly, he agreed with me that this was madness, but he wouldn't return them or try to explain to his father. He . . . only made me promise not to say anything . . . to anybody." The Captain's stomach muscles twisted, and he sobbed.

"Has he got them now?"

"I don't know. I haven't seen him for two days. He's been distracted."

The Colonel cleared his throat. "Now as to that American woman. She knew all about this, didn't she? It was her idea to have him take them for her, wasn't it?"

"No! No!"

The Colonel's knee pressed into the prone man. "*Wasn't it?*"

"O God!" and the voice cracked. "No, it wasn't at all."

The Colonel dragged up the dripping head, then pushed it away in disgust. Then he stepped back and spoke as if he were making a statement in court. "Captain Viktor Vorpovsky, you are under arrest."

A moment later the Colonel was in the doorway, his perfumed handkerchief against his nose. He turned to one of the policemen. "Make sure now that nobody knows about this—anything at all about it." He walked briskly out and down the hall.

In the tiny, overheated room there was a choking sound and one of the police officers went over to the Captain. He had no orders, but he could be kind. Reaching out, he pulled the bench away, and the wet body slumped to the floor. At least the Captain would rest more easily there. . . .

An hour and a half later, at precisely 8:30 A.M., Count Shuvalov himself stood with a briefcase at the entrance of Constantine's Marble Palace. A faint smile quivered around the corners of his mouth. The Grand Duke would receive him presently. The Count was kept waiting half an hour, but when Constantine arose from his desk to stand with folded arms, Shuvalov's look had become one of sympathy.

"I have unpleasant news for Your Imperial Highness." His face grew graver. "Let me say first that my intentions are of the best. I hope we may be able to forget our quarrel, and do what is best for our Tsar and our dynasty."

Constantine's voice was icy. "What are you talking about?"

Shuvalov cleared his throat. "Please be patient. I am talking about your son Nicholas. I have been trying to ease the shock."

Shuvalov still stood before him, but Constantine made no gesture for him to be seated.

"What shock?" The Grand Duke's mouth tightened.

Shuvalov looked pointedly behind him as if he wanted to sit down before going on, but Constantine's silence was inexorable. The Count said abruptly:

"It was your son who took the diamonds from the ikon." The Grand Duke moved forward, a terrible look in his eyes, and Shuvalov spoke quickly. "Wait, let me finish. We may be able to handle the matter. Trepov and I have found a person who is partially involved and who may be persuaded to take the full responsibility. If you will just work with us we can avoid a scandal; otherwise, the whole Court will suffer."

Constantine's voice trembled in anger. "The whole Court indeed! You've invented this, all of this, to spread it about me and my son! Nikki would never . . . never do a thing like that." Tears of rage came to his eyes. "You low animal, you want to take

216

revenge on me for our private differences by humiliating my son! I'll bring him in here, and I dare you to say it before him."

Shuvalov's face showed no emotion. "Please call him."

Neither of them spoke in the interval while Nikki was summoned. He came in, still in his dressing gown, his face puffy with sleep. At the sight of Count Shuvalov, he stopped in the doorway.

"Come in, my son. There is something I want you to hear." He turned contemptuously to the Count. "Repeat this fantastic accusation."

Shuvalov spoke slowly, with heavy theatrical emphasis. He told the few facts he had learned. He concluded:

"I am not at liberty to divulge our source of information, but we know that the story is reliable."

Nikki lunged wildly at him, but the Count stepped back in time to escape the blow and Constantine quickly moved to catch his son's arm. Shuvalov walked swiftly out, Nikki's shouts dying away behind him:

"Scoundrel, dog! You'll be sorry you ever started this!"

Constantine relaxed his hold on Nikki and looked at him searchingly.

"Now, Nikki, how did the Count ever get this idea?"

"This story is a weapon for him against us," Nikki said evasively. "I can't talk to you now, Father. Give me a little time more."

Constantine stared at him for a moment and then said:

"Very well. You must come with me tonight to the opera. Shuvalov has undoubtedly been boasting about this far and wide. We must show that we are not disturbed." He paused, then repeated the words as if in reassurance to them both: "We are not disturbed."

Nikki bowed. "I shall respect your wishes." For one second he fixed his eyes on his father's with the look of an imploring child, then he wheeled and left the room. In his own apartment in the Renaissance hall, he rang for Karpych. "Find out where Captain Vorpovsky is. Whatever he's doing, get him here."

As soon as the dwarf was out of the room Nikki went to the tall chest of drawers in the corner. He unlocked the last drawer and searched in it for something. But Karpych returned far more quickly than he expected and he slammed the drawer shut in alarm. The dwarf's voice was frightened.

"They claim he was taken away. No one knows where he is."

"Taken?" Nikki had grown deathly pale. "By whom?"

Karpych spread out his hands and said nothing. Both of them knew.

Before the afternoon was over, Count Shuvalov and General Trepov had jointly requested an extraordinary audience with the Tsar. Tsar Alexander received them unhappily.

"I think I can guess what you gentlemen have to tell me."

"Sire," Shuvalov bowed, "we should not keep this from you any longer. In fact, we cannot. Your brother and your nephew both refuse to co-operate. Grand Duke Nicholas Constantinovich swears at us. He will not admit a word of the truth, even privately. His father supports him." Shuvalov opened his hand. "Under the circumstances, how can he be shielded?"

"Be seated, gentlemen." The Tsar's weary voice had new firmness. "You have full proof that my nephew took the diamonds?"

Shuvalov dug into his briefcase. "Here is the deposition of Captain Vorpovsky, his aide."

The Tsar read the document in silence, reread it; then, with a sigh, he pushed it away. He raised his eyes.

"Is there a chance that the Captain might alone be responsible—that in confessing he told more than the truth?" His face indicated that he might have heard of instances in which Russian police captives told more than what had happened.

"Oh no, Sire." Shuvalov spoke quickly. "The Grand Duke is deep in the matter; we are sure of everything. As a matter of fact"—his tone deprecated his own police work, modestly—"it wasn't a very difficult thing. The Captain spoke frankly and readily."

The Tsar covered his eyes with his hand a moment. He said, almost inaudibly:

"In that case, question my nephew at once. If it seems necessary, you will arrest him like any other subject."

The two officers exchanged quick glances; they leaned forward, all sympathy, all regret. It was so unfortunate a matter . . . The Tsar got up heavily.

"That American woman?"

Shuvalov asked a question in reply. "Would it not be necessary, Sire, in developing all the facts, to get her story as well?"

Trepov added: "And then she has certain information about the Grand Duke's plans to leave the country. In fact, we are positive

218

that she encouraged this madness of his so that he could have funds to live with her in some extravagant fashion outside the country. She must have letters from the Grand Duke. And other possessions."

The Tsar nodded.

TWENTY-ONE

HATTIE LAY COLLAPSED ON HER BED; ONE ARM HUNG LIMPLY DOWN toward the floor, a handkerchief just barely clinging to her fingers. There were no more tears left, either of terror or desperation or exhaustion. She lay very still, but her mind would not quiet down. She lived over the terrible hour since she had stood in the early morning sun at the porte-cochere of the Winter Palace, holding the key that would not turn in Nikki's door. She had done all she could to get word to him—sent Joséphine after Karpych with plenty of rubles for possible bribery—and the note telling him that as this mysterious horror increased, so did her love. What did this mean—this action of Nikki's enemies and hers? Were they pouncing on his extravagant behavior since he had bought the Pink Palace as a means of separating them? Had their trouble all started with Nikki's mad indulgence in Italy? No, it had really begun in Vienna when Constantine had stopped their marriage. It had all worked together. She could not disentangle Nikki's present desperation from his family's harshness, both now and in the past.

But such thinking was useless, or worse. Whatever he had done she was his; whatever they tried to make her say . . . She opened her eyes. She hadn't really heeded his words about the danger of arrest for both of them. They had taken a Romanov into custody; why would they hesitate to take someone like her—because she was an American citizen? She remembered what Nikki had told her, that Mr. Schuyler would help her if she had difficulty at the border. A quick glance at the clock showed her it would soon be time for the Legation to open. She got up from the bed and went to her dressing table.

As she combed her hair back rapidly, she saw that her face was burning with color. She touched the back of one hand wonderingly to her cheek. It felt as hot as it looked. She had not been aware of fever; she had become used to a little of it with her cough. But this was no time for illness. When Joséphine came in, Hattie was ready to go out.

"Karpych has the letter," Joséphine told her in a reassuring voice. "He thinks he can find a way to pass it to him. He tells you not to worry, madame."

Nikki had told her to leave if he were arrested, but this was impossible until she knew what had happened to him. She would do the next best thing—try to prevent her own arrest.

The first clerks were just reporting for work when she reached the Legation and she had waited only a few minutes when Eugene Schuyler hurried in. When he saw Hattie he stopped abruptly. Without preamble, she said to him:

"The Grand Duke Nicholas has been arrested."

"I've just heard." Schuyler spoke quietly.

"I shall remain in Petersburg until I am assured of his safety. But . . . if there is official interference . . . may I count on the protection of my Government?" In the silence Schuyler cleared his throat. Apparently he was not ready to commit the Legation. In panic, she heard herself say the wrong things. "I'm still an American citizen . . . and I'm related to the McClellans and the Pattersons and the Holmeses of Virginia." She caught herself. Would she ever have thought she would go on like her mother, rattling off her family names?

"Please!" Mr. Schuyler's look was pained. "We will certainly do all we can, Mrs. Blackford, in the event of an . . . ah . . . awkwardness . . . but we can promise nothing."

Mr. Jewell, the new Minister, hesitated in the doorway behind them. He looked at Hattie with interest, obviously remembering her from the night at the theater. About to speak, she checked herself. There was nothing he could do for her now, either, and she suddenly felt an urgency to get home. There might be word from Nikki. She bowed to them both and left the room. Mr. Jewell paused a moment in the doorway to watch her go.

The day passed with no further word. When Joséphine brought food, Hattie sipped a glass of milk and pushed the rest away. At the window she watched the passers-by, none of whom turned in with a message for her. Among them a pair of men went steadily back and forth opposite the house. She was used to that now. When she fell asleep in late afternoon, she dreamed of Nikki in torment, weeping, and she awoke in terror. Joséphine had touched her shoulder and stood wordlessly before her, holding out a piece of paper; it was a page torn from a book, a few words scribbled on the margin in Nikki's handwriting.

"I am a prisoner, but I am patient, and have hopes that everything will be better soon. Please have courage; you know you have my love. N."

Hattie calmed down instantly. Asking Joséphine to bring tea, she sat twisting the plain band around her finger—her wedding ring. All might yet be well. She was able to eat some cake as well as drink the tea. There was a sound at the door. Hattie ran through the salon to open it herself. Mabel Grey stood there.

"My dear Fanny, will you let me come in?" The Englishwoman's eyes pleaded, as well as her voice. Hattie held the door open. She needed a friend too badly. As she came in, Mable caught at Hattie's hand. "I am sorry this—this happened between us." Tears were in her eyes, and Hattie was touched.

"That's over now," she said.

Mabel took her in her arms. "Oh, Fanny, I gave them information, you know. I suppose I didn't realize how much harm it might do . . . but I was jealous." She kept her head averted. "I came because of something I heard a few minutes ago. Shuvalov and Trepov are with the Tsar this minute! If they get what they are asking for, they'll arrest you."

Hattie moved out of Mabel's arms. Though her pulse pounded, her voice was calm. "So it's going to happen, then?"

"Isn't there anybody you know who can help, anybody with influence?"

Hattie hesitated. Even in this new mood she would not tell Mabel of the visit to the Legation. She shrugged her shoulders in a show of helplessness, which was genuine enough, and asked Mabel to sit down. But they had said all they had to say to each other. As Mabel left, Hattie saw a familiar figure coming in the front door. She had forgotten that she had a dressmaker's appointment at 5:30.

About to ask the woman to return later, Hattie remembered Nikki's earlier words: "Keep on as if nothing had happened." She held the door open. The woman came in with a look of eager interest, her protruding eyes darting about her. So the story was well over Petersburg by now. Hattie pretended an interest in the silk spread out for inspection on the sofa.

"This is a nice pattern . . ."

Joséphine burst in upon them. "Five carriages have stopped outside, madame."

In a moment there was a violent ringing of the doorbell, a pounding and shouting at the front and the back doors of the apartment. Before Joséphine or the maid in the kitchen could open them, the doors gave way. Fifteen or sixteen men, some in blue coats, others in civilian dress, poured into the rooms. With a cry, the dressmaker hastened out, leaving all her materials. The gendarmes hardly noticed her departure. They were standing in a ring around Hattie and Joséphine. A uniformed officer advanced toward her.

"You are Madame Lear?"

"I am Mrs. Blackford."

He clicked his heels. "We are here in the name of the Tsar and by order of Count Shuvalov. To search your premises."

She replied, with more firmness than she felt: "I am an American citizen. Before you do this, you must get in touch with the American Legation."

"Impossible!"

"Some of the Legation staff should be here," she cried helplessly. The men had already begun to fling open doors, pull out drawers. The officer's eyes blazed. "You say you are an American, but you choose to live under our Russian laws, don't you?" he demanded, and she knew it was hopeless.

"At least let me dress." She retreated into the bedroom, and when she saw that the men there had no intention of leaving she stepped into her little dressing room and closed the door firmly behind her. She managed to dress rapidly before the door was opened by the impatient officer in charge.

"Madame Blackford, the search means also that you are under arrest."

As she watched, they examined purses, books, beds, linen closets; from outside came several big trunks, into which they dropped account books, telegrams, letters, magazines, monogrammed cigarette cases, silver tableware, ornaments. As they dumped trays and threw clothing to the floor, she tossed her keys to them. "You needn't break the drawers." All the time, out of the corner of her eye she watched the little table by her bedside with Nikki's letters in it. It had not yet been touched.

She suddenly realized that Joséphine was no longer in the room. From the Breton's chamber down the hall she heard a thin cry. "Madame, help me!"

Wildly thrusting aside a gendarme who tried to stop her, Hattie raced past him to find Joséphine in the middle of her room, her clothing in shreds, her face bleeding, as she scratched vainly at two men who held her. With something of Nikki's authoritarian manner, Hattie cried to the gendarmes to let go of her maid immediately. To her amazement they did. Joséphine collapsed on the bed and Hattie stood beside her. A man who was standing on a chair to search the top drawer of Joséphine's chiffonier held up some money in triumph.

Joséphine protested weakly. "Mine, my savings."

The man pocketed the money with a grin. "It's that one's"—he jerked a thumb at Hattie—"that she took from the Grand Duke, or if it's yours"—he grinned at Joséphine—"you stole it from *her*."

Hattie cried out in indignation. "Madame Arnault has been with me for years, and of course it belongs to her." She turned helplessly to the commanding officer, who had followed her into the room. "This money has nothing to do with me." His face was impassive, and she said defiantly as the bumbling hunt went on around her: "There's nothing you want here. Hadn't your spies told you?"

By this time, the officer had reached the same conclusion. "You will be able to tell us later where we can find what we want!" He jerked a thumb toward the door and started out of the room. Soldiers fell in on each side of her and she was marched out of the apartment into the hall. Her mouth still bleeding, Joséphine limped behind her. "Madame," she whispered, "where are they taking you? . . . Are they taking you to Siberia?"

Hattie turned her head and said almost inaudibly, "The Legation . . . Schuyler . . . tell him everything that's happened."

"None of that!"

The commanding officer pushed Hattie forward. Outside, hatless, her yellow hair streaming, she faced a hundred staring people. The police carriage stood at the curb; at least it was only a few steps away. But the officer in charge entered the vehicle alone, and her involuntary movement toward it was held back by the men on either side of her. She stood still for a second, in shock, and one of the guards tugged at her arm: "This way . . . walk!"

They started forward, past the elegant doorways, pushing through the clustering crowd, which was silent with some of the awe and sympathy the throng at the dock at Nijni-Novgorod had shown on that faraway summer day. The memory was not reassuring. She was being walked rapidly down a street leading off the Millionnaya; the apartment houses were beginning to look cheap and run-down.

"Is it far?" she asked.

"Not far to the House of Detention," one of the men told her, "but there's a lot of walking ahead of you before they're through."

The grip on her arm grew tighter, the pace more rapid. They were approaching a bleak gray building. Entering the heavy front door, they faced a flight of dark, narrow stairs. "Up!" one of the men said. A stale smell of cabbage and dirt enveloped her as she started to climb, but she could make out almost nothing in the dim light. She stumbled and fell, but was dragged to her feet again quickly by the guards. From somewhere ahead she heard a woman's cry. In her terror the cry sounded as if it came from anguish and physical outrage. She had chosen to live under Russian law, the police officer had said. She could expect to be treated as they would treat the worst of their own. Her only hope was that Joséphine would get to the Legation in time.

General Trepov bent over the tight-faced Nikki. They were back in Nikki's apartment in the Marble Palace and he was under what was politely termed "house arrest." This meant that he was confined to one room under constant questioning while officials ransacked the other rooms. General Trepov's voice had grown a little hoarse, but he persisted.

"You certainly must remember what money and jewelry you gave the American woman from the time you met her. Don't you realize we're trying to make this easier for you?" Nikki's lips contracted slightly. "Didn't she influence you in your buying—tell you what to order and how much?"

225

All at once Nikki spoke. "Whatever happened, you fool, she had nothing to do with it. Leave her out of this. Leave her out!"

Trepov tried another approach. "But, Your Imperial Highness . . . a woman of her charm . . . she must have tricked you into signing papers for her, getting you to do certain things."

"Don't be an ass." Nikki folded his arms.

An assistant entered with long pages of documents—a partial listing of Nikki's astonishing purchases. Trepov exclaimed aloud as his eye ran over the equipment for the hothouse, the statues, the Chinese ornaments, the tropical fish and birds. Nikki barely noticed him. As he had done many times before, he begged:

"Let me see her. Why can't I see her?"

An assistant questioner made notes; each time Nikki asked this the fact was put down. An official beckoned Trepov to the door.

"Look, Your Excellency," and he handed his superior a pawn-broker's receipt, which he had found in a drawer in Nikki's desk. Trepov lifted his brow; the date was fresh, April 10, but the amount so small—only 200 rubles.

"He could hardly have got so little for the diamonds. But send one of the men to check."

Trepov was more interested in the next find: several neat packages of currency in another drawer.

"Thirty thousand rubles." The assistant totaled it, then rubbed his chin. "If he sold the diamonds, or pawned them, this might be the proceeds."

Nikki heard them. Jumping up, he grabbed one of the thick ledgers and pointed to a recent entry. Trepov and the others looked over his shoulder. The thirty thousand rubles had been received from the sale of his horses.

Later that day, a bookkeeper was called from the Court. He had been there only a short while when he reported:

"His Highness is solvent, sir. True, he hasn't much left after his recent purchases; he sold too many things for too little, and he paid too much for what he bought. Still, he's solvent."

Trepov showed his annoyance. "How can you be sure without a much longer study?"

"But, Your Excellency, in my office we are supposed to keep a close watch over the financial affairs of the Grand Dukes." The bookkeeper held his ground. "This simply confirms the impression we already had."

He was about to launch into a full explanation when the man who had left with the pawnbroker's ticket ran back into the room.

"Your Excellency, look what I found—from that little receipt."

He opened a tightly clenched hand. In his sweaty palm two great diamonds shone like the superb stones they were. There was a shocked silence, and Nikki averted his eyes.

"For two hundred rubles!" Trepov finally spoke. "And when he already had so much." He gestured toward the package of money for the sale of horses. He shook his head and turned toward several elderly-looking men who until now had remained in the background. They were doctors, ordered by the Tsar as part of a special commission, including Shuvalov, Trepov, and several others, to investigate the sanity of the Grand Duke. Trepov shrugged toward one of the doctors. "It's your case."

A bearded man stepped forward. He was Doctor Balinsky, celebrated professor of the Medical Academy, who would direct the medical phases of the commission; and now, with his assistants, he took over. Through all that night and the next one the questioning went on, and steadily its tone became harder, more intensive.

"How did you feel when . . . ?" "When did you first . . . ?" "Had you quarreled with your mother?"

Nikki gave varying answers, sometimes clipped, again long and rambling. He grew annoyed, and then he didn't care; for a time, he ignored them all. Hour after hour, the doctors wrote their many observations.

Toward two in the morning of the second night, Nikki suddenly closed his lips. Relays of medical men pressed their queries, insisted on answers, demanded them! He watched them through half-shut lids, confused and frightened. Then he rose with a shout and began to talk in exclamations and cries that they could barely make out. Their pens raced across the pages. From sheer exhaustion, his tirade quickly reached an end. He sank back into his chair, muttering:

"Let me see my lady. Bring her to me, for God's sake!"

The renowned doctor nodded to his colleagues.

"His Imperial Highness must be taken away for further inquiry. To a hospital."

Nikki sprang up. "A prison, you mean!"

The doctor did not reply; instead, he looked toward the door, and from there came a quiet voice.

"No, Your Highness, no prison. A hospital, where you will get the attention you need."

The words were regretful; the face, and the smile, were those of Count Shuvalov, who had been waiting for this moment. As Nikki leaped toward the police officer, screaming his rage, four guards caught him and held him back. They led him out, his feet half dragging against the floor. He managed to gasp out two words:

"The Tsar . . ."

Count Shuvalov, with a quickness of movement that surprised his associates, darted ahead to face the young Grand Duke.

"You don't understand, Your Imperial Highness. This is done by the Tsar's orders."

Where was his love to tell him his old black dream was a lie? . . . Behind him, while the members of the commission gathered their papers together, a young doctor paused for a reflection.

"A temporary strain, and, of course, his mother's jewels are back. He should do well enough when we find the condition that produced the strain, and perhaps the woman would help him, at that!"

The naïve young doctor looked up, expecting to find relief that a member of the Imperial family would soon be out of disgrace, but at Shuvalov's swift scowl he realized his mistake. From the hall, the young doctor heard the voice growing smaller as the guards drew the Grand Duke away.

"I've got to see her. Why can't I see her?"

228

TWENTY-TWO

It was 9:30 at night and four hours after her mistress had been taken away. Joséphine lay helpless where she had fallen with a serious hemorrhage. Finally, the frightened little kitchen maid brought a doctor.

"No, you can't get up," he told Joséphine. "By no means." As he left, he temporized. "If you wish, I'll try to see that a message is sent when I come back tomorrow."

Joséphine sobbed and prayed. It was terrible to delay this way, yet what could she do? At a light knock at the door, she thrust herself up and cried out in relief. The maid ushered in a terrified Karpych, who had heard the news of Madame's arrest. Joséphine's cry came to him as soon as he entered the door. He must go to the Legation, immediately! But Karpych looked doubtful.

"They are watching everything now. They will not like this."

"Do you want to help your master and Madame Lear—or their enemies?" Joséphine's gasping voice had a fierce note. "You're disloyal, that's it," she snapped, "a traitor to them!"

Sniffing to himself, Karpych took her orders and started out. "Tell just how it happened." . . . He repeated her words to him. Downstairs, he dashed across the sidewalk and in one leap bounded up beside Fyodor, Hattie's coachman, summoned by Joséphine's helper only a few minutes before.

"Don't talk, just drive off, fast . . . to the American Legation." As he spoke, he glanced nervously behind him. Yes, there was a carriage—not one but two of them—in the dimly lit street.

Fyodor whipped at his horses. Karpych was keeping an eye on the carriage lights behind them; they were definitely following, and had been joined by a third, a still larger one.

229

"Don't slow up!" he cried to Fyodor. "Get around this corner on two wheels, and then up the other street."

The lurching turn gained them time, but the pursuing carriages were drawing closer. Karpych leaned forward, shouting at the horses. The pounding of the hoofs behind was thunderous. Ahead lay the Legation. Before their horses had stopped in front of the doorway, the dwarf had jumped out and was half sliding, half crawling over the sidewalk. The carriages behind had pulled up in a confusion of rearing horses.

Karpych pushed at the gate. It was locked. Between the horizontal top of the gate and the arched ornamentation he saw a narrow space, less than a foot across at the widest point. The dwarf caught at the top of the low gate, drew himself up with a powerful movement of his shoulders, and pushed halfway through. He could go no farther; he was stuck there, and the pursuers were jumping out of their carriages, racing up to the gate.

Hands grabbed at his tiny boots as Karpych gave another powerful shove, thrust himself forward, and fell to the courtyard on the other side, leaving his scarlet trousers and furred boots behind him in the hands of his pursuers. He was through. "You can keep the boots!" he yelled. While the men outside shouted to him, he made his way to the portico and pounded until Mr. Schuyler and a butler simultaneously opened the door. The secretary jumped back in alarm as a red-faced dwarf darted in, his coat torn back over his shoulders, nothing over his hairy, bowed legs. Karpych shoved the door shut with his posterior, crying:

"Madame Lear! The Grand Duke! Madame Lear!"

When Schuyler finally understood, he gave directions. "Find something to cover this man's . . . nudity," he ordered. "And we'll keep him here at the Legation a few days. Bring him some whisky. I'm going up to see Mr. Jewell."

The Minister was troubled. "It's a hard case," he said finally. "She's not the usual citizen whose rights we have to protect. . . . There seem to be involvements with the Imperial family, which make this very touchy." Schuyler nodded. "And in this country it's difficult, in any case, to protect the rights of the citizens of another nation."

In the silence, the two men eyed one another. Jewell, inexperienced in diplomatic duties, showed his uncertainty, and though

230

Schuyler completely disapproved of Hattie, he took the first step. "Still, she *is* an American."

"Then"—Jewell looked relieved—"then we ought to do something. We must find her and help her."

"Shall I go to General Trepov, the first thing in the morning?"

"Could you, maybe, tonight?" Jewell suggested. "We've heard of their tactics. . . . And she could be shipped off so easily."

Schuyler showed no hesitation at all; he left immediately. Jewell tried to go back to sleep, then resigned himself to the situation. He'd never rest until he heard from Schuyler. He turned on the water in the bath next to his bedroom. He had hardly slid into the tub before the butler knocked to announce the return of Mr. Schuyler, and Jewell called out to the secretary to come in.

"Bad news," Schuyler reported. "They said he wasn't at home. But I have reason to think that he was."

"Then we must send off a note, right now," Jewell decided.

The butler brought a box of paper, and Schuyler sat down on a three-legged stool to write.

It was under these circumstances, as the Minister soaped his chest, that the representatives of the American Government drafted their message to the chief of St. Petersburg's police. As they worked over it together, they decided that the tone should be firm but not peremptory.

"It's a delicate affair," Jewell murmured. "We have hardly any example to follow, have we?"

As he dried himself, Minister Jewell propped the note against the shaving stand and read it aloud:

"The Envoy Extraordinary and Minister Plenipotentiary of the United States of America presents his compliments to His Excellency Aide-de-Camp General Trepov, and has the honor to say that the apartment of Mrs. Blackford, an American citizen, was entered this afternoon by the police; that the apartment was searched and many objects were removed therefrom; and that Mrs. Blackford herself was arrested.

"The Envoy hopes that the General will inform him—to-night, if possible—as to why the police have arrested Mrs. Blackford and searched her apartment, of what crime she is being accused, and where she is at present. The Envoy does not wish to hinder the administration of justice, but since he

231

believes he already knows the cause of this affair, he assumes that Mrs. Blackford will not be deprived of the due protection of the law."

They stared at one another. "Tonight, if possible . . ." Jewell read the words again. "That's one reply we won't get." Then he went on: "Due protection of the law . . . that's a phrase they'll find hard to understand." As they nodded good night, each man felt an anxiety he would not admit.

The next morning they waited nervously together in Mr. Jewell's study. Finally, at noon, an officer with a noncommunicative look delivered a note:

"Aide-de-Camp General Trepov presents his compliments to His Excellency Marshall Jewell, Envoy Extraordinary and Minister Plenipotentiary of the United States of America, and in response to his note of April 28 has the honor to inform him that it is in pursuance of the orders and dispositions of Count Shuvalov that Mrs. Blackford has been transferred with all due care and attention to a place where she will not lack for anything, and where she will be in good health and in the best of spirits."

Jewell touched his whiskers. "Passing it on to somebody else, eh? . . . Count Shuvalov." He paused. "That brings it pretty high, I suppose. 'Good spirits and health.' . . . I very much doubt it!"

The note had only increased his alarm, and Schuyler reflected his feeling. "And of course there is no mention of the charge against her," he said thoughtfully.

"Well, I suppose I shall have to go to the Minister of Foreign Affairs," Jewell said, getting up.

"He's gone off for the summer."

"So he has. The summer, and it's only the end of April! Well, I'll see his assistant, that fellow Westmann."

Jewell came back within an hour. His face was angry. "We forgot. It's the Tsar's birthday, and every office is shut."

They could only draft a note to Westmann. They had written the inquiring note to General Trepov in French; this time they used the accustomed English of the Legation's communications to the Ministry of Foreign Affairs.

"A request, Schuyler, not a demand." Jewell paced the floor as the secretary scribbled. "A note so that Westmann can consider it all in the light of a personal interview. After all, the Imperial family is involved." Jewell let out a long breath. "It's hard to handle this as if she were—well, of the highest reputation. Still, such a lovely woman. I certainly hope they'll"—he hesitated—"use discretion in handling her."

He saw that Schuyler's face was completely expressionless. The secretary made no comment, but continued to write the last few lines of the note. Then he read it to Jewell. The message stated rather than complained.

"... When the search and arrest took place, Mrs. Blackford desired that this Legation be informed of the facts and requested the presence of one of the members of it, and these requests were not granted.

"May I be informed why the arrest took place, of what Mrs. Blackford is accused, and in what place she is confined? I also request that permission be given her to communicate with her attorney or with this Legation."

On further thought, Jewell wrote a private note to Westmann, in French:

"I have reasons to think that a very highly placed personage is involved and gravely accused in this affair. Wishing to avoid doing anything that may prove disagreeable to the Russian Government, I regret that I am obliged to send this official note today, and I hope that the whole matter may be arranged in a manner that will allow me to withdraw from the case."

Nearly a day had passed and they had made no progress at all. They had failed to find where Mrs. Blackford was being held; they could discover no accusation against her; and they had no assurance that she was even in Petersburg, that she had not been removed already. Theft of Romanov jewels, undue influence over the nephew of the Tsar—these were not minor offenses in Russia.

But still, what more could they do? It was the second night after Hattie Blackford had been arrested, and the two officials slept uneasily. The next day, no reply came from Westmann, the assistant to the Minister of Foreign Affairs. When Schuyler went to the Ministry, he was told that the Privy Councilor could not be seen.

Jewell was shocked. "Deliberately avoiding a representative of the United States!"

"I'll try his house tonight," Schuyler said.

There, on the evening of the second day of their efforts, he cornered a Russian official at last. Westmann was panic-stricken.

"Mr. Schuyler!" Westmann cried. "Leave me out of this! It's a matter of *extreme* delicacy. The Tsar himself is directing it, and Count Shuvalov. We in the Ministry of Foreign Affairs know nothing about this, nothing. Don't you understand that the secret police are above us?"

Schuyler nodded. "Very well, we will see Count Shuvalov. We will appreciate it if you will take Mr. Jewell to him tonight, or at least tomorrow morning."

"No! No!"

"Then why don't you take it up yourself with Shuvalov, unofficially?" Schuyler's exasperation was beginning to show.

"Not even unofficially, and I advise you and Mr. Jewell to make no effort to see the lady. Such a request is sure to be turned down." His look was pained. "Most earnestly I advise you to drop the whole matter. Our government would be forced to let the United States know how strongly it resented this interference."

Schuyler sucked in his breath. He left Westmann's presence and made haste back to the Legation.

"A mess," the Minister said when he told him, "and possibly a dangerous one." He stroked nervously at his side whiskers. "Do you think we ought to ask the advice of people more experienced in the capital? . . . How about the Portuguese Minister? He's lived here and in America for years; he knows protocol and backstairs procedure in both countries."

The Portuguese Minister received the American Minister with affability and listened carefully. Then he spoke.

"Very difficult, my dear fellow. If you don't get satisfaction soon I should call for a meeting of the whole diplomatic corps, for advice. Don't wait too long! You mustn't give them time to pack her off to Siberia. It would be too late for any intervention if they did that."

In his eyes the Portuguese Minister seemed to be conjuring up the Siberian marshes, and rather enjoying the vista. Jewell rose, his nerves on edge. A little later, he saw the British Ambassador, Lord Augustus Loftus, who agreed with the Portuguese Minister. "The rights of all foreigners are at stake. Yes, a meeting of all of us would be a good thing."

Jewell hastened back to the Legation. "Schuyler, Schuyler, where are you? We've got to act. She may be taken off already, or dead, or . . ."

Schuyler came in, gingerly holding a piece of much-folded paper at his fingertips. "She's alive, at least," he said. "A policeman just brought this a few minutes ago. From her."

On the night of her arrest, as she was led along the narrow, chilled hallway Hattie tried to hide her terror. It was important. She must hold out until some kind of help came, and she had to make them understand that she would not give in to whatever they asked of her.

A guard took out an enormous key, which grated in the large iron lock. She was shoved forward, and locked in. The walls seemed close and overpowering, the room like a small locked box. Realization of her complete helplessness swept over her. In the dim light that came through the grating from the hall outside, she felt her way to the low cot, threw herself upon it, and began to cry, her convulsive sobs echoing through the corridor beyond the slatted door. As she cried, she began to cough; her cold had grown worse.

An attendant shook the grated door. "What's the matter?"

"Nothing," she answered through chattering teeth. The room was icy.

"If you're hungry, I'll get you tea and bread. Do you want it?"

"Yes," she said briefly, and added, "and roast beef and butter and champagne!"

He made no answer to her defiant flippancy, but was back shortly with coarse dishes rattling on a tray. He was accompanied by a heavy red-faced woman who came into the cell with him and remained when he left, locking the two women in together. Was this one of the women guards? Hattie remembered what Katya had said about them and stepped back involuntarily. The woman spoke to her in German.

"I am to stay here with you."

"Why?"

The woman shrugged. "I am a police matron. It is customary in such cases. Well, eat." The woman indicated the food on the tray, an unpalatable paste of strong-smelling meat, some black bread, and dark tea. Hattie had eaten practically nothing for two days. She could eat even this. From her coat the woman brought a bottle and gestured. "Vodka."

Hattie put out her hand, then drew it back. She was on her guard again. The woman's next words were clumsy, and even in this setting sounded melodramatic. "I've heard that the Grand Duke gave you fine jewels. Were they pretty?" Hattie did not answer, and the police matron observed: "*You* won't have to worry, with those nice papers you had him write out for you."

Hattie had already discovered more from the matron of what they knew of her than the matron had learned in her clumsy questioning. The woman's stupidity set Hattie's mind at rest. The secret police were far more subtle. This woman had been told something, enough to know why she was guarding her, but she could probably be managed. Hattie asked the woman's name and where she came from.

"I am a German from Riga. My name is Caroline."

Hattie's new composure vanished. She asked inaudibly if she might not go to sleep now. Caroline nodded stolidly and helped arrange the cot, even producing a ragged fur robe. She curled up herself on a sheepskin in the corner.

They had left Hattie her fur-lined cape, and with the robe beneath her and the cape wrapped tightly about her, she was warm enough to sleep, but she kept waking, each time wondering where she was, each time feeling terror at the pit of her stomach as the knowledge came to her all over again. The matron was snoring in her corner. For the first time since her arrest, there was no one to defy, and Hattie's thoughts were released. Nikki, Nikki . . . Could he too be in this same dreadful building? That would hardly be possible. Wherever he was, she knew he ached for her and cried out for her, as she silently did for him. She prayed for the night to end, then thought, "No, let it go on forever." She was more afraid of the morning.

Sometime after dawn, Caroline shook her. "Breakfast." Light had sifted into the cell, and Hattie could see it for the first time. The walls were yellow-gray, the ancient paint falling away in strips, drops of water standing out at the corners. By now, her

236

arms and legs were so chilled that she had trouble in moving. She sat up stiffly on the edge of her cot. Her teeth could not work through the hard roll and she gagged at the strong, bitter taste of the tea but she kept the cup in her hands for warmth.

"Are there any messages for me?" she asked.

"No messages are delivered here."

Terror swept over her anew. Would the American officials be denied the right to communicate with her? As far as that went, how did they know where she was? Joséphine had not known when they took her out of the apartment. Despair made her calm. She turned to Caroline.

"Can I have some water?"

Caroline went to the door and called out something. In a few minutes, the door clanged open and five heavy guards rushed in, caught hold of Hattie, and thrust her heavily onto the cot. As she cried out, Caroline shoved the men aside in annoyance and ordered them out of the cell. The woman actually looked ashamed, and explained:

"They didn't understand me. My Russian isn't good. They thought I wanted them because you were trying to attack me." Hattie looked up at the heavy-shouldered, sober-faced woman in front of her and started to laugh. Caroline clearly thought she was hysterical and brought out the bottle again. "Something to drink, madame."

Why not? Hattie took several sips of it. Caroline, swallowing larger mouthfuls, pressed more upon her. After a time, as the morning passed and afternoon began, Hattie felt a lightness in her head. . . . There was nothing to worry about. The people at the Legation would come and get her out, soon, and Nikki would be released at the same time.

Caroline leaned forward, suddenly confidential. "Madame there's a way to get out. Just give them a few things they want and answer a question or two! Your friends aren't bothering about you. You have only yourself to think of." When she got no answer, she tried the confidential approach again. "The Grand Duke Nicholas, he's friendly with our peasant people, isn't he, madame—like his father? I've always been one to think that we need more freedom in this country."

Hattie sat back, dizzy and silent, and Caroline went on: "Every-body knows how sympathetic he and his father are to the poor,

237

and all those crowds around the Grand Duke when he came back from the victory in the provinces—they were for him and his father, not for the Tsar's soldiers." Hattie's heart beat harder. She began to understand how devious and how well planned Shuvalov's work with the Tsar had been. Neither she nor Nikki had guessed what might have been behind the Tsar's accusation at Vilno that Nikki had ordered the demonstrations for himself.

Caroline's informative monologue was interrupted by the key in the lock. The door opened and a police officer walked in.

He made a sign and the German woman left. He took a few steps farther into the cell and bowed. The major was probably called handsome, Hattie thought; his thin hair was strikingly blond and his eyes a pale, hard blue. His look was polite, but his eyes darted from the inch of her ankle that showed to her small waist and the outlines of her breasts. Hattie had risen to face him. She drew her cape around her and raised her chin.

"Madame Blackford," the major began, "I have a few matters to take up with you." Hattie moved a step or two and braced her back against the wall; she shook her head to rid herself of the buzzing dizziness in her ears. As the major continued, she listened with determined concentration.

"Madame, it must surely be painful and disagreeable to you to be here, but haven't you suspected for a long time that something like this was going to happen?"

Hattie put her hands back against the cold, flaking plaster of the walls. The room was still unsteady.

"I have suspected nothing. Perhaps you will tell me why I am held."

The major shrugged. Then he said bluntly: "You have in your possession jewels and certain valuable papers." He paused. "We must have them."

"I am sorry. I can't give them up."

The major's pale eyes grew chill. "You understand your position?"

She nodded. "I suppose I do."

"I am not sure that you do. You are entirely in our hands." He spoke slowly, emphatically. He hardly looked like a brutal man, but she glanced down at his hands; in odd contrast with the effeminate face, they had a brown, hard look, and the right one was crossed with a jagged scar. He went on: "I should advise you

238

to give up any hope that friends will save you. You will stay here until we are ready for you to leave."

He took a step closer and, with an effort, she looked up from his hands and managed to show a defiance that she did not feel.

"Then I must stay here!"

He flushed. "Very well, we will give you time, a little time, to reflect."

As he left, she felt a rush of relief. Despite the chill in the building, the perspiration had collected in her palms and at the back of her neck. She knew she had been close to physical violence. When she heard a noise at the door, she cried out but it was only Caroline, with food and vodka. Hattie pushed the bottle aside and made herself eat the unsavory stew.

As the afternoon passed, Caroline took out a deck of dog-eared cards and played a quiet game in the corner. She offered to tell Hattie's fortune; then, suddenly, began to talk of the secret police.

"Some are very nice." She grinned obscenely. "If you want to get along easily here, you can. But if you make things hard——" She shook her head. "They have ways of handling troublemakers, you know. I've seen them put a girl naked in one of the cellar rooms; that's a good way to get pneumonia."

Was the woman telling her these things to frighten her? The day was interminable. Steps in the corridor outside went by. She dreaded to hear them stop at her door, for they might be those of the major come back—and longed to have them stop, for they might be those of an emissary from the Legation. The dark of her second night in prison came on. She tried to sleep. After a while she dreamed of Nikki, but he was elusive, changing, fading like a ghost. The old nightmare returned. Her father led a crowd that hurled mud and stones at her. "Harlot!" they shouted. "Harlot!" When dawn came, she sat up, biting her lips. Had the world forgotten her; didn't anybody care what happened to her?

"How long can they keep me here?" she asked Caroline.

The woman raised eyes to the ceiling as if in calculation. She answered, with satisfaction:

"Let's see, there's one woman back there that's been here fifteen years. . . . Why don't you give them what they want?"

Hattie did not answer her, but lay back on the cot, and there was silence in the cell for a number of hours. In the afternoon,

Caroline, standing at the little grilled window, turned her head toward her prisoner.

"It's the promenade hour outside. Don't you want to see it?"

In her distress, Hattie had not even looked at what lay outside the prison. Now she rose and stood on tiptoe to watch the carriages and the couples along the street. She saw the tops of the carriages like toys far below. In them were tiny figures. How casual and heedless and uncaring they were! She dropped back into her cell. As she did so, she heard footsteps at the door. The blond major came in for his second visit. He attempted no preliminaries.

"Well? . . . We will not wait forever."

"I have nothing to tell you."

"I needn't remind you that we have ways of persuading people."

"Do you have anything to suggest?" she asked. He stared back at her helplessly. By now, she should have been weeping at his feet. Her calm was a new and puzzling thing. He gave her a cold nod and disappeared.

She realized that she had baffled him, if only temporarily, and perhaps at greater cost to herself later on, but her pride remained. She paced up and down, phrasing an account of this as she would tell it to Nikki. . . .

"They don't realize that nothing is giving me this calm and force but absolute despair, and they don't understand that if it were a matter of cutting a finger, I would cry and implore, but since they threaten to cut off a whole hand, I'm quite prepared to endure it without murmuring and to dig a hole to bury it with my other hand. . . ." Nikki would like that, both her spirit and her expression of it, but her heroism suddenly collapsed. How did she know that she would ever be able to tell him this or anything else?

She ranged up and down the cell while Caroline's eyes followed her back and forth. She actually began to wish for the appearance of the official again. She had something that he wanted. She would at least bargain verbally to the extent of finding out what was happening to Nikki. By now, she hardly noticed the cold, the dirt, the lack of air. She ate and slept, without protest.

On the morning of the next day she awoke looking forward to the visit of her questioner. She had been stupid not to question him in turn. Then as the day went by and he did not come, his

240

absence made her uneasy. Was he planning something, some terrible instrument that he would bring, or someone with him to whip her in front of him? Stories she had read in Philadelphia years ago came back . . . the story of a tsar who had had a hostile noblewoman stripped to the waist and the flesh flayed from her back. That was centuries ago, but her whole feeling of time had collapsed. This was only the third day and she felt as if she had been in prison as long as the woman down the hall.

The major arrived at last, alone and carrying nothing. He locked the door behind him and stood with white-gloved hands folded in front of him: "Madame?" She faced him, and made her carefully rehearsed demand.

"I need someone to advise me. I must have someone from the Legation. That is where I keep everything."

"You will do what we tell you. What do you call everything?"

"Jewels, my jewels, and papers. His letters to me. Documents that he signed, pledging settlements to me."

The major's face had a new and eager interest. "Exactly! I will bring you paper to write to Mr. Jewell, asking him to send these things here."

"I will do no such thing."

"I believe you will. If you are wise, you will not provoke us any more."

She was obstinate. "I want Mr. Schuyler to come here and talk to me."

"Impossible!" Then his tone changed. "Of course we're interested in the jewels. But suppose we let you keep them. Would you give up the letters?" He spoke more slowly. "Also, what price would you ask to give up those papers—the settlements he pledged?"

She shook her head. "They are not for sale. I don't want anything. That is, all I want is to see Nikki."

"You are certainly not helping him now. He is suffering because of the way you have behaved, the unreasonable way——"

At that moment, just down the hall she heard a heavy sound, which she imagined was that of a man being dragged, and a scream, as if some creature was being torn apart. She could not contain her wild, illogical conviction that this might be Nikki himself.

"Are they doing anything to him?" Her voice broke and she

felt a tightness in her throat. "In the name of God, tell me!"

The officer pressed his advantage. "All I can say is that you're not helping him at all. Why don't you give back those two documents that we want for . . . say . . . fifty thousand rubles? You could keep the jewels, after we inspected them to make sure that none was his mother's."

"I don't care what you do . . . Give me the paper. I'll sign it."

"Sit down, then," he said, "I'll get you the paper, and you can write this to Mr. Schuyler." He added quietly, "Then you will be able to see him all you want."

Did he mean Nikki or Mr. Schuyler? She was afraid to ask. She wrote the words he dictated.

TWENTY-THREE

AT LAST THE CELL DOOR OPENED AGAIN, BEHIND THE MAJOR WAS Eugene Schuyler. Hattie's involuntary cry of welcome embarrassed him and he spoke nervously.

"Madame, Mr. Jewell and I have spent most of the past four days hunting for you." He told her, with the utmost brevity, of the steps they had taken.

When he had finished, she impulsively held out both her hands to him. Schuyler touched the finger tips of her right hand, then let his own hand drop. She smiled faintly, and asked:

"My boxes? Did you bring them?"

Schuyler's answer seemed to be addressed more to the major than to her. "The Minister and I thought it wise to wait a bit, to find out whether your letter had been written under duress."

The major's hard blue eyes turned to Hattie. She hesitated for only a second, then said firmly:

"I agreed to it of my own free will. The only 'duress' was the fear that my action might harm the Grand Duke."

Schuyler looked quickly at the major, who frowned. "Madame," he said, "the Grand Duke is certainly 'safe.' He remains in custody, but he is not being—'harmed.'" She was not reassured. She knew those phrases: "custody!" He turned to Schuyler. "We have arranged with Madame Blackford to pay her well for certain documents and letters given her by Nicholas Constantinovich."

The American's eyebrows raised, and he spoke in dry disdain. "I have nothing to do, sir, with any financial arrangements that Mrs. Blackford may choose to make. They are her affair. I will consult my superior about the matter of allowing the boxes outside the Legation."

"This is Madame Blackford's wish voluntarily stated." The major showed his tension. The matter was now between the two of them, and they debated as if the person of Mrs. Blackford were a diplomatic phrase, not a living and disturbing woman only a few feet away.

"Our concern," Schuyler said, "is to protect her interests as an American citizen. What would happen if this settlement *were* made?"

The major's expression showed clearly that he was affronted by this American arrogance. He returned contemptuously: "And what would happen if it *were not*?"

Schuyler's eyes flashed. "I repeat—we are not concerned with the settlement, but we *are* concerned with her release. If she is still detained, I expect a diplomatic incident."

"So?"

"So! Mr. Jewell has not acted without advice. It is probable that the whole diplomatic corps will hold council. The rights of all of us are involved." The major's face showed little change of expression, but Schuyler could sense that he was impressed. Schuyler's voice took on a persuasive tone. "In any case, if there *is* a settlement between you, she will go completely free?"

The major hesitated, then spoke. "Yes. Though she would be required to leave Russia."

Required to leave! Hattie thought. This was what Nikki had told her to do before he was arrested. Their only chance of reunion lay outside Russia. It was what she wanted with all her heart.

Schuyler nodded coolly to the major. "I shall take up the matter with Mr. Jewell."

The major's heels snapped together. "And I with my superiors."

As Schuyler bowed to Hattie in farewell, she said softly, "I can never thank you enough for coming here, for all that you've done. They'll have to honor their word now that you've found me."

"We shall see that they do," Schuyler said dryly, and followed the major out into the hall.

Late the following day, the two men appeared again. Schuyler, with a look of disapproval, set a box on her cot and stood back. Hattie opened the box, which held her jewels. A swift glance revealed that all the little leather and velvet boxes were in it.

244

She picked them up, one by one, pressing catches hurriedly, and saw that necklaces, bracelets, pins, and rings were all there.

The major bent over her shoulder. She held her breath as he picked up the leather box containing Eugénie's diamond bracelet. He opened the box and looked at it for several minutes. Almost dreamily, he drew out the bracelet and swung it back and forth in front of his eyes, which were no longer cold. Mr. Schuyler cleared his throat, and the major dropped the bracelet again into its white-satin hollow. He snapped the box tight and tossed it back among the rest, with an affectation of carelessness.

"You may keep them," he said. He turned to Schuyler. "The documents, sir?"

The American reached calmly into his pocket. "These were the two of greatest interest, I think. We found them with the lady's letters. With your approval . . ." He gave them first to Hattie, who scanned them, then handed them to the major.

After a swift inspection, he pocketed them and handed Schuyler a document of his own. It promised, in the name of the Imperial Government, to pay Mrs. Blackford fifty thousand rubles, as they had agreed, "less ten thousand rubles to cover a letter of exchange signed by Madame Blackford to the Grand Duke's order, but not yet cashed."

Schuyler protested. "The note of exchange was signed on the same day that the Grand Duke gave Mrs. Blackford the other two documents. Since they are considered invalid, the note must be also."

The major's eyes hardened. "A matter of bookkeeping, Mr. Schuyler."

This arbitrary decision might set a dangerous precedent, but Schuyler hesitated. His face showed distaste for the whole situation. He glanced at Hattie, who said impatiently, "Oh, please don't hold this up any longer!"

Schuyler sighed and turned to the Major. "Very well."

Hattie took the pen the major held out to her, held the paper up against the cracking wall and scrawled her name.

"I can go now?" she asked him, as she handed it back.

"Presently." The major spoke impatiently. "My superior must receive this before an order can be given. I suppose it will come around five o'clock."

Eugene Schuyler turned to Hattie as he left. "Let us know as soon as you reach your home."

"I will indeed. Please present my compliments to Mr. Jewell."

She had been here so long, a few hours more should hardly matter. They were the longest of her imprisonment. The near possibility of walking in the street, looking up at open sky, seeing Joséphine again, and, above all, managing to get a note to Nikki, made her frantic.

At five-thirty, she was shaking the bars of her door to summon the guard. The jailer was noncommittal. "Orders? We have heard nothing." He looked at her as if she must be imagining them. She began to wonder frenziedly if she were. Five hours later, Caroline came into the cell. By then Hattie was weeping, and exhausted. The jailer swung the door open, standing back.

"Well, are you ready to go?" Caroline said, and Hattie ran out, stumbling in the dark hallway. With Caroline close behind her, she went silently past three or four guards and down the stairs to the outer door. When Caroline took out a key and unlocked it, Hattie found that her knees were trembling. The clean night air hit her face with a rush and she breathed deeply. "Now . . . if I can get a carriage."

"Our carriage will be here in a minute." It was the voice of a man behind her and, turning, she saw that the three gendarmes she had passed had followed her down.

"Ours?"

Caroline nodded: "We will stay with you for a while, madame."

They were whittling away at her freedom the way they had subtracted from their original promise of fifty thousand rubles. "But I am to be completely free! Where is the major?"

As on the day of her first arrest, men came up behind her on either side, each taking an arm. "Come along, madame."

At least she had learned when resistance was futile. She got into the carriage. Several more men in uniform stood before the apartment building on the Millionnaya. She found two in the marble entrance hall; one of whom unlocked the door of her apartment for her. Two others and the blond major were waiting for her in her salon. She looked around helplessly.

"Where is Joséphine Arnault?" she asked the major.

"She's in a quiet place," Caroline answered for him. "She has been ill. I am to be your maid."

246

"I will not be a prisoner in my own house!" Hattie advanced on the major in sudden fury. "Why are you here?" She had difficulty in controlling her voice.

"For the time being," he answered, "you are under house arrest. A last point or two have to be settled. Won't you sit down?" Ironically, he indicated one of her own chairs. Although her knees were shaking, she refused to sit. He went on. "After further thought, we have decided it would be best to look at all of your papers. . . . You were ready to show them a few days ago before the American Legation intervened. Now if you'll simply write them another note . . ."

From the writing desk—obviously he knew his way about her apartment very well—he drew a sheet of paper. This last humiliating detail was too much. She ripped the sheet in two and threw the pieces on the floor at his feet. The major looked at her for a moment in silence, then took his leave.

"I'll return tomorrow. You don't seem happy to be back here at all. Perhaps we should return you to the other place—one of the rooms in the basement this time, smaller than the one you know, and colder." At the door, he turned. "And you are to communicate with no one."

That night, and again the next morning, Eugene Schuyler was halted at Hattie's doorway by uniformed men. When he told the Minister, Jewell was furious. Only the night before, his diplomatic fellows had congratulated him on the skill and decision with which he had handled "l'affaire Blackford," setting an important precedent.

"So they've broken their agreement, definitely." He got up. "Let's get to the heart of it—Count Shuvalov."

The officer in charge of the Count's reception room gave Schuyler a brilliant smile. "The Count left for England last night with the Tsar."

Schuyler's color rose. "Whom did the Count leave in charge?" he asked precisely.

The official hesitated. "I believe it is Count Levashev."

Levashev was pleasant, but not helpful. "It has been decided, definitely, that we must look over the Grand Duke's letters to Madame Blackford—all of them. They were together for more than two years, you know, and there are indications that they planned"—he paused—"matrimony." He gave the word a distasteful sound.

Schuyler sighed. "Very well, then, we will suggest to her that she allow this."

But when he called at the Millionnaya apartment, with the major, Hattie refused. "No! Those letters are private, and I will not show them to anyone. The Imperial Government has broken its word twice. What good will it do me to give in any more? And the Grand Duke? How do I know whether these letters will help him or whether they'll give the police an excuse to hurt him? I have nothing more to say about it."

At the Legation, in Levashev's office, then in the study of the friendly Portuguese Ambassador, acting as intermediary, there followed conferences and searching of protocols, diplomatic precedents, and the souls of the diplomats. Finally, they returned to Hattie with new proposals and new assurances. Schuyler spoke patiently.

"Suppose the letters are read by the major in my presence, and none taken from you unless the Legation agrees?"

At that, finally, Hattie gave in. "Very well. Please get it done soon." She turned to the major. "I can have my maid Joséphine back? Please tell me how she is."

The major shook his head coolly. "Madame Arnault is not in custody. She has been in the hospital. You may see her when the house arrest is lifted—after *we* have seen the letters."

The two men spent more than an hour, late that afternoon, going through the box of letters on the small table in front of Hattie. She was calm as she watched the two pairs of cold and impersonal eyes flicking over the well-known handwriting.

The table on which they leaned their elbows was exquisitely inlaid; its secret drawer was still filled with letters they would never see.

At length the major picked up three of the letters, considered a moment, dropped one, and turned to her: "We want these two, very much." He picked up another, then another. "I should like these two, also."

She went over them; they referred to times she and Nikki had spent in his father's palaces in Petersburg and Pavlovsk. She wadded her handkerchief tightly in her hand as she read, and then pressed her fist against her mouth, looking down. After a moment, she took her hand down and spoke with trembling lips.

"Very well—if you can answer a question, major?"

"What is it?"

"Please, do you think it possible that the Grand Duke will be released?" Her hand touched his sleeve; her dark eyes were imploring. "Your honest opinion?"

Mr. Schuyler looked down, and the major's voice softened. "It is not decided, madame, but I should say—not." She handed over the letters mutely and he saluted and left.

Several hours later, Hattie saw the solid Caroline buttoning herself into her sheepskin coat.

"Where are you going?" she asked, hardly daring to hope that she would be left alone.

"Your other one is on the way," Caroline said briefly. She walked out of the door without a further word.

When Joséphine's beloved figure finally appeared in the doorway, Hattie threw her arms around her. Joséphine was white, and her chin was still bandaged, but she was alive and back.

Joséphine reassured her; she had not had another hemorrhage, and she was now well enough to be up and around. No, they had not returned her money. Not a franc. "But what can one do? You have found that out as well as I, madame—even the Grand Duke is helpless."

"What have you heard—what?" Hattie demanded.

"Oh, madame, those first few days before they took me off, the gendarmes came every day and asked for something special of yours—one of your little pillows, your empty jewel box, and such things. I couldn't guess why they wanted them, they had so much already. Then, accidentally, I heard that the Grand Duke himself was calling for the things, hoping you'd slip in a message to him. They said he ripped the pillow apart until the room was filled with feathers. They kept telling him that you'd deserted him, that you didn't want anything more to do with him. They even claimed you testified against him."

Joséphine sighed: "It's impossible to get any word to him now. They search everything that goes in and out." As they gazed at each other despairingly, Joséphine added, "They say the Grand Duke has only just found out that you were locked away. They claim he's not given in yet; he fights back and causes trouble.

249

Breaks things—and he's always asking for you, says he won't give you up. Oh, madame, don't cry!"

Later Hattie asked: "And what about Viktor—where is he?"

"They say he's sick somewhere, but he'll be all right. Oh, madame, when can we leave?"

"I don't know yet," Hattie said wearily. "As soon as they tell us we can."

The guards had left the apartment, but the two in the hall were still on watch. The next morning, one of them presented Hattie with a note. It informed her that Count Levashev, taking Count Shuvalov's duties in the latter's absence in England, would call at noon that day about the details of her departure. She put the note down with an ironic smile. She knew the Count; the new official was one of the *vieillesse argentée* that she had met at the supper party on the night of her arrival in Petersburg. He should remember her well. She had no wish to see him, though she supposed she had no choice. Still, there might actually be some advantage in it. Perhaps he would tell her something more of Nikki.

She was dressed in soft white silk and her hair was arranged as only Joséphine could manage it, when Levashev entered, precisely on time.

"Ah, Count, it's good of you to come to me." She hoped her inner irony would not disturb the pleasant impression she wanted him to have. This was the first time she had ever seen him sober. "How handsome you look in your official medals!" He kissed her hand and put the call on a personal level at once.

"My dear, I'm desolated by this affair. If I had known in time, most of it would not have happened."

"It helps me to know that." She could not keep a light edge of sarcasm from her voice, and suddenly felt defiant. What would he tell about Nikki?

He looked embarrassed. "We are only soldiers of His Majesty, you understand. Only orders, no choice." She was silent and he asked, "Your plans, my dear?"

"To sell nearly everything here, send the rest to Paris, and leave as soon as I can."

He appeared relieved. "When will that be?"

"Oh, in some weeks' time." She was sure her indefinite answer would horrify him.

250

He answered as she had expected. "Oh no, you must go at once! As long as you stay, the scandal keeps up."

They ended with the understanding that she would leave by the week's end. The belongings that had been taken from her apartment at the time of the search would be returned to her. This settled, she asked the Count something else.

"Please do a small favor for me." She described the way Joséphine's money had been taken. "Can't they give it back to her?"

He nodded. "I will see to it." He cleared his throat. "Oh, and one thing more, madame . . ." Apparently the bargaining was still going on. "I neglected to say that our great specialist, Balinsky, wishes to ask you about the Grand Duke. He will come to see you here."

Her heart beat faster. "I shall be most happy to see him. But why am I accorded this honor?"

"He wishes facts about the Grand Duke's . . . mental condition."

She looked at him steadily. There was a saying in Petersburg that if a patient were dying, he had to crawl through the streets before he could see Balinsky. They must be putting a great deal of dependence on this part of the case against the Grand Duke.

"I'll be happy to give him the facts!"

That night, they brought back her possessions—books, bills, picture albums, the blotting pads they had taken. Clasps and snaps had been broken, pages torn, bindings loosened; a silver cigarette case was gone, a gold pencil, and other items, but at least Joséphine's francs were back, and that was the most important thing.

The officers who had returned the things had hardly gone when a new visitor stood at the door. His self-important manner identified him. It was the great Balinsky. He was a pale, weedy man, with hair that looked almost orange. His eyes were deep-set and probing.

As he crossed the room to sit down on the sofa she indicated, it seemed to her that he looked slightly deformed. She saw that he had an almost imperceptible limp. When he had seated himself, a wide notebook in his lap, two assistants entered to take silent places behind him.

He began to ask questions: When had she first noticed that the Grand Duke was nervous? What were his expressions when he was disturbed? Did he talk of death . . . the Tsar . . . his mother . . . ?

"Yes," she replied to the last. "He talked of the Grand Duchess Alexandra, and of his father, and of his brothers and sisters. I talked of my family, too. That seems to be usual between two people in love," she added dryly.

The doctors and his helpers wrote furiously.

"As a matter of fact," Balinsky looked up suddenly, pointing his pen at her, "you know that he's insane."

"I do not," she said. "He is as sane as you! . . . You are sane, aren't you?" she asked innocently.

The doctor frowned. His assistants lowered their heads and this time they did not record her answer.

All his questions were accusations. But perhaps this man was Nikki's only hope for understanding treatment. She made an effort to reach him.

"It may be true," she temporized, "that he took things from his mother's room and pawned them. Certainly it was at a time of great anxiety for him. How many other sons have done the same? If he were a peasant boy, he would be free today." She threw out her hands to Dr. Balinsky. "You know how badly he has been treated! How many things all his life have led to this single confused, rebellious act! You know he'd be well if he could leave Russia with me."

The doctor looked at her as if her appeal were an indication of madness of her own. His eyes hardened. "Do you realize that the Grand Duke has spent most of his time in a strait jacket because he has behaved so irrationally?" The doctor closed in for the real point of his visit. He looked genuinely puzzled. "Madame Lear, this extraordinary influence you have over him—how do you explain it? He never stops demanding that you be brought to him."

Her heart was sick at the thought of what this man had done and could do to Nikki. "Love is a strange mental condition, isn't it, Doctor? It's the only explanation for my 'influence.'"

The interview was hopeless, and she realized for the first time that if this treatment went on, Nikki would never be released. She could not keep back her angry, despairing tears; and the faces before her watched with a cold, analyzing curiosity. At a nod from the doctor, her callers rose and left the room together.

Joséphine came in with the real news of Nikki's condition. She had picked it up from a governess in a count's family. "The Grand Duke has been in bed for a week now with a very high fever from all that questioning, and the way they keep at him. They're even at him now when he's sick, and some say they've allowed the guards to hit him when he won't answer." Already unstrung by her interview with Dr. Balinsky, Hattie sobbed aloud. Joséphine went on: "Yesterday he told them he *would* go crazy if they wouldn't let him see you. They still wouldn't, so he lay there till a servant left the room for a minute. Then he got up and smashed everything there—mirrors, chairs, tables, windows." Ah, what Dr. Balinsky could make of that! . . . and there was nothing she could do. There was no way to get to him, and she must leave Russia within the week . . .

The next day, she and Joséphine discovered that the amiable Levashev's promise of freedom was no more reliable than anyone else's. Men were stationed at all entrances and exists of the building; every move that they made was observed. When they got into a carriage, two men followed and sat silently opposite them with arms folded. "I might have known," Hattie said with a sigh. "They promise something and they almost do it, but not *quite*."

Through the week, she and Joséphine worked in the apartment, setting aside things to be retained and crated for Paris, summoning dealers to sell the rest. The merchants paid very little, though Joséphine brought rumors that her furniture was fetching enormous prices from customers, and wild tales were being told about the various objects. "This is the couch where the Grand Duke and that woman . . . you know." Or, "They say she was stretched out on this when he first came in—completely naked, eating an orange."

The pile of crates in the apartment grew higher. There was so much that she could not give up. The Renaissance chair from his wing in the Marble Palace, the table that reminded her of one on which they had breakfasted at Naples, the oil painting that had been an Easter present. She saw Nikki in the whole apartment, in everything. As she decided to keep various things, she realized that she was holding onto them because they might be things that he as well as she would want later on. She would not give up the idea, wild hope though it was, that this furniture would someday be theirs together again.

On Saturday morning, the day before her departure, she went for a last drive through the town, along the breadth of Nevsky Prospekt, over the bridges that crossed the Neva. When they approached the Fortress of Sts. Peter and Paul she called to the coachman to stop.

Inside, she walked past the resting places of Nikki's ancestors, as she had done with Nikki on that other last day before his departure for the war. She went from one tomb to the other, bowing her head, remembering. It was here that Nikki had given her the family cross, presented to him when he was a boy. It was here that he had asked her never to forget him. And she had promised. Her eyes blurred as she knelt before the tomb of the great Peter.

When she came out she directed the coachman toward the Church of St. Nicholas. She would offer her prayers not only to the ancestor who was their protector, but also to Nikki's patron saint. The church was almost deserted. There was no singing, no murmuring throng. The quiet and emptiness gave her peace.

On the way back to the apartment they passed the ornate Pink Palace, now a monument to Nikki's tragedy. Boards crisscrossed the windows, and a single officer walked back and forth in front of the door. She thought of the reclining marble statue of herself among the birds and greenery in the fantastic hothouse. There would be that much of her left in Petersburg. What a symbol for people to peer at, whisper over!

How long would it take for the stories to die away? There was no way of making any denial of them public before she left. The newspapers? In Russia, where newspapers printed no news? Not a line of the matter, she knew now, had been permitted to appear, and none ever would. Perhaps another change in Romanov politics would mean Nikki's release, sooner than she could hope; but perhaps the Tsar would not relent, and would be succeeded in time by Sasha, from whom there would be no possibility of justice. . . . She could only hope and pray. Someday they might be together in America. She clung to the thought as tightly as her fingers clung to the band of gold on her left hand.

At the entrance to her building on Millionnaya, a soldier waited. "General Trepov pays his respects and requests a final interview with you." Her face lighted up. This man had authority; he could give the order that would let her see Nikki. She would beg, she would do anything, if he would let her talk to him again, see him, touch him. . . . Her face was white as she followed the soldier.

A few minutes later, she waited in a palatial office. The spectacular ornamentation, the superb curtains and furnishings, seemed ugly and frightening. She knew what agony they covered. The clerk bowed.

"His Excellency is ready."

As Trepov rose to greet her, his look was affable, his bow courteous. They spoke pleasantly enough of the train she was to take, even of the weather. As she realized that she would presently be dismissed, Hattie's poise broke down.

"Please"—she held her hands closely together as she spoke— "Your Excellency, there is something else." She drew a deep breath. "No matter what the Imperial Government thinks I have done, won't you let me see him again—for the last time? Just a few minutes, even with one of your guards present!"

The General's affable smile disappeared. "Enough, madame!" He spoke in measured tones. "Whatever you say, it will do you no good. Do you understand? You will never, never see him again as long as you live."

She covered her face with her hands. Her only defense was not to believe him. When she lifted a white, composed face, he looked at her directly, in an appraising manner.

"After all, madame, you didn't handle yourself particularly well."

"I don't understand you."

"Just that." He shrugged. "For a woman who is supposed to be so intelligent, you behaved very clumsily, and very foolishly. Didn't you know that even after we had arrested you, you had us in *your* power? We had to have those documents. You could have set the terms higher—a hundred times higher. We would have objected, but finally we would have paid because we had to. After all, they were at the American Legation, and we couldn't deal with you as directly as we might have in other circumstances."

Her voice was low. "I was told by your representative that what I did would help Nikki. I was afraid for him as well as for myself."

He smiled. "Indeed? They put our case skillfully, I am sure." He chuckled, as if to himself.

"I had no one to advise me," Hattie murmured. To herself she was thinking savagely of the letters she still had, of what she would do with them to tell her story and Nikki's once she was out of this country. But suddenly Cora Pearl's words came back: "Lovey, you've never made the most of your chances." They all said it; it was probably true.

By this time, Trepov was speaking again. "Madame, I'd like to make an observation. You are an extremely attractive woman, still young . . ."

It was the truth. Trepov probably thought her younger than she was, but she was not quite twenty-seven.

Trepov's look became still more friendly. "In Vienna, Paris, wherever you go, you should have no trouble finding friends, a protector . . ."

She got up. "I don't think you called me here to give me—paternal advice. I shall not be in a position to take it in any case. I shall be waiting in Europe for the Grand Duke."

"It may be longer than you think. I wouldn't advise you to wait *that* long, madame." This time there was no amusement in the voice, and the heavy door shut sharply behind her as she went out.

At noon of Sunday, May 10, 1874, with a gendarme to make certain of the fact, Mrs. Harriet Blackford and her maid, Joséphine Arnault, boarded the train for Paris. As on the day of their arrival, there were no friends at the station, no one they knew. Even now, Hattie could not feel fully at ease. Would there be some further incident, a seizure of their trunks, additional questioning? She needed no indication other than the faces of the two men in the adjoining compartment to understand that they were police agents. By now she could tell one half a block away.

At the border station, the two men got up, lifted their hats to her, and went quietly out. One fear was over at last.

TWENTY-FOUR

THERE WAS NOTHING TO DO NOW BUT WAIT AND HOPE, IN THE PRIvacy and freedom of Paris. But Hattie learned quickly that whatever happened to her now would not be private. The first night they went out to dine, a crowd gathered in front of the Grand Hotel to get a glimpse of her. Although she was used to crowds in Russia, it was a shock to realize how the stories had spread. Continental newspapers must have carried wild stories about her for the past month.

In the café that night four reporters converged on her table. "Please, madame, a few questions . . . We represent the press of three nations."

She felt that they were giving her the same cold, curious look that she had had from Dr. Balinsky and his medical assistants. Her color deepened.

"Gentlemen, I am being treated like an animal in the zoo. I don't know what kind of story you want to print, but I will tell you nothing."

"Madame, you are news," the London *Times* man reminded her cautiously.

Hattie looked up at the faces surrounding the table. The men stood their ground, pads and pencils poised. Her voice rose unsteadily.

"I shall never answer another question. I have had enough."

They shifted their feet a little, but gave no signs of leaving. The eldest in the group looked at her almost angrily. "Come now, Mrs. Blackford, you might as well co-operate with us." She had a hysterical sense that gendarmes might appear at any minute. Those dreadful euphemisms: "Co-operate . . . just a few questions."

257

She rose from the table, tight-lipped. "Come, Joséphine." She swept out of the dining room, the train of her skirt rustling angrily. Heads all over the room turned to watch her leave. She had not even been able to begin her meal. "We will go back to the hotel," she said to Joséphine, "and have our meals served in our rooms from now on." She gave Joséphine some coins. "Get me the papers."

Upstairs, the silent Breton handed her the day's newspapers. There was a long, garbled story on the first page of one of them. She had been the Duke's accomplice in a systematic rifling of Romanov jewels, involving untold millions.

She threw the paper to the floor. An even bigger headline ran in another journal. It told of "strong evidence" of a revolutionary conspiracy in which the American was implicated, and which had seriously embarrassed the American Legation in St. Petersburg. The next account suddenly made her laugh. An American paper reproved Secretary Schuyler for carrying Hattie's letters to her apartment in the last stages of the affair. He had acted unbecomingly; there was a hint that the prim gentleman had an unusual interest in the beautiful Mrs. Blackford. "We all know that Mr. Schuyler is a very learned gentleman and we read with pleasure his elaborate articles on Russian literature, but we never expected him to push his love for 'literature' so far." She hoped that the Legation saw the American papers regularly.

A London dispatch drew her attention. Reports were spreading that the whole matter had developed because of Grand Duke Constantine's interest in greater liberties for the people; his enemies had helped build the guilt of his son and the American to such remarkable proportions as a means of damaging him. "Their evil hands were too short to touch him, and so they struck at his poor son." This was probably the closest to the truth of anything she had read.

The Tsar was now visiting his daughter Marie at Buckingham Palace; in spite of every precaution, the affair was being thrown up to him on all sides. Russian exiles in England and Switzerland had taken up the scandal for their own purposes. One wrote satirically to the *Daily News,* sending a copy of a letter he had written to the Tsar at Victoria's Court: "Congratulations on the thievery of your own regal nephew! Members of your family apparently sin by stealing, but not by possessing humane ideas and

258

feelings—for which you, of course, have such thorough antipathy and which you persecute so mercilessly."

The papers lay in a heap at her feet and she stirred them thoughtfully with a toe. Would all this help Nikki, or hurt him, and when and where could she ever lead a private life again?

The next week, an envelope without a signature brought her a batch of hostile clippings from America. Papers in New York, Baltimore, and Philadelphia were carrying even more fantastic stories than the Continental ones. Strangely, some had an undertone of pride. She showed a concluding paragraph to Joséphine: "Better sun yourselves in the smiles of opera singers and ballet dancers, ye gentlemen of royal blood, and let these keen-witted American adventuresses alone!"

"Adventuress," she repeated the word thoughtfully to Joséphine. "It's better than some, isn't it? Now 'Jezebel' has a nice Biblical touch to it, but I don't think I care for 'loose female,' do you?"

Joséphine looked fierce. "The ones that make their living from mud have only mud to throw."

It was inevitable that a certain type of man would be much intrigued by the stories about her. She received offensive notes, and developed the habit of veiling herself heavily and taking a carriage for even short trips, to avoid being accosted by quite well-dressed men who would approach, smugly sure of a welcome. "Madame Blackford, I thought we should meet. We know so many of the same people. . . ." The variations of the approach were many but the tone was the same.

She had been at the hotel several weeks when the incident occurred that led her to leave. Three American women were crossing the sidewalk one morning when her carriage drew up at the door. As she stepped out, her blond hair gleaming unmistakably under her veil, Joséphine behind her, the first of the women turned and murmured to her companions. They stopped, and walked slightly to the side. For a moment, no word was spoken; then one of them turned her head sharply toward the two women about to go through the door. "Whore." She said it almost without emotion, in a voice that carried clearly across the sidewalk. Hattie was trembling as Joséphine caught her arm and hurried her in, chattering angrily, half to her mistress, half to herself. Her nightmares, like Nikki's, had been prophetic.

259

The next morning, Hattie went out to look for another place to live. On a fashionable street in the Faubourg Saint-Germain she liked a small elegant house; she hesitated over the price, then agreed when the agent said it was available immediately.

Soon after she moved in, a note arrived from Petersburg, the first communication she had had from Russia. It was from Mabel Grey telling her that after a short time in a private hospital, Nikki had been taken to one of his father's smaller villas at Koirovo, near the capital. Hunting through an atlas, Hattie found the name; it made her feel closer to him. She wrote a long letter to Mabel, thanking her for the news, then rewrote it, to make it as cordial as possible. This might be the only way she would get information. But a few days later, she received a letter without greeting or signature, forwarded to her from the American Embassy in Paris. The postmark was unreadable, but the stamps were Russian. The letter began guardedly:

"A friend thinks you should know this. In spite of the efforts of the Grand Duke Constantine and the protests of his mother, the Grand Duchess, Nicholas gets no better treatment. The doctors visit him frequently and still try to make him say what they wish. The Tsar's personal physician has been assigned to the matter. Your informant thinks of this as a new outrage. The other day the physician ordered children's toys brought to the Grand Duke; when Nicholas protested and broke them, he reported another instance of the Grand Duke's destructive tendencies, together with a statement that Nicholas himself had first called for the toys."

She read on: the commission in charge was studying an appeal from Nikki which he had managed to present to the Tsar in writing. "Am I insane or am I a criminal? If I am a criminal, put me on trial and sentence me. If I am insane, your doctors should treat me so as to give me hope that someday I may again see life and freedom. But what you are doing to me is cruel and inhuman." How true and how fair his statement was, and what agony to read it at second hand, when she could do nothing. The note ended by saying that the commission was using the fact that the appeal was unfinished—Nikki had left it so out of a feeling of helplessness —as proof that he was unbalanced. Reports grew stronger that he was to be "sacrificed" as a means of striking further at Constantine and those who thought as he did.

The message closed abruptly, with no signature. She searched the letter carefully and in the middle of a line she found a curious curlicue. Twisting the paper around to get several slants on it, she saw an unmistakable pair of initials: "V. V." Viktor Vorpovsky! At least he was alive and able to write. She gave thanks for that, and wished that she were able to write to him as she had to Mabel —and with how much more emotion!

Saddened again, she tried to distract herself. She decorated her house to frame the pieces she had brought from Russia. She would always wear white, for Nikki had loved it, but she would make this room look like the apartments he was used to in the Romanov palaces they had visited together. She chose crimson Moroccan covering for the chairs in the dining room. She covered the drawing-room pieces in black satin with red fringe, and she hung her bedroom in black velvet. She indulged in a sudden caprice; irregular pearl-like ornaments, oval-shaped, were hung at intervals against the dark background. When Joséphine first saw it she turned pale. "A weeping chamber, madame. So many tears." She shook her head. Hattie herself had not even realized what she had done, but the design was elegant as well as sadly appropriate. She took a certain melancholy pleasure in it. All her glassware and china from Petersburg, and photographs of Nikki and other Romanovs that he had given her, were in every room.

She felt much as she had during her two previous visits to Paris. At the time when she was expecting to hear from Nikki after their quarrel in Friedrichsruhe and also at the time when he was on the battlefields of Central Asia, she had wanted to see no one. She had lived all her inner life around her imaginings of the places he might be. She knew that this was a hopeless way to behave now but she could not help herself.

She had lost track of all of the friends she had made in the Paris of 1870; that Paris could have been a century away. She heard nothing of Cora Pearl, who had vanished with the unknown protector whose money had helped Hattie to go to St. Petersburg. It was hard to meet new people without being misunderstood. Besides, she felt an odd lethargy. It was as if she were drained of all energy and emotion, except when she thought of Russia and Nikki. Even to walk a little way on the street tired her.

She spent long hours on a chaise longue reading, drowsing, rising only for brief visits with her next-door neighbor, a shrewd, pleasant Parisian named Madame Colbert.

It was Madame Colbert's tact that had first won Hattie. She had not referred to her neighbor's past life, which she undoubtedly knew. Hattie suspected that she herself had once been an actress. She was well dressed, yet her make-up had a slightly theatrical emphasis. Hattie in turn did not pry. The friendship, begun cautiously, became a pleasant feature of her new life.

But all of it paled when she got her infrequent news of the Romanovs. One day, after she had been in the city three months, the mail brought her a note from Captain Viktor that electrified her. Without warning, the Tsar had called Shuvalov to congratulate him on a new "promotion" as Ambassador to England. The man who had guided the vital Third Section for years could only thank His Majesty. The reason? The master spy Shuvalov had himself been spied upon; while drunk, he had announced that, having all but broken one intriguer, the Grand Duke Constantine, he would soon strike at another, the Tsar's mistress, Princess Dolgorouky. The Tsar had acted immediately. She went on hastily to the heart of the letter. The Captain could hardly tell how Shuvalov's demotion would affect Nikki. He suspected that here, as in other matters, the Tsar simply couldn't make up his mind; and it was evident that Sasha, the heir apparent, opposed any freedom for Nikki. Finally, the Captain passed along a glimpse of Nikki that made her shudder. A group of officers, riding by the villa, occasionally saw him taking a walk, moving slowly in a semicircle of bayoneted guards; they reported him saddened, defeated. A few who had resented him halted their mounts a short way off to watch. When he cursed at them, they rode away to tell of his madness.

It was months later, in the summer of 1875, that the next blow came. Mabel Grey passed it on. Several of the doctors who handled Nikki's case had been refusing to declare him insane; but now the Tsar's commission acted, stamping the diagnosis and the sentence upon him. He lost command of his regiment and all other rights of a Grand Duke.

When Hattie read the letter, she came to a decision that she had pushed to the back of her mind ever since those first weeks when she had been hunted by the press. Nikki's brilliant, lucid letters from Khiva, the whole story of their love and life together, must be published in defiance of the secrecy in Russia, the distortion of the newspapers in the rest of the world.

Despite her weariness and the cough that she did not seem to get rid of, she set aside a few hours every day sitting at her desk, going over his letters and her own journal, plunging back deep into her memory. Some of the times made happy writing and her pen could not go fast enough; the excitement, the tenderness, the brilliance and beauty, they had shared together. But she forced herself to make the picture complete, to remember the time he had locked her in her room at Pavlovsk, the quarrel at Friedrichsruhe, and all the distress and anxiety of the end. She rose from writing of this kind trembling and exhausted, and Joséphine, bringing in hot milk, forcibly putting her mistress to bed, was darkly disapproving. "What good will this do you, madame?" She had heard Madame Colbert say that money could come from the book, but not the kind of money Madame Lear needed. Better that her mistress should spend her days with a kind new protector than to ruin her health over something that was done. New bills were coming every day. Despite every effort Joséphine made, the jewels were beginning to go. Madame had never learned economy.

Several days before Hattie finished her story, she had more encouraging word from Russia. Nikki had been sent to the city of Tver, between Petersburg and Moscow. Were they keeping him near the capital so they could call him back eventually? In better spirits than she had been for months, she took her manuscript to the publishing house Madame Colbert had recommended.

The publisher thumbed negligently through the pages. "I'll let you know, Madame Lear. . . ." Fanny Lear was the obvious nom de plume and the name that belonged to Nikki and his story.

Two hours later, his carriage was at her door, and he was leaping eagerly up the steps. He looked curiously, and she thought sympathetically, around her crimson-hung drawing room, and bent with interest over a picture of Nikki and his sister Olga. Then he turned to her.

"Madame, this book will cause a sensation. We shall call it simply: *Le Roman d'une Américaine en Russie.*" He hesitated. After he had asked for a minor change or two—initials only for the Court figures, a less realistic portrait of Shuvalov—he said

263

respectfully, "Madame, you write amazingly well." He blushed and changed the adverb—"particularly well."

She shrugged her shoulders, but she was pleased. In his sympathetic and respectful manner she saw the response she hoped the book would find in other readers. He picked up his hat and bowed low to her. "We will go to press with this at once."

When the first copy came to her hands and she read it in type, the past came alive with remarkable vividness; how much more vivid than anything that had happened to her since!

She looked with pride at a paragraph on the title page: "Against public offense, it is not only a right but a duty to defend oneself publicly"; then with tenderness at the dedication—"To one who called me by the name of Fanny Lear, who gave me an enchanted existence."

The preface stated her purpose admirably: "My intention is simply to establish facts distorted by ill-informed or ill-intentioned writers. . . . I know well that in my situation I have no other weapon but the truth."

But a few days later, the publisher returned; he was perspiring heavily. "Madame, a terrible thing has happened—an unprecedented thing!" Before his office had opened that morning, government agents had come with a cart; they had forced their way in and carried away every copy of "Le Roman . . ."

Hattie was stunned. This was Paris, not St. Petersburg. Slowly she motioned for him to sit down, and sank down herself onto one of Nikki's chairs.

"But what is the explanation of this, monsieur?"

The publisher would not sit down, but paced agitatedly up and down in front of her. The explanation was easy enough. Since the Prussian conquest and the Commune, the French Government had been weak. The Tsar's friendship was most important as a bulwark against Germany's continued greed. The shadow of Russia as a powerful protector lay over France. The French Government had been told how the Tsar's representatives felt in this matter.

The publisher's indignation sputtered out when she asked him what he intended to do. "If they're so determined to stop this, monsieur, they must be afraid that people will really want to read it!"

He spread out his hands in a gesture of helplessness. "What do you suggest that one can do, madame?"

264

She could think of nothing. But as she bade him good-by, her determination rose. She would go to Brussels, where she had heard that Lacroix et Cie was a firmly established printing house.

She sent Joséphine for a holiday in Brittany and went to Belgium herself, believing that her stay there would be brief. The publisher, she was assured, had considerable influence; no one would dare suppress his books. Lacroix accepted her volume. But there were delays in printing, a little more rewriting, and she lived for two months in meager solitude until the day the book appeared on the bookstands.

That noon, as Hattie passed a bookstore she noticed two policemen standing in the middle of a crowd around the doorway. With sudden panic she pushed her way through. Each one of the gendarmes had a fresh pile of paper-bound copies of her book in front of him. Methodically, carefully, they were tearing out the last twenty pages of each—the pages dealing with the diamonds taken from the ikon. Hattie felt as if she herself were being ripped apart. She fled to the publisher's office on the Rue de Ruysbroeck.

He attempted to quiet her. "It's not entirely bad, Madame Lear. This may run the demand way up." But later in the day, a new police order was issued and every copy was confiscated. Lacroix too had a political explanation. She was sure it was true. Belgian trade was beginning to move toward the rich mines of South Russia, and the Belgian authorities had no wish to endanger promising relations.

Wearily, she returned to Paris. Sitting on the bed in the chamber draped in black velvet, Hattie faced a tearful Joséphine.

"I'm going on to Italy now. I'm going to try to publish there, but I can't drag you along with my troubles any longer. I know how you've been marketing—using your own savings."

Joséphine shook her head and wiped her eyes in silence.

Her mistress went on gently: "I'll sell all this." She gestured toward the pearl-hung hangings with no regret. She hesitated. "And I'll pawn my Fabergé pearl collar."

"Oh, madame!" Joséphine exclaimed in horror, but after a pause she went on sadly: "I know I'm really more in your way than I am help right now, and my daughter wants me to come to her. But if you ever need me, madame, I'll come. No matter where you are, you must send for me." The swollen gray eyes looked at her sternly.

"You know I will." Hattie got up resolutely and patted Joséphine's shoulder. "And now perhaps Madame Colbert will know of a dealer . . ."

Hattie watched while the auctioneer shouted the merits of her furniture. The highest prices, though all were low enough, went for the portraits of the Romanovs and her Russian bric-à-brac; she could hear the excited whispers as each object was presented. As the crowd drifted away at the end, Hattie was approached by a thin man in a derby. "Madame Lear?"

She thought he was an assistant of the auctioneer's and when he declared his purpose, it was a shock to her. The French Government wished her to understand that it would be best that she should not return to Paris. She did not have to ask why; the Imperial Russian Government had used its influence again. Well, she was ready to go.

The final parting with Joséphine was hard. Her maid accompanied her to the station and settled her mistress's bags in the compartment for the last time. But she smiled as she turned to go.

"Good fortune, madame. You and His Highness will be together again, and then you will call for me. You'll see, you'll see."

"Write to me," Hattie begged, "keep on writing. Let me know how you are—and keep on saying what you've just said!"

She had returned to Italy, where she and Nikki had once gone from town to town with the ridiculous Imperial entourage . . . Italy once so blooming, so joyous. Now its only virtue was that at least the Government and the press were leaving her alone. Her book was finally published but, although there was no attempt to suppress it, it created little notice. Was it the little local publisher's almost furtive presentation? The printing was cramped and hard to read. The Belgian edition had been beautifully spaced on smooth paper. This one was on cheap, crinkled yellowish paper. There were only half the number of pages for the same text.

The word from Russia came infrequently; for months, there had been a gap, and with reason. Russia had declared war on Turkey. Nikki, Viktor had let her know, had petitioned to be allowed to fight with his former regiment and was rejected. Like her, he was shunted to one side.

Disheartened, she moved for a time up and down the peninsula, trying to recapture some of her own memory of it, but it was useless. She settled down in Rome. There was little now to give her spirit; there was no one to whom she could talk of the world that had been hers, and of Nikki . . . always Nikki. She kept seeing him in the streets, hearing voices from casual passers-by that reminded her of his. The nights when she lay alone and remembered the times she had rested in his arms were worst of all.

Early one morning, brushing her hair in the growing light, she found her first gray hair. She looked at herself carefully for the first time in months. Her complexion was as clear and glowing as ever; there was even a new kind of fragility to her face, which was very appealing when she was rested. But her hair! "My little blonde," Nikki had called her. She knew how Joséphine would disapprove, but she began to experiment with hair colorings. The new brightness was at least as brilliant under gaslight as it had ever been, and she kept it up.

The next startling news from Russia came when she had been in Italy two miserable years. She read it in the newspapers, in hurried paragraphs from Mabel, in a guarded note from the Captain. General Trepov, of the Petersburg police, was dangerously wounded. He had ordered a university student brutally flogged, close to the point of death. A little later, the boy's sweetheart, a sixteen-year-old girl, had called on Trepov at his office and suddenly drawn out a revolver from her skirt. Hattie thought of her poor Katya and Anton, her student, of the day she herself had faced Trepov in his ornate headquarters.

A little later, she heard the sequel. The girl, tried by jury, was acquitted. As she left the court, Trepov's police tried to arrest her again, but the crowd beat them back, rescued her, and now she was abroad. Tension was growing all over Russia; the latter-day repressions were having their effect. She remembered Viktor's words in Brindisi six years ago:

"Give justice, grant people their rights, and they will not rise to kill for them. . . . One day we may have to pay for such mistakes in blood."

The violence broke out again. Shuvalov's successor as head of the secret police was stabbed to death. Not long afterward, a terrorist fired, unsuccessfully, at the Tsar himself; the boy turned out to be a young nobleman, like so many of the new conspirators.

267

What was Nikki thinking when he heard the report? If only she could know his thoughts, share them, share his life again! She heard nothing.

There was news of Nikki's family. His aunt, the old Tsarina, died, and within six weeks Alexander II married his Princess and legitimized his children by her. Hattie felt only bitterness when she heard it. This was no help for them now. But a letter from the Captain was exciting, and almost reluctantly she allowed her hopes to be stirred again. Great changes were in the making for Russia. The Tsar's new wife had shown herself to be on the liberal side. Now she was telling the Tsar that changes must be made, if only to satisfy the rising demand. Let Alexander give the country what many had long wanted—a constitution. Constantine seemed to be returning to favor, working again with the Tsar, helping him prepare for the new rights. Sasha, the heir apparent, was sulking and furious. He approved no such concessions. But, meanwhile Constantine got on well with the Tsar's new wife, and they shared a concern in advocating the constitution. The Captain predicted that before another six months had gone by Russia would be a constitutional monarchy, and its influence as a modern state would be felt in world affairs.

Hattie's thoughts were in a tumult. Constantine had always puzzled her, and she had never trusted him. Yet, back in authority, wouldn't he do everything he could to bring his son out of his long, punishing obscurity? But the newspapers had nothing in them for her, and for months no more letters came. Her discouragement pressed in upon her again.

She still held a few possessions, which, sold one by one, netted her a slight income. She managed on less than she would ever have thought possible, simply because she had to. From time to time her mother's letters followed her from America, and now Caroline pressed her daughter: Since Hattie moved about so much, why didn't she return home, at least for a while? Between the lines Hattie read loneliness and a desire to see her, and she was moved. Unexpectedly, she found she could think of Philadelphia without anger, without any emotion. The McClellans, the Elys . . . Her feelings were gone.

Yet she stopped herself. Suppose the long-awaited word arrived that Nikki had found a way to join her? No, she would stay in Europe. Whenever she heard a sighing wind outside her window,

268

her mind went to an evening in Petersburg. A certain light at dusk, as a haze rose along the hills, brought back the hours at Nikki's summer palace. . . .

One day at her hotel in Rome, an attendant brought her a card. She recognized the name, that of a young count who was a natural son of King Victor Emmanuel. She glanced across the lobby. The count was standing near the door, bright, handsome; he carried his head slightly to the side, in a way that reminded her of Nikki. She held the card in trembling fingers. Her life had been waiting and waiting, so long. Was she merely watching it dwindle away? She remembered the bills increasing in her desk. Perhaps it might do no harm to meet the man, at least. . . .

Within the hour, they had lunch together on the terrace. She found him pleasant and witty, with the same irony that the earlier Nikki had shown. He had to attend a meeting now, he told her, but he wondered if they could spend the evening together. She consented, yet when she was alone she felt oddly guilty. She thought she was being very foolish, but the feeling persisted. Perhaps she should leave, and be gone when he came?

She never found out what her decision might have been. Before the time when the young count was to call for her, an unexpected name was announced. A cold-eyed man introduced himself. He was from the chief of police, and he had a brief message for her. They would be pleased if Madame Blackford would leave the country, and in point of fact, leave Rome that very night.

"May I ask why?"

"I think you know why, madame. Let us say only that the Royal family is disturbed."

Should she go to the American Ministry again? She sighed, and the silence was so long that the official was forced to use the persuasion he had hoped would not be necessary. "We will be happy to pay your bills, and to send you to any place you wish."

Hattie's bright head dropped in her thin hands. In an odd way, this international reputation was helpful at last. She looked up at the man. "Any place I wish to go? Very well. . . . I'll leave if you will send me to America."

The official blinked rapidly, but he agreed. From the point of view of the police and the Royal family, the price would be cheap at that.

269

TWENTY-FIVE

HATTIE FOUND PHILADELPHIA IN THE 1880's MORE OF A FOREIGN CITY than Paris or Vienna. There were new buildings, strange street names; many old landmarks were gone. Her mother's little house on Fourth Street seemed in more of a backwater than ever, for the town's activity had expanded away from the river. Yet her mother had hardly changed. She had been old before Hattie had left twelve years ago, and now she was only a little grayer, a little more tremulous. Her life had been tranquil enough, with the exception, of course, of the reports about her daughter; but Hattie was sure she had tried to ignore these, as she did now.

They embarrassed each other. The difference in their interests, their years, and their lives was unbridgeable. Hattie trusted her mother's old friends to have passed on the most unpleasant stories about her. Caroline must actually have heard many tales that were not true, and Hattie longed to tell her everything. She had dreamed on the voyage home of making a full confession to her that would make her mother understand at last.

But after she had been there only a short time she realized that this was impossible. As they sat together those first afternoons, having tea in the little living room among the sacred polished furniture, her mother spoke nervously of the tourist sights and historical monuments of France and Russia. Even when Hattie tried to talk with her on this level she was frustrated. Her too accurate descriptions of the famous old Romanov palaces sent Caroline into a flutter and a quick change of subject.

"She's a little in awe of me, and rather frightened," Hattie thought. It would have been a relief to receive the upbraiding she had expected, but that meant recognition of sin. With all her

270

own loneliness and bitterness, Hattie felt sorry for her mother. Had Caroline deliberately turned her face from life always, or had she lacked the capacity to deal with it on any terms?

Perhaps even more embarrassing was the fact that they had not shared the life Hattie had led in Philadelphia before she had left. Caroline spoke gingerly of people whom she knew her daughter had known. When Hattie ventured a question about George Madison, her mother gave her a sidelong look.

"He's dead, Harriet—only in the last year." She hesitated, and then generously gave her daughter news that she thought might please her. "His marriage with Miss Newell never did turn out very well. He used to come around and bring flowers to me and ask me what I'd heard from you."

Hattie was touched, but only briefly. That life seemed in another century. She wondered why she had come home. She did not want to see any of the gay group she had known before, to raise the hue and cry of those first days in Paris . . . and the days with Caroline were too sad.

At night, Nikki moved in her dreams, tall and full of that frightening nervous vitality and magnetism that had first stirred her so much. She saw his quizzical green eyes, the way he raised his light eyebrows, his habit of holding one shoulder higher than the other. The background of the dreams was the marble and cast-iron stateliness of St. Petersburg; then, increasingly, she saw the haze and the chestnut trees of the Paris boulevards. She and Nikki seemed to be together in the French capital, safe and happy. Each time she woke to a fresh realization of her loneliness.

She lay in bed in the mornings, too miserable to get up. Her mother hovered over her, alarmed over her daughter's lack of spirit and her fatigue. Hattie herself began to realize that she was coughing a great deal, but she attributed her exhaustion to her unhappiness. It wouldn't do her any good to see a doctor. She had never felt really ill, and she would not let her mother make an invalid of her now.

One day, on a shopping tour with Caroline, Hattie saw someone in front of a store window staring at them. It was a woman with glasses, whose face puzzled her.

"Why, it's Madge!" her mother cried, and hurried Hattie toward her.

Obviously, Madge did not know whether or not she should

speak; several times in the past, Hattie recalled, she had ignored her. But Caroline's presence forced the issue. "I hope you're well, Harriet." After going for years without the spectacles she needed, Madge had them now, but she still squinted. Hattie looked at her in horror. Madge had grown so peaked, so pale. Her complexion was bad, her cheeks were withered; yet they were the same age, weren't they? Thirty-four.

As they parted, Caroline said, "Now wasn't it nice to meet an old friend? Everybody says her husband is doing well—assistant manager of the new branch of the bank. Three children, and they're very happy. I hope you'll be seeing her again."

Madge did not seem happy; in any case, why had she let herself look so bedraggled and old? Hattie looked in the mirror at herself when she got back, with new critical attention. Her hair did look a little metallic, but her pallor was quite different from Madge's dull gray. Even though the lustrous, radiant air that Nikki gave her was gone, she could see why men in the street still turned to look at her. Yet that thought made her uneasy, too. She had been wearing the least chic of her street costumes in the hope that she would not be recognized.

It took the reporters three weeks to discover her; as a matter of fact, only two days after the encounter with Madge. Hattie suspected that this was more than coincidence when, one by one, the brisk young men knocked at the front door. The hunt had begun again. Hattie refused to go through with the disturbing indignity. She might have borne it alone, but Caroline was in a panic. She decided to make preparations to leave. Caroline sighed wistfully at her decision, but Hattie sensed her relief.

She had still not set the day of her departure when it was forced upon her. Soon after the reporters had sniffed her out, other callers arrived. These men were elderly, firm-eyed, and dour. When she met them in the parlor, their leader, a man with a mane of white hair, stepped forward.

"Harriet, I have come in memory of your departed father." His deep-set eyes missed no detail of Hattie's appearance: the new brighter shade of her hair, the cut of her gown, the slight shadow of sleeplessness under her eyes. He went on: "We have come to pray for your soul, Sister Harriet—to beg you to give up your sinful ways!"

To her astonishment, he lowered himself to his knees. As she watched in horror, the others followed him, taking their places among her trunks. "O Shepherd, thy mercy be on this erring sheep . . ." As the voices chimed in with the leader and gained in strength, she was terrified. The door had been left open and other members of the congregation were gathering in the hall. The leader's voice rose and fell with cadences that brought back her father's sermons. The group gathered for prayer was like so many she remembered from her childhood. It was as if she were ten years old again, obediently about to take part. But this time she was the center, the outcast. Reality and nightmare, childhood memories and present indignation, were so confused within her that for several minutes she stood still. The "Amen" of the group refrain, when the leader paused for breath, galvanized her. Trembling violently, she looked wildly about her for escape. She ran from the room, pushing aside the people in the hall, stumbling up the steps to her own bedroom, slamming the door behind her. Caroline had left discreetly when the visitors entered. Now Hattie heard her rustling down the stairs to apologize.

That night was the worst she had known in years. Hattie lay in bed unable and afraid to sleep. If only Joséphine had been there, first to chase these dreadful strangers out of the house, then to reason her out of her low spirits.

In the morning over her coffee, she read the paper's strongly exaggerated version of the visit, its scathing summary of her career. Regardless of her turbulent life, it admitted, she remained a beautiful woman. Hattie smiled grimly. Then she read the last line of the account; it gave her address.

Within the hour, she had a ticket for New York. She was not prepared for Caroline's final act. When the time came to say good-by, her mother pressed a thick envelope into her hand.

"Harriet, you are to take this—and I won't hear a word from you. All those years you sent me money regularly and a lot of times I didn't need all of it, or nearly all of it. I put some aside for you, and I want you to have it. Things will be better for you. But it will help for a while."

Caroline Ely's hand trembled as she pushed the envelope into Hattie's pocket. For one of the few times that Hattie remembered, her mother was resolute. Then Caroline said a thing Hattie had never expected to hear:

"You've been good to me, child. Nobody can say you haven't

been. And I know it's partly because of me that you have to leave home again. . . . Come back when you can. The talk will die down someday."

This, finally, was recognition of her daughter's tragedy, but Hattie knew it was a rare instant and could not be prolonged. Speechless and in tears, she took her mother in her arms for a long moment, then ran swiftly out to the waiting carriage.

On the train, she tried desperately to decide where she would go now. New York could only be a way station. Her longing for Paris had returned, yet she was barred from it. It was the only place where Nikki would look for her, where she could be found when word arrived, if it ever did. She felt cold as she realized that for the first time she had used the word "if."

In New York, when she stepped from the train, the cries of the newsboys rose as if they had been waiting for her arrival. She snatched a paper from one of them. *Sensational News from Russia.* She stood still, in the middle of the surging crowds, and skimmed the story rapidly. Tsar Alexander had been killed by a revolutionist's bomb. He had died in the arms of his young wife, his legs blown away, his body badly shattered. There were rumors of arrests and other killings; Russia's future hung in a shaky balance. . . . On the day of his death, the Tsar had planned to declare the long-promised constitution in effect. Now nobody knew what would happen.

Hastily she found a hotel room. Her own decisions would be influenced by this. The next morning she hurried out for further news. Alexander III—Sasha—had taken the oath. Sasha, who hated Constantine and Nikki! She read the paper with extreme care and was rewarded by a small note on an inside page. Grand Duke Nicholas Constantinovich, cousin to the new Tsar, and long in disfavor at Court, had appeared suddenly near St. Petersburg. He had been arrested by order of Alexander III. There were rumors—thus far without confirmation—that he had been one of the plotters of the assassination of Alexander II; another report had it that Nicholas's father, Constantine, was in custody because of a secret connection with the nihilists.

She discounted this at the start. Constantine was getting all he wanted for Russia through his brother, and in the way that Nikki had said they both wanted it—through orderly change. Neither one of them would ever have been involved in a plot that would elevate the reactionary Sasha, whom they hated, to a place in power. If only she were in Petersburg now and could hear, immediately, what was happening, frightful though it might be! Forlornly she waited through the hours for the next morning's papers. Constantine was free, they reported, but Nikki's arrest was confirmed, though no reason for it was given. The stories that followed were as she had expected. The new Tsar issued a proclamation declaring flatly that he had inherited—in his own phrase—an "autocratic government," and would continue it. He refused to promulgate the constitution that his father would have declared within another twenty-four hours; and he had ordered a succession of new arrests, repressions, and executions.

Over and over, during the weeks that followed, while Hattie did little to establish herself in the city, but waited for news, she told herself that Nikki's worst enemy had become Tsar and they could expect nothing from him. Yet it was a shock to hear from Viktor that Nikki had been sent into exile to the Cossack steppes near Orenburg. Orenburg! She put down the letter, remembering Nikki's words, written from there before he plunged into the vastness of Asia during the Khivan campaign: "The farther my body draws away from you, the nearer my soul comes to you." Then she had believed it. Now, it was harder. She could not add another three thousand miles to her exile and isolation. Above all things, she wanted to be back in Paris.

She sailed for London, and went directly to the French Embassy upon arrival. What harm could she do now? Couldn't they inquire of the Russian Government, which surely had no further interest in her?

At the end of several weeks, she received her answer. It was "unofficially" dispatched, but the content was direct. Madame Blackford still possessed certain letters and documents from the Grand Duke Nicholas. Perhaps she would be willing to give them up? She was puzzled.

"But they've been published!"

The secretary gave her a doubtful look. "It is known that you still have several more that have not appeared, which might be a cause of embarrassment to the Imperial Government."

Back in her hotel, she copied them. At least she would have his words forever. She knew them almost by heart, anyway. When she returned the original letters to the Embassy, she gave her word:

"I have no future plans to make my relationship public in any possible way. There will be no further 'embarrassment' for the Russian Court. None at all."

It was settled. The following week, as the roofs of Paris came into view at the approaches to the Gare du Nord, she wept, silently.

She found a small room, away from the boulevards. She would content herself with walks in the park, hours on the benches in the sun. Again she had come to Paris in the spring. Under the chestnut blossoms, in the vibrant sun, her health improved. She still coughed, but she continued to defer her visit to the doctor.

She had scant desire to do anything or see anyone. She had been there several months when a note in one of the gossip sheets made her pause. The Grand Duke Constantine had come to Paris to live in a modest apartment, leaving both his families behind— his Grand Duchess and his ballerina. The new Tsar had removed him as head of the Navy and Chairman of the State Council; his days of influence had ended.

Unconsciously, after that she looked for him in the streets, and in the carriages that rolled past her as she sat on a bench in the Bois. Then one day she saw him. He was sitting at a table not far from her in an outdoor café.

This was the third time. There had been that morning in Nikki's bedroom in the Renaissance hall, the morning he had prevented their marriage, and now this day of exile for them both. Would he tell her about Nikki if she asked him? Yet, as she sat still staring at his profile from several tables away, she felt a fierce resentment that he was free and Nikki was not. He had done so little to help his son, and of all who had stood between her and the man she loved, none had done more to injure her than this man. She did not want to look at him, but there was a certain tilt to his head, a Romanov arrogance, that reminded her so of Nikki that she was transfixed. Then, suddenly, that was the very thing she could not bear any longer, and she got up and walked hastily away.

Shortly after that, she had her last message from Viktor. Nikki was still in Central Asia; he had a certain amount of freedom and

276

his old friends knew that he was working quietly at some kind of irrigation scheme for the natives. But odd stories were told. When the old Tsar died, Nikki was supposed to have cried out that he, Nicholas, would come before "my Russian people" and that they would rally to his support instead of to his cousin's. Here was one reason that the new Tsar had acted so harshly. And Viktor had a final item of news; he had heard, indirectly, that even now Nikki called for her. "They say he's never forgotten you." Thank God for Viktor! She kissed the letter with the word that she had wanted so desperately to hear. . . . But the Captain wrote no more; it was months later that she received a brief note from Mabel Grey. Viktor Vorpovsky had died of fever during the winter. Mabel added, smugly, that she herself expected "to be married soon, and well." Then from her, too, Hattie heard nothing.

There was total silence now from Russia—and the years were going by with nothing to mark them. She had reached the summer of 1885. Could it be eleven years since she had left St. Petersburg? There had been nothing in those years but the news from Russia and the restless, unhappy moving. She was nearly thirty-eight, and she could not bear to look in her mirror. Glances on the street still came, but the new little lines deepening about her eyes and mouth terrified her. Nikki had called her beauty perfect—without fault or blemish. He had said when they first met: "It would never be possible to look enough at you," and he had felt that way until that last afternoon when she had seen him walk out of the apartment on Millionnaya Street. Would he feel so now? She was afraid to think of it.

She was afraid of other things. After discounting her illness and her fatigue, the coughs and the pain in her chest, she began to see blood on her handkerchief when she coughed. It frightened her so that she refused to admit that she was aware of it. A torn vein in her throat, perhaps? But as it grew worse, her alarm would not be contained. She went to a doctor and heard his words.

"Madame, it's consumption. You must have known." She could not believe it at first. "But it's well advanced, Madame Blackford. Like this." He drew a design that meant little, except for the words that accompanied it. "You must be careful, very careful. You must have rest and sunlight—drink plenty of milk, eat eggs and red meat. Do you have someone to care for you, day and night?"

When she got to her rooms, she could not put off thinking of his advice any longer. She was panic-stricken. Her mother was far away; Madame Colbert had left Paris. But Joséphine . . . in Brittany! Would she come? She sent a wire to the Arnault house. Rest, milk, eggs, meat—the regime she had prescribed for Nikki. She remembered his terror over her last cold in Petersburg, his frantic ministrations. She presumed she would hear if he died. But would he hear when she did? Not when—if. Joséphine's wire telling of her arrival the next day made her hope again. . . .

When Joséphine entered Hattie's room, she gave a sharp cry, then caught her mistress in her arms. "Madame, you haven't looked out for yourself!" So she had always been told. "We'll make you in good health again," the Breton said firmly. She herself was stronger than ever, fresh from a life spent mending nets for her fishermen brothers.

Before they even began to tell each other what had happened in the interim, Joséphine made Hattie lie back and drew a quilt over her. Joséphine's voice quivered a little. "When did you last see the doctor? We must see him again."

"It's been the heat," Hattie murmured, "enough to make anyone ill, even with nothing the matter. . . . Do you remember, Joséphine, when the Grand Duke took the villa for us at Pavlovsk?"

Joséphine remembered everything, but she preferred to talk of Paris in the old days, in the house on the Boulevard Malesherbes, to talk of Madame's plans to enjoy the city again as it should be enjoyed. . . . But the winter was early and hard, and the doctor's face stayed grave on his visits to the house. Finally, in March of 1886, he told her what his face had said already.

"Madame, you haven't responded to the treatment. There's only one thing left—the southern coast." He bowed himself out abruptly, taking no responsibility for his expensive prescription.

"I can't afford it." Hattie's voice was low. "I couldn't pay for even a single bedroom down there."

Joséphine scoffed. "Madame, you were never good at handling money. You've got no idea how much you have in reserve. From now on, I'll look after that part of it, the way I used to . . . and the places to stay . . . If one has sharp eyes, they are there."

By April, Hattie watched the Mediterranean waves from the window of a small villa in Nice. Joséphine was near at hand always, not too far away, so that Hattie could talk to her without raising her voice.

On the afternoon of May 15, Joséphine brought her knitting and sat near by.

She talked of their first days in Paris, their rides, the balls at the Hôtel de Ville, and the sight of Eugénie, a figure in trailing blues and greens. . . . Hattie's smile faded as she listened. The diamond bracelet had gone so long ago, but her fate had been like its first owner's. She had feared it—so superstitiously, she had thought—in Munich when Nikki had first fastened the bracelet on her arm.

"Do you remember, Joséphine, what you promised when I went to Italy—that I would be with the Grand Duke again? But I won't, will I?"

Joséphine did not answer. Gently she handed her mistress a handkerchief for the tears that rolled down her cheeks, and went to get her brandy and milk.

Hattie tried to swallow it, but could not. She lay back again for a time. The sound of the waves was lulling, and a sparrow chirped among the leaves that touched the window sill. Suddenly, Hattie wanted to change her dress.

"This is so plain and ugly. . . . A white one. No, not that one, the other." She pointed to a thin summer silk.

Joséphine stood there uncertainly. "It's too flimsy for you. You'll get a fresh cold." Then she looked at her mistress's face and gave in.

With many pauses for rest, the silken folds of the dress were finally settled into place. Joséphine deftly drew the silk closer over the wasted chest and pinned the folds with the little gold brooch.

When she was finished, Hattie lay back, the afternoon sun moving across her face. Her eyes were tired and she shut them. She seemed to drift for a time, in a slow, sunny haze out toward the waves. But then she opened her eyes. She was thinking of a letter Nikki had written her. He had wished that when she lay dying she would remember how much she loved him and say that she had never loved anyone else more than she loved him. Ah, she hadn't, before or since. Her eyes widened. Dying! No, she mustn't die. She had to stay alive. Suppose Nikki were to come to France and not find her?

The window began to darken. Had dusk fallen so soon? Someone was sitting beside her, looking at her, someone lean and tall and smiling. He held out one of his long tanned hands and touched hers. The green eyes were intense and smiling. They had said she would never see him again! Yet now he was with her once more, just as she'd known he would be. She tried to lift her fingers, but they would not move; it didn't matter. Nikki was there, so near.

The room grew darker still, and now, oddly, it didn't seem to be Nikki at all there beside her. Had they tricked her? That dark face—whose was it? Yes, her father—with the reproachful look, his lips moving as if he were trying to say something. No words came, and she was glad. She did not know whether they were reproving words, condemning her, or whether he forgave her as he had forgiven those other women like her. . . . She tried to talk, but her father's look had changed to tenderness. He understood and agreed and there was nothing she had to say.

Joséphine touched her hand. "Madame, it's time for your medicine. . . . Madame!"

Over the sound of the waves, Joséphine cried out, softly, despairingly, and reached over to close the dark eyes.

EPILOGUE

IN ST. PETERSBURG, YEARS LATER, THE GRAND DUKE NICHOLAS'S youngest brother, Constantine, received a note over which he pondered for a long time. Nikki wanted a favor of the new Tsar —his cousin Nicholas, who had succeeded his father, Alexander III. Couldn't his brother persuade the Tsar to agree to it? Constantine, who had become a lyrical poet of some distinction, was touched by his brother's request. He went to the Tsar, spoke to him eloquently, and the wish was granted.

By train, wagon, and sled workmen brought a heavy marble object to the far-off sands of Turkestan. There, in the tent where Nikki lived, it was installed—the long, reclining figure of a woman —Solari's marble creation of years ago.

The pale stone gleamed in the half-darkness of the tent; and in the evening, Nikki, stretched on his cot, could reach out to touch the image made to her measurements. Thus, after so long, he brought Hattie Blackford to share his exile. Long before then, he had given her jewels. Now he did the same thing. Ordering bracelets, rings, and necklaces, he covered the statue until it glittered in the dusk.

He stayed on, outliving one after another of his contemporaries, surviving Sasha's regime, then another—an enigmatic personage who puzzled the other Romanovs.

He was never allowed to leave his exile at the outer fringes of the Empire. Moving about the desert edges of the country, he astonished some of his opponents by launching a magnificently successful irrigation project. He proved himself a man of business, a flamboyant figure with a following among the natives. The

281

last was his undoing. It disturbed his enemies and gave them am-munition for arguments that he continue to be kept in exile. Nikki was altogether too friendly with those people, riding on the box with his coachman, greeting anyone on the street.

He lived through the 80's and the 90's, and into the twentieth century. He was still in his remote banishment when the Russian Revolution broke in 1917. The Empire was gone, the Tsar and his family under arrest, and a moderate provisional government took over. From Tashkent, Nikki sent a telegram of greetings to the new regime. Its text was widely published, a wonder to those who knew nothing of this Romanov exiled by other Romanovs.

"I'm free at last," he called out to the natives as he walked along the streets of his exile. "After all these years, I'm going back to Petersburg—as soon as things settle."

Things did not settle. A few months later, Lenin seized author-ity and civil war broke out; eventually, the Tsar and his family were shot to death in a cellar, and other Grand Dukes, including one of Nikki's brothers, were executed.

The problem of his own future was solved in another way. He died soon afterward, in January of 1918, at sixty-eight, thirty-two years after Hattie Blackford. He died of pneumonia in his palace at Tashkent while a file of friends and servants, mourning their brilliant, quixotic leader, stood outside.

With his last look at the world, he saw her. Directly before him, through an open door, in the main room of the house, she lay in her eternal symmetry, the warm marble preserving her for his eyes and the world's. In the dimness, the bracelets gleamed and the diamonds around her neck caught the glint of the light beside him.